GHOST DANCER

As Howie's eyes became accustomed to the night, he saw a dark figure on the road in front of him coming his way. At first Howie thought he must be mistaken. Who would be in this lonely place at night? But there was someone there. He heard the soft but unmistakable sound of footsteps.

The shape came steadily closer, some dim, terrible thing coming his way on this empty mountain road where no one should be. He strained his eyes trying to see better, but he could only make out an outline of living darkness. . . .

As Howie watched, the ghostly figure raised a shotgun high above its head.

And then it began to dance. . . .

"A superb debut novel!"
    —Carolyn Hart, author of *Death on Demand*

"Mystery readers, rejoice! . . . This gripping tale has an authentic Southwest flavor—don't miss it!"
    Francis Roe, author of *Under the Kinfe*

GHOST DANCER

A Howard Moon Deer Mystery

Robert Westbrook

A SIGNET BOOK

SIGNET
Published by the Penguin Group
Penguin Putnam Inc., 375 Hudson Street,
New York, New York 10014, U.S.A.
Penguin Books Ltd, 27 Wrights Lane,
London W8 5TZ, England
Penguin Books Australia Ltd, Ringwood,
Victoria, Australia
Penguin Books Canada Ltd, 10 Alcorn Avenue,
Toronto, Ontario, Canada M4V 3B2
Penguin Books (N.Z.) Ltd, 182-190 Wairau Road,
Auckland 10, New Zealand

Penguin Books Ltd, Registered Offices:
Harmondsworth, Middlesex, England

First published by Signet, an imprint of Dutton NAL,
a member of Penguin Putnam Inc.

First Printing, October, 1998
10 9 8 7 6 5 4 3 2 1

PUBLISHER'S NOTE
This is a work of fiction. Names, characters, places, and incidents either are the
product of the author's imagination or are used fictitiously, and any resemblance to
actual persons, living or dead, events, or locales is entirely coincidental.

This book goes with love to the Solar Slums:
Me'l Christensen, Seth Rolland, and Gina Azzari

PROLOGUE

Body Piercing

"Is this the first time you've made love at thirteen thousand feet?" he asked with his well-practiced boyish grin.

"The first time," she agreed. "But I'll bet you've done it before up here, haven't you?"

"Never!" He laughed, and flashed the famous grin again. "Well, maybe once a long, long time ago. But it doesn't count."

"Oh, no?" She nuzzled playfully, her brown eyes lit up with mischief. "And just why doesn't it count?"

"It was summer. There were wildflowers on the high meadows. Very pretty, actually . . ."

"I bet!"

"But I've never done it in the winter, not at thirteen thousand feet in a blizzard. You, my dear, are the very most delicious, most cuddly first . . ."

They giggled and played. He was old enough to have gone through a kaleidoscope of fashions, and seen most things recycled a time or two. But, my God, the kids these days! As the millennium approached, staying hip was turning into a full-time job.

It wasn't the nose ring that bothered him. He had gotten used to that, the delicate small gold loop that pierced the skin of her left nostril. But the ring through her clitoris was another matter. This was weird. Still, he had to admit, it never failed to excite him when his hand wandered into that nether region. An interesting aesthetic: smooth metal against moist flesh. A slippery foreign object where you least expected to find one. Kinky, to say the least. Especially when she explained that her husband had a gold ring just like it through his scrotum. They were a perfect Generation X couple, apparently, with matching genital wedding bands.

Well, we're from different worlds; it's part of the fascination. Sixty-three and twenty-four, he told himself as he gently stroked her stomach. It seemed to him miraculous, this subtraction of thirty-nine years. A sign from heaven of his own eternal silver-haired youthfulness. They lay on a narrow cot in a small avalanche hut high on the ridge above the ski resort. A propane heater sent a hissing glow into the room, reflecting against the window and the girl's bronze skin. She had an athletic body, compact and strong; her dark gold hair tumbled in thick curls onto her shoulders. Even on this wintry morning, she seemed to him full of sunlight; she was like holding a summer's day in his arms.

The shed was twelve feet by eight, not exactly the honeymoon suite. The radio equipment and boxes of explosive grenades left barely enough room to stand. Fortunately, the bed made standing unnecessary. Outside the snow swirled around the window.

"Hey, it's ten o'clock," she said, glancing at her watch. "You said you had a meeting this morning."

"Damn! Is it that late?" He never carried a watch—one of his eccentricities, though he prided himself on his innate sense of perfect time. "It can't be more than nine-thirty. You just want to be rid of me."

"No, honest. Look at my watch. You told me to remind you."

"Damn!" he swore again. He picked up his ski clothes from the floor. She started to dress as well; this wasn't a place to lounge around naked. Bra first, then panties, long silk underwear, black snow pants, thick gray wool sweater, and finally a red jacket with a large red cross on the back—the emblem of the ski patrol. He slipped into his own underclothes, then a dark blue powder suit and his Nordica boots. He grabbed his gloves and goggles and hat from where he had left them on the table by the radio.

"The morning went by too fast," he told her. "When can I see you again?"

"I don't know. I think my husband's getting suspicious. He's starting to give me these long pleading looks."

"Is he? Poor guy!" Her husband was a ski instructor, the same age as she was, and he felt a pang of unexpected empathy for the young man.

"I'll put him teaching Beginners' Week—that'll keep him occupied."

"You're bad!" she said with a coy smile.

"Not as bad as you are," he whispered back.

He kissed her weather-cracked lips, feeling the momentary cold touch of her nose ring against his own nostril. Then he was gone, stepping out from the avalanche hut into the storm. She watched through the frosty window as he got into his skis and pushed off over the cornice of the mountain into the steep chute below. As soon as he was out of sight, she opened a zippered compartment of her red backpack, took out a small cell phone, and punched in a number.

"He's on his way," she said into the mouthpiece.

She refolded the phone and put it away. Finally she took off her Eddie Bauer wristwatch, pulled the small silver knob on the side, and reset the time—correctly now—back one-half hour.

How glorious to ski waist deep, off-piste, through steep virgin powder! This was Beethoven's *Ninth,* and then some. He sang the "Ode to Joy" at the top of his lungs as he swept down from the high ridge toward the chairlifts and trails below, sending up a plume of white snow in his wake. No, he did not feel sixty-three years old. Not when he could still climb nearly seven hundred and fifty vertical feet to the avalanche hut in a storm, satisfy a young woman, and then ski down again with effortless ease—and all before noon!

In a few minutes he came down from a wide glacier bowl onto the ski-area proper and joined those below—not many in this weather—who had come to spend the day on the slopes. Slower, losing ecstasy as he lost speed, he descended partway down an intermediate trail. Finally he stopped and moved along a small path through the trees to the clearing where he had arranged his meeting this morning. He was the first to arrive. He stood by himself in the falling snow and sighed. He remembered that he had a problem. A big problem, possibly. But if all went well . . .

His mind wandered. He laughed suddenly, thinking of the girl's clitoral jewelry, wondering what a Generation X couple said to the guard at the airport when their genital wedding bands set off the alarm at the security check? It was not a par-

ticularly profound thought, but as it happened, it was the last
clear thought he ever had.

He heard a sound behind him. He turned with a smile still
on his lips. His lovely, boyish smile. But as he turned, something struck him in the chest with enormous force—an iron
fist, a locomotive, a battering ram, but stronger still. It shook
every part of him and made the world go dim and woozy. He
stood stupidly in shock, his mouth open.

His eyes traveled downward: My God, there was an arrow
sticking out of his blue powder suit! A wooden shaft, colored
feathers at the end to guide its flight. An arrow had pierced his
chest! He stared at the thing in astonishment. Just to make certain, he reached with one hand and touched the shaft. . . . It
was real, all right, no hallucination. Someone had shot him
with a goddamn arrow!

He looked up with genuine curiosity to see who could have
done this terrible thing. But his head was heavy. He struggled
to squint and focus his eyes. There seemed to be a dark figure
standing in the snow in front of him. Hardly more than a black
outline against the blinding white. A ghost, perhaps—that's
what it looked like to him. And the ghost was coming toward
him. Floating just a little. Twirling to some distant music.

The ghost was dancing. He saw that now. A dancing ghost
with a bow in hand, come to take him home.

PART ONE

Philosophical Divisions at the Top of the Food Chain

1

Howie met the Lady in White and her daughter on a chairlift in a late-season storm. He didn't learn her real name for some time, so that's how he continued to think of her, as the Lady in White. For a day that soon turned ugly, she made an attractive start. The memory of her became forever linked in his mind with the white sky, the mountains, and heavy snowflakes floating down so soft and silent, it was like standing inside a winter's scene from one of those old-fashioned crystal paperweights.

It was April Fools' Day, and Howie should have been more on guard. By mid-morning nearly twenty-six inches of fresh powder had fallen from the sky, hiding the scars of old turns left behind by last week's marauding college kids on spring break. The small resort village at the base of the lift looked like some Hollywood fantasy of old Bavaria. But it was all make-believe. The gingerbread houses with their steep roofs sold goggles, gloves, and skis, and the thing that looked like a church steeple was, in fact, the top of the Winterhaus Inn. This was not the Old World but the New—the northernmost mountains of New Mexico, close to the Colorado border, with a lot of set decoration thrown in to provide the proper atmosphere.

Howie and Jack had just pushed forward out from the front of the lift line onto a red plastic strip half buried in the snow that said LOAD HERE. Jack drifted past the mark by a few inches, and Howie had to pull him back by the belt.

"Load here, Jack," he said.

Overhead a huge wheel moved the heavy cable. Behind them an empty chair was making a U-turn and coming their way. Howie was thinking that a chairlift is certainly a splendid thing, to ascend a mountain upon huge steel pylons during a winter storm, traveling where a clever eagle might hesitate to

go just for the hell of it. But then without warning, the huge
wheel ceased turning and the lift came to an abrupt halt. The
two men were left standing foolishly on the red plastic strip.

"What's happening?" Jack asked.

"Someone probably fell getting off at the top. Jack, are you
sure you want to go through with this?"

"I'll be fine."

"You still can change your mind, you know. Wait in the
lodge with a nice hot toddy while I take care of business."

"Don't worry about me. I used to be a very good skier, you
know."

"I still think this is crazy."

"Relax, Howie. I came in third in the National Junior Slalom
Competition in Stowe, Vermont," Jack said with dignity.
"Back in '62."

For Jack Wilder, 1962 was clearly a vintage year, a much
better year than today. He was a large man in his early fifties,
six feet two inches tall, about thirty pounds overweight, with a
well-trimmed gray beard and curly gray hair. He carried himself with a kind of stately resolve. You could tell he must have
been handsome in his youth, before stress and various culinary
pleasures had broadened his features and added a comfortable
belly to his physique.

This morning Jack looked like an overdressed bear in a gray
powder suit that was padded from underneath by a thick white
sweater his wife Emma had knitted for him. He wore a blue
and gray wool scarf wrapped tightly around his neck, and there
was a dazzling red ski cap you couldn't miss in a blizzard
pulled down over his ears. The scarf and cap were crochet
work, also from Emma Wilder, who spent each evening in her
rocking chair near the fire, with two cats at her feet, and with
knitting needles or crochet hook working away at a great clip.
This meant she was always seeking new victims for her
work—obscure nieces and nephews in Iowa or San Diego
might unexpectedly receive oversize sweaters at odd times of
the year, usually July. Howie too was wearing one of Emma's
ski caps, an orange and black thing that made him feel like a
Halloween decoration. It was not his idea of style, but he hated
to hurt her feelings. Despite the storm, Jack wore goggles with
a lens so dark his eyes were invisible. Between the goggles, the
ski cap, and the scarf, there wasn't much left of Jack to see.

They had been waiting less than two minutes when Howie heard a child's eager voice behind them.

"Mommy, let's get on *this* chair!"

"Angela, wait!" came an adult voice in alarm. But it was too late. The child had moved forward from the line, sliding in between Jack and Howie onto the red LOAD HERE strip. She was about five years old, dressed in a candy pink snowsuit, cute as she could be—a cherub with plump cheeks and long blond hair falling down from her pink cap. Her mother appeared a moment later by her daughter's side.

"It seems we're joining you," she said with an apologetic laugh.

"Quite all right," Jack told her gallantly.

Howie was unhappy the mother and daughter had effectively separated him from Jack, but there was nothing to be done. The woman, he saw, was dressed completely in white—powder suit, gloves, hat. Even her expensive German skis, Volkls, were mostly white. How he knew that she was an attractive female of the species, covered up as she was in powder suit and goggles in a snowstorm, is one of the sweet mysteries of nature. His nerve endings simply whispered sex; though as a civilized male in the age of AIDS, he did his best not to show any interest. He smiled instead at the little girl. The child was adorable on her shorty skis, and she grinned back, her eyes ablaze through the yellow lens of her goggles. They were fresh as an ad for toothpaste, this lovely mother and daughter pair. But Howie wished they had stayed back in line.

With a groan of moving cable, the machinery started and the four-person chair was once again coming their way. A lift attendant whacked the seat with a broom to get some of the loose snow off. The effort was perfunctory, faintly ridiculous in a storm like this.

"Here we go, Jack," Howie said over the heads of the mother and daughter. "When you feel the chair against the back of your legs, sit down."

"Yes, yes, of course." Jack hated to feel helpless, and there was a note of irritation in his voice.

The Lady in White glanced toward Howie, studied him briefly, and then turned to inspect Jack. In her effort to get onto the lift with her daughter, she had not looked closely at her co-riders until just this moment. Now a small shadow crossed her brow as she sensed that in some undefined way they were out of place. But if she had any doubts about riding with Jack and Howie, it was too late for her, just as it was for Jack and Howie, because a moving chairlift is an inexorable thing.

Jack managed the first obstacle. The chair arrived, and he collapsed onto it, putting his arm anxiously around the metal bar at the side. They lurched forward together, their four pairs of skis gliding over a mound of snow, then falling off into empty space. They cleared the first tower and suddenly found themselves high above the white ground and climbing fast into the frozen sky.

2

Skiing is a white, white sport.

Anyone who does not believe that there are two Americas neatly segregated one from the other, should spend a winter in the mountains among the privileged class. Howie found it telling that here at San Geronimo—in the town itself, that is, fifteen miles away—the population was dominated by people of color, mostly Hispanic. But at San Geronimo Peak, high in the snow, there was nary a red, nor brown, nor black face in sight. Which is why Howie was so out of place.

The little girl had been studying him with huge eyes through her goggles ever since he got on the chairlift. She was too young to disguise her curiosity, to know that strangers are dangerous in this world and must not stare at one another. Finally she just came out and asked him: "Are you an Indian?"

"Native American, dear," the mother corrected quickly, a delicate blush of embarrassed P.C. in her voice.

Howie smiled at them both. He couldn't hide it, he supposed, his round full-moon face and flattish nose. Even the long black hair in a ponytail down his back—a ponytail, which despite his every effort to look like some hip rock entrepreneur, summoned instead a hint of ancestral forests and plains.

"Why, sure, I'm an Indian," he told the little girl.

"Then where's your bow and arrow?"

"Angela!" cried Mom, scandalized.

"Quite all right," he assured the woman. He peered into the little girl's grave, curious face. "Well, naturally I have a bow and arrow," he told her. "Lots of arrows, as a matter of fact. But generally I leave them back at the wigwam when I go skiing."

"Why?" demanded Angela.

"You think I'll need them skiing?"

"Indians are *supposed* to have a bow and arrow," she insisted.

"Well, I guess I could shoot a few Texans who are hogging the trails," he told her.

The mother laughed. Everybody's got to hate somebody, and in New Mexico people hate Texans. It was only natural. Just as Oregon loathes California, and northern California despises southern California, and southern California detests the brown-skin masses who live farther south still—there exists among humankind an entire chain of loathing in which everyone feels superior to someone, except perhaps the people who are so far south, metaphorically speaking, that there is no one left to hate except themselves. (And as an Indian, Howie had some knowledge of this last category.)

"He's teasing you, sweetheart," the mother said to her daughter.

The little girl smiled, serene in her own fantasy belief in storybook Indians who roamed watercolor pages with bow and arrow in hand. Normally Howie was not wild about too-cute children, but Angela seemed the authentic article, still young enough to pull it off. A year from now she would go to school and learn which lunch boxes were cool to have, and what TV shows she must watch to be part of the right crowd; she would discover she was blond and pretty, and probably become awfully stuck-up. But at the moment the little girl appeared that rare thing in today's world, a truly innocent child. With her plump cheeks she reminded Howie of the sort of angel you might find on a Renaissance ceiling—one of the small chubby kind that is usually found near the corners of the frame blowing trumpets at the clouds.

Now that they were chatting, Howie was able to inspect Mom more closely. His male antennae received a kind of high-voltage electrical zap. There was a great alertness to her, a surplus of energy, as though her emotional core was burning close to the surface. Her complexion was pale, rosy cheeks in the snowy cold. Her features were delicate and well formed. She had short dark hair cut in a cute, feathery way, almost as black as Howie's. Her eyes were large and animated, and he wondered what color they were beneath the orange lens of her goggles. There was not the slightest doubt in Howie's mind that she was well educated and came from money. He was willing to bet that men had loved her, and probably had suffered for it too. When she had first joined them on the chairlift, he had estimated her age in the mid-twenties—the same as his own. But looking at her more closely, he revised that figure upward ten years. She was a childlike woman, small and elfin, but an aging child nevertheless.

She was studying Howie too, in a certain anthropological way in which white people tend to look at Indians.

"Are you from the San Geronimo Pueblo?" she inquired.

"No, I'm a Lakota Sioux. From South Dakota originally. I've only been in New Mexico a few months."

"Really? And what brought you to San Geronimo?"

"Blind fortune," he told her with a smile. She smiled back. It didn't really mean anything, only a polite facial gesture signifying courtesy. Yet for all that, it was a nice smile, and he was inclined to elaborate in order to keep the conversation going: "I was in Europe for a year, and I met an American couple in Paris who offered me use of their guest cottage here. I'm a graduate student working on my Ph.D. dissertation—long overdue, I'm afraid—and I needed a quiet place to write. Unfortunately, Bob, my friend from Paris, twisted his knee in early December and gave me his ski pass to use. That was the death knell for me as far as academia is concerned."

"You're neglecting your studies to ski?" she said with mock severity.

"You bet. And how about you?" he asked. "Do you ski here often?"

"Only when I can. Not as much as I'd like these days. . . . So where are you doing your graduate work?"

"Princeton," he told her.

She raised an eyebrow—just slightly, but he saw it. As an Indian, Howard Moon Deer was accustomed to Anglo curiosity, and he could see the big question mark in her eyes: How did this kid from the res get to a fancy East Coast school? The answer, in fact, was not complex. He had simply gone where the scholarships were, first to Dartmouth, which had been chartered originally as an Indian school—a noble New England urge to educate the heathen—and then on to Princeton for his master's and finally his endlessly dangling, often interrupted Ph.D. It was the rich schools that tended to be the most generous with selected minorities, and as a Native American,

Howie was lucky to find himself on the receiving end of a lot of well-honed guilt.

The Lady in White could not read him, or fit him within any category that she knew, and he could tell it bothered her a little. He smiled vaguely but did not help her out. She gave him an odd look, and they fell silent for a few hundred feet, passing over a stand of Douglas fir whose branches were heavy with new snow. Jack, at the far end of the chair, seemed deep in his own thoughts. The little girl meanwhile had fled the adult world completely and was swinging her short skis back and forth in rhythmic boredom, singing a song to herself.

They had exactly nine and a half minutes to share their ride from the base to the mid-mountain station at 10,455 feet. It is an unusual interval of time, nine and a half minutes, to be trapped together with a beautiful stranger of the opposite sex, traveling in intimate proximity on a chair dangling twenty or thirty feet above the earth. Howie was determined to make the most of it.

"So where are *you* from?" he asked the lady. He was betting she would say Santa Fe because she had the look. But he was wrong.

"San Geronimo."

"You've lived here for a while?"

"Not really. I'm one of those dreaded newcomers," she told him.

Howie laughed. After Texans, everyone in New Mexico hated newcomers next—a rich vein of loathing, since there were newcomers here galore.

"What do you do in town?" he prodded.

He felt the slightest hesitation on her part. "I'm a doctor," she said guardedly.

This surprised him. She appeared too young to be a doctor. Too pretty, perhaps, though certainly this was a sexual prejudice on his part. "I bet a small town like San Geronimo is always in need of a good doctor," he mentioned.

"Actually, my practice is in Albuquerque."

"You *commute* to Albuquerque?"

"It's not so bad."

"It's three hours each way!"

"Well, I only work three-and-a-half days a week, so that

makes it easier. And I've been studying some language tapes in the car to fill the time."

"No kidding? Which language?"

"Swahili." She said it with a shrug of her shoulders as though it were no big deal.

"I'm impressed," he said. "But why Swahili?"

For a bold modern woman, she seemed unexpectedly shy. "I have a fantasy of starting a medical clinic in Africa . . . I don't know where exactly. Probably Swahili won't do me any good. But as a doctor, I long to be . . . well, useful."

"I can understand that," Howie answered, thinking, hot damn! This is *my* sort of Lady in White, from head to pretty toe. An idealist, even. He was looking at her perhaps too intensely, for he felt her consciously break the connection.

She turned deliberately to Jack, who had been sitting without expression throughout the conversation, as though he were not on the same chair. For a big man, Jack had a curious ability to disappear when he wished.

"Are you an academic as well?" she asked.

Jack smiled with a dormant sadness Howie had often seen in him. "Oh, no! God forbid!—I'm only a cop," he said with modesty. "Or rather, I used to be."

"Jack here was a big shot in the San Francisco Police Department before he retired," Howie explained to the lady doctor, feeling an odd need to speak up on his friend's behalf.

"Is that so?" said the doctor. But she did not seem pleased at the idea of sharing a chairlift with a police officer, highly ranked or otherwise. "What exactly did you do?"

"Oh, mostly office stuff, really. The great bureaucratic tango," he said vaguely. "But it's past history now. These days battling grasshoppers in my garden is about the extent of my excitement."

"You live in San Geronimo?"

"In town, yes. My wife inherited a house here."

"You must be glad to be away from all that big-city violence," she remarked.

"Actually, early retirement was somewhat forced upon me," he told her gently.

The lady doctor smiled vaguely and decided not to pursue the subject. They passed over an expert run, Apache Chute—a name that was sheer fantasy, since Apaches had never lived in

this particular corner of New Mexico. The white man—
Howard Moon Deer often noticed—did not burden himself un-
necessarily with historical fact. Below the chair two beginner
skiers had appeared on the slope, coming out from the trees
onto terrain that was clearly way over their ability. Probably
they had dared each other to do this run. One of the men wore
a moose-head ski hat with antlers on it. The other had no hat
at all, but he carried a can of Bud in one hand, a bit of Milwaukee courage. They disappeared below with a good deal of
laughter and shouting, barely upright, their skis in a wide
kamikaze stance pointed straight down the mountain.

"My God!" said the lady doctor scornfully. "Budweiser!"

Howie was amused. "You think it would have been any better if they were drinking Grolsch?"

She shook her head mournfully, momentarily robbed of
words by the sight of beer-drinking yahoos. Howie imagined
only expensive wine would dampen her own pretty lips, for
she was on the other side of a huge culinary chasm. Meanwhile
the magic chair kept gliding ever upward into the heavens. The
little girl, Angela, yawned and began to make a snowball from
the fluffy powder that had fallen in her lap. The lady doctor
wiped her goggles clear of snow with the backs of her gloves.

"I hate skiing when I can't see," she said.

"On a day like this, forget your eyes—use your feet to see,"
Howie told her.

She glanced at him skeptically. "You're kidding. Your
feet?"

"Sure. Let your feet guide the way over the terrain. There's
an exercise I did once in a ski clinic—the instructor had us go
down an intermediate slope with our eyes closed. What you do
is imagine you have eyes in your big toes. You sort of caress
the snow, feel your way down the slope, delicate as a pussy
cat. It improved my skiing a lot."

"Yes, but what if you encounter a tree?" she asked archly.

"Well, there are limits of course to every theory," he admitted. "During the clinic, the instructor naturally kept his eyes
open and told us where not to go."

"Hmm . . . I'm not sure what I think of these fancy ideas. I
learned to ski as a kid in southern California, and we just did
it without a lot of conceptualization."

They were coming up fast now to the end of their ride. They

lifted above a final stand of evergreens, and Howie could see the attendant standing with a shovel by the warming shed near the huge wheel that would turn the chair around and send it back toward the base of the mountain. Talking with the pretty doctor, Howie had almost forgotten Jack. The responsibility of taking care of him returned with a shot of anxiety.

"Jack," he said over the heads of the doctor and her daughter, "put the tips of your skis up. I'll tell you when to stand up . . . about fifteen seconds now."

He grunted irritably.

The lady glanced curiously at Jack, and then at Howie.

"Is he going to have trouble getting off?"

"Jack hasn't skied for some time," he explained.

On a chairlift with strangers, skiers bond for the few minutes of allotted time, then disengage as they near the top. Jack Wilder, Howard Moon Deer, and the mother and daughter sat together now without speaking, watching their ascent past the final tower into the approaching station. They readied their poles and adjusted their gloves and goggles.

"Here we go, Jack!" Howie said with forced optimism. They glided the last few feet into the station. "You can stand . . . *now* . . . upsy-daisy. . . ."

The lady doctor helped Angela hop from the chair, since the little girl's legs weren't quite long enough to reach the ground. Four abreast, they rose from the seat and began to slide along the gentle decline from the lift.

"Jack, ski slightly to the right," Howie suggested. "We'll coast to the flat spot about twenty feet ahead . . . You're doing fine. . . ."

Jack pushed the backs of his skis out to make a small wedge. This slowed him down so that he was no longer abreast. Moon Deer skied ahead with the lady and the little girl. They stopped at the crest of a small knoll.

"This way, Jack," he called. "Come over here and stop . . . I want to check my bindings."

Jack skied to Howie and snowplowed to a halt—stolid and clumsy, but Howie was relieved to see he was in control. The lady stooped down to fasten the snaps on her daughter's boots. When she stood up, she regarded Howie with a smile.

"Good luck with your dissertation," she said.

"Good luck with your doctoring," he told her in return. "Bye, Angela," he said to the little girl.

The doctor nodded curtly at Jack, who had not won her heart. Then she turned, skated a few feet to gather speed, and skied away with her daughter, who followed like a duckling in her mother's wake. Even on the flat knoll Howie could tell the Lady in White was an expert skier; she moved with the effortless grace of someone long accustomed to easy gliding on snow. The little girl lacked her mother's form, but she too was entirely relaxed and fearless. Howie watched the mother and daughter disappear over the lip of the hill toward the maze of trails below.

Howie liked his snow maiden just a little less in that she had so obviously not liked Jack, but had seen in him only her own projection of a certain type: a cop. That seemed shallow to him, and a disappointment. Still, they were a scrumptious pair, and when they were gone, he felt a sudden angst of female deprivation. Like the feeling you get if someone snatches away a plate of food you are about to eat.

Would he see her again?

Would he ever find true love everlasting?

Jack heard the involuntary sigh escape Howie's lips. "Forget her," he said.

"That's easy for you to say, Jack. You're fifty-two years old and happily married. I'm twenty-seven and single."

"We'll discuss your love life another time, Howie," he said. "At the moment we have work to do."

And indeed they did. For they had not come skiing today for frivolous reasons, but to meet the very first client of their newly formed enterprise, Wilder & Associate, Private Investigations. But first Howie had a problem on his hands: he had to get Jack to the next chairlift, then up to the top of the mountain and down the other side.

The problem was that Commander Jack Wilder, medically retired from the San Francisco Police Department, was totally blind.

3

A young woman from the ski patrol stood watching them from the side of the trail. She wore a red jacket with a cross on the back, and Howie was certain she was going to bust them for reckless endangerment. Probably felony foolishness as well. She had curly dark gold hair and sun-bronzed skin, and for some reason she was studying Jack and Howie with intense interest.

"Be cool, Jack, and just follow my voice," Howie said softly.

Fortunately, the hill here was not steep, and they made it past without incident. He even managed to flash a smile to show how relaxed he was. A pretty girl, he noticed. One of those blond Wagnerian ski goddesses you see at places like San Geronimo Peak, a body bursting with athletic health. As he skied past, Howie saw she had a small gold ring piercing her left nostril. This seemed fairly hip for the ski patrol, mildly intriguing.

Then he forgot about her because he had his hands full with Jack. They entered an intermediate run called Jabberwalky, and suddenly this was not a game anymore, this was really skiing. Howie stayed close to Jack, barking out the turns like a drill sergeant: "Right! . . . Left! . . . Right! . . . Left!" The snow was swirling around them so thickly that even for Howie there was little visibility, hardly more than a few feet.

"See the terrain with your feet, Jack!" Howie urged him, just as he had said to the lady on the chairlift. "On a day like this, I'm skiing blind, the same as you are."

"Yes, yes," Jack said through gritted teeth. "But spare me the pep talk, please."

Howie laughed when seconds later Jack took a spectacular

fall, headfirst, and came up sputtering snow. Howie had to pull him to his feet.

"You look like a snowman, Jack. Do you want to rest?"

"No. Let's go on."

Jack certainly had nerve. He had lost his sight four years ago, and Howie was always astonished how incredibly hard Jack worked to overcome his limitations. In town, he spent hours every day memorizing where things were. Not only his house—he had memorized that long ago—but the street outside his house, the walk to the park ten minutes away, even the downtown grid. He had worked out a navigational system, steering to the warmth of the sun in his face, depending on the time of day. It worked on sunny days at least, and with a few routes. But he suffered countless falls and collisions as well. Howie's big fear was that one day Jack would have all of San Geronimo memorized, just as some developer came to town and changed it all.

They continued down the white trail. Howie managed to get Jack into a dancing rhythm, one turn after another, warning him of the obstacles ahead, as far as he was able to see them himself. It was obvious that Jack had been a good skier at one time, though he bobbed up and down a great deal and kept his feet too close together in an Austrian style of skiing that was now thoroughly out-of-date. But Howie was impressed that Jack could manage at all.

Jabberwalky led to the Peak Express, a two-person chair that carried them from mid-mountain to the very top, an elevation of over twelve thousand feet. The snow was blowing hard on the summit, and they ducked down quickly onto the back side of the mountain, which was more protected from the wind. Finally, after ten minutes and nearly as many falls, Howie told Jack to stop. They had arrived at an unobtrusive bend in the trail where a separate track disappeared beneath the snow-heavy bough of a blue spruce. Howie led the way into the forest, talking Jack along the bends of the trail, moving slowly. There were signs people had been here before them— three separate ski tracks whose outlines had not yet been entirely obscured by the new snow. But the clearing itself, when they arrived, was empty of life. Not a soul. Nothing but the snow coming down.

"What time is it?" Jack asked. He hadn't had this much exercise for years, and he was panting for breath.

"Ten-forty-three," Howie answered.

"We're late, Howie! We were supposed to be here at ten-thirty! You should have told me."

"Jack, under the circumstances we couldn't have gotten here any faster."

"Then we should have allowed more time."

"Anyway, our client is late as well. In a storm like this, everybody gets slowed down."

"All right, then. We'll wait."

Howie had been here before. The spot was officially known as Phoenix Rock, because of an oddly shaped granite obelisk that rose nearly thirty feet high in a suggestively phallic manner at one side of the clearing. But the locals generally called it Doobie Rock, because of the smoking activity that went on here. The clearing stood at the very edge of the mountain, and in good weather there was a spectacular view of the desert thousands of feet below. On pristine days you could see hundreds of miles to distant mesa tops, all brown and dreamy on the western horizon, and even see a hint of the Rio Grande. Most skiers Howie knew paused here for a beat or two, while stuffing their pipe back into their pocket, to contemplate the grandeur of planet Earth. But today there was no visibility at all, just the blank whiteness of the storm.

The minutes ticked by. It seemed to Howie miraculous they had a client at last—a local big shot even: Senator Kit Hampton, the owner of San Geronimo Peak and descendant of a ranching family whose roots went back more than a hundred years in New Mexico. In terms of the local Spanish and Indian Pueblo cultures, this was no time at all, of course, about as nouveau as a microscopic meal in the center of a huge plate. But it was said that Kit Hampton was distantly related to his namesake, Kit Carson, the wily explorer who had once tramped about in these mountains, and this made him aristocracy as far as the Johnny-come-lately Anglos were concerned.

As for his political career, that was a thing of the past—it was now more than a decade and a half since he had lost his seat in the U.S. Senate to a Republican challenger, a man who had labeled him sarcastically as "the Jerry Brown of New

Mexico." Many people said he had been smeared, and there
was an ancient sex scandal connected to the lost campaign
whose details Howie had long forgotten. Still, for all that,
small towns love their celebrities, and Kit Hampton would always be known fondly as "the Senator," regardless of scandals
and election results.

Howie had never met the man in the flesh, though he had
seen his photograph in the local newspaper often enough, at-
tending this or that art opening or charity luncheon: a fit, silver-
haired man of distinguished appearance who was about
everything you'd want to find in a local aristocrat. Not only
did he run the ski area—San Geronimo Peak stood on family
land, part of the old Hampton ranch—but he had served on the
board of directors of the Santa Fe Opera, he was a past president of the San Geronimo Art Association, and he was still a
force in all sorts of high-minded civic ventures to protect the
environment from out-of-town real estate developers who
were always threatening to build shopping malls and golf
courses. Some might say that a ski resort was itself not exactly
a friend to the environment—but you didn't say that, apparently, if such downhill pleasures were the main source of your
own personal fortune.

The big question in Howie's mind was why such an exalted
individual wanted to meet with a dangerously overeducated
Indian and a retired police commander from San Francisco.
Senator Hampton had answered their small advertisement in
the *San Geronimo Post*. He had spoken to Jack on the telephone yesterday, suggesting they meet him on the slopes today
at Doobie Rock. This seemed an odd request, but rich people
reserve the right to be odd. Senator Hampton explained only
that he had a problem, and Jack would understand the situation
more readily if he could rendezvous with him at this particular
place. Most considerately, he had arranged free passes for
them at the ticket office. Howie's guess was that the Senator
was going to ask them to spy on his employees and inform him
who was smoking Mother Nature on company time. Howie
was not thrilled about the prospect of being a narc, but Jack refused to do divorce work and there was not otherwise a huge
demand for two would-be private investigators in the small
town of San Geronimo. Their ad had been running for two

months, and this was their first serious response. How could they turn it down?

After nearly ten minutes of waiting, Howie finally spoke: "Jack, are you certain it was actually Senator Hampton who called you yesterday?"

"Of course I'm certain. Why?"

"Well, it *is* April Fools' Day. I hate to say this, but maybe someone's just having a bit of fun at our expense."

"No, that's not possible. I know his voice."

"You've met him?"

"Of course, I've met him."

"You didn't tell me that."

Jack shrugged. "It was a number of years ago, in the late eighties. I helped him out of a jam in San Francisco. It concerned his daughter, Josie. She was a junior at the Art Institute going through a rebellious phase. One of my detectives picked her up in the Haight during a drug sting—she was dating one of the dealers, only indirectly involved, in the wrong place at the wrong time. So I let her go."

"Was she pretty?"

"What do you mean, was she *pretty*? What the hell kind of question is that?"

"I'm trying to imagine you as a softie, Jack. Maybe the heart of Commander Wilder was melted by a pretty face."

"Her looks had *nothing* to do with my decision," Jack said stuffily. "I was after the big boss, not small-fry and bystanders. However, her father was grateful. He stopped by my office when he came to California to fetch his daughter back home, and we ended up having quite a long talk. When he saw our ad in the paper, he remembered my name."

"So you don't have a clue what he wants now?"

"Howie, I've told you this about five times—he said he would explain everything once he had shown us Doobie Rock."

Howie smiled. "He hasn't seen you for years. I bet you didn't tell him—did you?—about your eyes. . . ."

"My health is not his concern," Jack interrupted testily. "What time is it now?"

"Nearly eleven."

"We'll wait another fifteen minutes."

It was a big thing for Jack to be working again as a detec-

tive, and Howie hoped their mysterious client was going to
show. When the minutes ticked by and no one appeared,
Howie felt more and more badly for him.

"Time?" Jack asked.

"Eleven-fourteen."

"Well," Jack said finally, "maybe this *was* an April Fools'
prank, after all."

"Not if you actually recognized his voice, Jack. Probably he
didn't think we'd show up in this weather, and he's down at
the bottom waiting for us in his office."

"He would have phoned. Or sent someone up here with a
message."

"We can wait a few more minutes, if you'd like."

"No," he said with a discouraged sigh. "We might as well
go. Hell with it."

"Just gotta pee," Howie told him. He slid his skis close to
the edge of the precipice. Astronauts probably have an easier
time taking a pee than a fully dressed alpine skier. Howie
planted his poles in the snow, then took off his gloves and im-
paled them upon the poles. Next he opened snaps, undid the
belt around his waist, and pulled down the zipper of his snowsuit from neck to torso. Then he only needed to search through
layers of shirts and long underwear with a cold blue hand until
locating at last that shriveled thing, a penis in a snowstorm,
which was not exactly an object of manly pride at such a time.
Howie did his best to redeem his ego by peeing in a mighty arc
out beyond the precipice, sending his small stream a thousand
feet into the storm. Adults may put on a fine pretense of civi-
lization, but few of us entirely outgrow the infantile pleasures
of the toilet.

Howie peered over the precipice as far as he dared, hoping
to see how magnificently far he could send his yellow river
into the wide world. And that's when he saw a pair of skis,
blue Rossignols, on a narrow ledge about fifteen feet below
him. And then he noticed a leg protruding from the snow at a
very odd angle. Howie was so startled, he dribbled on his boot.

"Oh, Jack! . . . Oh, Jesus, *Jack*!"

"What is it, Howie?"

"I think I've found our client."

4

When Howie was ten, he discovered the dead body of his Uncle Wilbur Fat Cloud in a '57 Chevy pickup, collapsed on the steering wheel, and he had nightmares about it for years. Fat Cloud earned his name because he ate twice as much as anyone else on the reservation and he weighed close to three hundred pounds; he departed this world on the wings of a heart attack with a pleasant, mildly surprised look on his face. Such was Howie's single contact with a dead body before this moment. Like most Americans, native or otherwise, he had done his best to keep the "great trickster" a distant concept.

Now, on this April Fools' Day in the snow, Howie found himself fascinated and repulsed. He couldn't bear to look at the broken thing on the ledge below; yet it was impossible to tear his eyes away.

Jack skied closer.

"Don't move!" Howie screamed at him. "Don't get too close to the edge! Man, you're going to give me a heart attack!"

"Good God, Howie, chill out! There's no reason to get so excited."

"I'm an intellectual, Jack. I don't come across dead bodies every day. . . . I think I'm going to puke."

"Go ahead," Jack suggested coldly. "Maybe it'll clear your head."

Howie tried. But he could only give a few dry heaves, nothing very satisfying.

"Howie, I want you to take a few deep breaths and tell me how much exactly of the body can you see?"

"Only the legs and torso."

"What about the ledge it's on? How far down is it?"

"Ten, twelve feet. Far enough."

"And how wide is it?"

"Maybe eight feet wide. It's only an outcropping of rock. Then after that, it looks like there's nothing, just empty space all the way to the desert below. But I can't see too far because of the snow."

"You feeling a little better now?"

"Yeah, sure."

"Good. Now, I'd like you to look at the ledge and tell me this . . . is there any way you can get down there?"

"*Down* there? Are you kidding?"

"Take your time and study the terrain, Howie. That's all I'm asking. If you can't get down safely, we'll go and call the ski patrol. But if there's any chance at all . . ."

Howie sighed, feeling very put-upon. He was fearful of heights, particularly the extreme vertical kind where one could fall screaming through many thousands of feet of empty air. "Man, I don't know . . . there's a tree, an aspen. It's growing up from the ledge against the side of the cliff. Maybe I can use it to sort of shimmy down."

"The tree's strong enough? It's not rotten?"

"It looks okay. Hard to tell this time of year . . ."

"I don't want you to do anything foolish."

"Believe me, I'm not *planning* to do anything foolish." Howie studied the aspen tree, the side of the cliff, the narrow ledge below, and the legs and torso and Rossignol skis for about another five minutes. Nothing changed in that time except more snow drifting down. He was frankly terrified.

"How you doing?" Jack asked quietly.

"I'm scared shitless, Jack, if you really want to know the truth."

"Naturally. Anyone would be frightened to climb down there. Let's get the ski patrol."

"No, I'm going to do it," Howie insisted. *Why* he was going to do it, he did not precisely know. It seemed that Indians, even the Ivy League sort, had to be brave; it was engraved in his genetic engineering, and if he didn't give this a try, he was going to feel like a failure. "I just need a few minutes to psyche myself up."

"Okay. But don't turn this into some rite of passage. It's a physical problem, not spiritual. Why don't you step out of your skis and look it over some more. Is the aspen really strong enough to hold you? Are there any places in the rock where you can get a foothold? These are the only questions you need to ask yourself, not whether you are brave enough."

And so Jack talked him through it—standing safely, it might be noted, in the center of the small clearing, well away from the edge of the precipice himself. Howie stepped from his bindings into waist-deep snow, and experienced an unpleasant thrill to the testicles. He had forgotten that his snowsuit zipper was still open to the crotch. It woke him up big time. He zipped himself up, got his gloves on, and scrambled onto a rock that had been mostly cleared of snow by the wind. From here he was able to take hold of the trunk of the aspen. It was a lithe, slippery young tree only two or three inches in diameter. But it seemed anchored solidly in the ledge below, so he gave it a try.

The moment he climbed aboard, the tree bent like a rubber toothpick, and for a nasty second Howie thought he was going to plummet to the desert below. He hung on tenaciously and somehow slid down a few feet to where the trunk was thicker and more solid. From there he managed to wedge himself between the tree and the cliff, using the rigid toes of his ski boots to find a sort of steep staircase in the rock to descend to the ledge below.

"I'm down, Jack," he called finally. His hands ached, his shoulders hurt from tension, but he was in one piece.

"Good. Now, tell me what you see."

The dead man was in a stylishly cut dark blue powder suit, facedown in the snow, his arms outstretched as though he were embracing the mountain. At least Howie assumed it was a man from the angular lines of the figure, though the person was half buried in fresh powder and it was impossible to be sure of his gender, let alone his identity. The bindings had released upon impact, as they were designed to do, so that the skis had separated from the skier and stuck into the snow at odd angles near the body. As Howie's gaze traveled from the boots upward, he could tell there was something very wrong about the head. There were some unappetizing tufts of white hair and congealed bubbles of blood. The skull looked more like a smashed melon than anything human. From where Howie was standing, he was not able to see Jack in the clearing on top, but he shouted all this grisly information up to him, feeling like he was addressing some all-powerful god.

"Is it the Senator?" Jack called down.

"Maybe. Maybe not."

"The next step is going to require a strong stomach," Jack warned. "I want you to turn the corpse over onto his back so you can get a better look."

"Good God, you want me to *touch* him?"

"He's not going to hurt you, Howie."

Howie complained loudly. He told Jack he should climb down and do it himself. But since this was out of the question, he gritted his teeth and pulled the body loose from the snow and got it turned over on its back. The corpse was not entirely frozen, but it was stiff enough, and turning it over was not easy because of its outstretched arms. It was a man—Howie had been right about the gender identification, which can be tricky in these androgynous times.

"Holy shit," said Moon Deer, contemplating the unfortunate spectacle of human meat once the soul had departed. The top of the forehead was a bloody pulp, and below that two bulging eyes stared off in different directions. His mouth was frozen in a strange smile that showed several teeth broken off like a berserk Halloween pumpkin.

"I'm almost certain it's Senator Hampton, Jack. But I've only seen photographs of the guy, and this . . . this *thing* doesn't look like anything I would recognize except in a bad dream."

"Take a guess about the cause of death."

"That's easy. He fell and hit his head against the rocks. The front of his skull is crushed in."

"Much blood?"

"Some. It's congealed on his forehead, and there's blood in the snow from where I lifted him out."

"You're doing great. Now, Howie, strictly speaking, we should go report the death to the proper authorities, without disturbing the body anymore. I certainly don't want to lead you into breaking the law. Nevertheless, this particular opportunity to gather information may never present itself again."

"What do you want me to do, Jack?" Howie asked with resignation.

"I want you to search through his pockets and tell me everything you find. . . ."

For the next few minutes, under Jack's persistent orders, Howie searched through the dead man's zippered pockets. He found a billfold in an inside breast compartment. The victim was indeed Kit Armstrong Hampton of 197 Nuevo Año Rd., San Geronimo, New Mexico, according to his driver's license. There was also every kind of credit card, gold and platinum, as well as two hundred and seventy-three dollars in cash and a set of keys on a lucky rabbit's foot charm—which had not done Senator Hampton a great deal of good in this instance. The billfold contained nothing personal, no photographs of loved ones, or phone numbers scrawled on small pieces of paper. And most importantly, no indication of why Jack and Howie had been summoned there that day.

It was while putting the billfold back into the inside breast compartment, that Howie touched something unusual: the jagged end of a wooden shaft that had broken off and was embedded into the chest just below the sternum. Howie retracted his hand quickly and found it was sticky with dark, globular blood—blood that had changed in consistency from the cold and had become rubbery as chewing gum. Howie wiped off his hand with an urgent motion in the clean snow nearby.

"This is going from bad to worse," he said to Jack.

"What's going on?"

Howie was about to say that he did not have a clue what was going on, but then he saw a small wedge of colored feather sticking out of the snow about a foot from the body. He reached for the feather and found it was attached to a few inches of wooden shaft.

"My God, Jack! It's an arrow!"

"A *what*?"

"A broken arrow! . . . Kit Hampton was shot with an *arrow,* for chrissake! I didn't see it at first because it got broken off, probably by the fall. It was almost buried in the snow."

Jack was silent for a moment. Then he asked: "What kind of arrow?"

Howie was outraged by Jack's calm. "What do you mean, what *kind* of arrow? It's just an arrow."

"A hunting arrow? A target arrow? What?"

"I know this is going to surprise you, Jack," said Howie with superb patience. "But despite what I told that little girl this morning, I've never actually shot a bow and arrow in my life. I know nothing about them. I've never scalped anyone either, though I have been tempted upon occasion."

"Do you have that out of your system, Howie? If you've got any more comments about your cultural identity, I'm ready to listen."

"No, that'll do for the moment," Howie said with a sigh.

"Good. Then, let's get back to the arrow."

"It's just some cheesy thing from a sporting goods store. For shooting at targets, I suppose."

"Describe the feathers to me."

"They aren't real feathers, just colored plastic bristle. Two of them are bluish-green and the third is yellowish. . . . Jack, I'm starting to get kinda cold down here. Do you think we can wrap this up? I'm beginning to feel we should maybe tell someone about this."

"Yes, yes . . . we'd better get the ski patrol," he agreed reluctantly.

Howie was glad to leave. Death by an arrow bothered him a great deal more than death by falling off a cliff. It brought out some atavistic Indian horror of his own ancestral past, and made him think that maybe he should get his red ass back to Princeton, New Jersey, where people killed each other in more up-to-date ways.

He left the dead man on the ledge, his arms outspread so that he looked crucified on the rocks. At least nature was kind enough to provide a shroud. The soft flakes sifted down, covering the agony of death with the white cool mercy of snow.

5

There was to be one more adventure for Howard Moon Deer
and Jack Wilder before they made it safely to the bottom of
San Geronimo Peak. As a lapsed Jungian, Howie thought of it
later as not so much an accident as synchronicity—the not-so-
chancy coming together of fated objects.

It happened below Wizard on an intermediate trail called
White Fox. (More synchronicity!) Jack was skiing fairly well
but Howie was spaced-out, pondering the meaning of life and
death, and the very thin line between the two. Unfortunately,
it's not a good idea to ponder major philosophical questions
while moving at a brisk speed on skis.

Howie was deep in his thoughts when he became aware of
two figures appearing suddenly from a merging expert trail on
his right, Sipapu Drop. They were skiing fast and sweet. It
took him a moment to realize it was the Lady in White with
whom he had shared a lift earlier in the morning, with her
daughter taking up the rear. The mistake Howie made was to
stop and look at them for a few seconds, for he was in a
dreamy mood and the mother and daughter made a pleasant
sight. The lady doctor was skiing superbly well, moving almost directly down the steep fall line in soft rhythmic turns, a
delicious zigzag through the powder. The little girl followed
fearlessly in her mother's tracks about fifteen feet back, without much form but managing the difficult slope like a pro.
After the horror on the ledge, Howie was enchanted to see
such prettiness.

Then he remembered Jack. The lapse of concentration was
nearly fatal. When Howie came out of his reverie and turned
downhill, he saw that Jack was about to ski off the trail into a
pine tree.

"Jack! Do a hockey stop! Turn right!" he shouted.

Jack responded immediately. He turned out of the fall line away from the tree, but then lost his balance at the end of the turn and fell. Howie skied down after him, concerned that Jack was all right. But now he was not concentrating properly on his own skiing. He hit a small bump beneath the new snow, fell back too far on his skis, and nearly took a nasty tumble. He managed to stay upright, but he lost control for a moment and swerved too far to the side of the trail. All this time, he had been looking only at Jack, but now a blurred motion to the side of his vision made him turn abruptly toward the merging trail. He saw, to his astonishment, that he was on a collision course with the Lady in White. The fault (if there was one) was hers—she was skiing entirely too fast from the expert slope onto the intermediate terrain where Howie was still struggling to stay on his skis. She came like an eagle swooping down while Howie could only stand there flapping like a befuddled turkey.

When the Lady in White saw that she and Howie were destined to crash, she tried to cut her speed with a heroic hockey slide that sent a plume of snow fifteen feet into the air and turned Howie into an instant snowman. But it was too late. They met face-to-face with the inevitability of Newtonian physics. Howie opened his arms so he wouldn't hurt her with his poles, and he caught her in a bear hug. His right ski, a purple Elan, slipped in suggestively between her two white Volks; their legs became intertwined as closely as lovers, and they fell in this intimate embrace upward into the hill.

"Uumph!" she cried in surprise. "Damn it!"

"Sorry," Howie told her. "Are you all right?"

"I didn't see you," she said more calmly. Then she added, "I'm okay . . . anyway, it's my fault."

"No, it's my fault," Howie insisted. "I was off balance."

Howie became gradually aware that this was a uniquely interesting situation; he was holding in his arms a very beautiful woman. Every nerve ending of his male being sensed the slim curves of her body beneath her snowsuit. Her cheeks were glowing pink with exertion, and he could smell the warm clean fragrance of her skin, a girl smell that was a thousand times better than any perfume. Her breath was hot against his cheek, and their legs were interlocked, thigh-to-thigh, in a position Howie used to think of in his early teenage years as "the dry hump." He did his best not to smile, knowing that a single smirk could lose her to him forever.

"Shall we try to get out of this?" she asked calmly.

"We'll have to do it in unison . . . on the count of three?"

Howie and the lady struggled to stand up and separate, but it was no good. It can be difficult on skis under the best of circumstances to get up from an awkward fall, but wrapped up together as they were on a steep slope in fresh powder, it was nearly impossible. The new snow was like quicksand. They managed to get halfway to their feet and then fell back against the hill in a tighter embrace than before.

"Slide backward," she told him.

"I can't," he replied. "The backs of my skis are buried. Why don't you try."

"No, I can't move, either."

"Then, I guess we're stuck with each other," Howie admitted, risking the smallest smile.

They had been holding each other cheek-to-cheek. But now the Lady in White leaned her head backward so she could get a better look at him. Her goggles had come off in the fall, and Howie found himself staring into a pair of large and intelligent brown-gold flecked eyes. Her lips were extremely close, only millimeters away. She was regarding him just as intently as he was staring at her. She must have seen something in his face— something Howie could only guess at—because suddenly she decided the situation was funny. Her eyes sparkled, and she threw back her head and laughed.

"Mommy! I'm cold!" said the little girl, who had stopped on the slope a dozen feet below.

"Yes, what's happening here?" Jack added grumpily. He was still sitting on the snow, not far from where the child was standing.

"Well, I can't say this hasn't been interesting. But I think we're going to have to separate," the Lady in White told Howie with a subtle smile. "Have you any suggestions?"

"I'll get out of my bindings," Howie told her.

He reached down behind himself to the plastic release lever on his uphill ski. He stepped out backward waist-deep into the snow, and in a moment they were able to pull free from one another. The lady kicked her skis loose from the snow and gave Howie a final appraising look. Howie wanted to say a hundred things to her, but the frankly sexual manner in which she had examined him left him tongue-tied. He could only give her a goofy smile. Like he was some moronic thing from the backwoods who had never seen a woman before.

Then he made it worse. "I hope I run into you again sometime," he said. He didn't even mean to be funny; it was simply the only inanity he could manage to come up with.

She arched her eyebrow at him and turned away. Then she skied down to the little girl.

"Come on, Angela—let's go, sweetie."

They skied away down the hill. Howie watched her as she made impeccable parallel turns into the great snowy distance below.

"I wish I could ski like that," Howie said with longing. He was pretty good, but watching her he realized he worked at it too hard. Probably he was too far down on the food chain ever to fully relax into frivolous play. He was willing to bet she had a husband who drove a Porsche and made a million dollars a year and was an even better skier than she was.

"Let's get going," Jack said wearily. "My rear end feels like a block of ice."

Jack's rear end was not nearly as enjoyable to contemplate as the Lady in White's. Nevertheless, Howie gave Jack a hand up, and then he talked him down the mountain, turn by turn. Thinking to himself: Holy shit! How many times in a lifetime does a woman like that come sailing into your open arms? . . . and I blew it! I couldn't think of a clever word to say . . . and then, worst of all, I let her go!

6

When Howard Moon Deer looked back over his life, wondering how he had gotten himself into this weird predicament—a seeing-eye Indian to a blind detective—he had to place the blame squarely on his own fatal curiosity. From his earliest childhood, Moon Deer had always found white people wonderfully exotic. Laughable, certainly, comically full of delusions and lies, but a strangely moving race. He had devoured tales of the paleface world with the same wide-eyed interest that an earlier generation of white children once read about Indians. He dreamed of New York, London, Paris, St. Petersburg. He literally read his way out of his dysfunctional corner of Paha Sapa, which is the name the Sioux gave long ago to the Black Hills of South Dakota. For Howie, books were the wings that carried him away from his Airstream trailer, the dust and wind, the sheep grazing outside among rusting cars, his alcoholic father, defeated mother . . . an entire tribe of diabetic, overweight relatives who made him feel ashamed.

In later life white friends sometimes asked him in accusing tones, where was his Indian pride? He tried to explain that in his childhood, Indian pride was not even slightly in the picture; it had died at Wounded Knee and a thousand other places in a century of demoralized captivity on the reservation. Personally, Howie was fixed upon his own bookish path. As a Sioux, he was impressed from an early age that General George A. Custer had graduated last in his class at West Point, the Class of 1861. It seemed to him there might be some correlation between this fact—Custer's last standing, academically speaking—and Yellow Hair's porcupine ending at the Little Big Horn at the hands of his ancestors. Howie was determined to do better in school himself.

He was fortunate in this task to have the help of his sixth-grade teacher, Miss Fransworth, a gray-haired, flat-chested, leather-faced spinster from Nebraska. He was Miss Fransworth's pet, her pride and joy, and probably the only tangible success she ever had as a teacher on the reservation. He read every book she gave him and was hungry for more. Miss Fransworth shared a house with another gray-haired, flat-chested, leather-faced spinster named Miss O'Dowell, who was the librarian in the nearby town of Red Creek. Together Miss Fransworth and Miss O'Dowell planned and plotted his future. For Howie's junior year in high school, they managed to get him a full scholarship to a fancy prep school in Vermont, the Putney School, where the regular students paid over twenty thousand dollars a year for the privilege of having a classmate like him who was an authentic Native American.

And that was Howard Moon Deer's early ticket out of South Dakota. From Putney to Dartmouth, Princeton to Paris, he followed the scholarship trail and became the sort of Indian rich people liked to invite to their summer homes. It was an interesting life, not bad at all; though New York, London, Paris, and St. Petersburg were a disappointment when he finally arrived in these fine places, for they could not possibly live up to his perfect childhood conception of them. White people, he concluded, were about the same as red people, only they had a lot more toys.

It was at Princeton that Howie had begun to suspect that human beings were creatures of appetite, and that society was nothing but a kind of henhouse pecking order in which the strong ate better—and ate a good deal more—than the weak. It was a terrible vision, really. Suddenly everywhere Howie looked, he saw an open mouth that was poised to gobble something (or someone) up. This vision gradually matured into a new academic field he called culinary psycho-sociology. He titled his Ph.D. dissertation, "Philosophical Divisions at the Top of the Food Chain," and he set out to show how the American Dream had turned into the Great American Divide through a giant but basically simple case of acute indigestion. Budweiser versus Grolsch . . . iceberg lettuce versus arugula and baby greens . . . the sort of person who said "shrimp," and the very different kind who said "prawn"; these were the issues, he believed, that divided America in two, a seismic cultural split that was of a more profound and fundamental nature than Republican versus Democrat.

His culinary studies led him to Paris eventually on a grant from the Betty Crocker Foundation—American indigestion was always his primary concern, but he was looking for international comparisons and, of course, some fun. He met Bob and Nova Davidson at a small café on the Boulevard Raspail—they were at the next table one day and started a conversation with him. The three soon became the best of friends in a way that is only possible among ex-patriot travelers. Bob and Nova were from San Geronimo, New Mexico; he was from Red Creek, South Dakota—from the vantage point of a Paris café, it felt like they were almost neighbors, part of the same American West. Bob and Nova were both artists, quite talented in their separate ways, but lucky to live on Nova's trust fund rather than the less reliable whims of the marketplace. They had taken a flat for six months near the Luxembourg Gardens, and soon Howie and they were doing nearly everything together. When the Davidsons returned to the States, they made him promise to visit in New Mexico as soon as possible, and stay as long as he liked in their guest house. In the intensity of their foreign adventures, they had started to feel inseparable.

Howie too went home eventually, but with a sad heart. There had been a woman in Paris, a fiery redheaded philosophy student, an American girl taking a year off from Radcliffe who threw him over eventually for a black rock musician from Nigeria. Even at the time Howie understood perfectly well that she chose the African because her parents would be even more shocked by him than by Howie, a mere American Sioux. Nevertheless, this did nothing for Howie's self esteem, and he was in a funky mood. His dissertation seemed suddenly hopeless and boring, not nearly as interesting as the hot wounds of love. He was ready for a break from academia, and from Paris he headed directly to South Dakota, determined to rediscover his roots. For a few months he wore a lot of feathers and buckskin and turquoise, and was about the most Indian Indian you'd ever want to meet. Howie's parents, who ran a gas station on the reservation, thought he was nuts.

He soon realized, of course, that there was nothing for him in South Dakota. He had been away entirely too long, and he had never really fit in there in the first place. Even Miss

Fransworth and Miss O'Dowell were gone, their dry bodies blown off by the prairie wind to some new destination. So Howie took off his feathers, buckskin, and turquoise, and wondered what to do next. As far as he could see, he was neither fish nor fowl. His education had resulted only in a grand dislocation: he did not belong anywhere. For a few weeks Howie considered suicide by overeating, but he could not quite settle on the menu. In the end he decided to take up the offer of Bob and Nova, the nice couple he had met in Paris, and become their houseguest in New Mexico.

And that's how he came to meet Jack Wilder, on a day in September only a few weeks after he had arrived in New Mexico. The weather was extreme that day, breathlessly clear in the morning but by the afternoon the wind had come up and the sky was suddenly black with thunderclouds. For no particular reason, Howie decided to borrow Bob's mountain bike and take a ride, little suspecting that his life was about to change. He pedaled out onto the two-lane highway with his ponytail flapping in the wind. When no one was looking, he did a papa-wheelie. He was twenty-seven years old, a creature of academia; but riding a bicycle made him feel like he was twelve.

The sky grew darker, rain fell, lightning crackled in the heavens. Howie didn't care. He cruised down a long grade into the eastern edge of town, and soon found himself on Kachina Lane, a new residential street carved out of the desert that was lined with freshly planted cottonwood trees all in a nice straight row. Kachina Lane led into Calle Santa Margarita, a narrow gravel road. Here he entered an older part of town, a mixed neighborhood of old money and even older poverty, side by side. As Howie rode, the rain began pelting down harder and the wind was furious. Occasionally the lightning struck so close that he could see where it hit the ground in front of him. Through a break in the black clouds, San Geronimo Peak in the distance was bathed in a single swath of sunlight, fantastical.

It was an unaccountable afternoon. Moon Deer ran his bike through a big brown puddle and found himself letting out a high coyote war cry he had learned as a child. He pedaled up a steep grade and then flew down the other side. And that's when he saw a large and ungainly figure, a gray-haired man struggling in the front yard outside an old adobe house, trying unsuccessfully to get a blue plastic tarp tied down to protect his ripening tomato plants from the driving rain. He made such an odd picture that Howie stopped in order to see him better. The man was framed against the black sky, and the tarp was flapping wildly in his grasp, as though he were wrestling with an angel. The scene was almost biblical. There was a dog, a wet German shepherd, dancing about excitedly at the man's heels. It looked as if the wind was going to pick up the man, the tarp, and the dog as well and carry them all off together into the black heavens.

Howie got off his bike to see if he could be of help. The man didn't see him, and the flapping of the tarp covered the sound of his footsteps. Then the dog noticed his presence and leapt his way as he approached.

"Who's there?" the man cried, spinning about. Just at that moment, a flash of lightning illuminated his face and Howie was filled with terror. The man did not seem human. Water ran down his stony cheeks; his gray hair was tangled by the wind and rain. There was a scar on the left side of his face. But what terrified Howie most were the man's eyes, fixed and bulging, staring at him hideously. As he stood gaping, there was a crash of thunder, a huge exclamation mark. Howie screamed and tripped backward and fell into the mud. The German shepherd was on him immediately. At first Howie thought the dog was going to eat him alive. But the animal only licked his face with a scratchy tongue and vast enthusiasm.

"Katya!" the man shouted. His voice was low and powerful, like a thunder god. "Katya, come here!"

The dog obeyed reluctantly, slinking away from him, tail wagging, moving to the man's side. Howie sat up in the mud, feeling foolish and miserable.

"Who are you?" the man demanded. And there came another boom of thunder, as if on command.

Howie was terrified. "I'm . . . I was riding by . . ."

"Yes! Speak up!"

"I was riding a bike," Howie managed. "You looked like you needed help."

"You stopped to help me?"

"Yes, I thought . . ."

"Well, get hold of the other end of the tarp, then," the man said gruffly. He added more gently: "There's no reason to be frightened. I'm not Frankenstein, for chrissake. . . . I'm only blind. And as a matter of fact, I would appreciate a hand if you have a moment."

Howie laughed at his own terror. This wasn't some unholy spirit after all, but only a blind man in the rain having trouble with a household chore. So he stood up from the mud and helped the man tie the ends of the tarp to an apple tree at one end of his tomato patch, and a picnic table at the other. The wind was so ferocious it took nearly ten minutes to get this done, even with the two of them at work. The dog worried Howie at first, but she turned out to be a real softie, wagging her tail like crazy, overexcited by the drama of the storm and the black afternoon. They were soaked to the skin by the time they were finished, and the blind man invited Howie inside for a cup of tea.

"The name's Jack Wilder," he said. "Thanks for stopping by."

"I'm Howard," Moon Deer answered, doing his best to re-trieve his fine Princeton persona. "Glad I could help."

The house was a true adobe, probably very old, with thick walls of mud and straw and big old timbers holding up the roof. The kitchen was a large room with a low ceiling and a kiva fireplace at the far end. Howie had an impression of wooden surfaces and many knives and kitchen utensils; cast iron pots and pans hanging from hooks; shelves crammed with jars of spices and food. There were potted plants on every win-dowsill as well as on the tables and counters. A few geraniums, a cactus, but mostly spices, since this was a working kitchen— thyme, oregano, basil, chives, parsley. There was a round table of thick dark wood near a window with two rocking chairs set against it, all very snug.

Jack tossed Howie a towel and told him to have a seat in one of the rocking chairs while he went upstairs to change into dry clothes. When Jack returned to the kitchen, he was wearing dark glasses, and this made it easier to share his company. Jack made a pot of Earl Grey tea and poured a shot of brandy into their cups.

"You're Indian?" he asked, handing Howie his cup.

"Lakota," Howie agreed, surprised a blind man could tell,

for he had worked hard to erase his past and imitate the trans-
Atlantic accent of his intelligentsia East Coast friends.

"It's the way you laugh," Jack explained. "A kind of *hey-hey*
rather than a *ha-ha*. They took you off the reservation, didn't
they? Sent you to a lot of white man's schools?"

"I'm working on my Ph.D.," Howie replied, a touch defen-
sively.

"Are you? What's your field?"

"Culinary psycho-sociology."

"Good God, what's *that*?" Jack laughed. He added: "I don't
mean to be rude, but back in my day we had things like English, math, and biology. I'm not sure I've even heard of this
culinary what's-it of yours."

Howie smiled tolerantly. "Basically, I investigate the connection between diet and behavior. What I'm trying to show,
is how the cultural divide in America between the Left and the
Right is connected to how people eat."

"No shit?"

"No shit," Howie assured him.

"So you plan on teaching this stuff eventually?"

"Not if I can help it."

"Why's that?"

"Frankly, I'm sick of school. I'm ready to try something
else."

Jack grinned. "Try what, for instance?"

Howie wasn't sure why he was opening himself to this blind
man. "I don't know," he admitted. "I used to think academia
was my bag. But now I'm just not sure. . . ."

Jack's smile seemed to grow and grow. "Have another cup
of tea," he said.

And such was his first odd encounter with Jack Wilder.
Howie ended up staying for several hours, much longer than
he had intended. It was the start of many long, rambling conversations that he and Jack were to have in that kitchen. After
the second cup of tea, Jack began to shell peas into a bowl as
they spoke. It was a rhythmic, soothing motion, and after
Howie watched him a few minutes, he offered to help. Jack
gave him the bag of peas and moved on naturally to other
kitchen chores, standing at the cutting board and using a large
chef's knife with great skill to dice up a yellow onion, red pepper, a jalapeño, Greek olives, a tomato, garlic, fresh thyme,

and oregano. He minced and sliced more quickly than Howie
thought possible, never nicking a finger. The man fascinated
Howie. Though he was blind, he moved about his kitchen with
absolute assurance, reaching for jars on the shelves, sniffing
occasionally to make certain what they were, hardly wasting a
gesture.

Howie stayed for dinner and met Emma when she came
home from her job at the library. She was a handsome woman
in her early fifties with short dark hair that was touched only
at the very ends with gray. Howie was sure that in her youth
she must have been a knockout. Now, like Jack, she was a little stout, and she was not the sort of older woman who spent
much of her time on clothes or trying to look young. She once
told Howie, months later, that one of the benefits of being married to a blind man was not having to worry about her appearance.

Jack and Emma . . . they became for Howie a second home.
In the beginning he dropped by just to say hello, but after a few
weeks he began to do odd chores around the house, read to
Jack, and chauffeur him to the market when Emma was at
work. When Jack tried to give him money for these services,
he at first said no. But before long they formalized their relationship, and Howie accepted a salary—the money, in fact,
was a godsend since he was broke and psychologically in need
of paying Bob and Nova some rent for use of their guest house.
Oddly enough, however, he had no idea Jack was an ex-cop
until nearly two months after they met. Jack simply never
mentioned it.

And then one afternoon Howie came across an envelope ad-
dressed to Commander Jack Wilder. When Howie asked what
sort of commander he was, Jack said he had been a cop in San
Francisco, the head of a special investigative unit until an accident nearly four years earlier had forced his retirement. The
"accident," how Jack had lost his eyesight, was kept deliberately vague; Howie was not to learn the details for some time.
But he came to suspect that Jack had left the envelope deliberately for him to discover, for it heralded a sea change in their
relationship. A few days later he told Howie his plan to start a
private detective agency in San Geronimo, and he invited
Howie to become his assistant.

"But, Jack! I don't know a thing about being a detective!" Howie objected.

"Of course you do. For the past decade, that's about all you've been doing—research. Digging about in libraries and finding things."

"Yes, but that was for school."

"Basically, there's no difference. We'll simply venture out of the library into real life. Frankly, I think this could be good for you, Howie."

Howie had to admit that this was the most interesting proposal that had come his way in a long time. Girls, he thought, would be a lot more attracted to a private eye than a graduate student with a dangling dissertation. And so Jack got his license, which in New Mexico is mostly a matter of paying two hundred dollars and undergoing a cursory background check. Then Jack put an ad in the local paper, and they were in business, Wilder & Associate, with their office in Jack's kitchen.

For Howie, it made a fun anecdote to tell Bob and Nova, and he began to sign letters to friends back east as Howard Moon Deer, P.I. All in all, quite amusing, he thought, and utterly harmless. Basically, Howie thought they were just playing games.

Until April Fools' Day, when the game turned serious and they found their first client dead in the snow.

7

Death has its formalities, and it was not until late in the afternoon of April 1, when the day was fading to a dim and stormy twilight, that Jack and Howie finally made their way to the Winterhaus Inn. The bar was crowded, and there was a whiff of wet ski socks and soggy gloves in the air. They collapsed into a booth near the huge stone fireplace. Jack was visibly exhausted, hardly able to drag himself another step. A Yule log was burning in a hearth that was big enough for a Texas barbecue. The heat felt good on their snow-reddened faces.

A waitress in black jeans and a tight turtleneck sweater appeared at their table. Probably a college girl, Howie judged, taking a year off from school to find herself—i.e., ski and party with the opposite sex—while Mom and Dad paid the greater part of the bills.

"Hey, guys!" she said, eyeing Howie as a possible party mate, barely seeing Jack. "What can I get for you?"

"A transfusion," Jack told her wearily. "Or rather, if you will—a glass of your best, blood red wine."

They settled on the wine of the week, a Clos du Val zinfandel. Jack told her to bring the whole bottle, please. They had spent the past several hours repeating their story to a wide variety of officialdom: first the ski patrol, then the San Geronimo County Sheriff's Department, and finally the New Mexico State police. The press showed up as well, a local reporter from the *San Geronimo Post,* and later a TV crew who arrived from Santa Fe, but Jack skillfully ignored their questions. Howie had never been involved in a newsworthy situation before, and he had an odd feeling that it was all make-believe, a group of children playing self-importantly at true-life drama. The ski patrol had been the most difficult encounter. They were furious that Jack had skied without the required orange

"Blind Skier" vest to warn others of his handicapped condition.

Wilder & Associate were now waiting to see Josie Hampton, the young woman Jack had helped out of a jam in San Francisco more than a decade ago. Josie had risen far in her father's hierarchy since those days of youthful folly, all the way to the number two position at the ski resort. She had been tied up throughout the afternoon in various urgent meetings, but had sent word through the ski patrol that she wanted to see them. Could Jack and Howie meet her about four o'clock at the Winterhaus? They could. Particularly with a glass of good red wine to warm their innards.

Josie was nearly half an hour late. Jack and Howie were sitting in a semi-stupor with their wine, half hypnotized by the heat of the fire, when a woman with long black hair appeared at their table. She was short and attractive, a compact woman in her early thirties with a smooth brown complexion. Howie would have taken her for Spanish except for her light blue-gray eyes, which gave her an oddly displaced appearance, as though someone else were inside her body looking out.

"Commander Wilder?" she asked in a tentative voice. "Is it really you?"

Jack turned his wraparound dark glasses toward the sound of her voice.

"Josie, forgive me if I don't rise. This is my assistant, Howard Moon Deer. I'm terribly sorry about your father."

She seemed dazed. "I still can't absorb it yet. My God, who would shoot him with an arrow? And *why*? It's just so crazy."

"Let's get you a drink."

Josie was dressed in jeans and a fluffy white sweater. She was the sort of woman people describe as cute, rather than a beauty. But her voice wasn't cute. It was low and growly, at odds with the rest of her appearance. It was a voice accustomed to giving orders and holding its own among the boys. She raised a finger, and the waitress appeared immediately. Josie ordered a double shot of Courvoisier.

"I was sorry to hear about your eyes, Commander . . . the ski patrol told me you were blind. How in the world did it happen?"

"An accident," Jack told her briefly. "But I'm doing very well."

It was obvious Jack didn't want to talk about his blindness, so Josie turned her attention toward Howie. "You're . . . Cheyenne?"

"Lakota," he told her. And then he saw something about her, a mannerism that would be nearly impossible to describe to a non-native. "You're Indian too, aren't you?"

"Half and half. My mother was from the reservation here. But Dad was about as Anglo as they come, of course. Such is my schizoid heritage."

"If you feel up to it, I'd like to get your family picture straight in my mind," Jack told her.

"Sure. Ask anything you want. I'm okay, really . . . I suppose this will hit me later, but right now I only feel numb."

"I seem to remember that your mother was Kit's second wife?"

"Not wife. Girlfriend. They never got married." After a small pause, she added with a subtle smile: "That makes me 'a love child,' you see—that's the phrase my father liked to use."

Jack nodded in an encouraging manner.

"My family history's a little complicated," Josie continued. "Cynthia Hampton was Dad's wife—she's the mother of my half sister, Alison, who's a few years older than me. But Dad was always big on the ladies, and in the mid-sixties he had a hot affair with my mother, Maria Concha, who worked as a cashier here—she was only seventeen at the time. When Maria got pregnant with me, Cynthia was not amused, so she split with Alison to California and filed for divorce."

"This was when your father was a U.S. senator, I presume?"

"No, I was born in 1967 when Dad was still running the ski area. He got interested in politics a few years later—he was in the Senate from 1972 to 1984. During the period when he was in Washington, San Geronimo Peak was put in a blind trust and managed by a Swiss outfit."

"Let's get back to your mother—how long were she and Kit together?"

"Just a few years. It ended pretty soon after I was born. The cultural gulf between them was too much, I guess. Dad went to Harvard, you know. Mom never finished high school."

"Did your father ever marry again?"

"Never. Cynthia was the one and only legal union. I guess he decided life was best as a carefree bachelor."

Jack frowned. "So you grew up with your mother?"

"That's right, on the reservation. I never even knew I had an Anglo father until I was twelve. I guess I looked different from everybody else with my blue eyes, but Indians can be fairly nice about stuff like that, and no one made a point of it. I thought my father was a guy named Manny Trujillo, whom my mom married when I was two. Manny wasn't from around here—he was a Chicano dude from Los Angeles. But he didn't have blue eyes either, so I guess I should have figured some-thing was up."

"How did you find out who your real father was?"

"My mother told me finally. She was drinking—she and Manny drank pretty heavily for a while, and the story just sort of tumbled out one night. I was blown away, as you can imag-ine. Not only did I have an Anglo father, but he was a million-aire, apparently—a U.S. senator, to boot!"

"You must have been curious to meet him."

"Well, yes and no. It's hard to describe—I mean, I already *had* a family and a life on the reservation. Anyway, this was during the time Dad was in Washington, and he hardly ever came to San Geronimo, so it wasn't like I had the opportunity to show up on his doorstep even if I wanted to."

"Did he take care of your mother financially?"

"Yes, he did. I have to say that for Dad, he was never stingy. I grew up in a nice house, and we had everything we wanted. I didn't realize, of course, where the money came from until I was twelve—up to that time I assumed Manny earned it."

"So when did you get to know your father?"

"When I was seventeen, in '84 after he lost the election and returned home to San Geronimo. Suddenly he was very curi-ous about me, this daughter he didn't know. Maybe there was something about losing . . . he was wounded, I guess, feeling rejected, looking to reestablish family connections. I'll never forget the day I met him. It was right after I graduated from high school. He simply showed up at the house one day, this handsome man with silver hair saying he was my father. I had been fighting with my mother about that time, and I couldn't stand Manny ever, so it was sort of a fantasy come true. Like I was a swan, you know, not a duckling, and I belonged to a whole different life."

"Like a fairy tale," Jack agreed.

"We took a trip that summer to Europe, just the two of us, to get to know each other. Dad was the perfect guide—he spoke fluent French, he knew tons of fascinating people, we tripped around the great cities of the world staying in fancy hotels. I thought he was fabulous. When we got back to the States, he wanted to send me to college, and that's when I enrolled at the San Francisco Art Institute."

Jack was nodding. "This is coming back to me. You have to excuse my memory, Josie—the old brain gets overcrowded when you're my age, and things get lost. Your father actually told me a bit of this story when I met him in 1987."

"When I had my little escapade with the law, you mean," she said ruefully.

"Yes, your little escapade. You were what, twenty-one?"

"Twenty," she told him. "I'm thirty-one now."

"I see. Now, Josie, I seem to recall there was a scandal that was responsible for your father losing the '84 election, and that it had something to do with this story . . ."

She laughed. "You bet it did! Those Republicans did a real smear job on Dad in '84. Somehow they found out about Maria and me—that Dad had an illegitimate child. It was kinda the last straw. For months they had been painting him as 'the Jerry Brown of New Mexico,' this total flake who was into New Age meditation and dating Hollywood actresses, etcetera. It was a very effective campaign, extremely well organized. They saved the juiciest bit, that Senator Hampton had an illegitimate daughter stashed away on an Indian reservation, for just two weeks before the election. It was what really did him in. He even lost a lot of his liberal supporters over it—the fact that my mom was underage when he started up with her, and that she was a disadvantaged Indian, and all that. The Republicans made it seem as if he had abandoned us in a very heartless manner, which wasn't true, actually, at least not in terms of money and child support. But the tactic worked."

"So your father decided to get to know you. I'm surprised he didn't feel, well . . . just a bit sour about you. In effect, you were the reason he lost the election."

"No, Dad wasn't like that. He was very fair. It's strange, I think he had forgotten my existence up to that moment. But once he was reminded, he decided to do the right thing."

Josie seemed to enjoy talking about her father; perhaps it

was a way to deny his death. But suddenly she bit her lower lip to keep from crying. "Poor Dad! I still can't get over it . . . an *arrow*!"

"An arrow *is* very odd," Jack agreed. "Tell me, Josie—is there anyone down on the reservation who bore your father some sort of grudge?"

She looked at Jack in astonishment. "The *reservation*? You think maybe an Indian did it? . . . Good God, none of those guys could shoot a bow and arrow if their life depended on it! Not this century, anyway."

Josie drained her cognac and held up the empty glass in an imperious manner for the waitress to see. "Excuse me, but I think I'm going to get a little sloshed tonight," she said. "How are you two doing?"

"Just fine," Jack told her. "Back to your family, there are only two children, then—you and your half sister Alison?"

"Yes. Actually, I don't know Alison very well, since she grew up in California. But she's moved back to San Geronimo recently, and I'm hoping we'll become friends."

"I'll want to talk with her. Do you have a telephone number?"

"In my office. We can stop off there afterward."

Jack was just warming up with his questions. But Josie had a few of her own. She wanted to know what Jack and Howie had been doing at Doobie Rock. So Jack went patiently through the story once again, from the phone call he'd received the day before to finding the Senator on the lodge. It was a story that raised more questions than it answered, and at the end, Josie could only shake her head.

"What in the world did he want to talk to you about? And why meet you *there*, of all places?" she wondered.

"He didn't tell you about our meeting?"

"Not a word. I'm mystified, really. I know pretty much all there is to know about the business—I'm the general manager, you know. So if it was something about the ski area, I'm sure he would have told me."

"Your dad said he wanted to *show* me something at Doobie Rock, and that we would talk about it afterward. Does that ring any kind of bell with you?" Jack asked. "Something a person might *see* there?"

Josie shrugged. "Not really. Unless it had to do with dope—

that's what skiers generally do at Doobie Rock, you know.
They stop there to get a buzz."

"I've heard that. Was your father concerned about drug
use?"

"Not particularly. All employees have to sign a statement
agreeing to random drug testing, but that's mostly for our insurance. I've never heard of the rule actually being enforced.
Basically, Dad had a live-and-let-live attitude about stuff like
that."

"So you would say that everything's been going smoothly at
the resort?"

"Couldn't be better. *Ski* magazine gave us a huge write-up
three years ago; said we had better snow and terrain than any
place in Colorado—since then, we've hardly been able to keep
up with the crowds."

"Tell me a little about how San Geronimo Peak is struc-
tured. It's a private corporation—is that right?"

"That's correct. My dad is . . . *was* the main stockholder. He
owned ninety-five percent of the land that the ski area is actually on—it's the old Hampton family ranch, you know. But
there are a hundred and forty-eight investors, all in all. Basically, whenever Dad wanted to put in a new lift or expand the
boundaries, he'd invite in some outside money."

"I'll want to have a list of those investors, if that's all right."

Josie seemed doubtful. "I hate to bother any of them. But if
you think it's absolutely necessary . . ."

"It's necessary. Now, who owns the remaining five percent
of the land?"

"There's just a small chunk on the back of the mountain
that's not ours, about fifty acres. It was added back in the mid-
sixties when Dad decided to expand that side of the resort and
build two new quad lifts. Most of the parcel is leased from the
U.S. Forest Service, but about nine acres is Indian land, part of
the reservation—we have an arrangement with them."

"What about Doobie Rock?" Jack asked. "That's on the
back side of the mountain. Does it belong to the old ranch?"

"I'm pretty sure that's family land back there, but I'd have
to check the plat. Do you think it's important?"

Jack shook his head. "I doubt it, Josie. I'm just trying to get
a general picture of things in order to figure out why your dad
needed a private detective. You say business has been good. Is

there anything else you can think of? Was he cheerful recently? Worried? Preoccupied about anything?"

Josie was silent as the waitress appeared with her second snifter of cognac. She took the glass and held it for a moment against her cheek, feeling the smooth surface against her skin.

"I'm not sure I can really answer that. He always acted like everything was wonderful. He was very charismatic, you know, my father. Very entertaining. It's like he had to seduce everyone with his charm . . . maybe that's what drew him into politics. But what he actually thought about, if he was worried about anything in particular . . . it's terrible to admit, but I just don't know. And I guess I'll never find out now either. . . ."

It seemed to be hitting her now, her father's death. Or maybe it was the cognac loosening her up. She was wandering off into some personal realm of grief, and Jack had to work to hold her:

"Tell me, Josie—if you had to take a guess at who killed him, who would it be?"

"Just a wild guess? Well, it's crazy, but when the ski patrol phoned and told me the news, my first thought was, *the assholes finally got him!*"

"Who got him? I don't understand."

"The people who destroyed him in 1984."

Jack was trying to follow her logic. "You're saying he was killed by an old political foe from fourteen years ago?"

"I told you it was crazy. But those right-wingers hated him. It went beyond any kind of logic. It's like Dad symbolized something for them that set all their bells ringing. . . . I'm not certain you can even call it politics, that sort of hatred. It was more like cultural warfare. I mean, those people wanted to annihilate him."

"You say 'those people.' But who were they, Josie? Was it a group?"

"I guess so, I don't know for sure. Probably you think I'm nuts, but you *did* ask my opinion."

"No, I'm very interested," Jack assured her. "When you talk about the past, and the people who wanted to destroy your father, is there any single individual who comes to mind? . . . I'm trying to remember the name of the Republican who won his seat that year. . . ."

"James Corman? No, he was a total nonentity who got

drummed out of office after one term. He was only a puppet
for a bunch of right-wing interests who were behind him.
Probably you're going to laugh, or think I'm being horribly
New Agey. But the way I see it, when you're rich, smart,
healthy, when you live a privileged life . . . when you have
everything . . . you end up creating this terrible opposition, this
pool of resentment. And suddenly a big dark fist comes out of
nowhere, and it wants to smash you . . . I'm not putting this
very well. Do *you* understand what I'm saying?" she appealed,
turning to Howie for support, settling her light blue eyes on
him.

Strange eyes, he thought. It was the first time she had really
looked at him since the start of the conversation, and once
again he had the odd sense that her eyes didn't fit with the rest
of her face. It worried Howie a little.

"*Do* you?" she insisted. Her voice was breaking with some
emotion Howie could not understand.

"Well, sort of," he told her cautiously. "Perhaps it's what
the Greeks called hubris."

But Josie Hampton was no longer listening. Suddenly she
was weeping hot tears into her Courvoisier, bursting with grief
for her dead father. Yet it seemed to Howie as if the faucet had
been turned on deliberately. He gave her some privacy by
looking away.

"So a big dark fist out of nowhere?" Howie said to Jack, as
he led him through the parking lot toward the old Toyota
pickup truck that was the Wilders' second vehicle.

"Anything's possible," Jack replied vaguely.

"Personally, I like the idea of cultural warfare," Howie said
happily. "Maybe the God of Budweiser wanted to murder the
God of Chardonnay."

The storm had ended with the usual abruptness of weather
in New Mexico, and there were bright hard stars twinkling in
the night sky. Jack held onto Howie's arm as they trudged together through the snow. The Toyota was buried in the snow,
hardly more than a white lump in the parking lot. Jack stood
thoughtfully to one side as Howie got busy digging them out
with his hands and a whisk broom he found under the seat. A
shovel would have been nice.

"Howie," Jack said after a while, "stop what you're doing

and tell me something. I want you to remember back to when we were just entering the trail to Doobie Rock. You described the path to me so I'd know where to go. What did you tell me?"

"I said we were going to follow a pair of tracks into the woods, and that you'd better keep your head down as we went beneath a big old blue spruce tree. You didn't duck low enough so you got dumped with snow."

"Yes, yes," Jack said irately. "So there was only one pair of ski tracks into the clearing?"

"No. If I remember, there were three tracks, side by side. One was fairly deep, and that's the track I followed because I knew you were getting tired, and I didn't want us to work any harder than necessary breaking new snow."

"And the other two tracks?"

"One was so light I could hardly make it out. The other was a little deeper, but not as deep as the one we followed."

"So we have three tracks," Jack pondered. "For the sake of convenience, let's call them Papa Bear, Mama Bear, and Baby Bear. Now, as a great Indian tracker—how would you interpret them, Howie?"

"There's no need to be sarcastic, Jack."

"I'm being perfectly sincere. Tell me what you think."

"Easy. The snow was falling at about an inch an hour. Baby Bear was the oldest track, nearly covered. Mama Bear was made maybe half an hour before we arrived, and someone used Papa Bear shortly before we got there."

"But there could be another explanation, couldn't there, for one set of tracks being deeper than the others?"

"What do you mean?"

"It's possible that elapsed time may not have been so much a factor as the *weight* of the skier. Do you see what I'm saying? Three people may have entered Doobie Rock simultaneously side by side, and the lightest tracks could have been made by . . . a young child, for example."

Howie blinked at Jack in astonishment.

"I think I've figured it out," he said slowly. "It was that cute little girl we met on the chairlift. Probably she went to Doobie Rock to sell drugs and found Kit Hampton on her turf, so she shot him with her bow and arrow and pushed him off the cliff."

Jack put on his most annoyingly patient voice. "Howie,

we're simply looking at every possibility. I don't know if this means diddly-shit, but it's important to avoid a personal bias when interpreting evidence. So tell me, could a young child have made the third track, Baby Bear?"

"Well, theoretically, Jack, sure. . . ."

"And what about Mama Bear? Could that have been made by a light woman?"

"I suppose so."

"That's all I want to know. Now, let's get the hell home. I've had enough of this mountain for one day."

8

April 1 might have been winter, but April 2 was decidedly spring—at least down in the town of San Geronimo, which stood at an elevation of a mere seven thousand feet. Spring is always a fragile event at such altitudes, with snowflakes never far away, but by April 3, the warmth seemed even more established, penetrating deep into the cold bones of the earth. The sun shone brightly, birds sang in the trees, and the melting snow turned the land everywhere into a big happy mud puddle that was conjugating with the stuff of life.

Howie felt the onslaught of warm weather in every pore of his body. There was a fragrance in the air that filled him with longing for sweet, dreamy things. At night he tossed restlessly in his bed as he fantasized different endings for what might have happened between him and the Lady in White had they collided thigh-to-thigh in a less constrained world. As for Jack, he kept to himself for an entire day after the murder. Howie wasn't certain whether the exercise on the slopes had been too much for him, or he was simply gathering his thoughts. But on Friday, April 3, Jack phoned Howie early in the morning and told him to come by as soon as possible. They had a full day in store.

"My God, Jack! You got a haircut!" Howie laughed when he drove over to Calle Santa Margarita in the red Toyota truck, the Wilders' second vehicle, which he had on a kind of semi-permanent loan. "And look at those new clothes!"

"It was overdue," Jack muttered, stepping into the cab of the truck.

Howie couldn't get over it. Normally Jack looked like a big shaggy Russian bear. But today he was almost sleek. His curly gray hair had been neatly trimmed, and even the anarchy of his beard was momentarily under control, short and almost mili-

tary in appearance. From the foot up, Jack was wearing: highly
polished brown leather shoes, beige slacks, a pink dress shirt
with a button-down collar, a dark burgundy-colored tie, and a
gray tweed herringbone sports coat. Everything was so new
you almost expected to find the price tags dangling. He even
had a new pair of dark glasses, aviator style, that made him
look like a Hollywood celebrity or a drug dealer.

"Pretty sharp, bro!" Howie told him, grinning like crazy.

"Okay, okay—enough already about my appearance. Emma
took me to Santa Fe yesterday, and we picked up a few things.
It's no big deal."

But it *was* a big deal, Howie was certain. Part of some mind-
set, a new beginning, a morale booster. Commander Jack
Wilder back on a case again after four blind years. Howie felt
like teasing him some more, but decided to leave it alone.

"So where to?" he asked.

"The pueblo, of course."

Howard Moon Deer was as much an outsider at the San
Geronimo Pueblo as Jack Wilder. Howie's ancestors, the
Lakota people, were hunter-gatherers, nomads, and warriors,
itchy-feet Indians who liked to roam. The Pueblo Indians were
just the opposite: town folk, a conservative, stay-at-home people who had their own language, their own ways, and had
never liked outsiders even in the old days before the white man
arrived.

The San Geronimo reservation was situated on a 90,000
acre swathe of land to the west of San Geronimo Peak. It was
good land, reaching far up into the high mountain valleys,
though it was only a fraction of what the Indians here had once
called their own. The pueblo itself, the village at the heart of
the reservation, dated from the early fourteenth century, and it
was a maze of adobe condos, rooms built one on top of the
other two or three stories high, with wooden ladders connect-
ing the different levels. It was very picturesque, often pho-
tographed, but no one actually lived in these ancient rooms
anymore—the historical part of the pueblo existed now mostly
for tourists, and for traditional ceremonies that were closed to
the public.

Howie parked in the central plaza, an unpaved, muddy
square of ground that was surrounded by gift shops. There was

a smell in the air of burning cedar from kiva fireplaces. Old men sat in the sun with nothing much to do. Howie had only been to the San Geronimo Pueblo once before, but he found the Indian-ness of it deeply familiar. Too familiar, really. He went inside a gift shop to seek directions to the home of Mrs. Maria Trujillo. The woman inside the shop regarded him warily; she did not ask his tribe, or offer him refuge from the white world that Howie had learned to call home. Being on the reservation made Howie feel very edgy.

"There's no Maria Trujillo living here," the woman told him.

"No? Her daughter, Josie, told me there was."

"Not Trujillo. She calls herself Concha again, ever since Manny took off to Oklahoma with some hippie girl."

"So where can I find Maria Concha?"

It was work to get directions from this woman, but Howie kept at it. He was in a sour mood by the time he stepped back into the cab of the truck.

"Listen, don't start having some kind of Indian identity crisis on me," Jack told him.

"What, Jack? What did I say, for chrissake?"

"I just feel it coming. I *know* you, Howie. And there simply isn't time for it now. We're investigating a murder, and I need you to be solid."

Howie sighed with exasperation. "You're on the wrong track, Jack. You're talking to a guy who's melted in the great American pot—I'm hardly more Indian than you are Irish."

"That's bullshit, and you know it. Now, please drive."

"Unbelievable!" Howie muttered. He got his jeans muddy putting the front hubcaps into four-wheel drive, and then he drove along a narrow dirt road that was deeply rutted with puddles of melting snow. They passed through a neighborhood of modest adobe homes, each with a small yard and a TV antenna on the roof, but soon the houses became less frequent. After a while they crossed a fast-moving stream on a rickety wooden bridge and headed toward the mountains.

"You know, Jack, I don't mean to spoil the fun, but the truth of the matter is we don't have a client," Howie mentioned as they bounced along the bad road.

"Of course we have a client. He is simply deceased," Jack countered.

"And where are you planning to send our bill? Heaven, perhaps? Or is our particular benefactor down below?"

"We'll worry about money later," Jack said breezily.

"You think Kit's going to come back to life with a nice fat retainer in hand?"

"What I think, Howie, is that someone phoned me for help, but by the time I got to him, he was dead. So we're going to find out, you and I, exactly how this misfortune occurred."

Howie was surprised by the anger in Jack's voice. "What is it?" he asked. "You feel you owe him something?"

"Not a bit. It's bad for business, that's all. To have only one client, and then that client gets killed—that's a one hundred percent failure rate, and people aren't exactly going to beat a path to our door if the word gets around."

Howie didn't have the heart to say the obvious, that no one was beating a path to their door anyway, and business couldn't be any worse than it already was. They drove the rest of the way in silence, not entirely happy with one another. Maria Concha lived about twenty minutes from the tourist part of the reservation in a damp, steep valley that did not receive much sun this time of year. Her house was low and light brown in color, and it seemed to Howie almost a caricature of mid-Americana: a front yard with a satellite TV dish, a two-car garage, a living room shaped like a loaf of bread with other little boxlike rooms connected to it. The house had been quite modern at one time, but chintzy. Now it looked as if a good wind could blow it all away. There was a huge American car in the driveway, an Oldsmobile, a classic gas guzzler from the late seventies that was dented in a number of places and had seen better days. Howie parked behind the Oldsmobile and guided Jack along the short path to the front door.

The door opened before Howie could knock, revealing a middle-aged Indian woman. She was short and stocky, and there was a haggard fleshiness to her face that suggested alcohol. She regarded her visitors in an unfriendly manner.

"Yes?" she demanded.

Jack let go of Howie's arm. "Good morning," he said pleasantly. "Are you Maria Concha?"

She did not reply, but fixed Jack with her stare. Jack reached into the inner breast of his new sports coat and handed her a card from Wilder & Associate, Private Investigations.

"Senator Hampton was my client, Ms. Concha—we're investigating his death. We spoke with your daughter, Josie, and she suggested we talk with you."

This was not true, but Jack said it very well. The woman studied the card carefully; she even glanced at the back.

"Well, come in for a few minutes, I guess," she said reluctantly. "I told the cops everything I could think of yesterday, which wasn't much. I haven't seen Kit in months. We don't exactly hang out in the same circles these days."

The interior of the house reminded Howie of a motel. There was insubstantial, anonymous furniture. Even a tourist photograph of the Rio Grande on the wall. The focus point of the living room was a huge old TV set toward which every chair and sofa faced as though it were a holy altar. Maria Concha lit a cigarette and sat in an overstuffed armchair whose springs and stuffing were leaking out. Howie guided Jack to the sofa and sat at his side. He tried to see in Maria Concha something of the pretty seventeen-year-old Indian girl who had caught Kit Hampton's roving eye thirty years ago. But there wasn't much. Indian women can age quickly on the reservation, their nubile girlhood only a brief window of opportunity that closes fast. Howie had an idea that this was what Josie would look like when she was older, particularly if she kept downing double cognacs to ease her pain.

"I'll try not to take too much of your time, Ms. Concha. I was hoping you might tell me about the last time you saw Kit Hampton?" Jack asked her.

She took a long drag on her cigarette.

"He showed up unexpectedly," she said on the exhale. "It must have been January. A few months ago, anyway. It surprised me because I hadn't seen him for about ten years before that."

"He came here?"

"That's right. He showed up one morning at the house, just like you did, without calling first. I made us a cup of coffee. I should have slammed the door in his face, I guess, but I was curious why he had come."

"And why had he come?"

"To talk. Hang out a little."

"What did you talk about?"

"Nothing much."

Jack was patient. "So after ten years he simply shows up one morning and wants to hang out? Didn't that strike you as strange?"

She shrugged. "I don't know. Kit and I go back a ways He seemed tired and out of sorts, and he just wanted to relax with a friend."

"You consider yourself a friend?"

"Not really. But what the hell—the bad stuff between us happened a long, long time ago."

"So he was out of sorts. Did he say what was bothering him?"

"The Peak. He said it was a hassle to run a big place like that. Too much work, too much stress. Insurance costs were going sky-high, everything had become very difficult. He said he was thinking of giving the whole thing up and retiring to the South Pacific. But first he had to get everything in order."

"What did he mean by that, get everything in order?"

"He didn't say, and I didn't ask. It was all bullshit, of course—I used to hear him talk about retiring to a tropical island thirty years ago. It was just something he would say when the mood was upon him, usually to some girl when he wanted to get into her pants. His eyes would get all dreamy, and he would go on about palm trees and making love on the beach under the stars. That was Kit. You couldn't really believe a word he said, but it sure sounded nice."

"So you don't think he actually planned to sell the resort?"

Maria laughed sharply and shook her head. "No way. Owning a fancy ski resort was what made Kit a big shot in New Mexico, now that he's not a senator anymore. He wouldn't give it up for anything."

"So what else did he talk about? Did he say anything about Josie? Or his other daughter Alison?"

"No. Like I told you, he just wanted to sit quietly for a few minutes. He left after maybe half an hour."

Jack frowned. The Senator's visit to Maria didn't make sense to him. "Did you get the impression he had come to the reservation that day to do some other errands here? To visit someone else besides you?"

"Maybe. He knows a lot of people at the pueblo."

"But he didn't tell you?"

"No, he didn't say."

Jack, Howie, and the Indian woman sat quietly for a moment. Somewhere in the house there was an old grandfather clock ticking. Tick . . . tock . . . tick . . . tock. Time can pass slowly on a reservation. When Jack finally spoke, Howie was astonished, because he took a huge leap.

"Ms. Concha, in 1984 when Kit was running for reelection, it was you, wasn't it, who spoiled his chances?"

She didn't reply. She took another drag on her cigarette and watched him. Jack simply waited as though he possessed as much time as the grandfather clock.

"Don't call me *Ms.* Concha," she said after a while, mockingly. "I don't like that Anglo shit. Call me Maria."

"Very well, Maria. You went to the Republicans who were running James Corman for the Senate, and you told them that Kit had seduced you when you were seventeen and that you had an illegitimate child with him. I'm not saying I blame you for what you did. What I want to know is who you spoke with?"

"That was a long time ago. I don't remember."

"Try to remember, please."

She finished her cigarette, then she lit another. Howie didn't think they were going to get much out of her, but then she seemed to change her mind and decide she was in the mood for talk.

"I hated Kit for a while. The bastard used me, and I didn't like that one bit."

"Used you in what way?"

"My Uncle Raymond was the cacique."

When she didn't elaborate on this statement, Jack turned to Howie for help.

"The cacique is the tribe's spiritual elder," Howie told him.

"I still don't understand," Jack said, turning back to the woman.

"To get the lease. Kit wanted me to use my influence."

"Ah!" said Jack with understanding. "We're talking about the nine acres of Indian land that Kit wanted in order to expand the ski area! What year was this? 1967?"

"It was sixty-six, back when we first started fooling around. And those nine acres were crucial; I didn't realize that at the time. It was where they happened to be located, halfway up the one narrow place where he could build a chairlift on the back side of the mountain. Without those nine acres, San Geronimo Peak would have always remained a dinky little family mountain for beginners."

"So he wanted you to convince your uncle to agree to the lease?"

"You bet. Only Kit was so slick, he got me to think it was my idea. I offered to do it. I thought it would make Kit love me more. And when Uncle Raymond said no, he was against leasing Indian land to a ski resort, I went to the tribal council and I convinced them. There was a lot of money in it for the reservation, and we were able to build a new school."

"How long is the lease for?"

"Ninety-nine years. Long enough so we'll all be dead at the end of it."

"So the lease did not actually need the cacique's approval?"

"Hey, we live in a democracy here. Uncle Raymond only gives his advice, and these days not many people listen to it. But he has a lot of prestige, and it helped with the tribal council that it was Raymond Concha's niece who had come to them."

"So you were very useful to Kit?"

"You're damn right I was! And when he got what he wanted from me, he dropped me like a brick."

"I can understand why you hate him."

"Can you? Well, I did hate for a while, at least. But as I say, it was a long time ago. And to tell the truth, after Manny Trujillo, Kit Hampton started to look maybe not so bad."

Jack smiled. "I gather you haven't been lucky in love?"

She didn't smile. "No, not so lucky."

"So you went to the Republican who was running against Kit in 1984," Jack said, guiding the conversation back to his earlier question.

"Yes, I did," she admitted. "I spoke to some guy in Corman's office, I don't remember his name. I told him that Kit had got me knocked up with a kid when I was seventeen. They sent some photographers to the reservation, and for a while I blabbed my head off to anyone who would listen."

"Kit must have been furious with you."

She shrugged. "Well, not really. He showed up on the reservation maybe a month after he lost the election. I was a little scared really, what he might do. But he smiled at me in a sad way and said that he understood why I'd done it, that he was the one who had been wrong. And that was when he started taking an interest in Josie. I was glad when he took her away from here because I was afraid Manny might be messing with her."

"Messing with her sexually?"

"I never knew for sure, but when Manny was drinking, he'd screw a donkey. So I was grateful Kit took her off the reservation and gave her a chance to make something of herself. It's funny, but I got to thinking Kit wasn't such a bad guy after all."

"Interesting story," Jack told her. "So you became friends again?"

"Not really friends. But when he showed in January, I guess that's why I didn't slam the door in his face. He was a bastard, but he had done right by Josie. I guess she's going to run things up there now that Kit's gone."

"So did he say anything else that day? Anything at all peculiar?"

"Well, there was one thing," she mentioned. "It seemed a little peculiar—he talked about the end of the world."

Jack's eyebrows went up. "How did this come up?"

"Just out of nowhere. He used the word millennium. He asked me if I knew what it meant—in the old days, Kit was always trying to teach me things, you know. I told him I had heard the word, but I didn't really know what it meant. So he explained that a millennium was a thousand years, and that throughout history whenever people came to the end of a millennium, there was always a lot of magic and mystical things going on, and people saying that the world was going to end. He even told me there was a name for it: millenarianism. He said this millennium coming up soon was going to be no exception. Things were going to get really out of hand, so we'd better be ready for it."

"It's in the Book of Revelations," Jack told her. "Revelations, 20, to be precise—after a thousand years, Christ was supposed to return and usher forth a new epoch of holiness and peace on Earth."

"That's right. That's what Kit told me. He said a thousand years ago, people went pretty crazy waiting for Jesus to come.

But they prayed and waited, and prayed some more, and Christ still didn't come."

"Millennium!" Jack wondered, shaking his head. "I wonder why Kit was thinking of that?"

"The end of the world!" Maria agreed cheerfully. "Well, personally I'm going to have me a beer."

She walked to her refrigerator and offered them to join her in a can of Old Milwaukee, but Jack and Howie politely declined.

"So who killed him, Maria?" Jack asked as she drank from the can.

"How do I know?"

"Take a guess."

She shook her head. "It wasn't an Indian, anyway."

"No? An arrow rather suggests an Indian, you know."

She continued to shake her head. "No one on the reservations uses a bow and arrow anymore. Everybody has a nice hunting rifle these days from Wal-Mart."

"Everybody?"

"Sure, why not? Everybody except maybe my Uncle Raymond. He's an old-fashioned man. He hates the modern ways. Poor guy, doesn't even have a TV set."

"I'd like to meet Raymond, actually."

She grinned so widely that Howie could see a few of her back teeth were missing.

"I hope you got snowshoes. Raymond lives, well . . . just a little ways off in the woods."

9

Howie did not have snowshoes, but he did have use of a pair of cross-country skis that belonged to his friend Bob. First Howie drove Jack home, because this was not going to be an expedition for a blind man. Then he stopped by Bob and Nova's, borrowed the skis and boots—they were half a size too large but close enough—and returned alone to the reservation. By keeping the Toyota in four-wheel drive, he was able to make his way about half a mile past Maria Concha's house on a dirt road that climbed into the high pastures, until he arrived at a snowdrift that completely blocked forward progress. He parked, slipped into the skis and poles, slung his day pack on his shoulders, and set off into the wilds.

It was after two o'clock by the time he got underway, a brilliant afternoon, though the shadows were beginning to lengthen, and there was a cold bite to the breeze, a wintry current beneath the spring warmth of the sun. Howie found himself on a flat plain, a valley bordered by piñon-covered hills that gradually narrowed into a V as it approached the south face of San Geronimo Peak, the opposite side of the mountain from where the skiing was. At first Howie had to step around numerous spots of bare ground where there was mud and running water, but as the altitude increased, he was soon in unbroken snow—crunchy corn snow whose crystals glittered in the sun. He skied with long strides in a rhythmic motion, working up a sweat. There were animal tracks in the snow, but no human had come this way since the April 1 storm. According to Maria Concha's map, he was to cross the valley and enter the narrow part of the V, and from here climb along the stream bank until he came at last to Uncle Raymond's cabin, a distance of perhaps seven or eight miles. Howie hoped he hadn't started too late in the afternoon to get there and back before darkness fell.

After nearly an hour of strenuous skiing, Howie stopped for a drink of water from the plastic bottle in his daypack. He was alone in a remote part of the reservation. As he stood quietly, he heard the wind rustle the trees and the gurgle of a stream nearby. But there was no human sound other than his own breath and the beating of his heart—no cars, no voices, not even an airplane overhead. The land was so vast and wild, it scared him a little. Suddenly there came a shriek overhead. Howie looked up quickly to see a huge dark bird fly across the sun. Was it a hawk? An eagle? A vulture? He had been too long in cities and classrooms, and couldn't tell.

He returned the water bottle to his pack and set off again, but now there was a small knot of fear in his stomach. The unspoiled woods were still a delight, but he had to admit that the familiar sight of a road or a telephone pole would have been a welcome relief. He tried not to think too much about the loneliness of this place, and concentrated instead on his skiing. Another hour passed as he skied deeper into the wilderness. As the valley narrowed, the trees crowded closer around him, and Howie had the odd feeling that he was being watched. He could sense motion just off to the side of his vision, but when he jerked his head to look, there was nothing to see but dense forest.

Howie was uneasy. Indian land had a different feel than other land. The wind itself seemed alive and restless. There was a kind of sparkle to things, as though there were spirits lurking just out of sight. Howie came at last to the end of the valley and began a steeper ascent by the side of a fast-moving stream. The trees were larger at this altitude, huge old firs that creaked eerily in the wind. He climbed by sidestepping in the steepest places, and sometimes heading straight up the mountain in herringbone fashion where the terrain was more gentle. Several times he fell; he was wearing touring skis that were designed for the flats, and they did not have metal edges to grab hold of the slope. Howie was sweating freely now from his exertion, but he was glad to keep moving. Whenever he stopped a moment to rest, it seemed to him that invisible things of the forest began crowding in around him.

Hold on a minute! I'm a doctoral candidate at Princeton

University, he told himself firmly. *I don't believe in Indian spirits!* But, in fact, though Howard Moon Deer might not believe in Indian spirits when he was in New Jersey, or sipping a glass of wine in town, or riding around in the Toyota with Jack—here in this remote and ancient forest, it was quite another matter.

"Ah-hem," said a voice, clearing his throat.

Howie nearly jumped out of his skin. There was an old man standing on a rock above him, a giant of a man who looked as if he had appeared suddenly from an earlier epoch of the earth.

The old cacique was powerfully built and well over six feet tall. He had a face that was like the side of a granite mountain, long white hair in a braid down his back, and eyes that could have been plucked from an eagle. He was wearing a bearskin cape, leather pants, and high deerskin boots that were laced with rawhide straps.

He spoke to Howie a few words in a language that sounded like what trees would say if they could speak.

"I'm sorry, I don't speak Tiwa," Howie told him.

"Then, I guess I'd better talk American. I've been watching you for the past hour, boy. You sure make a hell of a lot of noise in the woods. Where are you from?"

"I'm Lakota."

"Are you? Good people, the Lakota. The Oglala too. I went to a powwow up there once, must have been about 1962. But you look more like you've come from Los Angeles, or New York City."

Howie smiled. "Have you ever been to New York City, old man?"

"You bet I have! Washington, D.C. too. I met the Great White Father there—the President of the United States, Richard Nixon."

"Nixon hasn't been President for a few years now."

"No? Well, good riddance. He was not a person with an honest manner. So what brings you to see Raymond Concha?"

"I wanted to ask you about another Great White Father— Senator Kit Hampton."

Raymond Concha threw back his head and laughed. "Kit? He wasn't so great! I guess he was a father, though, and he was white, at least, I'll say that for him. Right now, I hear he's one hell of a dead white man . . . well, too bad for him."

"How did you hear he was dead?"

The old man grinned. "Maybe the wind told me. Come on, let's have a cappuccino."

"A *what*?"

"Isn't that what you young braves like to drink these days?"

Before Howie could answer, the cacique took off with long strides uphill through the forest. He was wearing snowshoes and he moved quickly. Howie estimated he must be in his late sixties, but with an Indian like Raymond who lived in the woods, this was a whole different age than it would be for a white man. The old man appeared as strong as a buffalo, and he soon left Howie far behind. Fortunately, it was an easy matter to follow his tracks in the snow. A few minutes later Howie came out into a small clearing in the trees and saw an adobe hut with a thin stream of smoke coming out the chimney. Howie left his skis by the front door and walked inside. It was a hermit's hut, about as primitive a dwelling as human shelter can be: one small room with a dirt floor and an adobe fireplace at one end. There were two low stools, a low table, and a wooden chest. When Howie came in, the old man was putting a heavy metal kettle onto the fire. The cappuccino turned out to be the instant kind from a jar, but nevertheless, Howie was astonished.

"Coffee's my weakness," Raymond admitted. "It makes me feel very wide awake and warm inside."

"You must go into town occasionally for supplies."

"No, not for years now. But town comes to me. Whenever friends show up, they bring me a present. Everyone knows I like coffee, and someone brought this the other day. I hope you have come with a present too, my young friend."

Howie solemnly opened his day pack and brought out the orange and black ski cap that Emma Wilder had crocheted for him. Howie should have felt guilty to give away such a personalized belonging, but in fact, it was a fine opportunity to get rid of the thing, and he could not think of another offering on the spur of the moment. Raymond Concha accepted the gift with ceremony and dignity, placing the cap on his head as though it were a jeweled crown.

"Very warm. Very nice. I will wear this, and I will remember our meeting."

"The colors suit you," Howie assured him.

"Very nice," the old man said again. "I will give you a present too, but first I need to know you better. We will have coffee, and then you will tell me your story . . . sugar?"

"Please."

Howie felt oddly comfortable on the hard wooden stool near the open fire, drinking a cup of instant cappuccino with the old cacique, Raymond Concha. Like most Pueblo people, the old man let himself be known by his Spanish name, which was the least sacred of all his names. He would have an Indian name too, of course—several Indian names, most likely—but these he would keep secret from Howie, who was not of his tribe. And there would be at least one name, his real name, that no one knew except himself. Secrecy was a very large part of native religion.

Howie thought it best to simply tell the story of how he had met Jack Wilder last fall; how they became friends, set up a detective agency, and went to Doobie Rock to find their first client with an arrow in his chest. Indians love a good story, and Howie spent nearly an hour narrating these events as vividly as he was able in storybook order, from beginning to end. Raymond listened appreciatively. He was particularly interested in the fact that Jack was blind, and asked about this several times, nodding with satisfaction when Howie described how well Jack was able to navigate his dark world.

"Yes, this is good," the old man told him. "You should stay with this blind man, Moon Deer. I think he is part of your journey. Personally I have never been one to say that we cannot learn from the white man. I would have them leave this sacred mountain, but I do not wish them any harm. They could be happy across the Great Water, where they have come from. As it is, it is very sad to see such a restless and rootless people who have no real land of their own. We must wish them a safe journey home."

Howie laughed. "Old man, the white man isn't going to return across the Great Water anytime soon. In fact, there are more of them on their way, and they're in a rainbow of colors—brown men, yellow men, you name it."

Raymond did not answer, nor did he speak for quite a long time. "They will all go away," he announced finally. "I have seen it. Perhaps it will not be soon, but it will come."

There wasn't much Howie could say to this, since the phrase "I have seen it" did not invite discussion. Howie debated how best to proceed with the old man, and he decided to plunge right in. "Jack wants to know if an Indian killed Senator Hampton. That's why I'm here, to find out about this murder."

Raymond shook his head. "Indians don't kill white men anymore. Those days are over, Moon Deer."

"Not even a land-grabbing white man? Someone who turned a sacred mountain into a ski resort? I understand you were opposed to leasing those nine acres of Indian land to the Senator."

"Yes. I was against it. This land has been put into our keeping, and we must protect it."

"Yes, but the money from the lease built a new school on the reservation, and probably did some other good things as well."

"Money!" he said scornfully. "You think any good can come from exchanging our sacred land for money? . . . No, it cannot. This is not good. But no one listened to me. It seems that these days all the people are bewitched; they have forgotten the spiritual life. Even here on this reservation, every house has a television set. You know what a television set is, Moon Deer? It is evil magic that robs a man's soul and destroys his mind. But they will see in the end, I think, that I was right."

Howie laughed because he did not particularly like television either. "We'd all like to return to simpler times," he told the old man. "Do you know this place where Senator Hampton was killed? The place the skiers call Doobie Rock?"

"I know it. That is not its real name, of course."

"What is its real name?"

The old man shook his head. "This is not for you to know."

"Well, whatever it's called, Josie wasn't certain if it was part of the Indian lease or the old Hampton ranch."

The old man seemed astonished. "This is *all* Indian land here! What are you talking about? How do you think Kit's parents got this land? They robbed it from the Spanish people, who stole it from us! They are all thieves, these people!"

"But Doobie Rock itself—this is what I'm asking about.

Was this part of the nine acres that the reservation leased to the ski resort in the mid-sixties?"

Raymond seemed to take a special effort to speak carefully. "This rock you are asking about is a very special place for my people. It has been in our keeping since before time began, and it will be in our keeping after time has ended."

"It was part of the lease?"

"Yes, and it was the reason I advised the council to turn down Kit Hampton's offer."

"A sacred place!" Howie said. He should have realized it earlier, for Doobie Rock was just the sort of odd place Indians would find special. "Then, it's a great sacrilege that white people are there—skiers go there to take drugs."

Raymond only shrugged. "Well, it doesn't matter. The land is very patient. The land will be still be there after the skiers have gone."

"What about Kit Hampton?"

"What about him?"

"You must have hated him for spoiling this special place."

"No, I did not hate him. He was the father of my niece's child, so I have never wished him any harm. He was not the sort of man who saw things deeply, but there are many people like that, red men as well as white."

"Who do you think killed him?"

"That's very obvious. I'm surprised you need to ask. The mountain killed him."

Howie raised a questioning eyebrow. "You think mountains can shoot a bow and arrow?"

The old man nodded. "Yes, I think so. Some mountains can do whatever they want."

Howie grinned. "I doubt if the cops are going to be pleased with that answer, Raymond. They want someone they can put handcuffs on."

"That is not my concern," he answered simply.

Howie sensed that Jack would be better at this sort of interrogation. In his own way Raymond Concha was as illusive as a stream of fast-running water.

"Maybe you gave the mountain a helping hand, Raymond?" Howie asked. "Did you shoot Senator Hampton with your bow and arrow?"

Raymond smiled at the thought. "Do I look like a killer to you?"

"I'm not sure. Doobie Rock isn't very far from here, is it? I bet you could probably hike there in a few hours, even in a snowstorm."

"Less than that. Forty-five minutes, perhaps."

"Well, then? Did you decide to do a little housekeeping on behalf of your sacred mountain?"

The old man narrowed his eyes and regarded Howie with a particularly serious expression. "I think you should go now, Moon Deer," he announced finally. "These are Indian matters, and you have chosen a different path. You would not understand if I told you the truth, for your eyes see in a different direction. I don't say you are on a wrong path, for a man must decide his own journey. But you do not see what I see."

"Try me. Maybe I can understand."

But Raymond Concha shook his head, as immovable as the mountain that was in his care. Howie was annoyed to have the conversation end so abruptly, but he saw that Raymond had made up his mind. Howie kept at it for a few more minutes, but the old man seemed to go into a trance where he did not even hear him. Finally, there seemed nothing left to do but stand up and go.

"Before you go, I have a present for you," the cacique said, coming out of his trance. He walked over to the wooden chest at the far side of the room and reached inside. Howie was a skeptic, a new generation of educated Native American. But still, he could not help being a little thrilled to receive a gift from the holy man. He wondered what sort of magical fetish it might be.

The gift was a flashlight, an old dented silver Eveready.

"May this guide you on your journey home, my young friend," the cacique said elaborately.

Howie grinned foolishly. This was not what he had expected, but it turned out to be just what he needed. When he left the cabin, he found that night had fallen, and without Raymond Concha's flashlight, he would certainly have broken his neck getting home.

10

On Saturday morning Howie and Jack had breakfast at the New Wave Café, a renovated adobe on a narrow street just off the plaza in the historic district of San Geronimo. This was the quaint part of town where all the buildings, by command of the town fathers, were required to look old and atmospheric, even the McDonald's and JCPenney. The New Wave was where the arty Anglo set liked to hang out—they had poetry readings at night, and there was usually some fairly awful artwork on the walls, someone's latest show. As a crowd, the arty set were not Howie's favorite people; they liked to pretend they were on the cutting edge of things, but isolated in a small New Mexico town, it was obvious that the world had passed them by.

Everybody in town seemed to be talking about the murder. "You know what it is, don't you? The mountain simply decided to cleanse its aura!" one woman was saying in a loud voice at the next table.

"Strange how people have decided this crime is a metaphysical event!" Jack observed more softly to Howie.

"Well, that's San Geronimo for you. Welcome to the New Age, Jack."

Jack snorted and wiped cappuccino foam from his mustache with the back of his hand. Howie had it made among the New Agers, being an Indian, but for Jack it was clearly an uphill struggle to be hip.

"Tell me more about Doobie Rock," Jack said, continuing a meandering conversation that had been going on all morning. "What makes this place so special?"

"Okay, the first thing you gotta understand is that Indians don't have churches or temples, at least not in the way you pale persons think of such things. For an Indian, all of nature is a kind of open-air cathedral. The land itself is sacred, and there will be lots of special places scattered about the reservation—certain rocks, trees, streams, caves, hilltops, you name it. These are where you go in order to pray and perform various rituals. Doobie Rock, apparently, is a particularly sacred place, so it's really quite extraordinary that the tribe would agree to lease it to the ski resort."

"If the cacique is the tribe's spiritual leader, I'm surprised his opposition didn't kill the deal."

"Jack, a lot of Anglos I know like to romanticize Indians as one big happy tribe, but the fact is, Native Americans are every bit as divided as regular Americans, and pretty much along the same lines. Every reservation I've ever seen has a hot feud going on between its conservative and progressive elements—I don't know why things are set up like that, but it seems almost to be some kind of natural law, like yin and yang. With Indians the conservatives want to hang onto all the old ways no matter what: the language, the traditions, and most important of all, the religion. The progressives want to move forward into the modern world. They are the ones who are into education and decent health facilities, which is all very nice—but you have to watch these guys, because they are the ones who are liable to bring strip mines and nuclear waste dumps onto the reservation. Just like Republicans and Democrats, Indians can get pretty nasty with each other, depending on which side of the divide you happen to be on."

"So in this case, apparently the progressives won. I wonder just how bent out of shape Raymond Concha got over his loss? Tell me, Howie—now that you've met him, do you think he could have put that arrow into Senator Hampton?"

"Well, he *could* have, Jack. It's physically possible, at least. By car it's almost an hour's drive from the reservation to the ski area. But if you look at a map, you'd see that Concha's cabin, the way it's situated on the south face of the mountain, it's really very close to Doobie Rock as the crow flies. He himself admitted he could get there in about forty-five minutes. He must know all sorts of trails and shortcuts through that forest. But I don't see him as a killer."

"Hmm . . . I wonder," said Jack vaguely.

Jack was still wondering while Howie ordered another round of cappuccinos and croissants from Sarah, the pretty English waitress.

"Your turn now," Howie prompted. "How did you spend the afternoon?"

"Well, it's the damndest thing," Jack said finally. "While you were with Raymond. I had a visit from Captain Ed Gomez of the state police—he's been put in charge of the murder investigation, and he wanted to go over my statement. Not an especially bright guy. His mind is set on some sort of drug angle to the murder, just because it happened at Doobie Rock."

"And you don't think so?"

Jack shrugged impatiently. "Maybe drugs. Maybe not. It's really too early to say. Fortunately, while Gomez thought he was questioning me, I managed to pump him about the police investigation so far. They don't have much. Apparently, the Senator was seen riding the seven-forty-five A.M. chair up the mountain on April first—it runs at that hour for fifteen minutes for employees to get to work. The Senator rode by himself, and then it's like he disappeared off the face of the earth. No one saw him again. But there are a few troubling items that came out of the autopsy report. For starters, the coroner is estimating the time of death at ten A.M., half an hour *before* his appointment with us."

"Why's that so strange?"

"Howie, *think*! The weather was awful that day. Why the hell did Senator Hampton get to Doobie Rock half an hour early to stand around in a blizzard waiting for us?"

"Maybe he had an earlier appointment with someone else."

Jack shook his head. "It's one thing to go skiing in bad weather, quite another to linger on the side of a mountain at eleven thousand feet in a snowstorm holding meetings like you're in your goddamn office . . . no, I don't buy it. It's nonsensical in the extreme. And there's something else that's even crazier. . . ."

Jack was interrupted by Sarah, the English waitress, arriving with a tray. She had a croissant stuffed with green chile and feta cheese for Jack, a chocolate croissant for Howie, and two more double cappuccinos. One had to keep one's strength up somehow.

"Something else from the autopsy that's even more bizarre," Jack continued when she was gone, taking a huge, predatory bite from his pastry. He had to chew a moment before he could continue: "Senator Hampton had sex with a woman less than twenty minutes before he was murdered."

"No kidding? You know, I'm starting to like this old Casanova, Jack. I hope *I* have sex twenty minutes before I kick off."

"On a ski slope in a *blizzard*?" Jack roared so loudly that several of the people at other tables—doubtlessly in the midst of soft, artistic conversations—turned to look.

Howie shrugged. "Hey, it's a cold world. Sometimes you gotta take your pleasures where you find them, bro."

Jack and Howie had an appointment at Senator Hampton's house at eleven. Josie said she would be there to show them around, and also introduce her half sister Alison, who was coming to the house for a ten o'clock meeting with the family lawyer.

The Hampton residence was a few miles east of town, nestled in the foothills of the mountains among the piñon and pine. The entire estate was surrounded by a high adobe wall. It seemed to Howie a very lovely old wall, thick and rambling, faded ocher in color. But some local kids had scrawled graffiti near the front gate, the inchoate spray-can markings of their generation. Apparently, there was no escaping the modern world, no matter what kind of wall you put up.

Howie drove in through the main gate and up a long driveway that wound its way gently through a well-groomed forest. They crossed a small stream on a pretty wooden bridge, and came out after a few hundred yards upon the house itself—a two-story adobe villa that sat atop a small knoll surrounded by huge old cottonwood trees. There was a blue Jeep Grand Wagoneer outside the front door, and Howie parked the Toyota alongside. A Spanish maid answered the doorbell and led them into a huge living room. Howie helped Jack settle into a thick sofa and then he browsed around while waiting for Josie and her sister to appear.

It was everything a chichi New Mexican house should be: lots of natural wood, cool tile floors, Navajo rugs on the floors and walls, spectacular views of the desert and mountains. There was a nice Georgia O'Keefe painting on the wall; a study of rock formations, probably a landscape from her Abiqui home. A baby grand piano stood near the sliding glass

door to the patio, a book of Chopin *Preludes* open on the
music holder. Senator Hampton had been an avid Indian art
collector. Everywhere you looked there were kachina dolls.
Tony Da pots, Hopi baskets, and Navajo sand paintings. There
was even a twenty-foot totem pole outside the living room
window standing grandly at the far end of a lap pool. Totem
poles, of course, come from the Northwest not the Southwest,
and to Howie this seemed overdoing the Indian motif just a little. The pool was empty of water this time of year, and the
stacked faces gazed down on the concrete hole with frowning
malevolence.

Josie Hampton came into the living room while Howie was
busy describing these various house and garden splendors to
Jack. She was wearing a blue jogging suit and looked fresher
and more attractive than the last time they met at the Winterhaus bar. Once again, her light blue-gray eyes struck Howie as
odd in such a person-of-color face, giving her a kind of constantly startled, ironic expression. She seemed to be laughing,
slightly, at everything she saw.

"Commander Wilder," she said in greeting.

"How are you doing this morning, Josie?"

"Better. I've had a few good cries. But, you know, life goes
on. Running a busy ski area doesn't leave a lot of time for
grieving. Tomorrow's the last day of the season, and there are
a hundred things I need to do to shut down until next year."

Jack sniffed the air, which struck Howie as an impolite gesture, even for a blind man. "Is your sister Alison here?" he
asked.

"Oh, no. I'm sorry but you missed her. We moved up the
meeting with our lawyer, and she couldn't stay."

"This is a disappointment. Is she avoiding me, by any
chance?"

"Oh, no, no," Josie said hurriedly. "Alison's just like that—
always incredibly busy."

"Is she?" Jack asked wryly. "Well, I'll deal with your sister
later. Right now let's talk about your father's love life. I'm interested in current girlfriends."

Josie was clearly pained by the subject. She sat down into a
stiff, old, ornately carved Spanish chair and crossed her legs
primly. "This is a messy area, I'm afraid. Seduction was Dad's
stock in trade. He used to say it was what kept him young, all

that running around. In recent years there have been a whole
bunch of affairs, but nothing long-lasting."

"Who's his most recent conquest?"

"I really don't know. Frankly, I made a point of *not* knowing. The girls kept getting younger and younger as he got older
and older. You know the syndrome, I'm sure. Some of the girls
were younger than me."

"You didn't approve?"

"It's not quite that. It just began to seem sort of pathetic.
And I worried about him coming on to the female employees
at the Peak, that it would be bad for morale and lead to problems among the staff. You know, I wouldn't be entirely surprised if some jealous husband put that arrow in him!"

"Do you have any particular jealous husbands in mind?"

She shook her head. "No, I don't. I tried to tell him that he
needed to be more discreet, but he just wouldn't listen. It was
like the ski resort was his personal harem, his fountain of
youth—God only knows what he was really looking for, or
trying to prove. To tell the truth, it was a little embarrassing for
me as his daughter. Finally I decided, hell, it was his business,
and I'd better just butt out."

"So you really don't know his latest girlfriend?"

"Oh, I'm sure there *was* someone—there always was. But
no, I didn't ask, and Dad didn't tell me. Living together in the
same house, we both decided to give the subject a wide berth."

"You lived here with your father, Josie? I didn't realize
that."

"Yes, I've taken over the old basement family room during
the past few years and turned it into a kind of apartment. It was
supposed to be temporary, after I broke up with the rat-fink
boyfriend I was living with. But Dad and I got on pretty well,
actually, and it turned out to be a nice arrangement for us both.
We each had our own lives, of course. We came and went
sometimes without seeing one another for days at a time."

"And he never brought a woman here?"

"You seem to be obsessed with this one subject. Is Dad's
sex life really so important?"

"Yes, it is," Jack assured her.

She seemed exasperated. "Well, he never brought any of his
girlies here, anyway. But knowing Dad, he had some twen-
tysomething chick stashed somewhere."

"Stashed where?"

"God only knows. I certainly never asked."

"So sometimes he didn't come home at night?"

"I presume so, but I don't really know. I have my own entrance downstairs, and the house, as you see, is quite large."

"When's the last time you actually saw him, Josie?"

"Let's see . . . I guess it was the morning before he died. We had a quick breakfast together."

"What did you talk about?"

Josie shrugged. "China, believe it or not. Dad sometimes liked to spout off about politics. He was very opinionated, as you might imagine."

Jack pursed his lips. He sat for several moments in a profound silence, frowning, thinking, retreating deep behind his dark glasses. Josie watched him carefully, as though he were a dangerous animal who might strike unexpectedly, and Howie watched Josie watching Jack. The questions had come to a momentary dead end.

"By the way, I have that list of private investors you asked for, people who have money in the Peak," Josie said helpfully. "I can get it for you if you like—it's upstairs in Dad's office."

"Let's go together," Jack suggested, coming out of his trance. "It will give us a chance to see the house."

"You want the grand tour?"

"You bet."

With Josie leading the way, they toured the library, dining room, kitchen, back pantry, upstairs bedrooms, even the wine cellar. Howie felt like a running commentary from *Architectural Digest* trying to describe it all to Jack. Fortunately, Josie helped out when he faltered or ran out of breath, getting into the spirit of the occasion. As for Jack, his dark glasses constantly scanned his surroundings like two radar screens in motion, taking in impressions through senses Howie could barely imagine.

Pretty strange, Howie thought, to walk through the house of a dead man. Like inspecting the empty, cast-off shell of a hermit crab. In the Senator's library, there were novels in French—*Madame Bovary, Le Rouge et Le Noir,* Proust, Sartre, and more—which Josie assured them her father read for pleasure in his spare time. There was also a good deal of philoso-

phy, particularly of the Eastern variety—Zen Buddhism, Tao-
ism, the Vedantas, the *I Ching,* Alan Watts, Krishnamurti, and
company. The guy was nearly perfect, Howie had to admit.
There was an exercise room with a treadmill and Nautilus machine. Framed photographs in the hallways of Kit posing with
various celebrities, politicians, opera singers, movie stars,
even an Italian film director. A citation from the Sierra Club
for bringing high environmental standards to the ski industry.
A plaque expressing gratitude from the Santa Fe Opera, on
whose board he had served in the late eighties, doing his civic
bit for culture. And, of course, plenty of vanity photos of Kit
swishing down San Geronimo Peak on skis: Kit going through
slalom poles in perfect form, Kit in the air flying off sheer
precipices of snow, Kit skiing unfazed through a field of
moguls that were as big as VW Bugs.

Kit's upstairs bathroom was at the end of a walk-through
closet, and there were his-and-her sinks, a sunken tub big
enough for a Roman orgy, and a toilet with a superb view of
snow-covered San Geronimo Peak. Howie imagined it must
have been pleasant for him to sit on the can and peer out the
window to his source of wealth, imagining all those people
shelling out forty bucks apiece for lift tickets. Nevertheless,
there were sleeping pills and sedatives in the medicine cabinet.
This surprised Howie a little; apparently life was a bitch for
those who had, just as it was for those who had not.

"How did your meeting go this morning?" Jack asked Josie
as they lingered near the Jacuzzi.

"Meeting?"

"With your family attorney."

"Oh, yes . . . well, pretty good. He explained how everything was going to proceed—probate, estate taxes, and all that.
Dad has a safe-deposit box in town, but I gather we can't open
it without a representative from the IRS present. So we're getting the ball rolling on that."

"What is the lawyer's name?"

"Christopher Broach. He has an office in town."

Jack nodded in Howie's direction.

"I'm writing it down, Jack," Howie assured him.

"And what about your father's will?" Jack asked her. "Did
you discuss the division of the estate?"

"Yes, we read through the will together. Basically, my half

sister and I split everything, with a few small bequests to the San Geronimo Land Trust, the Santa Fe Opera, and KNME—that's the public television station in Albuquerque. Dad was always very big on public television. He left them twenty thousand dollars."

"And who will run the ski resort?"

"I will. Naturally, the Princess will get *her* share of the profits, along with the other investors."

"The Princess?"

"Sorry. Alison, my dear half sister."

There was something unpleasant in Josie's tone. Since Jack remained momentarily quiet, Howie decided to wade cautiously into sibling waters.

"It doesn't seem quite fair," he said, "that Alison should get half of the ski resort when *you* were the one by your father's side this past decade helping him run the resort."

"Oh, I don't mind," Josie replied. But she said it with a sharp laugh that belied her words. "Well, to be honest, there's *one* thing about the will that pisses me off just a little. . . . Dad left her the house."

"*This* house?"

"Yep. Dad just gave it to her—the artwork, the furniture, everything. Not that I care about the money, of course. It's more the idea of it. I mean, he *knew* how much I love this place. I only found this out an hour ago, so I haven't quite absorbed it yet. I'm feeling a bit evicted, if you want to know the truth."

"Wow, he gave her the artwork too!" Howie said with sympathy. "I noticed a Georgia O'Keefe in the living room—that must be worth a fortune."

"It's been valued at two hundred and fifty thousand dollars!" Josie said, suddenly angry. "And I really *love* that painting too!"

Howie looked over to Jack, certain he'd want to exploit this interesting twist to the conversation. But Jack was gazing back at him, the slightest smile on his face, a go-ahead. Howie saw that this was his chance to be more than Jack's errand boy. So he continued:

"Why do you think your father did it—left Alison all this in his will?" he asked gently.

Josie's expression was distant, full of old pain, old family dramas. "I really feel Dad tried to do his best by me, despite the late start. But with Alison, it was always different. She was the Princess from day one; she was the legitimate one. I mean, me, I was a quickie—I was conceived in a broom closet up at the ski area . . . I kid you not, by the way, my mother told me this a few years ago! But Alison, she grew up in a big house in L.A., she went to the best schools. She was always Dad's *real* daughter, the golden girl, and I guess she was important to him in some way that I wasn't. Probably I shouldn't say this. I don't mean to be petty, and I love my sister, I really do. . . ."

"No, say it. I'm curious."

"It's just . . . well, to be honest, Alison has a way of manipulating men, and then discarding them when she's gotten what she's wanted. She's a knockout, of course, totally beautiful. And men have always been wild about her. But she *uses* them, you know. And I really don't like that."

"Do you think she manipulated your father?"

"I didn't want to say it," Josie agreed, saying it anyway. "But it's true, of course. It's how she relates to men, by pushing their buttons. She's the sort of girl who just bats her eyelashes, and guys'll do anything for her. She really sucked up to Dad these last few months, and I think that must have *something* to do with why he gave her the house."

Josie peered at Howie, suddenly suspicious, as if he might be the shallow sort of male who could be seduced by the mere lure of flesh—her sister—rather than the purer gold of character, herself. Howie concentrated on looking as though sex had little interest for such a scholarly Indian, but Josie wasn't buying it. Somehow he had used up his window of opportunity with her. Jack had been listening carefully, and he decided this was the moment to take over the interrogation once again.

"So where are you planning to live, Josie?"

"Oh, I'll buy a house, I suppose. Actually. Alison's been very nice—she says I should stay here as long as I want. So probably I'm being very bitchy about her."

"Were there bequests in the will to any other friends, or employees at the ski area?" he asked.

"None at all."

"Women friends? Distant relatives?"

"No, nothing of that kind. The will was really very straightforward."

"If I may ask, how much money will you and Alison inherit?"

"Not counting the house, approximately four million dollars. After estate taxes, it won't actually be a great deal. . . . The main asset, of course, is the ski resort, which should give Alison and me an additional three hundred thousand a year. Maybe more. Of course, *I* have the responsibility and the work, while *she* will just receive her check in the mail."

"Yes, but your father did leave you with a rather good job," Jack mentioned. "How much salary will you draw for running San Geronimo Peak?"

"A hundred thousand a year . . . but believe me, I'll earn every cent of it!"

"I'm sure you will," Jack said in a most gentlemanly manner.

They continued with their tour of the house. The last room they came to was at the very top of the house, Kit's home office, a small third-floor tower that was reached by a narrow spiral brass staircase that looked like something you might find in an old lighthouse. Howie was partial to towers, ivory and otherwise, and he described the view glowingly to Jack, a panoramic view of the mountains, the desert, even a scenic slice of the town itself in the distance. There was a small adobe fireplace and a wonderful I'm-on-top-of-the-world feeling to things. Unfortunately, the family attorney, Christopher Broach, had removed all items of interest from the desk itself—the checkbooks, financial documents, and computer discs, taking these to his office to sort through at leisure. There wasn't much left of a nitty-gritty nature for two detectives to get excited about.

"Oh, look, there's Dad's watch!" Josie exclaimed. She bit her lip as she stared at it. It was a gold Rolex, and it was sitting on top of a new hardcover biography of Wolfgang Amadeus Mozart.

"His watch?" Jack asked with sudden interest. "Wasn't he wearing it the morning he was killed?"

"Oh, no, he never wore it. It was one of Dad's quirks. He used to say the electrical impulse of a watch—the battery, the metal, I'm not sure what—interfered with his inner equilibrium. It's a little loony, but people in New Mexico start be-

lieving stuff like this after they've been here long enough.
Anyway, Dad used to go on about how he had an almost perfect sense of time. He claimed he could trust his inner clock.
As for the Rolex, he usually kept it in a drawer, or he used it
as a paperweight when it got windy up here. Cynthia gave it to
him years and years ago."

"Did he ever ask people for the correct time?"

"Occasionally. When he had an important appointment or
something. But rarely."

Jack nodded somberly. "I see," he mused. "And you're *certain* he didn't have the Rolex with him on April first?"

"Absolutely. Captain Gomez is keeping all of Dad's personal belongings that were on him when he died until after the
inquest. . . . Ah, here's the list you wanted of the hundred and
forty-eight investors, along with their various addresses."

She reached into a file cabinet and handed several pages of
computer readout to Howie.

"Please keep this list confidential, by the way. The privacy
of our investors is naturally very important to us. If you actually decide to contact anyone, I'd appreciate it if you would inform me first."

Howie browsed the list as they descended the spiral staircase to the lower floors. There were names he recognized of
powerful New Mexico families. But most names he did not
know at all.

Money, money, money, he thought. Who has enough green
stuff to put a mil or two into a ski resort? The same sort of person, obviously, who had a gold Rolex to use carelessly as a paperweight. Just as Howie was about to fold the list and put it
in his pocket, he noticed a particular name on the second page
that made his eyes open wide. He took a breath to disguise his
excitement.

They walked together down the three flights of stairs to
ground level. Josie said good-bye to them at the front door, and
Howie guided Jack to the passenger seat of the pickup truck.
He walked around to the other door, slipped in behind the
wheel, and waited until Jack had his seat belt properly fastened
before delivering his news.

"Ready for a small revelation, Jack? Try guessing the name
of one of the investors?"

Jack turned his dark glasses toward Howie and frowned. "I'm not in a mood for any more guessing . . . who?"

"Millennium Investment Corporation, Colorado Springs, Colorado. Interesting, don't you think, that the Senator gave a little lecture about millenarianism to Maria Concha? . . . maybe the end of the world is coming after all?"

11

In Lakota, the language of Howard Moon Deer's ancestors, there was an old name for the white man who had invaded their country: *wasicu*. Generally this was translated into English as "the greedy one," but the literal meaning was more precisely "he-who-takes-the-fat." Whenever Moon Deer was inclined to forget the genius of his people, he reminded himself of this single word. *Wasicu.*

He-Who-Takes-The-Fat.

It was the perfect description of the white man, as far as Howie was concerned, and the birth of culinary psycho-sociology as well. In San Geronimo these days, if you wanted to take-some-serious-fat, the Blue Mesa Café was the place to go—the word "café" itself being wonderfully in fashion, chic but understated, belying the prices these cafés charged. On Saturday night, after his busy day with Jack, Howie was invited to a dinner party at the Blue Mesa by his friends from Paris, Bob and Nova Davidson. He was frankly glad to forget about Senator Kit Hampton for a while, and Jack Wilder too. He was certain Jack would disapprove of his fancy off-hour friends, and they in turn would find him gauche and much too old and married to be any fun. So he made an effort to keep the divergent parts of his life separate.

There were seven people at dinner that evening seated at a long, languid table in the outside courtyard. The temperature outside was probably in the low fifties, not exactly balmy, but there were clever gas heaters spaced about the courtyard hissing softly, wasting huge amounts of fossil fuel to create the illusion of a warm Mediterranean climate. The table itself was covered with white linen and good china, wineglasses and remnants of salads and appetizers. An attractive waitress came and went with a small army of busboys fluttering behind her.

She was a decorative young thing, their waitress, blond and
smooth, pretty as a plate of food, cross-dressed in a man's
white dress shirt and paisley tie. Howie always found himself
wondering where these waitresses came from, looking vaguely
erotic in their male attire; as far as he could tell, they appeared
in places like San Geronimo almost by magic, part of a culinary support system required at the top of the food chain.
Eventually, he imagined, they would be gobbled up by a rich
husband.

Howie was dressed down for the occasion, making a virtue
of his poverty, in old jeans and Birkenstock sandals and a
slightly tattered black turtleneck sweater. A fashion plate for
Generation X, his ponytail dangling over the back of his
sweater. At the far end of the table sat Nina and Diane, a pleasant lesbian couple who ran the Crystal Galaxy, a shop special-
izing in items necessary to channel energy, worship the
Goddess, and live a proper New Age life. Next to Diane was
Albert, a sculptor who worked in "found objects," as he called
them—unusual stones, used condoms, beer cans, driftwood—
anything the universe dropped on his doorstep, which he
welded and glued together into quirky shapes. Farther along
the table came Bob and Nova, talking a mile a minute, full of
fun. And finally, to Howie's right, sat Maddie Jessup, a terrif-
ically healthy-looking blond woman, twenty-nineish, big in
the bones with a pretty peasant face. Maddie was the chef at
the Corn Maiden, the second-best restaurant in San Geronimo
after the Blue Mesa, and Howie was aware that Nova had invited her along for him, a stray gal for a single guy. They eyed
one another with cautiously carnivorous intent.

"Have you tried the squash blossoms? They're yummy,"
Maddie said, passing him a plate of unborn zucchini—tender
budding orange flowers that had been plucked from the plant
at just the right moment, then stuffed with Greek goat cheese
and very lightly steamed so that the cheese was warmed but
the blossoms did not wilt. It seemed to Howie's native sensi-
bilities a tad decadent to eat such pretty-pretty food out of season, for it was not yet zucchini blossom time in New Mexico.
He put the blossom to his nose, sniffed it like a bumblebee,
then popped it into his mouth.

"Yummy, isn't it?"

"Mmm," he agreed. Though if Maddie said yummy a third time, he was tempted to dump the plate over her head.

"Have you gone to the bathroom yet?"

I beg your pardon?"

"The bathroom," she repeated. "On the way to the bathroom, you pass over the old well. . . ."

"Oh, yes, the well!" He was relieved they were discussing archaeology rather than scatology. After the food, the high prices, and the fashionable clientele, the big thing about the Blue Mesa was the fact that it was built directly upon one of the town's earliest wells, an earthen shaft that had been incorporated into the floor of the bar, covered with clear Plexiglas and lit from way down deep with hidden lighting. You could actually step on the Plexiglas on your way to the bathroom, if the vertigo view didn't bother you, and peer downward into San Geronimo's historical past. It was quaint to think of the early Spanish settlers digging for water, blithely unaware that someday in the future there would be an expensive restaurant built upon the spot, utilizing their primitive work for decoration. Humans had certainly come a long way. Now if you wanted water, you only had to ask the bartender for a San Pellegrino.

At the far end of the table, Bob, Diane, Nina, and Albert were discussing their "inner child." Albert had lost his, apparently. Misplaced the poor creature in the ceaseless bombardment of adult responsibilities: the need to pay bills and taxes and floss his teeth. With a glint in his eye, Bob launched forth on one of his favorite anti–New Age tirades, one that Howie had heard before. "People forget that all this goddess shit and inner-child nonsense are at best only useful *concepts*," he declared archly. "They're exactly like Freud's id and superego— they don't exist except as a kind of metaphor. The way a lot of people in San Geronimo talk about their inner child, you'd think they needed to change the damn brat's diapers every few hours!"

Bob could go on like this for hours. He was very bright and endlessly full of opinions. As far as Howie was concerned, the average *wasicu* of the past two generations did not need to discover his inner child as much as his inner adult—but he had learned to keep his mouth shut in these matters.

"You must tell me about Native American cuisine," Maddie

was saying at his end of the table. "I'd love to get some really native dishes onto the menu at the Corn Maiden."

"If you want to go native, you should try some nice raw buffalo heart fresh from the kill, still pumping blood," he suggested. He smiled a bit too brightly and added: "I can imagine the gurgles of delight in a crowded dining room. Serve it at room temperature, I should think, with chop sticks and perhaps a hot towel to clean off afterward."

"Hmm . . . with two scallions across the top of the plate," she mused, "like crossed arrows. Perhaps a small mound of pickled ginger and wasabi, like you serve with sushi."

"We'll call it mushi," he said helpfully.

Unfortunately, Maddie did not have a sense of humor. She pondered his suggestion quite seriously, wondering if it would help her break through the barriers of oral indifference into international fame. The challenge of today's culinary marketplace, of course, was to astonish the taste buds of people who had tasted everything; to come up with something continually new among all the contestants hoping to win favor in the modern mouth. Maddie was intrigued, but at last she shook her head. "No, people in this country hate innards. Anyway, Howie, Native Americans surely don't eat that way today."

"Not too often," he admitted. "Today we're more into refined sugar. You might do best to run a Mars bar special. Or corn dogs with lots of bright yellow mustard. Actually, as a kid I found corn dogs *very* yummy." He sensed he wasn't being very nice, but there was something about Maddie that rubbed him the wrong way.

"Howie, you need another glass of champagne," Nova insisted, refilling his fluted glass. They were drinking French champagne this evening in memory of Paris. Nova was red-complexioned, mid-twenties, and modestly attractive in a kind of Flemish way. Howie was her special project, and she gave him a look of warning that he was blowing it with Maddie and should make an effort to be nice. A few months ago, when Bob had been away in Los Angeles, Nova and Howie had nearly had an adventure in her hot tub. They were naked at the time and alone, so it was only natural. They necked a little, but then decided mutually that they simply could not betray Bob. Ever since, Nova had been doing her utmost to fix him up with a girl. Basically Howie was willing. In his own way, he was searching for Ms. Right as badly as she—he hoped—was out there somewhere searching for him. Yet it all seemed such a hard lot of work these days, the battle of the sexes. He was lazy, he supposed, looking for romance rather than a relationship.

"You're looking thoughtful," Maddie said.

"Probably he's thinking about a case," Nova suggested coyly.

"A *case*?" Maddie inquired, all ears—and she had quite large ears at that.

"Howie, tell us some of your lurid adventures as a private eye," Bob said, pivoting from one conversation to another.

"But I thought you were working on your Ph.D.?" said Maddie.

"I am. The detective thing is only a part-time job."

"Isn't it dangerous?"

Howie shrugged, hoping to look impossibly brave—like one of those bare-chested Indians on the cover of romance novels, a half-naked white girl collapsed in their arms.

"Tell Maddie about your case, Howie," Nova enthused, glad to keep him off the subject of buffalo hearts.

"Oh, yes! Tell me!"

"Well . . ."

"First you've got to tell her about Jack Wilder," Nova insisted. "I saw him once, Maddie—he looks like a cross between a Russian bear and Jerry Garcia. I swear, that's the only way to describe him. And, Maddie, get this . . . he's *blind*!"

"A *blind* detective?" she gasped. "But how can he solve anything if he can't see?"

"Howie here is his eyes," Bob explained on Howie's behalf.

Howie was about to explain about Jack Wilder, and the "case," such as it was, when the first of a series of shocking things happened that made this Saturday dinner party an event that was long remembered.

Howie smelled smoke.

Tobacco smoke.

They all smelled it at the same time, a heavy aroma on the evening breeze. At first Howie found the smell rather pleasant—it reminded him of France—until it fully hit him what a scandal it was that someone should be smoking a cigarette at the Blue Mesa Café!

Their nostrils all quivered with outrage. Nina, Howie observed, appeared as if she were trying not to breathe lest this terrible thing, secondhand smoke, make its carcinogenic journey into her lungs. Like everyone else, Howie's eyes were doing radar about the courtyard, searching for the source.

And then he saw her. It was his Lady in White from the chairlift. He was astonished to see her, particularly since she held a cigarette in her right hand, smoke curling upward into the late evening sky. Actually, she was no longer a Lady in White—she was dressed in black this evening, a simple but elegant dress that hugged her slim body. She was sitting near the center of the courtyard at a table for two with her daughter, Angela. The little girl was wearing an outfit of burgundy-colored velvet, and the mother and daughter appeared deep in a most adult-like conversation. Howie watched as two waitresses and the maître d' converged upon their table from different angles of the restaurant.

For the first time all evening, he was entirely awake.

12

Howie could see now what was only hinted at before—that his snow maiden, previously concealed in bulky ski clothes, was a very pretty woman indeed. Petite features, pale skin, and huge dark animated eyes. Her short feathery hair was hanging in bangs that were parted more or less in the middle in an attempt to make a passage for her eyes. It looked to Howie as if she were trying to grow her hair out, and the process was currently in an awkward phase. Yet awkwardness suited her. Even the cigarette in her right hand did not imply sophistication; she held it inexpertly like a twelve-year-old with a new vice.

"Do you know her?" Maddie asked, following the intensity of his gaze to its source.

"I ran into her once. She's a doctor."

"Hmm," she hummed with disapproval. "What sort of doctor smokes cigarettes these days, I wonder?"

Howie was wondering the same thing himself, and so apparently was the staff of the restaurant who were moving quickly to her table. The maître d' was a very Italian-looking guy with a soft pussycat face and a ponytail. He arrived at her table, bent forward, and said something that Howie could not hear.

"I'm awfully embarrassed," she told him. For a delicate woman, her voice carried. "I just took up smoking again after a break of eight years. The rules seem to have changed somewhat in the meantime. . . ."

The maître d' was sympathetic but unyielding. The lady took one final deep drag before she stubbed her cigarette out on the ground. It nearly gave Howie an erection just to watch her inhale like that. He had given up cigarettes back in his undergraduate days at Dartmouth, but watching her made him remember all the things he had loved about smoking. A cigarette after sex. A cigarette after dinner. We are empty vessels, Lord, longing for fullness, and for a moment he was tempted to forget petty thoughts of cancer and heart disease, and light up a whole pack of Lucky Strike, his old brand, and suck like crazy.

"Howie, you were telling us about your case," said Nova, trying to get her Cupid agenda back on track.

He surgically removed his attention from the attractive mother and daughter in the center of the courtyard. Nova sipped her champagne and gave him a loaded look. If he read her clearly, she was saying: Look, Howie, don't let your eyes wander upon someone else's dinner. You don't like Maddie too much, and I admit, she's a bit grating. But for heaven's sake, play your cards right, and at least you'll get laid tonight.

So he did as he was bidden and spoke amusingly about their dead would-be client in the snow. The murder of such a well-known figure in a small town like San Geronimo was big news, of course, so everyone around the table was fascinated with Howie's inside account. There was a lot of clicking of tongues and shaking of heads. Even Bob, the cynic, was temporarily forced into seriousness. "Man," he said, "that must really be a bummer to get shot with an arrow!"

"Goodness, can we talk about something else? Like how about dessert?" Maddie said brightly. "Personally, I want to try their yummie sorbet."

They were deciding on dessert when Howie noticed three strange-looking individuals, two women and one man, enter the restaurant and walk three abreast straight past the maître d's podium into the courtyard. There was something purposeful about them as a group, almost military, that caught his eye. The woman on the left was grim-looking, stout, and dark, in her late forties with her mouth sternly set in an inverted U. The woman on the right was younger and blond, but not in any way what Howie thought of as a sexy California blonde. She was skinny and tall, and there was something squashed about her face, as though her features did not quite dare assert themselves. The man sandwiched between the women was short and nebbishy with a bony, fishlike face. He was wearing an inexpensive suit that looked as if it were bought off the rack at Kmart. All three of them would have done better in jeans, that great fashion equalizer, but they had tried ineptly to dress up for the occasion.

"What is it?" Nova asked, following Howie's gaze. "Friends of yours?"

He shook his head. As an unabashed people watcher, Howie was perhaps too quick to pass judgment on different types. But he sensed that this threesome did not in any way belong to the very chic Blue Mesa Café crowd. It wasn't just their unstylish clothing. He knew by looking at them that they ate noodles rather than pasta, white bread instead of whole wheat; and that whatever they ate, they washed it down with a diet Dr Pepper rather than a good glass of cabernet sauvignon.

There was more: he could tell they were uncomfortable walking into this feeding arena where they did not belong, crossing the culinary caste lines of a divided America. They attempted to disguise their discomfort with hostile expressions. But they could not fool Howie, an Indian kid who had done some gate-crashing himself, entering with butterflies in his empty stomach the dining rooms of the rich.

"Howie, what *is* it?" Nova demanded.

"Probably nothing," he murmured. Yet his sense of unease increased when he saw the three march toward the table in the center of the courtyard, where his snow maiden sat with her cute daughter. The nebbishy man in the middle carried something in a shiny black plastic garbage bag in his right hand. The garbage bag was just one more element of wrongness in the picture. Why, Howie wondered, would anyone carry a garbage bag into the Blue Mesa? Then several synapses made connection in his soggy Saturday night brain, and the answer hit him like a blow to the stomach.

"Oh, my God!" he said, standing up. He saw clearly in his mind what was about to happen, but it was unfolding too fast to stop it. The three people reached the table in the center of the courtyard and came to a halt. The lady doctor looked up at them from her main course (the grilled Ahi, Howie observed, with mango salsa); her face seemed to drain of blood, and it was obvious that she too understood the meaning of the tableau.

"Baby killer!" the stout woman shouted in a dark, unnatural voice. And the other two took up the chant: "Murderer! . . . murderer!" Every eye in the restaurant was upon the man in the middle as he dumped the contents of the black plastic garbage bag upon the dinner table: it was an amorphous mess of afterbirth, a revolting gob of blood and slime that tumbled out upon the white linen. Howie was fairly certain the ghastly offering came from a cow rather than a human, but the effect could hardly be more horrible. From nearby tables he heard people gasping and retching, for it was far from an appetizing sight.

The little girl began to wail in terror. She leapt from her own chair into her mother's lap.

"God will punish you!" the stout lady shouted. And the nebbishy man and gangly blond woman, like a demented Greek chorus, continued to chant: "Baby killer . . . baby killer . . . Jesus has your number!"

The lady doctor stared at the bloody mess on the table in horrified fascination. For a moment there was pandemonium. The little girl's terrified wailing rose to a high-pitched scream that pierced every corner of the restaurant. Finally the mother wobbled to her feet, grasping her daughter protectively in one arm, and holding a butter knife in her free hand like a weapon. Things might have gotten very bad, but the maître d' jumped into the fray and stood between the intruders and the intruded-upon while another employee, a chef from the kitchen, telephoned the police.

The chef and maître d' managed to haul the protesters into a back room to await the authorities. They were Christian martyrs now, no longer terrified bumpkins, and they made their exit with their heads held high. They had done their duty as they saw fit, destroying the collective appetite of their culinary foes. As for the lady doctor, she and little Angela made a grand exit as well. Howie was watching closely as she moved from her table and walked very pale and proud from the courtyard, leading her daughter by the hand. He was certain he was not the only person at the Blue Mesa who wished to protect this lovely mother and daughter forever from fanatics who took themselves so seriously as to ruin a person's dinner.

"You know who that is? I recognize her now," Bob whispered into Howie's ear as the mother and daughter passed close to their table. "She's Senator Hampton's daughter."

"That's the oldest daughter? That's *Alison*?" Howie asked in astonishment.

"You bet. She was with her father at an art opening about six weeks back. I remember the legs."

Suddenly a lot of things made sense to Howie. Even how his snow maiden had come to be such a splendid skier. Her father had owned one of the most famous ski mountains in North America. And, of course, he knew now exactly what sort of doctor she was.

13

Howard Moon Deer rose to his feet. It wasn't so much a decision to follow her as an irresistible gravitational pull.

"Excuse me," he mumbled hurriedly at Nova and Bob. He nodded vaguely, apologetically in Maddie's direction and then hurried from the courtyard into the restaurant proper and on through to the lobby. He found Alison Hampton and her daughter near the front door talking with a cop. Alison's voice was calm and decisive. She was telling the officer that she would make a proper statement tomorrow but right now she *must* get her daughter home. The policeman was helpless against a woman like this who knew her own mind and spoke with such moneyed certainty.

Howie had no such certainty himself, he hardly knew what he was doing. He followed Alison and Angela out into the street.

"Excuse me!" he cried, running up behind them. "We met last week on the chairlift!"

He knew it was a dumb introduction. Skiing was the last thing on the lady doctor's mind, after what she had been through. She stopped and studied him with extreme caution, clutching hard to her daughter's hand just in case he tried anything weird. Howie saw that he had about ten seconds of her time before she screamed for the cop inside the restaurant doorway.

"My name's Howard Moon Deer. Remember, we had sort of a collision on the slopes? I was wondering if you needed any help."

From the blank way she regarded him, he doubted if Alison Hampton had understood much of what he was saying. But he was nonthreatening, and she seemed to relax a few degrees. He

smiled at the little girl, who was watching him with tear-filled
eyes.

"Hi, Angela. Remember me?"

"You're the funny Indian."

"That's me, sure. The funny Indian."

Angela grinned, and a small laugh of shy delight escaped
her lips. The little girl was recovering fast from the nastiness
inside the restaurant. But it was the opposite for her mother,
who had been icy calm and now was clearly about to fall apart.
She seemed unsteady on her feet.

"Look," he said, "why don't I drive you home? It would be
no trouble at all for me, and it's not a good idea for you to
drive yourself when you're so upset."

"Yes, thank you . . . I'd appreciate that," she managed. She
seemed not to have any clear idea who he was, except a strong
young man with broad shoulders and a safe, comforting voice
who had appeared at an opportune moment. Angela knew him,
though. She held her arms up and said, with childish certainty,
"Carry me."

"Up you go!" he said, lifting her into his arms. Carrying the
child, he walked with Alison across the street to where her car
was parked. It was an old MGB two-seater sports car, dark
green in color with a beige convertible top. Alison slipped into
the passenger's seat. Howie handed her the little girl, then took
the keys and went around to the driver's side. The interior of
the car smelled pleasantly of oil and leather. The engine was
deep and growly, but it came to life the instant he turned the
ignition. When he looked over at Alison, he saw she was crying.

"Sorry. So dumb to let those people get to me. But with my
father murdered, and those damn Christians, and everything
happening all at once . . . I mean, hell—I thought it would be
nice to take Angela out to dinner. Just her and me, ladies' night
out sort of thing. Away from everybody being so gloomy and
hypocritical about Dad's death. . . . My damn sister crying half
the time when it's obvious she's in hog heaven about the
money we're going to inherit. Even my mother got into the act,
phoning from California in this very fakey-fake voice full of
concern. But she's positively *gloating*, of course, that she actually outlived the son of a bitch!"

It was quite an outburst. "It sounds like a difficult period in your life," Howie admitted.

"Go straight," she directed. "I'll tell you when to turn."

"Have antiabortion protesters bothered you before?"

She flashed Howie an angry look through her tears, as though he must be very stupid even to ask such a question. "The CMA has been picketing my clinic in Albuquerque for nearly six months now. That's why I moved to San Geronimo—I thought Angela and I would be safe from those idiots up here."

"What's the CMA?"

"Christians for a Moral America. You haven't heard of them? Lucky you! They're a right-wing hate group that's based up in Colorado. Antiabortion protest is only one of their many activities. They also want to abolish the income tax and make life hell on earth for homosexuals. Gun control is their other big peeve. The list goes on and on. Public hangings of drug felons. And how about the death penalty for children?—now *there's* a good pro-life cause!"

"These were the people at the Blue Mesa tonight?"

"I assume so. The CMA's been stalking me for months."

"Stalking you? Really?"

"You bet. I'll be driving along, and suddenly there's a big American car on my tail, one of those hideous late-model things that all look alike. Take a look in the rearview mirror—I bet it's there now."

Howie was at a stoplight so he was able to lower the window and glance behind him. "There's a Peugeot station wagon behind us," he said.

"No, that's not them. They *never* drive foreign cars, of course. Well, I guess they figure they've done enough to me tonight, so they're taking a little vacation."

"This is pretty serious," he told her. "Stalking a woman is a crime in this state. You should report it to the police."

"The police!" She laughed bitterly. "Good luck!"

"Mommy, I don't want you to cry anymore," Angela ordered, looking up into her mother's tearstained face.

"I'm all right, sweetheart," Mommy said. And promptly cried a fresh river of grief.

They drove a few miles north on the main highway through town, and then turned west onto a dirt road into the desert. It was the little girl who gave Howie the final instructions to the house, temporarily reversing roles with her mother.

"Here," said Angela, pointing to a driveway that led to a strangely shaped solar home. The front of the house consisted entirely of two stories of glass facing a southerly direction. On the roof were photovoltaic panels and a small satellite dish, giving the place the appearance of an outpost on the moon. Howie parked in the driveway and went around to the passenger side to open the door for Alison and Angela.

"Thank you," the lady doctor said uncertainly. She seemed to have recovered herself somewhat from her earlier outburst. "You know, this is embarrassing but I was so upset I didn't really catch your name."

"Howard," he told her. "Howard Moon Deer."

She offered a crisp handshake. "Well, thank you, Howard Moon Deer," she told him. "I haven't met many chivalrous men recently. It was very nice of you to drive us home. We'll be fine now."

"No problem," he told her with a small smile. Grateful though she might be, he had served his purpose and she was dismissing him in the slightly awkward but haughty manner of an upperclass matron dealing with a delivery boy. He almost expected her to press a fifty-cent tip in his palm.

Well, what did he expect?

"Good night," he said. "Bye, Angela," he added with a small wave.

"Bye, Howard," said his friend, the little girl.

He turned and walked down the driveway into the dark starry night.

"Wait a second!" Alison cried after him. "What are you doing?"

"I'm walking home. I don't mind. It's not really far. I'll stick out my thumb when I get to the main highway."

It was clear that she had not thought about him enough until just this moment to realize the simple truth of his predicament: that since he had driven her home in her car, he was without transportation back into town.

"Wait, I'll phone for a taxi."

He tried not to laugh. "Dr. Hampton, there *aren't* any taxis in San Geronimo. But honestly, I'm fine. Believe me, I've walked longer distances before in my life. And it's a beautiful night."

"No, it's ridiculous for you to walk. After you've been so kind. Look, I'll tell you what—you can borrow my car and bring it back in the morning. I don't work on Sunday, so I'll have time tomorrow to run you wherever you want to go."

Now that the Lady in White had decided on doing the polite thing, Howie saw there was no arguing with her. So he took her car keys once again and assured her that he would return bright and early. He got back into the MG and fired up the motor. He supposed he was getting somewhere with her—he had her car, at least, so she would have to see him again. But Howie wasn't too optimistic.

He was pulling out of her driveway when he heard a scream. It was a terrible scream, full-throated, high and piercing. It scared Howie so much he bit his tongue when he slammed on the brakes. He ran from the car down the driveway and along a short path. The little girl was standing by herself, her mouth quivering, her entire body about to fall apart once again into huge sobs. But it was Alison who had screamed. She was standing by her front door looking with horror at something sticky on her right hand. Even in the darkness of the night, Howie could tell her hand was smeared with blood.

There was blood all over the front door, and more blood on the huge solar window alongside the front door. It took Howie a moment to see that the blood was streaked in patterns, and the patterns formed words. The words said: DEATH TO THE CHILD SLAYER.

She turned to him. Pale, shivering slightly, a lady in distress if he had ever seen one.

"Listen, I feel terrible asking you this, after you've been so nice already . . . but would you mind staying with me tonight?"

14

Howie was in a light sleep sometime in the dark hours, curled uncomfortably on the living room couch, when he was awoken by a rustling of soft material, a patter of bare feet. Then came a small explosion from nearby. POP! He jerked bolt upright, terrified, all his senses alert. Then he heard the swirl of liquid pouring into a glass, and the meaning of the sound became clear. He felt pretty silly almost wetting his pants like that over a pulled cork, but the last few days had shaken his faith in a safe world.

Alison Hampton was coming out of the nearby kitchen with a glass of red wine in her hand. She was in a silky white nightgown, barefoot, looking like some wandering Ophelia, floating ghostlike through the living room toward the stairs to the upper floor. The living room was dark, but a light from the upstairs hall illuminated her. Before she reached the stairs, she turned toward the couch and saw Howie watching her. She changed directions and came toward him.

"Did I wake you?"

"Not really," he lied. "Are you all right?"

"I couldn't sleep. All of a sudden I started worrying about our dog, Rusty. Just what I need—one more thing to worry about. But I haven't seen him tonight."

"Does he wander off a lot?"

"Sometimes. He's not fixed, so occasionally he has his little jaunts. Want a glass of wine?"

"Sure."

She set down her own glass on the coffee table and returned to the kitchen. Howie rubbed his eyes and yawned. The living room was unusual, very modern, a kind of solar atrium that was two stories high with one entire wall of glass on the south-facing side, and a flight of stairs on the north leading to a bal-

cony overhead where the upstairs bedrooms were located.
With all the glass, the living room was a veritable greenhouse,
a jungle of growth protruding from huge decorative pots
everywhere—a banana tree, bougainvillea, several orange
trees, a fig tree, even a few tomato plants bearing fruit. Howie
imagined in the daytime all these plants were very attractive,
but at night the shapes seemed spooky to him. Alison came
back with a second glass and a half-gallon jug of Gallo Hearty
Burgundy. In some odd way he was relieved she had plebeian
tastes in wine; she wasn't a perfect snow maiden after all. She
sat in a chair across from him with the light from the upstairs
hall behind her, casting her in a dark shadow so that he could
see only her luminous silhouette. She looked to him like a dark
angel with a halo around her head. She leaned back in her chair
and put her bare feet up on the coffee table.

"I haven't thanked you properly for driving me home and
staying here tonight," she said.

"You *did* thank me. And it's nothing, really. I still think you
should let me call the cops," he said—for she had insisted a
few hours ago that he should not.

"In the morning," she agreed. "Right now I don't think I
could take a bunch of cops asking endless questions. Tell me
something. Earlier, when I couldn't sleep, I phoned my sister
Josie. When I mentioned you, she said you're a private detective. Is that true?"

"Sort of," Howie told her, feeling like a fraud. "Jack's the
detective. Me, I'm just looking for creative excuses to avoid
my dissertation."

"Jack Wilder's the cop who helped Josie out of that drug
bust in California years ago, isn't he? I was wondering—why
do you think he let her go back, then?"

"I asked him that, actually. He said your sister was only a
bystander and that he was after bigger fish."

"Really? I was always curious how Josie wiggled out of that
particular mess. It astonishes me how everybody thinks of her
as this innocent, Miss Priss. Dad certainly did. She was perfect
as far as he was concerned. Quite the little helper."

"You're saying she isn't?"

Alison laughed. "Good God! *She* was the one who dreamed
up that drug scam back in college! Always the business-
woman—that's my half sister, Josie! The reason she and her

boyfriend were in Haight-Ashbury that night was to pick up a shipment of coke to sell at the Art Institute. But she smiles at the cops like some little goody-goody and gets off with a lecture, while the poor guy gets the shaft. Don't get me wrong, it's not that I begrudge Josie her one wild moment—it's just that I can't stand her being such a hypocrite about it."

"Don't you like Josie?"

"Well, it's complicated. An old family saga. I guess what I *really* resent is how Dad set up these roles for us—Josie was the good one, you see, who grew up poor but made up for it by being so levelheaded and working so hard. And I was the wild one, who grew up spoiled and rebellious and very impractical. Not that these roles were ever strictly true. I mean, here's Josie selling drugs in college, while I'm studying my ass off to get through medical school. But once your parents typecast you, it's like your character is engraved in stone, no matter what you do."

"What did you do that was so wild?"

"Oh, it was my attitude mostly. I did the usual teenage things—I played guitar, screwed around, took acid trips at the beach. You know." Alison took a sip of wine. "Anyway, it's funny, your father dies, and you think you should be grieving. But mostly I've been reprocessing all the old wounds."

Howie had a question he had been waiting for the right moment to ask. There was no right moment, but he popped it now:

"What about Angela's father?"

"What about him?"

"Where is he?"

She took another sip of wine, and her bare toes curled around the table.

"His name was Stephen. I meet him in Nicaragua, just at the end of the Sandinista era. He was an American, down there as a volunteer, like me. I was working in a medical clinic about an hour outside of Managua."

"He was a doctor?"

"No, a botanist. He was trying to improve the crop yield and teach the peasants organic farming. We were all so idealistic back then. It was just a brief affair. A kind of consolation, I guess, after America stomped out the revolution. Ronald Reagan and Oliver North! I've never quite understood why they hated the Sandinistas so much, but they did. Eventually there was nothing to do but come back home. Stephen never even knew I was pregnant."

"You never saw him again?"

"He phoned me once a few years later. It was a bit awkward really. Hot tropical romances don't travel very well back to reality. Then I heard that he was dead. It's ironic really. He survived the contras and the Sandinistas battling it out in Nicaragua, only to get home and be killed in a drive-by shooting in Los Angeles. A friend of mine sent me a clipping from the newspaper. Apparently Stephen was doing some work with the Chicano community in South Central L.A., building community gardens, trying to turn the slums into a green zone. I guess he was just in the wrong place at the wrong time."

"This is probably a bit personal, Dr. Hampton. But why . . . I mean, with your profession and all . . . why . . ."

"Why didn't I get an abortion when I found out I was pregnant?"

"Yes."

She laughed. "Well, here's another irony for you—I don't actually believe in abortion. Not for myself at least. I believe in contraception, and choice, and rational family planning . . . that's why I became an OB-GYN."

"Then, you *wanted* to get pregnant?"

"No. Actually I messed up," she admitted with an impish grin. "Left my diaphragm behind on a particularly lovely moonlit night on the beach."

"Ah!" said Howie. He tried not to imagine the scene too vividly, but he saw it anyway: the moon, the dark sand, palm trees waving in a warm breeze, and Alison Hampton naked and beguiling.

"Anyway, it was a shock when I heard that Stephen was dead," she went on. "I always imagined Angela would have time to get to know him one day when she was older. But history seems to repeat itself. Now she'll never know her father either, just like me."

"But you knew your father," Howie objected. "You ended up living just a few miles away."

"That doesn't mean I *knew* him. . . . Want another glass of wine?" she offered. "We can get drunk, and I'll tell you the awfully sad story of my life."

*   *   *

It was sad, all right. Alison grew up with everything, a nice
house in Brentwood, a swimming pool, her own horse at a
nearby stable, a car when she was sixteen, trips to Europe, and
other awful things like that. The bottle of Hearty Burgundy
went down considerably as Howie listened to this heartbreak-
ing tale. He knew he was getting drunk by the third glass,
when the Gallo actually started tasting good.

Alison had been three when her half sister Josie was born,
and her mother, Cynthia, took her off to southern California
and filed for divorce. Two years later Cynthia married a character actor, Ben Hammond, who made a good living playing
bad guys in the movies. Like a lot of actors who played bad
guys, Ben was actually a much nicer guy in person than most
of the actors who played good guys. His only major problem,
according to Alison, was that he was a weakling and a drunk—
not an abusive drunk like Josie's stepfather, Manny Trujillo,
but a drunk nonetheless.

"It's odd, isn't it?" she said. "Both Josie and I had alcoholic
stepfathers that we detested. Sometimes I feel like we're mirror images of each other, Josie and I."

"When did you discover you had a half sister?"

"Oh, I always knew about Josie, as long as I can remember.
Her existence wasn't public knowledge until much later, but
everyone knew in the family. Josie was the reason my mother
left Kit, and believe me, my mother used to go on and on about
it."

"But you didn't meet her until . . ."

"Not until I was nearly twenty, so it's all very strange. I fantasized about her all the time, of course—this Indian sister I
had somewhere. I was terribly envious of her, you know.
Being an Indian, living with a whole tribe of wonderful spiri-
tually minded people—it seemed a lot more attractive to me
than watching Mom and Ben drinking Bloody Marys around
the swimming pool . . . you're smiling?"

"Only because life on an Indian reservation isn't quite as
idyllic as your fantasy of it."

"Oh, I know that now, of course. But when I was a teenager,
I imagined that Josie had everything that I lacked. I was sure
that in Josie's Indian family, everyone sang and laughed and
had a great time. I thought she saw a lot more of Dad than I

did—I didn't realize until I was grown-up that Dad ignored
Josie just like he ignored me."

"Did you visit your dad often?"

"Not often, but from time to time. I went to Washington
once when he was in the Senate. One Christmas we took a ski
vacation to Switzerland. A few summers I stayed in Santa Fe,
where he had a house for a while. But he was always a
stranger. Once when I was thirteen I worked up the nerve to
ask him about my half sister, but he was very evasive. He gave
me some line about how I would understand when I was older,
so he wouldn't try to talk about it now. It only piqued my curiosity, as you can imagine. So it was a real disappointment to
finally meet Josie and discover she was quite an ordinary person who had spent her childhood being as envious of me as I
had been of her."

"Well, the grass is always greener," Howie acknowledged.

"She was so straight, that's what got me. I mean, *I* was the
Indian, in a funny way—for a time I even wore a headband and
went around barefoot. But Josie, all she wanted to be was Miss
All-American Middle Class."

"Buying drugs in Haight-Ashbury doesn't sound so middle-
class to me," Howie pointed out.

"No, I suppose not. But she wasn't actually getting high.
She only did it for money. She's always been very materialistic, you know, maybe because she grew up so poor. She's always craved nice clothes, cars, and things."

"The things you had, but didn't want."

"Yeah. It's a shame we couldn't just trade places. Poor
Josie! I guess she made Dad happy, though. After 1984, anyway, when he decided to acknowledge her. I mean, *that* was
pretty strange too, like something out of a Victorian novel, the
illegitimate daughter comes forward and takes her proper
place in society. But it worked out for both of them. She became his right hand at the ski area, the perfect daughter, all the
things he probably wished I would be. Josie stuck by him, I'll
say that for her. She's been horribly dutiful. Me, I've been a
big disappearing act."

"And yet, here you are—you moved to San Geronimo."

"Yeah, I guess I did. One more irony in the fire. It was
Dad's idea, actually. He suggested it when I started having so
much trouble down in Albuquerque with the protesters. He

was worried about Angela. And it seemed to me maybe a good idea too. I was hoping to get closer to Dad, although it didn't really happen. We certainly *saw* a lot more of each other after I moved here, but it was always awkward."

"Your father obviously cared for you," Howie told her, "or he wouldn't have left you his house."

Alison smiled. "Oh, Josie told you about the house, I see. She's pissed as hell!"

"Mostly I think she's hurt," he said judiciously.

"Well, she shouldn't be. Josie got what she wanted most—the ski resort. As for the house, it was just a guilt offering, anyway. Dad trying to make up for ignoring me most of my life. I'll never live there—frankly, I can't stand the place. It's awfully pretentious, don't you think."

"It's pretty grand," Howie admitted.

She poured them each another glass of wine, and then she studied him for a long moment.

"I like your hair," she announced.

"Oh, come on!" he laughed.

"No, really. Anglo guys always look ridiculous to me with a ponytail, like they're trying so hard to be hip. But with an Indian, it looks natural."

"That's because we've had a few thousand years to perfect our coiffure. The savage look, you know."

"You don't seem terribly savage to me, Moon Deer."

She reached for a pack of cigarettes on the coffee table. As she leaned forward, the light from behind caught the smooth surface of her chin. Howie was aware that her nightgown had opened at the top, and he forced himself not to peek down the front. Fortunately, he had always been proud of his remarkable powers of self-restraint.

"Want one?" she offered, holding up the pack.

"You bet," he told her, turning his back on six smokeless years without a qualm.

She used a Bic lighter, puffing first on her cigarette and then offering the flame to Howie. In the flickering yellow light, he could see her better. She had beautiful skin, smooth and radiant. He inhaled too deeply, and the smoke hit his lungs with a flood of thick warmth that made his head spin.

"I'm corrupting you," she said. "How old are you?"

"Twenty-seven."

"I'm thirty-four. Pretty ancient, huh?"

"You don't look very ancient to me, Dr. Hampton."

"Good God, you'll make me *feel* ancient if you keep calling me Dr. Hampton! Why don't you call me Alison . . . better yet—call me Allie."

"Allie," he said in an experimental fashion. It made him think of an alley cat.

"I think I'm going to call you Moony," she said with sudden whimsy. "Moon Deer with the round moony face. My man in the moon."

"Now, you're teasing me."

"No, I'm not," she told him softly, blowing smoke. "You're pretty naive, aren't you? I'm flirting."

Howie stared at her in astonishment, since, in fact, this had not occurred to him.

She had to spell it out to him: "I mean, here I am, sitting with very little on, drinking wine with you in a darkened room, telling you my life story at nearly two o'clock in the morning. Doesn't it give you certain ideas?"

He felt pretty foolish when she put it this way. "Well, yes, of course," he said weakly. "But you've been through a lot . . . I was trying to be sensitive."

She smiled. "You've been very sweet. And you've been trying awfully hard not to look down the front of my nightgown, haven't you? . . . but go ahead, if you want. Sometimes it's the nice guy who gets the prize. . . ."

He couldn't say with certainty what happened next. One moment he was staring at her a few inches away, thinking to himself: Holy shit! This is a beautiful woman who just said, if I heard her correctly, that she's mine for the taking! And then the next minute they were kissing. He didn't know who started it, if she leaned forward or if it was him. For a long time they didn't touch with their hands or bodies. Just lips and tongues, licking and tasting. She tasted clean and good, and expensive and well cared for; a complex, interesting flavor he imagined he could get to like.

Then they were tearing off clothes and falling over each other onto the hard floor. For a snow maiden, her skin was burning warm that first electric moment when they touched. When Howie thought about this later, he understood that any sort of euphemism would give the entirely wrong idea of what

had happened: this was not making love, this was screwing,
pure and simple. They rolled over onto a scratchy Navajo rug,
they banged into furniture, both of them grunting and panting
like animals. Howie started off on top, but soon she rolled him
over onto his back, and she proceeded to ride him like a horse.
He reached upward and held her small breasts, and they galloped off together into some ultimate Indian sunset. Howie felt
like he had been lifted up by an angel and carried clear into
genital heaven.

He felt pretty good, all in all. But while he was on his back
getting galloped, he had a glimpse of the moon through her
solar window, and he saw once again the words written on the
glass in blood. They were indecipherable hieroglyphs from his
position on the floor, but he knew what they said: DEATH TO
THE CHILD SLAYER. It cast a shadow on his lust. He remembered
that there was a murderer on the loose, and maybe it was a big
mistake to be playing doctor with the dead man's daughter on
her living room floor.

Somewhere in the desert, a coyote howled. The sound was
so eerie, goose bumps broke out all over his body.

"A ghost walked on your grave!" she whispered, feeling his
bare skin.

This too was not reassuring. But his waters were rising and
it was too late now for this particular salmon to turn around
and head for safety downstream.

Sunday morning he played catch with Angela in the front
yard while Allie cooked breakfast. It was another perfect
spring morning, unseasonably warm. The aroma of toast and
eggs and coffee drifted from the house. The little girl ran
around the garden with an ecstatic expression on her face as
Howie tossed her a soft purple Nerf football and made funny
faces and clowned. It was obvious that Angela adored having
a man around the house.

All the nighttime shadows were gone on such a sunny morning, and Howie was a happy man. Howie and Allie and Angela—it was a seductive picture.

"We'll call the police after breakfast," Allie had promised.
"You can call Jack then too, if you want."

"I'd better," he told her.

But they both wanted to put it off as long as possible. Reality. Cops knocking on the door, strangers intruding upon their intimacy. They were reluctant to turn their thoughts from wet thighs and kisses to blood on the window.

"Howie! Catch!" Angela cried. She threw the Nerf football as hard as she could, high into the air. A breeze came up and gave it some extra lift, and the football flew clear over the *latilla* fence into the sagebrush beyond.

"Wow!" Howie cried, congratulating her. "You're something!"

"Breakfast!" Allie called, appearing in the front doorway. It seemed to Howie almost like being in some kind of New Age Norman Rockwell painting: handsome young Indian, white lady doctor, angelic little girl.

"Be right there!" he told her. He jogged out the front gate and around the side of the *latilla* fence to fetch Angela's ball. The purple ball was easy enough to find in the open desert; he spotted it between an anthill and a small prickly cactus. But as he picked up the ball, he smelled something bad. When he saw the source, he nearly threw up. It was the family dog, Rusty, lying in the sagebrush. The Irish setter had its throat cut so violently that the head was nearly severed from its body. A swarm of flies had settled on the open gash.

Howie heard Angela running up behind him. He turned quickly and picked her up in his arms and carried her back to the house, a taste of ashes in his mouth.

15

After breakfast Howie telephoned Jack to say that he had found Senator Hampton's oldest daughter and that she was in trouble, besieged by fanatic pro-lifers who wrote messages on her window with the blood of the family pet. Jack had been unexpectedly angry.

"Howie, for chrissake!" he exploded. "Why didn't you phone me last night when all this happened?"

"Because the lady was exhausted, Jack, and she didn't want any more hassles. Anyway, her trouble with these Christians doesn't have diddly to do with our case, so I thought hell, the morning is soon enough."

Jack's voice was incredulous: "Howie, a man—our client—gets murdered, shot with an arrow, and then someone terrorizes his daughter, slits her dog's throat, and threatens to kill her too . . . you don't think there's a possible *connection* here? What kind of detective *are* you?"

Howie became emotional, due perhaps to lack of sleep. "Frankly, I'm *not* a detective, I'm a scholar, thank you—and if you don't like my work, you can shove it."

Jack seemed taken aback by Howie's tone. He spoke more calmly. "This is a murder investigation. Don't you get the seriousness of this?"

"I do, Jack. Naturally, I do."

"No you don't. We don't know who the killer is—it could be Alison Hampton, for all you know."

"Now, *that* is ridiculous!"

"You think so, do you? Howie, listen to me. When I asked you to be my assistant, I didn't know we were going to get such a heavy case the first time around. I thought I would have a little more time to teach you things. Now I'm telling you, boy—keep your dick in your pants, and your wits about you, or you could get yourself killed here. Am I making myself clear?"

"Obnoxiously clear."

Howie was so angry he nearly slammed the phone down. But it was a complicated situation because somehow he felt like a kid caught with his hand in the cookie jar. He knew he should have called the police last night, and Jack as well, and that he had not insisted on doing so because of his own not-so-altruistic motives—that a bunch of cops coming over would have interfered with his late-night opportunity to have Alison entirely to himself. This too was a cause for soul-searching. Maybe he should have kept his distance from the lady doctor. Howie had to admit that the whole thing felt a little wrong to him, and one day when he found truelove everlasting, there wouldn't be words written in blood and dogs with their throats slit lying in the yard.

Later on Sunday morning, Jack had Emma drive him to the house where he took charge in his most imperious manner. He told Howie to please look after Angela for an hour, take the little girl on a walk—something, anything to get the kid out of the house so Mom would be able to talk more freely. Howie felt himself unfairly exiled, but he made the best of it. He drove Angela to the Rio San Geronimo, a half mile from Alison's house, and showed her how to catch fish with her bare hands. It was one of the few really Indian things that Howie could manage. The trick is to lie down quietly on the bank, then reach into the water quickly and pull the fish out from beneath the submerged ledges, where they liked to hide. Howie and Angela didn't actually manage to land a single fish on Sunday, but they did a great deal of laughing, and they both got very wet.

By the time he got back to Alison's house, the state police were there, and Jack had even called the FBI, who were supposedly on their way. So much for the possibility of further intimacy with his snow maiden. Alison seemed so overwhelmed by the situation that she barely glanced at him, her sensitive Indian lover of the night before.

"Why don't you let me take you and Angela out for some pizza tonight," he asked, getting Alison alone for a second. "Maybe we can take in a movie afterward, just the three of us. Get away from all this hysteria."

But she only flashed him an exasperated look. "I can't, Moon Deer, not tonight. But soon, okay? . . . I'll give you a call."

"Sure," he said.

But when he left that afternoon, Alison had not even asked for his telephone number.

On Monday Jack sent Howie northward on a trip to Colorado Springs. His mission: to investigate the Millennium Investment Corporation, to learn who they were and why Senator Hampton had seemed so oddly interested in the word itself, "millennium," the last time he had visited his old girlfriend, Maria Concha. Howie sensed that Jack was deliberately getting him away from Alison. This pissed him off slightly, yet he was grateful for the five-hour drive alone. To sit with his thoughts in the cab of the pickup truck, just a speck on the horizon, driving through a high desert plateau on a two-lane highway with snowcapped mountains in the perpetual distance.

You could feel the difference almost the moment you crossed the border from New Mexico into Colorado, passing from the red desert and softly rounded Spanish architecture into a more verdant white man's land of trees and mountains and sharp angles. New Mexico was an Indian, feline place whose beauty was mysterious and subtle; Colorado was cowboy/canine, and there was nothing subtle about the Rocky Mountains. Such was the cultural divide. New Mexico generally voted Democratic; Colorado, Republican—with the exception of a few liberal pockets in such places as Denver and Boulder. It seemed astonishing to Howie how the world always broke down into this clever yin/yang divide. "Man, I guess you gotta have either an innie or an outie!" he said aloud, profoundly, as he pulled into Colorado Springs. It was his big thought of the day. He meditated awhile on Alison Hampton's innie, deciding that as these things go, hers really fit like a glove.

Colorado Springs was bigger than Howie remembered. An attractive town, very clean, nestled against the Front Range mountains with Pike's Peak in the near distance—the famous peak where a poet had once been inspired with patriotic fervor to write the verses to "America the Beautiful." Howie found his way out of the downtown grid into a well-manicured, residential section. There were a lot of *Leave It to Beaver* houses and station wagons full of moms and kids; this was a last bastion of Anglo-Saxon America, a besieged culture that had retreated from the multiethnic coasts to make a fortress in the Rockies. The fortress came complete with the United States Air Force Academy and some very secretive NORAD bunkers built into the nearby mountains. Colorado Springs had always been a Mecca for the right wing, a town that thought of itself as a kind of anti-San Francisco. Most of all, there were lots and lots of churches.

By consulting a map Howie made his way on Colorado Avenue past Garden of the Gods Park toward Manitou Springs. It was close to two in the afternoon when he finally located 3195 Patriot Drive, Suite 304, the address he had for the Millennium Investment Corporation. At first Howie thought there must be some mistake. The address took him to the Manitou Mall, a mid-scale shopping center with a JCPenney, Sears, movie complex, food court, and a variety of smaller outlets. To Howie's surprise Suite 304 was the administrative office of the mall itself, reached through a back hallway between the men's rest room and a bank of public telephones. Howie was about to turn away when he saw "MILLENNIUM INVESTMENT CORP." stenciled in small letters on one side of the glass door. He wandered inside.

"You must be the Easter Bunny," said a pretty young blond woman sitting behind a desk. It was a small, windowless office, hardly more than a cubicle. An athletic young man had been leaning over her, but he jumped back guiltily when Howie came in. It was obvious that he had been flirting with the pretty blonde, and he seemed uncomfortable at being found out.

Howie smiled at them both; personally, he was in favor of flirting and all activities that continued the species. But they did not smile back. The man had short dark hair, a low forehead, and a pudgy, babyish face. But his body was a more serious affair, a weight lifter's body of big shoulders and huge biceps. He seemed to be bursting out of his clothes, a short-sleeved polo shirt and jeans that were half a size too small for him. He stared at Howie without an ounce of friendliness.

"Well, I guess I'd better get back to work, Darlene," he said slowly to the woman at the desk. But his eyes remained on Howie's ponytail. "Call me if you need anything."

He snapped his fingers and clapped his hands together, meditating upon Howie's presence for a moment more. Then without another word, he walked from the office.

Howie turned his attention to the woman. She was in her mid-twenties, a blonde with big hair that swooped and dived in various directions about her head. Howie noticed (not necessarily in this order): red lipstick, a kind of permanent, orange suntan, blue eyes, a cute little snub nose, and huge breasts that were so picture-perfect and perky, one suspected a boob job. She was a cross between a Playboy pinup and an All-American cheerleader. A kind of Republican sex goddess, Howie decided.

She decided to smile at him. "I hope you didn't forget to bring back your ears and tail." Her voice was chirrupy and bright.

"I beg your pardon?"

"Weren't you the Easter Bunny?"

Howie spent a moment assuring her that no, he was not, nor had he ever been, a rabbit of any kind. Nor was he applying for the security job that had been advertised in the newspaper.

"Then what can I do for you?" she asked, not quite as chirrupy as before.

"I'm looking for the Millennium Investment Corporation."

"Oh. Well, they're not here, of course. This is the Manitou Mall administrative office."

"Yes, I see that. But there's a sign for Millennium on your door."

"Well, that's because Millennium Investments is the company that actually *owns* the mall. But there isn't anyone here from them."

"Where can I find their office, then?"

"Their office?"

"You know, office. Where they do business. Tables, chairs, a room. Maybe someone who can actually answer a few questions for me."

"What is it exactly that you want to know?" she asked, less friendly by the second.

Howie wasn't entirely certain why they were having such a

communication problem about something that seemed to him quite simple. He tried again:

"What I want," he repeated patiently, "is to know where I can find the office for the Millennium Investment Corporation."

She shook her head sadly, pouting just a little. The pout suited her. She was really very sexy, he saw, and he understood why the dark-haired hulk had been flirting.

"I wish you were the Easter Bunny," she said, "because then I'd be able to help you."

"I wish I was the Easter Bunny too. I'd multiply and do all sorts of fun things. So you really can't help me?"

"Perhaps if you tell me what you're interested in knowing, I might be able to answer your questions myself."

Howie saw he wasn't going to get past her without a story. So he got a tad creative: "Well, the thing of it is this. I represent a consortium of Native American ski interests. What we're doing, we're exploring the concept of a Sioux ski resort in the Black Hills, and the name Millennium came up, naturally, as an investment group with a long history of involvement with the ski industry."

"Oh, I think you must be mistaken," she told him with a thoughtful frown. "Skiing?"

"Oh, yes. I have a friend from San Geronimo Peak who suggested Millennium. Said this would be just the thing for them, right up their alley. Ski Sioux, we're going to call it."

"Let me make a phone call," she said vaguely.

Howie waited while she picked up her telephone, dialed a number, and spoke softly into the receiver. "This is Darlene . . . listen, there's a young man here. An, uh . . . indigenous person . . . no, not an *indignant* person, gracious me! *Indigenous* . . . that's right, an Indian. And he wants to talk to someone at Millennium about a ski resort. . . ."

She looked up at Howie with a cheerless smile. "I'm sorry I didn't catch your name?"

"Howard Moon Deer. I'm the vice-president in charge of development for the Black Hills Ski Association."

". . . Says he's the vice-president in charge of development for the Black Hills Ski Association," she repeated dutifully into the telephone.

She listened and nodded, and then she hung up the phone.

"I'm so sorry. Just as I thought—there's no one who can help you. But if you leave me your card, perhaps I'll be able to have someone get back to you."

Howie patted his shirt pocket. "Darn, I'm all out of cards. But maybe I can talk to the person you were talking to just now."

"I beg your pardon?"

"The person you had on the phone just now—was that someone over at Millennium?"

"Over at . . . oh, no!" She laughed cheerfully at his misunderstanding. "That was just Christie at the dental office—I thought she might have some ideas, but she didn't."

"What does a dental office have to do with Millennium Investments?"

"Oh, nothing at all," said the blonde graciously.

Howie was starting to wonder about this conversation. It was like trying to wade through a puddle of Velveeta cheese. He just couldn't get anywhere. Finally there didn't seem much else to do but write down his name and address and leave. He debated making up a fictitious address, but why add to the absurdity of an already absurd encounter? In the end he gave his proper address in San Geronimo, feeling he had done enough fibbing.

Howie left the office with a sense that he had failed woefully at a very simple task. Jack was going to be unhappy with him, and that was the last thing he needed after their fight. *Howie, you should have been more aggressive,* Jack would say. *What kind of detective are you, boy?*

But what was he supposed to do with a woman who had such a problem with basic communication? Break her arms? Jam toothpicks under her fingernails? *What, Jack, what?* Howie had to acknowledge that he just wasn't any good at this. He really had no idea how to make a person talk who was determined not to do so.

As he walked along the hallway from the office, he noticed a young woman coming toward him from the direction of the food court. She looked familiar, though he didn't know from where. She had thick dark blond hair and a Nordic face that was very tan. A pretty girl, all in all, a bit stocky, and Howie couldn't imagine where he had seen her before.

The hallway was narrow, and they had to pass close to one

another, since she was walking toward the office he had just
vacated. He saw, quite to his surprise, that she had a small gold
ring piercing her left nostril. This seemed very avant-garde for
Colorado Springs, if not positively counterculture. Howie
smiled at her as they passed, and she smiled back. It was the
recognition of people in a foreign land who come across someone vaguely of their own kind.

He was sure he had seen her before, but he couldn't for the
life of him remember where or when. Howie walked on a few
feet down the hall, but he was so annoyed at his lack of memory that he turned to give her another look. Strangely, she had
turned at just the same time to look at him. They laughed.

"You know, I'm trying to think of where I know you from?"
he said.

She shook her head. "No, I don't think we've ever met."

"Do you ever get down to San Geronimo?"

"Never," she assured him. Then the girl with the nose ring
turned decisively and walked away.

16

The food court at Manitou Mall was something—a huge atrium with a glassed-in ceiling and an updated, hygienic version of an old-fashioned carousel in the center to entertain the kiddies. There were brightly colored plastic horses and little chariots and moving benches that went around in circles to a recorded calliope waltz. Howie suspected the food court needed such Disneyland extravaganza in order to disguise the sad truth that the food itself was lousy and overpriced.

He personally was not fooled. He surveyed his culinary choices with a gloomy eye and opted for an Orange Julius hot dog and a lemonade. It seemed to Howie that his trip to Colorado Springs had been a bust. He took his plastic tray to a plastic table and watched the plastic horses go around and around. He knew that if he didn't come up with some better piece of detective work than what he had done so far, Jack was going to raise an eyebrow at him when he got home and make him feel like a complete idiot. But what could he do?

He took out a ballpoint pen and spiral notebook from his day pack and started jotting down ideas:

1) Phone the number I have for Millennium. Perhaps someone else will answer besides the Republican sex goddess, and I can "grill" her, as they say in the novels. (Note: Check the origin of this strangely culinary slant to detective jargon.)

2) Check the local phone book for other possible listings of Millennium Investment Corp. Who knows?

3) Stroll the mall pretending to be a happy shopper. Strike up impromptu conversations and ask assorted salespeople if they can tell me anything about who owns this building full of sleepwalkers who buy junk they don't need.

4) What else? Check with the Colorado Springs Chamber of Commerce? Meander into a local real estate office and ask if

anyone's heard the name Millennium? But will any of these upstanding citizens really open up to an Indian with a ponytail who is clearly not their kind?

Howie was debating these possible points of procedure when he saw the big-haired, big-breasted blonde from the office cross in front of the carousel and head toward the Mc-Donald's counter. She was waiting in a short line when she was joined by the man Howie had seen earlier bending over her desk, the baby-faced hulk with the muscular arms who seemed to be bursting out of his clothes. He whispered some sweet nothing into her ear, and she laughed. It was interesting to watch the body language of two people who were so obviously sex mates. It was as if the air between them was disturbed by some subtle electric charge. The blonde—Howie believed her name was Darlene—left her spot in the McDonald's line in favor of the Hulk, who was clearly a tastier morsel at the moment in her eyes. They stood together restlessly, waiting for something to happen or someone to arrive. It turned out to be the latter, and the someone was the girl with dark blond hair and the nose ring, who came into the food court from the direction of Radio Shack. Howie still had a maddening sense that he had seen her somewhere before. The group was a threesome now, and the Nose Ring Girl did not seem to fit with Darlene and the Hulk, at least not in Howie's culinary psycho-sociological scheme of things. She was a "pasta primavera," while Darlene and the Hulk were T-bone steaks. Nevertheless, they walked together toward the exit from the mall into the parking lot.

This was most intriguing. Howie popped the last bite of hot dog into his mouth and decided to follow. It seemed he might have a chance to do some detecting after all.

Outside the sun was shining, a bright, bland afternoon. Howie followed the threesome at a distance as they strolled up into the J section of the parking lot, entering a sea of asphalt and automobiles. Just in case they happened to look around, Howie pretended to be a befuddled shopper trying to find his car among a thousand others that all looked the same. It was a part he had practiced for many times in the past throughout the shopping malls of America, but the group did not glance behind them to see his fine performance. They walked clear to the end of the row to where a dark blue car of recent vintage was parked next to a stubby tree. It was a Detroit mobile, a large car now that wasting fossil fuel was back in vogue. Howie was uncertain of its make—Buicks and Fords and Chevrolets all seemed pretty much the same to him these days. There was a man sitting in the driver's seat waiting for them, and his window came down with a soft hiss. His face seemed very pale, and Howie had a glimpse of red hair. But the sun was reflecting on the windshield, and Howie could not see more than this. The Nose Ring Girl stood close to the open window and began talking with the man inside. Meanwhile Darlene and the Hulk stood quietly to one side. As meetings go, this rendezvous seemed to Howie to be of a suspicious and dubious nature. Unfortunately, he was too far away to make out a single word.

Howie, you really are a wimp! You mean you followed them out into the parking lot but you didn't get close enough to hear what they said?

Come on, Jack. What am I supposed to do? Sneak up on my hands and knees?

Sure, why not? Or are you afraid to get your Ivy League hands dirty? Maybe mess up your jeans?

Howie sighed. He knew there was no way he was going to be able to face Jack unless he found out what this parking lot rendezvous was all about. He studied the situation and decided to creep closer, hiding behind the line of parked cars. With luck he might get near enough to eavesdrop. He didn't want to do it, particularly, but he supposed he had better give it a try. He set off as quietly as possible, darting from car to car and feeling just a little ridiculous. In a few minutes he was close enough to hear voices. Howie hunkered down behind the rear fender of a GMC truck and strained to listen.

It was the Nose Ring Girl who was speaking: "No, that's totally unacceptable," she was saying. "Look, if you're not serious about this, you need to say so now . . . all right, I understand . . . yeah . . . yeah . . . well, I'll have to think about that and get back to you. . . ."

It was frustrating because Howie could not hear the response of the man inside the car, and the fragments of the girl's part of the conversation were meaningless to him. He wondered what Jack would do in a situation like this? Jack, that gung-ho idiot, would probably try to sneak closer yet.

Howie was on his hands and knees creeping along the pavement when he noticed two huge tennis shoes a few inches away. Howie looked upward, following the contour of two thick legs in tight jeans. He saw a silver belt buckle, bulging muscles in a sleeveless polo shirt, and finally a pudgy, baby face. It was the Hulk, and he did not seem pleased to see Howie.

"Hey, have you seen my car keys?" Howie asked. "I must have dropped them somewhere around here. They're on a kind of a roach-clip key chain that has a lot of sentimental value to me. . . ."

Howie thought he was pretty clever to think so fast, but apparently he was not clever enough. Without warning, one of the huge tennis shoes came up swiftly from the ground as though to punt a football, only in this instance, Howie's head was the ball. He took the kick on the chin as he was struggling to rise to his feet. The force knocked him backward. There was an explosion of light and a gush of pain. He lay on his back breathing heavily, tasting blood. He tried to sit up, but his head hurt so badly he thought it best just to lie there until the world was a nice place again.

A new face appeared above him. It was the man with red hair from inside the car. He had an unusual face, an El Greco face, elongated and strange, the sort of face you might see on a tortured saint in an old painting.

The face swam closer in Howie's vision. The red-haired man was kneeling by his head. He had something in his hand, Howie saw. A can of diet Dr Pepper. Howie noticed the soda because he was horribly thirsty. But the man did not offer him a sip.

"Does it hurt?" the man whispered. There was something compassionate about his eyes, as though he really wanted to know.

"Yes, it hurts," Howie managed, a dry croak.

"Then stop this foolishness, because it will hurt more the next time. And you mustn't cause us any further sin or none of us will go to heaven when the trumpets sound . . . do you understand what I'm telling you?"

Howie did his best to nod, though, in fact, he didn't understand a thing. All he really wanted to do was sleep for a very long time.

The redheaded man watched him for a moment, and then he committed a small but unpleasant crime: he took the final swallow of his drink and carelessly threw the can over his shoulder to the ground.

It was a while later. How much later, it was hard to say. Howie had managed to roll over and get up onto his hands and knees, and he was throwing up against the hubcap of a Mustang convertible. This was exhausting, and he collapsed into his own vomit.

Had he been able to see beyond the immediate extremity of his pain, he would have noticed the Nose Ring Girl pass close by. She hesitated briefly as she studied his condition, and then walked quickly across the parking lot. In her hand she carried a paper bag, and inside the bag, there was an empty diet Dr Pepper can.

She was a tidy girl, apparently, no litterbug. She opened the trunk of her car, threw the soda can and paper bag inside, and then took out a red day pack. There was a cell phone inside the day pack, and she punched in a series of numbers.

"It's me," she said into the receiver. "I'm afraid things are getting a little out of hand. . . ."

17

Howie must have slept for a while, because when he opened his eyes again, it was late afternoon and he was by himself. He was lying in his own vomit in the narrow space between two cars in the parking lot. Vomit was only part of the bouquet of smells; someone had dumped a bottle of liquor over him—muscatel, Howie deduced from the aroma. If anyone had walked by, they would have taken him for one drunk, low-class Indian. There was blood on his shirt, and he really was a mess. As he sat up gingerly rubbing his chin, a woman holding the hand of a small child walked by and caught sight of him. She clutched her child tightly and hurried on.

It took Howie a few minutes to rise to his feet. He was sore, he had a headache, but his body seemed more or less in working order. He wished he could say the same thing for his clothes, which were torn and filthy. The dark blue car was nowhere in sight. His first thought was to go inside the mall and find a telephone and call the police to lodge a complaint against the terrible people who had done this to him. But the way he looked, stinking of muscatel, he realized there was a very good chance that he would be the one to wind up in jail. In an amazingly short time, he had tumbled down the social ladder into an untouchable caste that made people avert their eyes and hurry away.

Clearly there was no more detecting he could do in Colorado Springs, not until he changed clothes and had a shower. At least he had gotten something from this trip that he could bring home to Jack: the Millennium Investment Corporation were suspicious bastards indeed, they were not even slightly pleasant people, and Wilder & Associate should investigate further. For now, this would have to do.

Sore and weary, Howie stumbled through the parking lot

until he found at last the Toyota pickup truck. He was very
glad to fire up the engine and leave Colorado Springs in his
rearview mirror. He drove for more than an hour on the open
highway until gradually his headache subsided. The sun set behind the western mountains, and Howie was glad for the darkness. It was a humiliation to be beat up and kicked around. An
assault not only on his body, but upon his fine opinion of himself. Sometime after dark he stopped at a small roadside diner
but they refused to serve him. He felt altogether too low in
spirits even to become angry.

Howie turned on the heat in the cab of the truck as he
climbed up the steep mountain pass that would lead him back
into northern New Mexico, a land more hospitable to Indians,
where he longed to be. About ten p.m., high in the mountains
and nearly out of Colorado, he noticed the same car had been
behind him now for quite some time, its persistent headlights
reflecting in his rearview mirror. He slowed down to let the car
pass, but it slowed as well and stayed in place about fifty feet
back. Probably it was nothing, just a station wagon full of
some all-American family. Yet he had a funny feeling, a cold
clutch of paranoia that he could not entirely shake.

He climbed higher along the lonely highway, passing an elevation marker that said 9000 feet. It was an obscure mountain
pass, not a well-traveled route, and at this time of night Howie
and the car in his rearview mirror were the only vehicles anywhere around. Maybe it's a cop car, he told himself, hoping to
nail me for speeding. For the next half hour, Howie kept his
speed obsessively at 55 miles per hour, the precise limit. He
made a game of it, watching the red needle on the Toyota dash-
board.

The road became very winding, and there were times when
the headlights behind him disappeared, separated by a curve.
Howie decided to try an experiment. He accelerated sharply as
he passed around one of the long mountain curves. When the
car in his mirror was momentarily lost from view, he slammed
on his brakes, pulled over quickly into a turnout at the side of
the road, and shut off his headlights. In a moment the car on
his tail glided past with a swish of tires and hum of engine, a
dark phantom speeding into the night. It went by so quickly,
Howie was not even sure what kind of vehicle it was, foreign
or domestic.

"Well, good-bye whoever you are!" Howie said aloud into the night. He turned off his engine and decided to wait a few minutes just to make certain he would not run into it again further along the road. It was a dark, cold night with only a thin sliver of moon hovering in a misty black sky. To his right there was a bare granite cliff, the mountain itself. To his left, a guardrail and a steep drop-off to a valley below. There was no other traffic now that the car in his rearview mirror had gone by. In the distance Howie could hear a stream of some sort, moving water. And the sound of the Toyota engine gurgling a little in the dark. It would have been peaceful, but the stillness of the night seemed spooky to him, and Howie would have been glad for a few friendly trucks going by.

And then, as Howie's eyes became accustomed to the night, he saw a dark figure on the road in front of him coming his way. At first Howie thought he must be mistaken. Who would be in this lonely place at night? But there was someone there. He heard the soft but unmistakable sound of footsteps.

Step . . . step . . . step. The shape came steadily closer, some dim, terrible thing coming his way on this empty mountain road where no one should be. Howie was fluttery with terror; there was a quivery feeling in his chest when he tried to breathe. He strained his eyes trying to see, but he could only make out an outline of living darkness that was more dense and solid than the darkness of the surrounding night.

Howie's hands were shaking as he pressed the plastic knobs on the doors to make certain they were locked. He turned the ignition, and the Toyota roared into life. With a grinding of metal, he forced the transmission into first gear and the pickup leaped forward onto the pavement. He drove blind for a moment, downshifted into second, accelerated, then flicked on the headlights so he wouldn't crash. The beams of light swept the road. And yes . . . there was a figure there. It was a dozen feet ahead of him on the road, an unrecognizable person, faceless in the sudden glare, standing by the guardrail on the left side of the road, holding an arm to its face as though to shield itself from the encroachment of light. The figure was holding something in its hand that was long and thin. It was a gun, Howie saw—a double-barreled shotgun.

Howie raced the engine in second gear, not daring to pause long enough to downshift into third. As he drew alongside the figure, he watched as the shotgun was raised and both barrels were pointed his way. Howie ducked down low in the cab and jammed his foot on the gas pedal. There was a deafening explosion. The rear wheels of the Toyota seemed to lose their grip on the road, and he started to spin as though he were skating on black ice. Howie sat up and tried to correct the steering. But something was very wrong with the truck. He was skittering out of control, heading toward the guardrail on the left side of the road. He stepped frantically on the brake, but it was too late.

When Howie saw he was about to crash through the guardrail, he experienced a moment of enormous calm. There seemed to be plenty of time. Quite calmly, deliberately, he unbuckled his seat belt. As the truck broke through the thin metal and flew out over the side of the cliff, he opened his door and jumped outward into empty space.

He was only in the air for a moment, and then came down free of the Toyota upon some soft brush. This seemed like a good thing to him, but he kept on rolling and hit something hard. He came to rest, his back against small hard rocks, the wind knocked out of him, a strange feeling in his lower body. He knew he was hurt, possibly hurt badly, and it seemed most unfair that such a thing should happen to him twice in a single day. Below him he heard the truck crashing through brush, bouncing against earth and rock, a jangle of shattering glass and metal. Then there was a whoosh of explosion, a fireball of light.

In the brief glare Howie had a glimpse of the shadowy figure watching from the road above. It didn't seem entirely human to him, but rather some nightmarish thing. As Howie watched, the ghostly figure raised the shotgun high above its head in a kind of triumphant jubilation.

And then it began to dance.

PART TWO

---∞∞∞---

THE BLIND DETECTIVE

1

Jack Wilder was having his recurrent nightmare when the phone rang. He always dreamed in color. Dazzling colors: lush living greens, blues as deep as paradise, reds straight from the fires of hell. Only a blind man in his dreams could see colors as rich as these, so beautiful and complex, swirling with electric presence.

He saw a sleepy suburban street, an expensive two-story white frame house, a front yard and trees. He was standing in the driveway when the garage door hissed open to reveal the blackest Mercedes Benz in all the world. The car was pure evil, and the headlights were eyes that searched to find him. Without a sound the machine came to life and leapt his way like a great hungry beast, seeking to run him down.

Jack drew his service revolver; he took the crouched stance he had learned so long ago at the police academy, feet apart, and he fired round after round into the approaching windshield. There were Chinese men inside the car, each of them dressed in dark blue suits and ties. He shot them all. *Blam! . . . blam! . . . blam!* One after another, he blew their heads apart. They exploded like overripe melons, bone and blood. But the car itself refused to die, it kept coming at him as he stood in the driveway firing his impotent gun. Finally he threw the gun away and attempted to vault over the hood of the Mercedes as it came rushing upon him, a kind of crazy handstand in which he hoped to get clear of the terrible machine. But he was a middle-aged cop, not a teenage gymnast; he flew into the air with the grace of an elephant and came down too soon, headfirst through the bullet-cracked windshield . . . his bloody head resting at last in the bloody lap of a drug lord.

Rivers of blood, dead Chinese gangsters in a car, a black Mercedes; in his dreams as in life, these were the last things

Jack Wilder ever saw. A drug bust that had ended his career. The irony was that Commander Wilder wasn't even supposed to be there; he was much too senior, a creature of the high police bureaucracy. He should have left the raid entirely to the people in his command, but had not done so for the simple reason that he was feeling bored at the moment, stale, going through yet one more midlife crisis.

Brrring! went the bedside phone. An old-fashioned telephone, with an actual ringer rather than an annoying digital beep—Jack insisted on it.

"Jack, shall I get it?" It was Emma's voice in bed next to him.

"I got it," he told her.

But when he opened his eyes, the nightmare began in earnest: He couldn't see, he was trapped in a bottomless well, a suffocating darkness in which he felt himself buried alive. This was a bad joke indeed, to see when his eyes were closed, when he was sleeping; but then see nothing when he woke and opened wide.

For a moment he couldn't bear it, the terrifying claustrophobia of blindness. A strangled cry escaped his throat.

Emma eventually picked up the ringing telephone. It was nearly eleven-thirty at night. There are sophisticated places in the world where this might be considered early, the start of an evening, but not in a small New Mexican town among people of a certain age. Jack and Emma had been asleep for a good hour.

She turned on her bedside light and glanced anxiously at Jack. She knew he had been having his dream, which happened at least once a week, sometimes more—though not as often as four years ago. Jack and Emma's bed was in a snug room on the second floor with a low ceiling of wood *latillas*— branches stripped of their bark that were set in a traditional herringbone pattern. There was a small adobe fireplace, round and smooth, at one corner of the room, and two well-fed tiger-stripe cats, Sushi and Sashimi, curled on the bed, fitting themselves wherever they could among the crevices and mountains of Jack and Emma's reclining forms. The cats were sisters, nearly identical. Katya, the German shepherd guide dog, was asleep nearby on the floor. Katya's personal tragedy was that she was not allowed on the bed itself, and the cats, of course, always lorded it over her.

"Yes?" Emma said into the phone. She listened for some time to what the voice on the other end was telling her, interrupting occasionally with questions. "But he's going to be all right? . . . . Oh, thank God! I see . . . well, don't worry about *that*—our insurance on the truck will take care of the medical bills . . . now, tell me about the accident. . . ."

She put down the phone and studied her husband. Jack was lying on his back breathing hard, his forehead shiny with cold sweat.

"Are you okay, honey?"

"I'm fine . . . it's Howie, isn't it? What's up?"

"He's in a hospital in Fort Willard, Colorado. He ran the Toyota off a cliff on a mountain pass."

Jack took a long breath. "How bad is he?"

"His right leg is fractured in two places, and he has a concussion, but he's going to be okay. You know these hospitals. Their main concern is that Howie doesn't have insurance."

Jack swung his legs from the bed onto the floor. "I'll need you to drive me to Colorado, Emma. I'll put on some coffee while you hunt up our insurance policy for the vultures. . . ."

He stood and walked toward the bathroom to splash some water on his face. Jack knew every inch of the house and moved with confidence toward the hallway. What he didn't know was that Katya had shifted from her usual spot on the scatter rug and was stretched out on the floor directly in his path. Emma saw the accident a moment before it happened, but by the time she called out, it was too late. Jack tripped over Katya's front paws, and all hell broke loose. The dog yelped in surprise and bounded away. Emma screamed. Jack swore. Even the cats yowled and leapt off the bed in different directions. In a normal household it would have been a laughable moment. But not so with a blind man. Jack tumbled forward, disoriented. He fell against a dresser and dropped hard on the floor with a cry of pain.

"Jack!" Emma cried, jumping to his side. "Oh, *damn* that dog!"

Jack sat up from the floor with a groan. "It's not Katya's fault. Usually I feel about for her . . . but I wasn't thinking. I was disoriented from my dream."

"Oh, Jack, you're bleeding! You hit your head." It broke her heart to see him like this, helpless and bleeding.

"I'm okay," he said stubbornly.

"You have a gash beneath your eye. I think you're going to need stitches."

"I'm okay, Emma!" he said irritably. He shook his head, disgusted with himself. "I'm sorry. I don't mean to take this out on you. Look, if you can just stop the bleeding . . ."

Emma went to fetch him a towel from the bathroom, leaving Jack on the floor. He hated the low comedy of this, to find himself a blind man who couldn't even make his way to the bathroom without tripping over a sleeping dog. *So what am I going to do?* he asked himself. *There are only two choices: I can put a pistol in my mouth and pull the trigger. Or I can pick myself up and try again.* Each day for four years, Jack had come to this same crossroads. It was always necessary to make a new effort, a new resolve. Tonight it seemed particularly hopeless. Howie in the hospital, himself on the floor . . . it was hard to imagine a less auspicious moment for the firm of Wilder & Associate.

They reached the hospital in Ft. Willard, Colorado, at nearly three o'clock in the morning. Emma left him alone in a chair in the waiting area outside the emergency room and went to investigate Howie's condition. Jack fought down the panic that came with being by himself in an unfamiliar place. He hated hospitals, and with good reason, knowing them too well. He needed to pee, but now he would have to wait until Emma returned to help him find his way.

He wondered whether he was in a large or a small room? It helped to define his universe, see his surroundings in some way . . . it was a small room, he decided from the close acoustics. There was a woman at the reception desk talking about her insurance policy; she had brought in her husband with chest pains, and now she was going through the paperwork to get him admitted.

I'm going to sit here patiently, Jack told himself firmly. *I will not panic!* Nevertheless, it was a relief when he heard Emma's footsteps and smelled her warm familiar scent.

"Sorry to take so long," she said. "They have him in intensive care—I had to wait until I could speak to the head nurse.

There aren't supposed to be visitors this time of night, but I talked her into it, since we came so far. We can go in and see him for five minutes . . . are you okay, Jack?"

"I gotta take a goddamn leak. Can you walk me to the men's room?"

"Of course, honey. There's no need for you to get upset."

"*Upset?* I can't even go the bathroom without asking my wife for help!"

"Only in unfamiliar surroundings," she told him mildly. Jack was having a bad night, but these moments came and went, and she knew from practice how to deal with them. She took his arm and led him to the door of the men's room. There was no one around this time of night, and she wished she could walk him into the bathroom and lead him to a urinal. But she knew it was better to let him pee on the floor than to destroy his dignity with her solicitude.

Howie would never suspect the price Jack paid for his apparent calm—that the facade he presented to the world was built upon sheer terror.

"So you thought Toyotas could fly, did you?" Jack asked lightly, standing by Howie's bed.

"Japanese ingenuity," Howie managed. His voice was slurred with painkillers.

Jack could hear the *drip drip* of the IV, and the beeps and clicks of the machines that were monitoring Howie's vital signs. All these sounds were deeply familiar from his own long convalescence. There was a sickly smell of fluids and bandages in the room.

"So how are you feeling, Howie?"

"They're going to set the leg tomorrow morning," Howie answered dreamily. "I'll feel better then. . . ."

"We're making plans to have you transferred down to San Geronimo," Emma told him. "We're hoping we can move you by ambulance the day after tomorrow. Meanwhile, don't worry about money. Thank God the Toyota was insured to the max . . . do you want me to call your parents, Howie?"

Howie shook his head. "Indians, you know . . . we don't make a big thing about pain. Better tell Bob and Nova, though. They'll be worried."

"I'll phone them first thing in the morning," Jack said.

"Look, we have only a few minutes before the nurse kicks us out. So tell me what happened."

Howie was floating in Demerol, only semi-coherent. "Man, there was a blonde with huge knockers. Do you like big knockers, Jack?"

"It depends to whom they're attached."

"I like small breasts myself. It's where I'm at on the food chain. I mean, nursing just isn't my bag. It's not what I'm looking for with a woman, Jack, to suckle . . ."

"Yeah, sure . . . but the accident, Howie . . ."

"I had a hot dog. People really eat badly up there."

"In Colorado Springs? Did you find out anything about Millennium?"

"They had an office in a shopping mall. That's where I met the blonde with the knockers. But she didn't respond to me. Maybe she sensed I've been weaned . . . there were two men, a baby-faced hulk with big muscles, and a red-haired guy with the face of an El Greco saint . . . the Hulk kicked me when I followed them out into the parking lot. Then El Greco said something to me . . . but I can't quite remember what . . ."

"Calm down, Howie," Emma told him. For Howie was suddenly agitated, trying to sit up in bed. "Jack, I think we should let Howie get some rest."

"We will, in just a moment, Emma. Now, Howie, I want you to concentrate and tell me about the accident."

"It was no accident . . . son of a bitch shot the tires out on the truck."

"*Shot* the tires? Who are you talking about? Was it your El Greco saint, or the Hulk with big muscles?"

"No, not *them* . . . aren't you listening, Jack? It was the Ghost Dancer. . . ."

"The *what*?"

Unfortunately—and most frustrating for Jack—the head nurse came into the intensive care unit. She was a middle-aged woman with dyed blond hair, black eyebrows, and a saccharine manner. "I'm sorry, but you have to leave now so our patient can get his beauty sleep," she said in a pleasant singsong.

Jack ignored her. "Howie, what are you talking about? What is a Ghost Dancer?"

"I didn't really see him . . . scared me to death the way he just came walking down that dark highway. . . ."

"I'm *very* sorry," said the nurse, more sternly now. "Perhaps you can come back during visiting hours tomorrow."

Jack was on edge, and this nurse was the last straw. He turned to her with haughty irritation. "Will you kindly shut up! Can't you see I'm trying to question this man? . . . Now, what the hell are you talking about?" Jack had turned his attention back on Howie. "What do you mean, a Ghost Dancer?"

But Howie could only shake his head. "Damn near scared me to death!" he repeated, awed by his own terror.

Meanwhile the nurse was going for help.

"Come on, Jack," Emma told him gently, taking his arm. "Howie needs to rest."

"But I need to know who shot at him!"

"We'll come back," she said patiently. "Tomorrow there will still be mysteries, my dear, left for you to solve."

2

Howie drove off the cliff on Monday night. On Tuesday Emma Wilder took the day off from work in order to chauffeur Jack around, fill out various insurance forms, and arrange for Howie's transfer by ambulance from Colorado to San Geronimo. But on Wednesday she returned to work. Emma held one of the two paying positions at the San Geronimo public library, and much as she loved Jack—much as she wished to be helpful—it was simply not possible for her to drop everything and become his all-purpose seeing-eye-wife in Howie's absence. She had a life too.

The San Geronimo library was housed in an old hacienda that had been bequeathed to the town by a rich and genteel old lady. It was said that Carl Jung had spent a night here on his trip to New Mexico to see the Indians, and that D. H. Lawrence and his wife Freida once had a tremendous shouting match in the courtyard. The house was quaint, but it made for an inefficient library—a warren of small rooms that were crammed floor to ceiling with books. At noon on Wednesday Emma left a volunteer in charge of the checkout desk and took her bag lunch into the Native Cultures Room, an oddly shaped area that had once been a back pantry. Emma pulled out a volume from the shelves and settled herself at the table, prepared to eat and do some research for an after-school literacy program she ran for local children.

She opened her lunch, wondering what culinary surprise Jack had for her that day. She laughed when she saw what it was: a peanut butter and jelly sandwich.

"Jack, you son of a bitch!"

Every successful marriage is based upon a fair division of labor; love alone, once the honeymoon has passed, does not cut the cake. In the Wilder household Emma did the house-work, and Jack did the cooking; such was the division they had settled upon a few months after he had lost his eyesight, for Jack had insisted he either must be useful or he would go mad with boredom and self-disgust.

Today Jack's skill in the kitchen was legendary throughout his social circle, but his culinary prowess had not come without cost. For nearly six months after he took over the kitchen, Emma suffered through meals of almost psychedelic disarray: food that was burned, or half raw, bizarre spices, ingredients that were comically wrong. In his blind impatience, Jack had used sugar instead of flour, soy sauce for oil, cayenne pepper for salt, and on one memorable occasion, a can of Katya's dog food which he mistook for refried beans.

Gradually Jack had learned to taste and smell and organize his kitchen in such a way that he knew where everything was; he had become a master chef, multiethnic, veering from sushi to enchiladas with delirious ease. All this made the peanut butter sandwich today a cause for some concern. Emma studied the sandwich thoughtfully, pondering its significance. As peanut butter sandwiches go, this was certainly the deluxe model—the bread was homemade, the jam was imported from England, the peanut butter was organic. Nevertheless, she knew her husband very well, and the lunch he had made for her today was a statement of his discontent.

"I am *not* going to feel guilty, Jack!"

She did feel for him, though; she knew that without Howie, and without her help, he was stuck at home today and most likely he was extremely grumpy about it. But she wasn't about to give up her own job. Certainly to be a librarian was not as glamorous as being a great detective; but then again, maybe it was. Who could say, perhaps one day she would give just the right book to just the right person, and it would have a more lasting impact on the world than all of Jack's running around?

Emma bit down rebelliously on her peanut butter sandwich. It was delicious, absolutely the best peanut butter sandwich she had ever tasted, due in large part to the whole-wheat bread that Jack had baked himself. Then Emma reached into the bag for a napkin and found a Godiva chocolate.

"Damn you, Jack!"

As always, he was manipulating her in his own sly way. But

what can you do with a husband who makes you perfect sandwiches and slips Godiva chocolates into your lunch bag? With
a sigh Emma closed the book she was reading, a collection of
Navajo coyote stories she was considering for her after-school
program. Apparently the local children would have to wait, because Emma Wilder had a husband who was a bigger child
still.

She put the coyote stories back on the shelf and then
searched among the books for quite a different subject. She
found three volumes that were helpful, and spent the rest of her
lunch break reading about a Native American cult of the last
century. A cult that was known in English as the Ghost
Dancers.

"How odd!" Emma said aloud. In general she was inclined
to like Indians and respect their customs. But there was something disturbing about these Ghost Dancers, not at all pleasant,
almost insane. She stared out the window for a moment, deep
in thought, and then she returned to the checkout desk to use
the telephone to call Jack.

But the phone rang and rang until she got the answering machine. Jack was not home, and this worried Emma too.

Where in the world could a blind man go?

Jack spent the first part of Wednesday morning in a deep
funk. It was extremely frustrating for him to be housebound
because there were so many things he would have liked to
do—drive to Colorado Springs, interview some people at the
San Geronimo Pueblo, even make a trip up to the ski resort.
But everything seemed impossible without Howie or Emma to
help him.

"So what now?" he asked the empty house. Jack sat in the
overstuffed platform rocker in the living room pushing back
and forth rhythmically with the toes of his right foot. While he
was rocking, he felt a long wet nose thrust itself into his lap. It
was Katya, hopeful of some affection. Often enough in the
past, Jack had pushed her away, for he did not particularly like
dogs. But Katya had caught him at just the right moment. He
put a hand on her furry head, and he felt the motion of her tail
wagging optimistically.

"Poor old Katya!" he said in a soothing voice. (He meant, of
course, "Poor old Jack!") They had always had a difficult re-

lationship together, man and dog. The German shepherd had
come to him in California from the San Rafael School for
Guide Dogs after a two-month training course soon after he
lost his sight. But Jack was a self-described "cat person," finding cats graceful and clever and independent, and dogs just the
opposite—klutzy and dumb and horribly dependent on people.
The last straw with Katya was that she liked to chase cats, although fortunately Sushi and Sashimi, the two tiger-stripes,
were more than a match for her. There had been an incident
shortly after Jack and Emma moved to New Mexico. While
Jack was walking around the block with Katya in harness, she
saw a cat, forgot all her training, and took off down the street
at a gallop. Jack was half dragged in a most undignified manner nearly up a tree; he vowed it was the last time a German
shepherd would ever control his fate. Of course, he should
have returned her to the guide dog school for further training,
but Jack couldn't be bothered. Katya was simply demoted
from guide dog to barely tolerated pet, and from that moment
on he had made a concerted effort to memorize his surroundings and get around with no one's help.

"Well, Katya, I haven't treated you very well, have I?" Jack
said to her this morning, scratching her ears.

Katya had been waiting years for this moment, just the tini-
est bit of affection from the man she adored. Dog that she was,
she became overexcited with the smallest encouragement. Jack
found himself licked in the face with her long tongue. She
slobbered all over him and tried to climb up into his lap. Jack
knew he must be in a very bad way, because it actually felt
good to have someone—anyone—drench him with such un-
critical amounts of love.

"Down, Katya, down!" But she could tell from his voice that
he didn't mean it. And in a moment he gave in to her completely; he wrapped his arms around her neck and buried his
dead eyes in the gorgeous warmth of her fur.

Half an hour later Jack and Katya stood on the front path together outside the Wilder home. Katya was in harness—Jack
had managed to find the contraption after a search in the back
of the hall closet. He held the stiff handle of the harness with
his left hand, and in his right he carried a white cane. It had
been a very long time since he had attempted this procedure,

and he tried to remember what he had learned from the two-month course he had taken. Guide dogs do not really look after their master; they are trained instead to avoid any possible danger to themselves, to stop at curbs and look for traffic so that they will not be run down. Most of the work is done by the blind person, who must listen and feel and be constantly aware of changes in the shifting environment.

Jack felt foolishly self-conscious as he stood there with his dog and cane, very much a handicapped person for all to see. He hoped none of the neighbors were looking, finding him in any way an object of pity.

"Okay, this is it, your big chance, Katya," he said to her in a stern voice—a voice that had once terrified uniformed officers and lieutenants alike. "You mess up, and you're dog food! You got that? . . . All right, what are you waiting for? Let's go . . ."

And off they went, late on a fine April morning, Katya leading the way down the sidewalk, tongue lolling, ears pricked forward. And Jack following behind . . . tap, tap, tapping with his cane.

3

Jack and Katya headed in the direction of Sisters of Mercy Hospital on the north side of town, where Howie had been transferred from Colorado earlier in the morning. The distance from Jack's house to the hospital was slightly more than a mile; as treacherous a mile as any he had traveled in all of his life.

Jack thought he had the route perfectly clear in his head. He had come this way often enough on walks with Howie in the fall—go north on Calle Santa Margarita, with his back to the sun; cross four streets, turn right on the fifth intersection and walk straight for about fifteen minutes until arriving at the main highway. The hospital should be on the right-hand corner. What could be simpler?

Katya did her part admirably, keeping him straight on the sidewalk whenever he had a tendency to swerve. She stopped at every curb, just as she had been taught, allowing him the time to perform his own well-practiced drill: to feel for the curb with his left foot, use his cane to seek out possible obstacles, and above all, to listen for traffic. The first two intersections went so smoothly he began to relax. But the third street was a disaster. He was halfway across the road when a carful of teenagers appeared from nowhere and nearly mowed him down. They yelled obscenities and howled with laughter to see a helpless blind man with a cane. Why this struck the little barbarians as funny, Jack could not say, but it made him so angry that he lost his orientation and forgot how many streets he had crossed.

All it took was for his concentration to waver just this much, and it was as if a magic thread had been broken. Before the teenagers appeared, he had been a man who knew exactly where he was; by the time they passed, he was lost in a featureless, all-embracing night. Jack continued onward, for there was no turning back. Somehow he turned too early and arrived at the main highway at a corner he did not know—a place full of strange smells and sounds that all mingled together in a chaotic way. For several bad minutes he felt himself on the edge of something he recognized as blind panic.

He was starting to hyperventilate, struggling to get a grip on himself, when he heard a wheezing voice nearby: "Hey, Cap'n! Can you help a guy out? Lend me three-ninety-nine?"

The voice belonged to an old street character named Tucson Tom, a down-and-out hippie who had arrived in San Geronimo with the counterculture invasion of the early seventies, and had somehow survived all these years. Jack knew who he was from Emma's anecdotes, for Tom generally slept in a small clearing behind the library. He stank of beer and dirty clothing.

"Why three-ninety-nine?" Jack managed to reply, breathing heavily.

"Get ourselves a twelve pack, Cap'n! We'll go to the park and do ourselves a little drinking. Whad'ya say? Hey, did I tell you? I was in the Vietnam War."

"Were you?"

"You bet I was! Man, I saw some terrible things over there. I'll tell you all about them over a brewski. . . ."

Jack made a deal with him: If Tom would lead him to Sisters of Mercy Hospital, Jack would gladly give him four dollars. He could have the twelve pack all for himself, the penny change, and even keep his war stories to himself. Tom said sure thing, Cap'n. He took hold of Jack's arm, but he was so drunk, he nearly pulled them both to the ground.

"*Don't* take my arm!" Jack said crisply. "Just walk by my side, please."

For Jack, this was a nightmare; the loss of dignity was nearly as bad as feeling so utterly lost. Tucson Tom pawed at him and spoke with semi-coherent nostalgia about the days when you could get drunk much more cheaply than today. When they finally reached the hospital, Jack found he had a new problem. He needed some seeing-eye help in order to pick out four dollar bills from his pocket; he had stuffed a handful of cash into his pocket before leaving home, but he did not know the denominations, and he certainly had no intention of trusting his drunken guide to choose the right amount.

Tom became belligerent when Jack refused to pay up on the sidewalk, suggesting instead that they go inside the hospital and find the help of some neutral person.

"I *am* going to pay you," Jack explained patiently. "But I will pay you *inside* the hospital."

The old drunk suspected a trick, and Jack thought he was going to have a fight on his hands. But then a nurse appeared from the parking lot and offered to help. She paid Tom from the wad of bills Jack pulled from his pocket, and then turned Jack over to one of the candy-striper volunteers inside the hospital. One volunteer took charge of Katya, because dogs were not allowed inside the hospital, not even a guide dog. Then another volunteer led him to Howie's room.

And so he arrived at last, exhausted and shaken.

My God! he swore to himself. People with the use of their eyes could barely imagine the adventure of traveling a single mile from home!

Howie laughed when he saw the expression on Jack's face as he sank into the chair next to his hospital bed. It was the first time Howie had laughed since driving the Toyota off the Colorado mountain.

"You look miserable, bro. How did you get here, anyway?—Emma phoned from the library a few minutes ago, so it couldn't have been her."

"I walked."

"You walked!"

"Naturally. What do you think I did? I put Katya in her harness, I used the cane, did my whole blindman's bluff."

"Jack! That's quite a ways to come from your house! I'm impressed."

Jack shrugged. "Well, don't be. I had the route memorized, so it was nothing . . . now, let's talk about you, Howie. How are you feeling today?"

"Better. I'm still doped up pretty good. I wish you could see me—I look like the Curse of the Mummy. Bandages wrapped around my head and my chest where I got bruised. My right leg is in a cast, suspended from a nifty little pulley system. The doctors say I can go home at the end of the week, but I'm not going to be able to do very much for a couple of months."

"That's too long," Jack grumped. "You've got to get well faster than that."

Howie grinned. "I'll try, Jack."

Howie shared the hospital room with a Spanish rancher who had hurt himself falling off a horse. The rancher had the TV set on to an afternoon talk show, and his wife was sitting at his bedside watching with him. Occasionally they talked to each other in soft Spanish. Jack pulled his chair closer to Howie.

"So tell me about Colorado Springs," he asked quietly. "I want to know what kind of hornet's nest you stirred up there on Monday that made someone try to kill you."

"From the beginning?"

"Every detail, my friend."

Jack listened to Howie's account without interruption. Then he sat very still. Jack was quiet for such a long time that Howie turned his attention back to the television, which he had been watching before Jack arrived. A lady named Antonia (who once had been a man named Tony) was talking about changing his/her sex. It was a simple operation, apparently: A surgeon turned your penis inside out, and you had yourself a brand-new vagina. In a very short time Howie had become an addict of daytime TV.

"The girl with the nose ring," Jack said finally. "Tell me more about her."

"I'll try. She was in her early twenties, sort of Nordic-looking, high cheekbones. A pretty girl, but not really in a distinctive way. I mean, it wasn't so much her features that you noticed— it was mostly that she was rosy-cheeked and blond and full of health. I would describe her as a type, Jack. The sort of Colorado girl who doesn't wear makeup that you'd expect to see charging up a mountain with a pack on her back. I bet she has muscular legs. Her hair was the nicest part of her, a kind of dark gold, very thick. But a guy looks at a girl like that; I don't think he even really sees her. He just fills in the blanks, what his imagination wants to see."

"*I* want you to see her. I'm interested in individuals, not types."

"Well, good luck! This is a collective world, bro. A mass culture we live in . . . what do you think a nose ring is?"

"You tell me, Howie."

"It's a badge. It lets people know you belong in a particular niche of the counterculture, and that you hold certain well-defined opinions. It lets other people with the same badge know that you are one of them. This is how people relate to one another in an overpopulated world. They send each other smoke signals, constantly seeking their own kind."

"So you're telling me a nose ring is not a form of self-expression?" Jack asked wryly.

"It's group expression," Howie assured him. "It's a uniform. But not a uniform I expected to find in Colorado Springs."

"You said she looked familiar to you. Where did you see her before?"

Howie shook his head. "I've been trying to remember, but I keep hitting a blank. Maybe I was mistaken. She was such a definite type, you know—perhaps that's why she seemed familiar. She could have been any one of a hundred women I've seen in the past few years."

"Could you have seen her in San Geronimo?"

"Possibly. Or maybe I met one of her many twin sisters."

"All right. We'll put her to the side for the moment. Let's discuss the person you saw on that dark mountain road. Hopefully he is more distinctive in your mind."

"Man, that guy scared me to death, Jack!"

"I understand. How tall was he?"

"Average. Not too tall, not too short."

"Was he slight? Or did he have a heavy build?"

"I didn't really notice . . . medium, I would say."

"Color of hair?"

"I didn't notice."

"Was it long or short?"

"Jack, I didn't see that either. Remember, I told you he held an arm up to his face, to shield himself from the glare of my headlights."

"So you saw nothing?"

"Jack, what I saw was a gun . . . a gun that looked about ten feet tall to me."

"A shotgun, you said?"

"Yes."

"Two barrels or one?"

"Two."

"And what arm was he holding it in?"

Howie had to think for a moment. "The left," he decided.

"So he was shielding his face with his right arm?"

"That's right . . . I think so at least."

"How was he dressed?"

"Pants. A jacket . . . but if you ask me what kind of pants or jacket, I'm not going to be able to tell you. I only saw him for a few seconds, and everything about the guy was washed out in the headlights, like a photograph that's overexposed."

"Okay, that's reasonable," Jack said patiently. "Now, tell me this—are you certain it was a man?"

"Good God! You think it was some sort of evil genie?"

"That's not what I'm asking. Could the figure have been a woman?"

Howie stared at Jack in surprise. "No," he said. But then he changed his mind. "Well, maybe."

"Is it no, or is it maybe?"

"I can't tell you for sure. It's like trying to remember a dream. Frankly, I was terrified, the way he appeared like that out of nowhere, and I didn't get a very good look."

"Up in Colorado, you described the figure as a Ghost Dancer. What did you mean by that?"

"Did I say that? I was half out of my mind that night."

"Naturally. But just try to remember what you meant."

"Well, the figure, *whatever* it was—it was damn ghostly. And when I was lying on the rocks, just before I passed out, I looked up and saw the thing in the light of the explosion, and it seemed to be dancing a little. Jumping up and down. Kinda a victory dance, like football players do after they've scored a touchdown. It was strange as hell."

"He reminded you of a football player?"

"Not really. I just used that as an example. He reminded me of a Ghost Dancer."

"Yes, yes," Jack said impatiently. "But what *is* a Ghost Dancer, Howie?"

"They were an Indian cult in the last century. In the 1880s, there was a Paiute holy man named Wovoka from Pyramid Lake. He came up with a kind of garbled version of the Christianity that had been preached to the Indians by the missionaries—that the world was about to end and a Red Messiah was going to appear any moment to bring all the dead Indian warriors back to life. That's why they were called Ghost Dancers, Jack, because they danced to resurrect their dead. They be-

lieved the buffalo would come back to life as well, and everything would be just like it was before the Europeans came,
only better. The evil white man, naturally, would be totally an-
nihilated. There was a lot of hocus-pocus . . . they wore magic
shirts they thought would protect them from the white man's
bullets, but this led to some major disappointments, as you
might imagine. Basically it was your classic messiah fantasy.
You get these things from time to time when you have a down-
trodden people looking for deliverance—just like the Jews
under Pontius Pilate. For a while the idea caught on among the
different tribes, particularly the Sioux. But it was a decadent
religion, Jack. Fanatic and awfully desperate, not the sort of religion that's born of love and light. You have to remember, the
Indians were in pretty bad shape in the 1880s and clutching at
straws. The white people, naturally, were scared to death of
this talk of a Red Messiah, and Washington sent Custer's old
outfit, the Seventh Cavalry to take care of the problem. The
massacre at Wounded Knee in 1890 was the result."

"And this cult, is it still going on today?"

"Not in any organized fashion. Every now and then some
guy on the res drinks a lot of beer on Saturday night, and
smokes enough dope, and suddenly he has a vision of white
people dying horrible deaths and the buffalo coming back.
We're not talking, Jack, about real Indian holy men—not
someone like Raymond Concha, for example. This is definitely the low-rent side of religion."

Jack was listening carefully. "Could anyone be trying to
bring back the Ghost Dancers?"

"If so, I've never heard of it."

"What about AIM?"

"The American Indian Movement? No, that's pretty much
dead now. Anyway those dudes like Leonard Peltier had a
much more modern outlook. They were seeking political rights
for Indians, they weren't religious at all—which bothered
some of the traditionalists. AIM would have found Ghost
Dancing an embarrassment. I think you're on the wrong track
here, Jack."

"Then why was the first description out of your mouth about
the guy who shot at you, that he was a Ghost Dancer?"

"I was stoned on painkillers. It was just a phrase I used without thinking."

"Sometimes those are the phrases we need to take most seriously, Howie."

"Well, I told you—he reminded me of a Ghost Dancer for that one moment when I saw him dancing in the light of the explosion. But on second thought, maybe the football image is a better one. He was doing a little touchdown shuffle. The asshole thought he'd killed me, and he was celebrating."

"I wonder," said Jack. "Well, this will require some thought. If I still had a big-city police department to play with, I'd send a forensic team up to the mountain road to where that dancing ghost nearly killed you. Then I'd send another team to Colorado Springs to trace your steps and figure out who you spooked. I'd also put a couple of detectives on Alison Hampton's problem, to find out who's writing bloody hate words on her house. But since there are just the two of us—and I'm blind, and you're laid up in bed—we're going to have to keep this fairly simple. We need to keep our focus on the heart of this case, Howie."

"And what's that?"

"April Fools' Day, of course. Why Kit Hampton wanted to see us at Doobie Rock. Why he got to Doobie Rock half an hour early . . . and most of all, what in the world he was doing having sex with some girl twenty minutes before he was killed. We need to find that girl, Howie. From now on she's our number one priority."

Being young, the word *sex* roused Howie's interest and stirred his imagination. "So Wilder and Associate are still in business, huh?"

"Of course, we are!" Jack seemed outraged that Howie might think otherwise, just because appearances might be against them at the moment.

Howie smiled. "Well, then, Jack—I have an idea."

4

There was a ski instructor named Zora Rousseau who was everybody's mother, a middle-aged woman who provided the best shoulder to cry on in San Geronimo Peak. Howie should have thought of her before. Zora had been working on the mountain every winter for nearly twenty years. The rest of the year she ran a successful business in town: Far Adventures. If you wanted to know who was screwing whom at the ski resort, she was definitely the one to ask.

"Well, I suppose she's worth a try," Jack agreed without enthusiasm. "What's this company of hers, Far Adventures? River rafting?"

"You'll see, Jack."

"No, unfortunately I *won't* see—that's the problem. And I've had enough adventure myself for one day, so just tell me, please."

"Oh, she arranges all sorts of exotic life experiences for bored trust funders who are trying to find themselves. Llama safaris into the wilderness, vision quests, fire walking . . . you name it."

"What's fire walking?"

"This is her specialty, Jack. It's an evening where she gets a bunch of people together to walk barefoot over a bed of burning coals. A kind of human barbecue—very hip, the absolute latest rage. First you need to face all your fears, of course, and do a lot of inner work on yourself to get into the proper spirit. Then you walk over the coals, and amazingly it doesn't hurt . . . as long as you remember to keep chanting your personal power mantra, naturally."

"You've done this?"

"You bet. Bob and Nova and I did it one night. It was kind of fun, actually, except one part early in the evening where you're supposed to team up with a partner and make goo-goo eyes at one another. New Agers are always trying to look deep into each other's eyeballs with a kind of fakey-fake expression on their faces that's supposed to resemble gentleness and love. It's a little embarrassing."

It all sounded strange to Jack, but Howie assured him that there was tons of money to be made leading the lost-and-wounded souls of San Geronimo over beds of burning coal. The office for Far Adventures was on Martinez Alley, a small cul-de-sac behind the downtown plaza. Jack and Katya were able to get a ride here on the hospital minibus that was run by the town as a service to help the poor and elderly get to their doctor appointments. The driver was very helpful. He parked the bus and led Jack into an office that felt small and over-crowded, and then he waited to see that Jack was all right before he disappeared. There was a musty smell in the room of patchouli oil and incense.

"Oh, what a pwetty, pwetty doggie!" cried a loud and enthusiastic lady in baby talk. She had a deep, earthy voice with a distant trace of Brooklyn in it.

"Are you Zora Rousseau?"

"That's me, by God . . . holy shit, you're blind! How utterly fabulous! You know, sometimes I go about for days at a time with my eyes closed."

"Why, for heaven's sake?"

"So I can really *see,* of course! All the truly important things are inside us, not outside. You blind people have such an advantage over the rest of us, getting in touch with your inner eye."

Howie had described Zora as forty years old and kind of goofy; frizzy hair, a short round body, and bright laughing eyes. Not the sort of slick body-perfect person you'd expect to find as a ski instructor at San Geronimo Peak, though, in fact, she could ski the pants off most of the younger guys. Jack sat in a leather armchair that was old and cracked.

"So!" she said happily. "I hope you're here to sign up for the fire walking this weekend. We're really going to make some breakthroughs and expand our limits."

"Perhaps another time," Jack demurred. He reached into the pocket of his sports coat for his business card. "I'm a private detective. Senator Hampton hired me shortly before he was killed, and I'm looking into his death."

"This gets better all the time! A blind detective!" she gushed. "But aren't there already a gaggle of cops investigating Kit's death? For days after the murder, there were detectives swarming all over San Geronimo Peak."

"Did they speak with you?"

"No. But I wasn't on the mountain when Kit died. My left knee had gone a little wonky, and I wasn't skiing for a few days."

"Well, there you are. All the cops in the world can miss the one potential witness who can bust a case wide open. Tell me something—I understand that Kit was quite the ladies's man?"

Zora let loose a big booming laugh. "You got *that* right! But, of course, he never made a pass at *me.* I'm everybody's mother, you know. Every ski resort needs a person like me so that the sex maniacs have someone to confide their deep, dark secrets to."

"Yes, and that's exactly why I've come to you, Zora. I'm hoping you can help me find Kit's most current girlfriend. I need to know who he'd been seeing."

Jack heard a note of caution enter her voice. "Why do you want to know?"

"I should think it's obvious. Kit's lover, whoever she is, probably knows more than anybody else what was going on in his life. She'll be able to throw some light on this case."

The gushing enthusiasm had drained from Zora's voice. "I can't help you. You know why people confide in me, Jack? It's because I keep their secrets."

"Then let me tell you a secret too. This is confidential police information, by the way, so please keep it to yourself. The autopsy showed that Senator Hampton had sex less than half an hour before he died."

"*Did* he?" She seemed interested.

"Yes, he did. And this is the most puzzling aspect of the case, as far as I'm concerned. The Senator was seen taking the early morning chair up the mountain, so he must have had his tryst somewhere on the Peak itself—but where in the world would a person go up there to have sex in a near blizzard?"

"Well, well!" she said. Avoiding a direct answer.

"You know, Zora, I think you can help me. And I really need your help badly to untangle this mystery."

She spoke reluctantly. "Well, there's the number three avalanche hut, of course."

"What's that?"

"There are several avalanche huts above tree line. You have to climb to them—they're way up on the ridge. The ski patrol uses them to watch the snow conditions and store the explosive canisters and grenade launchers. After a storm, they'll usually start a few controlled slides so that the snow doesn't avalanche on its own. At certain times of the year, they assign a patrol person to stay up in the huts during the day to keep an eye on things with binoculars."

"What's special about the number three hut?"

"It has a bed and a good propane heater. Believe me, it's seen some hanky-panky over the years. It's situated on top of El Lobo Ridge, and there's even a fantastic ski down, if you like the really steep terrain."

"Can the general public go there?"

"No way. It's roped off, definitely off-limits. Only the ski patrol is allowed on El Lobo, but occasionally they'll invite a special friend. You have to be an expert skier, of course, to even consider it."

"And Senator Hampton might go up there?"

"Of course. Kit was the boss. He went anywhere he pleased."

"My question was more, was he a good enough skier? He was sixty-three years old, you know."

"Kit could still manage," she said with a laugh.

"I see. Now, what about the other avalanche huts besides number three? Are *they* ever used for romantic reasons?"

"I doubt it, unless you like to screw standing up. The number one and two huts are about the size of a phone booth. Number three is the only one where there's a bed."

"Do the cops know about this?"

"Probably not, unless they've asked the right people. You're learning some of the deep dark secrets of San Geronimo Peak, Jack."

"And it's about time too!" Jack muttered. "So now the big question is this: If this hut is where Kit Hampton went on the morning he was killed, who was the woman he was with?"

"That I can't tell you."

"No? It would have to be someone on ski patrol, wouldn't it?"

"I would presume so."

"Well, how many women are there on ski patrol? There can't be many."

"The Peak has a little over forty people working ski patrol. Of that number, maybe one-quarter are female."

"So ten women . . . it shouldn't be too difficult to check them out and discover Kit's final lady friend. I would prefer it, however, if you would simply tell me, Zora."

"Why are you so certain I know?"

"Because I can hear it in your voice. And it would save me a good deal of time."

"Jesus, and I thought you were a nice guy when you first walked in here!"

Jack leaned forward. "Zora, there *are* no nice people in murder investigations. Now I'm going to get to the bottom of this one way or the other. So how about just telling me what you know?"

"Damn!" she swore sourly. "It's a complicated situation. If it's who I'm thinking of, the girl's married."

"If you give me the facts, I can approach her in a discreet manner. Perhaps some time when her husband's not at home."

"The guy's going to be devastated if he finds out. He's a ski instructor. A nice guy . . . well, he's a little weird, but I feel for him. All winter long he kept telling me how he was suspicious his wife was stepping out with someone. It was very painful, particularly since I knew it was true. It's something I learned by accident one night when I stayed late—I came across her and Kit kissing in the parking lot. They didn't see me, but I sure saw them."

"It was dark?"

"Yes, but not so dark that I couldn't see them properly. Anyway, I heard them talking as well. They thought they were alone, and they weren't being very careful. She was saying . . . well, how much she enjoyed having oral sex with him."

"When was this?"

"Sometime in late February. I forget the exact date."

"And you don't believe her husband ever found out?"

"No. As I told you, Donny suspected something was up, but he never knew for certain. I'm sure he never would have guessed in a million years that she was seeing Kit."

"Donny?" Jack urged. "What's his last name?"

"Oh, Jesus, I let that slip, didn't I? . . . Donny Henderson," she said with a sigh. "I really wasn't going to tell you this."

"And her name?"

"Crystal. She's good-looking, but she's certainly made life hell for Donny."

"Good. Donny and Crystal Henderson . . . I finally feel like I'm getting someplace with this damn case. Let's start with Crystal. Please tell me what you know about her."

"Not much. We've hardly exchanged more than a few hellos. She's ski patrol, of course, and they usually don't condescend to hang out with us mere instructors. Mostly I've just heard about her from Donny."

"Who are her friends up on the Peak?"

"I don't think she has friends. She's very aloof and standoffish. I know that Donny always felt he had to beg for her attention. She controls him."

"What does she do off-season?"

"She's an artist, or at least trying to become one. Donny says she does watercolors, but I've never seen any of her work."

"So Donny is really the one you know?"

"Well, I can't say I *know* him, but we work together. There's a lot of time riding the chairlifts to talk about stuff. Donny's big obsession, of course, is Crystal. He's always asking my advice—what should he do so she'll be more interested in him? Poor Donny, he's one of those guys who always has a kind of hurt look in his eye, which isn't so attractive to women. I tried to tell him he needed to forget her and work on himself."

"Do you think Donny is capable of violence?"

Zora laughed. "Oh, no! *Donny* didn't shoot Kit with that bow and arrow! . . . To be honest, I almost wish he had—the guy really needs to get in touch with his anger. But he's more the type who mopes and worries. Frankly, I'd nominate him as a candidate for suicide, not homicide."

"Sometimes there's a very thin line between the two," Jack told her. "You said that he was a little weird. What did you mean by that?"

"Nothing much. They're both into body piercing, that's all. I certainly consider myself a progressive person, but I have to admit, self-mutilation turns me off."

"Body piercing?" Jack wondered. It was a subject he had never much considered, and it took him a moment to realize the importance of what she was saying. "By any chance does Crystal Henderson have a nose ring?"

"That's right. Through one of her nostrils. It caused a bit of a sensation on the ski patrol when she did it this winter, but Kit said it was all right . . . *that* should have tipped Donny off right there! Actually, when Donny and Crystal got married, they got pierced in some intimate places that aren't so obvious . . . this is something Donny told me, by the way—I'm glad to say I haven't seen it for myself firsthand. They have matching wedding bands. His is hanging from his scrotum, hers is through her clitoris."

Jack shuddered. "Let me make sure I have the right person—she's in her early twenties? Not too tall, a kind of pretty, Nordic face? High cheekbones, thick dark gold hair?"

"You must have seen her somewhere. That's Crystal exactly."

Jack permitted himself a smile. "It's my inner eye," he assured her. "It never misses a thing."

5

Jack and Katya were in a fine mood. Man and dog made their way, with the help of a passing tourist, half a block down Martinez Alley to the New Wave Café, where they sat at a picturesque table on the outdoor terrace and waited for Emma to get off work at the library. Sarah, the English waitress, made a cappuccino for Jack and a special doggy milk shake for Katya, and they split a giant cookie between them.

"You're looking awfully chipper," Emma observed when she drove by to pick them up at a few minutes past five. "You must have had one of your famous breakthroughs."

"No, not really." Jack was superstitious enough never to claim victory until the final snap of the handcuffs. But, in fact, he was very pleased with his progress that day. For the first time in this confusing case, he saw a clear line of attack. He would question Crystal Henderson, find out about her affair with Kit Hampton, and ask what she was doing in Colorado Springs the day Howie was nearly killed. New obstacles would certainly arise on the path to truth, but Jack no longer felt helpless. He was a man with a plan.

"Emma, would you mind stopping off somewhere for just a little while? There's a girl I need to talk to."

"A *woman*," Emma corrected. "We don't call them girls anymore, Jack, unless they're under the age of twelve."

"Well, I'm a creature of old and wicked ways," he told her. He placed his hand suggestively on the upper part of her leg as she drove.

"You're a dinosaur," she agreed. "Complete with green scales and a horny old tail."

"A horny something," he admitted. "I thought we'd have dinner in bed tonight, and maybe a nice bottle of wine. . . ."

"You think I'm going to let myself be seduced by someone who's still living out gender roles from the late fifties?"

"It was a sexy time, the late fifties. All that slow dancing to corny love songs. Us dinosaurs enjoyed it a lot."

Jack's hand was creeping higher. Howie would have been surprised at the extent of the Wilder's sex life; it was stout sex, certainly, and not quite what young people fantasize. Yet the passion was still there after many years together, and this moment in the car could have been interesting. But suddenly Katya pushed her nose forward from the backseat, and with a small squeal of delight, she licked Jack directly on the mouth. Emma laughed, and the romantic moment was gone.

She drove to the address that Jack had gotten from Zora for Donny and Crystal Henderson. The house was a small pseudo-adobe on a narrow lot on the south edge of town. There were two cars in the driveway, both aging four-wheel drive Toyota Tercels.

"Someone must be home with two cars in the driveway," Emma told him. "Why don't I drop you off? I'll run into town and get us pizza to go and a bottle of wine while you do your nasty old detecting. I can be back in twenty minutes. Then we'll go home and get a little cozy."

"You've got yourself a blind date," he grinned. When a case was going well, Jack had a tendency for atrocious puns. "Just get me to the front door, and I'll take it from there."

They left Katya in the car, and Emma guided Jack along a short path to the front door. There are happy houses, and there are sad houses; you can often tell from the outside how life is going for the occupants inside. This, thought Emma, was a sad house. The yard was barren, there were few shrubs and plants, and the curtains on the windows were closed even though it was still daylight. Emma didn't see a doorbell, so she knocked on the front door. To her surprise, the door was not completely closed. It swung open on its hinges with the pressure of her hand.

Jack suddenly took hold of her arm.

"Get me the gun in the car!" he said quietly.

"There *is* no gun in the car."

"Yes, there is. Look in the trunk. It's in the compartment with the tire jack. Get it for me quickly, and don't make any noise."

Emma didn't like guns, but there was something in Jack's tone that made her decide to save her lecture for later. She left Jack for a moment, jogged across the yard, and found—to her dismay—a Smith & Wesson .38 just where he said it would be. She came back to the front door not certain whether to give it to him or to hold onto it herself. Jack held out his hand, and she gave it to him.

"Jack, I don't like this," she whispered.

"Neither do I, Emma. I think there are some dead people inside this house—I'm not sure how many, or what exactly we're going to find. If you want to wait in the car, you should."

"No, you need my eyes."

He smiled weakly. "As a matter of fact, I do."

Emma pushed the door completely open, and now she too smelled what Jack had noticed first with his sharper senses, the unique odor of death. Jack put one hand on her shoulder, and she led the way into the house. Emma stepped into the living room. It was a cheaply furnished house, old couches and secondhand tables and chairs from the thrift shop. She gagged as her eyes scanned the room and came to rest upon the small dining alcove.

"Tell me," Jack ordered.

As the wife of a policeman for many years, Emma had seen a few terrible sights in her time, usually in photographs. She had never gotten used to it. She took a deep breath and tried to remain calm.

"There's a young woman lying on her back on the floor by the dining room table. She was shot in the throat."

"Does she have a nose ring?"

Emma peered closer. "Yes . . . a small gold loop through her left nostril. She's blond, and it looks like she was quite pretty, poor thing . . . what a shame to die so young!"

"That's Crystal. What about Donny?"

"He's slouched backward in one of the dining room chairs. It's pretty gross, Jack. He shot himself in the mouth."

"What makes you say he shot himself?"

"There's a pistol that's fallen to the floor a few inches from his right hand."

"I hear something. A kind of hum."

"It's a computer that's been left on. It's on a desk by the window."

"It's *on*? Be careful not to touch anything, Emma. Tell me what's on the screen."

Emma laughed darkly when she saw what it was. "This is suicide the modern way, Jack. It's a note."

"Read it to me, please."

"It's short and to the point, and very tragic. Five words, all in capital letters: 'TILL DEATH DO US PART.' "

6

On Thursday morning Dr. Alison Hampton took her five-year-old daughter to work with her, leaving her house in San Geronimo at five-thirty, the usual time of her commute, well before even the first hint of dawn. It seemed almost cruel to bundle the half-asleep child into the ancient MG for the three-hour drive to Albuquerque. Supplies were necessary: a banana, a giant oatmeal cookie (a bribe), a purple dinosaur (Barney), a coloring book, and a box of Legos to keep Angela occupied later in the day.

This was the third consecutive day Alison had brought her daughter to the clinic with her. Normally on the days Alison worked, an elderly Spanish woman named Viola Suazo took care of Angela in the early morning until it was time to drive the child to the Bright Rainbow Preschool in town. But after such a crazy weekend—the incident in the restaurant and the blood on her window—Alison had suffered an attack of nerves. It wasn't a rational decision so much as a gut feeling that with hostile forces all around her, Angela must be kept very close at hand. At first the little girl seemed to enjoy the special time with her mother, driving back and forth to Albuquerque. But as the days passed, it became obvious that this arrangement could not go on forever.

On Thursday morning Alison half listened to the news on National Public Radio while Angela sat dreamily in the passenger seat hugging her purple dinosaur and staring out the window. The sun rose, lighting up the desert and mountains with a burst of living color. On the half hour NPR broke off for local news of New Mexico. There was yet more violent death to report from San Geronimo, an apparent murder/suicide yesterday of an unhappy couple. The police reported that the young man had shot his wife before turning the gun on himself. Good Lord! Alison sighed. For a picturesque little town, San Geronimo was certainly getting its share of brutality these days! But New Mexico was an unexpectedly violent land, not quite the paradise one imagined.

Angela stretched restlessly in the passenger seat.

"How you doing, sweetie? Want me to tell you a story?"

"Yes. A story!"

"How about 'The Frog Prince?' " Alison offered.

" 'Red Riding Hood!' "

"Well, that's a grisly tale, but all right."

Alison turned off the radio, and it was at this point, as she leaned forward, that a glint of reflected light in her rearview mirror caught her eye. It was the fender of a black Ford pickup truck behind her. Extended cab, balloon tires, tinted windows, CB antenna. This was not the dark car she sometimes feared had been stalking her the past few months, but nevertheless, the truck caused instinctive worry, since it came from the other side of the great American divide. She knew she was being jumpy, but she couldn't help it.

"Mommy, tell me 'Red Riding Hood.' "

"Well, okay . . ." Alison did her best to forget about the truck in her rearview mirror and get on with the fairy tale. At Angela's preschool, the teachers liked to tell an altered "Red Riding Hood" in which the Big Bad Wolf and Little Red Riding Hood talked things over, did some creative problem solving, and parted as friends. But Alison was against such revisionism. She told the tale as she herself had heard it as a little girl, believing some degree of terror was not amiss in the world, and that innocent little girls must indeed be on the lookout for wolves.

Alison took St. Francis Drive through Santa Fe on her way to the interstate. At a stoplight she studied her rearview mirror for the black pickup, and was relieved to see a green Volvo station wagon behind her instead. You knew what sort of person drove a Volvo station wagon, a person like yourself. But as she accelerated onto a southbound lane of Interstate 25, she glanced in the mirror and the black Ford was once again on her tail, sleek and aggressive on its oversize tires, only a dozen feet behind.

Surely it's nothing, she told herself. Yet it was impossible not to worry. The reappearance of the Ford bothered her so much that she allowed the tale of "Red Riding Hood" to drift to an inconclusive pause at the climactic moment, just as the Handsome Woodcutter was about to bring back Riding Hood and her Grandmother from the very jaws of death.

"Mommy, what happens next?"

"You *know* what happens next, sweetheart. The Handsome Woodcutter hacks away at the Big Bad Wolf with his sharp ax—he cuts open the wolf's nasty old stomach and out pops Grandmother and Riding Hood, and everyone lives happily ever after. . . ."

"From the wolf's *stomach*? Weren't they all yucky and chewed up?"

Angela asked this same question each time she heard the story, and Alison always gave her the same answer: "No. And you know why? Because that nasty wolf was *so-oo* greedy he ate them up with one huge bite, and they got swallowed whole, just like Jonah in the whale . . . now Mommy needs to concentrate on driving."

"Mommy, I think that Howie looks like the Handsome Woodcutter," Angela announced seriously. "When I grow up, I'm going to marry him."

Probably it was a good thing that Mommy wasn't listening. She slowed from 70 to 55 to encourage the truck in her rearview mirror to pass. But the truck did not pass. It slowed to match her new speed and remained in place twenty feet back, confirming her worst fears. Alison made certain her daughter's seat belt was tightly fastened, then she put her foot on the gas pedal and moved into the passing lane. The MG accelerated quickly past two huge trailer trucks and a blue Honda, returning to the right-hand lane at close to 85 miles per hour. The road ahead was clear. But in the rearview mirror the black pickup was still behind her, matching her new speed.

"Damn!" she swore. A black pickup truck with tinted windows and a CB antenna was a terrifying sight, a vehicle onto which a woman could project her every fear of rape and mayhem, the male violence of the American highway. Alison looked about wildly for a police car, hoping for a speeding ticket, any miracle to save her. But there was no police car, no help in sight. Then she saw a freeway sign announcing a rest stop one mile ahead, and this gave her an idea. She eased her foot from the pedal and slowed gradually to 65. The truck stayed on her tail, slowing down as well. Her plan was a simple one: to swerve into the exit at the last moment and hope the truck would speed past on the interstate and be unable to back up. If this failed, if the truck followed her into the parking area, she wasn't quite certain what she would do. Hopefully there would be other people around to help.

As Alison approached the exit ahead, she maintained her speed at exactly 65 so as not to alert the black truck to her plan.

"Hang on, sweetie," she said to Angela.

She was about to brake and swerve when an odd thing happened. The Ford simply moved into the left-hand lane and passed her. Was it possible the truck hadn't been following her after all, but was simply going on its own merry course through hell? Alison caught sight of a bumper sticker on the tailgate as it sped past. The sticker read:

DON'T LIKE MY DRIVING?
CALL 1-800-EAT-SHIT

Incredible! It was only blind anger speeding down the highway; road rage that had nothing to do with her personally. By the time Alison read the bumper sticker and understood the danger was over, she had already overshot the exit. She pulled over to the shoulder of the interstate, her hands shaking and her heart beating so fast it was difficult for a moment to breathe. *I'm going crazy,* she thought.

Angela was studying her with huge worried blue eyes.

"Mommy?"

"Yes, darling?"

"What were you and Howie doing on the living room floor? You didn't have any clothes on."

All of Alison's tension exploded into laughter. "You *saw* us that night? . . . Well, it's called sexual intercourse," she explained as seriously as she was able. "And *you* don't need to know anything more about it than that just yet, young lady!"

Alison continued into Albuquerque. Thinking, My God! It sure as hell isn't easy to be a parent these days!

The Women's Cooperative Family Planning Clinic was located in a bad part of town, a converted Victorian house on the far eastern end of Central Avenue, a dissolute area of shabby motels, Pussycat adult theaters, Chinese restaurants, and businesses that always seemed to have signs in their window announcing a going-out-of-business sale. The area was well-known locally for prostitution, drugs, and violent crime. The co-op was located here for a good reason: This was the only part of the city where Alison could find a landlord who was willing to shrug off bomb threats and the possibility of arson to rent to a medical clinic that performed abortions.

On Thursday morning Dr. Hampton parked her car and held tightly to her daughter's hand as she led the way up a cement path to the entrance of the converted Victorian house. This was always the worst part of the day, entering and leaving the clinic, passing the line of protesters from Christians for a Moral America. In the past few months Alison had come to hate these people with all her heart and soul. About a dozen protesters were already in place, waving placards and gruesome photographs of mangled babies. When they saw Alison, they began to chant in unison: "Abortion is murder! . . . Abortion is murder!" Months ago, when all this first started, Alison had sometimes shouted back comments of her own, wondering aloud about these people, who apparently cared so very much about the sanctity of life, where had they been when the United States was dropping napalm on Vietnamese villages? Or supplying weapons and "advisers" to the military dictatorship in El Salvador? And why weren't they marching against the death penalty? "You're not *pro*-life! You're just *anti*sex!" she had shouted at them once. But it was hopeless, and she had ceased long ago trying to have a logical dialogue with the CMA, even in her own mind.

After nearly six months of protest, she and the Christians had come to a kind of status quo. The Albuquerque protesters, in fact, appeared intent on obeying the letter of the law: They remained the proscribed distance from the co-op entrance, thirty-three feet, and although they shouted a good deal at clients going in and out of the building, they did nothing physically to stop business at the clinic. Nevertheless, every muscle in Alison's body clenched tight as she walked up the path to the building holding her daughter's hand. It was terrifying, the angry voices beating down upon her. She looked neither to the right nor the left, but hurried straight ahead. She was not a particularly brave woman, but she was proud, and all her life she had despised bullies. "Come on, Angela," she said grimly. "Don't even look at them. They're only nasty old bullies!"

"Nasty old bullies!" Angela mimed, sticking out her tongue briefly at a thin woman holding a sign.

Once inside the building, it was a typical morning. Dr. Hampton's first patient was an eighteen-year-old girl who was pregnant for the third time and appeared blissfully ignorant of the facts of life. Alison first made certain that the girl was indeed pregnant, and then, on condition that she promise to use birth control pills in the future, she set up an appointment for a D & C. Next came a twenty-two-year-old secretary who wanted to go off the pill and be fitted for a diaphragm; Dr. Hampton always felt a moment of small triumph when a few of these young women actually used contraception. After that she did a pap smear, examined a patient for genital herpes, and finally, late in the morning, performed a suction aspiration, the simplest form of abortion, on a sixteen-year-old girl who was pregnant only a few weeks, still in the first trimester. The procedure was little more than inserting a catheter inside the uterus and sucking out a few cells. It was this act that the religious fundamentalists outside called murder.

Angela meanwhile spent the morning playing with her Legos on the floor of the receptionist's office. Alison visited with her daughter for a moment or two between each patient, and then during her lunch break they went to her own office on the second floor. Lunch was sent over from the Sichuan Palace nearby: sweet-and-sour chicken (Angela's choice), shrimp with asparagus in a black bean sauce, fried rice, two spring rolls, and two fortune cookies. The lunch was delivered in cardboard cartons with handfuls of napkins, disposable chopsticks, plastic spoons and forks, and a sea of condiments in annoying plastic containers that you needed to tear open with your teeth—enough trash to fill a small corner of the city landfill.

Alison was eating a spring roll, chatting with her daughter, trying to act like everything was peachy keen normal, when she could not resist the temptation to glance out of her office window and check on the protesters outside. Her heart sank as always and her mood darkened to see that they were still there, the men in business suits, the women in polite church dresses, waving their placards. Couldn't they simply go away? Didn't these people have lives of their own somewhere? As Alison watched, a late model Cadillac DeVille drove up to the line of protesters, and a large man emerged. The Cadillac made Alison immediately wary. It was a dark burgundy in color, a flashy car, an automobile from a different segment of society than the black Ford pickup this morning. But it was the enemy nonetheless—a quintessentially Republican car, as Alison thought of it. A sort of anti-Volvo.

The man from the DeVille shook hands with several of the antiabortionists, and then he stepped out in front of their line onto a flower bed that was adjacent to the clinic. Alison had planted those flowers herself in an attempt to make the clinic more homey, and it annoyed her greatly to see them trammeled underfoot. "Damn him!" she swore. Somehow this was the last straw! She had endured too much already: a bloody afterbirth thrown at her in a crowded restaurant, her daughter's dog butchered, hateful words shouted at her month after month. For some reason—she could not adequately explain it later— something in her snapped as she watched her flowers being crushed by fundamentalist shoes.

"Wait here!" she said tightly to Angela.

She walked downstairs and passed through the reception area with such military resolve that Suzie Gonzales, the receptionist, looked up from her work with a feeling that something terrible was about to happen. Alison marched out the building without bothering to close the door behind her.

"You goddamn son of a bitch, get out of my flower bed!" she screamed at the man from the Cadillac as she approached where he was standing. Her voice was shrill, almost crazy. "Don't you have *any* respect for living things?"

The man gaped at her in astonishment. Alison's fury was like a hot wind sweeping down upon him.

"You son of a bitch! *Get out of my flower bed!*" she shrieked.

The man had never seen anything like it. As it happened— and though Alison did not realize it at the time—she was addressing Dr. Fred J. Doron himself, the director of Christians for a Moral America. Dr. Doron was a tall man with broad shoulders, and he looked a good deal more like a high school football coach than a religious figure. At the moment his size thirteen shoes were planted firmly on the green shoots of a not-yet-budding daylily.

Alison stood inches from the man, tiny by comparison, shivering with rage. She made an effort to control her voice.

"If you don't get off that flower, I'm going to take my scalpel and cut your balls off, I swear to God!"

Dr. Fred J. Doron's eyes went very wide, and he stared downward at the small figure before him as though he were seeing the Devil herself. He had always suspected the Devil was a woman.

"Move!" she screamed.

The head of Christians for a Moral America literally jumped back onto the paved sidewalk, as though his feet had touched burning coals.

7

Dr. Fred J. Doron suffered a delayed reaction from the indignity he had just endured. As soon as the lady abortionist returned to her clinic, he turned red in the face with fury and embarrassment. A group of people gathered around him to offer spiritual solace, but he wasn't consoled. Then he did something he knew he shouldn't: He jumped back onto the flower bed and took out his frustration by grinding the daylily under the heel of his shoe. He pulverized the poor plant.

Finally he got a grip on himself.

"Observe what the Devil can do to a Christian soul!" he said mournfully. "I shouldn't have let that creature get to me."

"Anyone would be upset after an experience like that, Fred," one of the women nearby told him in a kindly voice. "Why, I've never heard such language in my entire life!"

"No, Praise Be—I should have been stronger. If you don't mind, my friends, I think we'd better gather in a circle for a moment and bow our heads and pray. . . ."

Dr. Doron was in particular need of prayer today. He had been out of touch for a week, snowbound in a Montana cabin where he had gone to hunt elk and grizzly bear with one of CMA's most generous supporters. On his return to Colorado Springs the night before, he had gotten an earful of what had been going on in his absence, and he didn't like it one bit. This morning he had been up since five, tearing up the asphalt in his Cadillac DeVille, doing the 350-mile drive to Albuquerque in a little over four and a half hours. None of this put him in a good mood. The moment he and the abortion clinic protesters said amen and released hands, Fred raised his eyes across the circle and glared at his two boys, Luke and Dwight. Both boys were dressed this morning in conservative gray suits, expensively cut, clean white shirts and ties, black shoes shined to a high polish. They were big boys, both of them over six feet tall, but they jumped when their father called them, and followed him to the Cadillac.

"Get in, you damn fools!" Fred ordered, punching the master button to open the computerized security lock. Though he was a religious man, he was not adverse to a little swearing when he was mad; he was certain that Jesus didn't want American men to act like sissies. Luke slipped into the front seat, and Dwight into the back. Both boys recognized the signs of extreme paternal wrath, and from long experience knew how to deal with it. This was the time to say, "Yes, sir," "No, sir," and keep their eyes lowered and their manner respectful. Luke, the oldest, was thirty-three; he had light red hair, pale eyebrows, and a strangely elongated face. Dwight, the younger boy, was twenty-seven; he had dark hair and a low forehead. He was nearly an inch shorter than his brother but muscular as a bull.

Fred was so angry he didn't allow himself to speak a word until he had reparked the Cadillac behind the clinic in a place where no one would hear them.

"Okay. Now, you tell me what the hell is going on here?" Fred demanded, turning off the engine. "Exactly what do you sons of bitches think you've been *doing*?"

"Yes, sir," said Dwight from the backseat. "You're probably wondering about what happened in the restaurant, sir."

"You're goddamn right I'm wondering about what happened in the restaurant, sir! You know I told you specifically, no funny stuff in New Mexico. What we're waging here is a war of public relations. So whose idea was this, to get some damn fetus and dump it on the lady doctor while she's eating dinner?"

Dwight temporarily sidestepped the matter of authorship. "It wasn't actually a fetus—just some afterbirth from a cow. Betsy Winthrop did it with Arnold Shipley and Alice Larkin. You know how deeply committed those people are, Dad."

"Yes, and I also know how stupid they are. There's no way they could have pulled off this stunt without help—finding out where that doctor was eating dinner and terrifying her like that. Don't try to bullshit me, Dwight—I recognize a certain hand."

"The hand of the Lord," said Dwight with the smallest

smile. "Don't worry about this, Dad—Betsy, Arnold, and Alice are taking full responsibility, saying they did it without the knowledge or participation of CMA."

Fred snorted. "And how long do you think *that's* going to last? They're in jail, I presume?"

"No, they're out on bond. But they'll keep quiet, I promise you. What we are talking about here are Christian martyrs."

"Before I left for Montana, we discussed all this in detail, didn't we? What did I tell you, Dwight? That everything we did in New Mexico had to remain strictly within the limits of the law! And why did I tell you this, Dwight? Why?"

"You said we didn't want any adverse publicity."

"That's right. No adverse publicity. That's what I told you. We don't want John Q. Public to think we're a bunch of damn extremists. Particularly right now, when we have some very delicate deals in motion. So you tell me—I'm waiting *patiently* to hear—why you allowed this goddamn stupid thing?"

What happened next was a watershed moment in the Doron family history. Dwight Doron met his father's challenging stare and said simply: "I disagree with you that it was stupid. I think it was the first clever thing we've pulled off in months."

"You . . . *what*?"

"Look, Dad, we had the local media at the clinic for exactly two days six months ago when we started up our Albuquerque operation. No one really gave a damn. I mean, big deal— Christian protesters march around in front of an abortion clinic. It's been done to death. None of the national media showed up at all, and even the local papers lost interest fast. There's only one way to get the attention of the American public. You gotta give them just that little jolt of violence."

Fred stared at the boy as if he had never really seen him before. "A little jolt of violence, huh?" he repeated with outrage. "What are you? Some kind of bomb-throwing anarchist?"

"Not at all. This is simply show business, Dad. You know that, and so do I. We could parade up and down in front of that clinic until doomsday, and nobody's going to pay us the slightest attention without that little added something. And look what happened. The day after that restaurant business in San Geronimo, we were the lead story on the local news all over New Mexico. The day after that, we got CBS and NBC down

here. The story went coast-to-coast, and we got national expo-
sure."

Fred tried to stare down his son, but Dwight refused to look
away. "I'm not saying you don't have a point," the father
agreed. "But in this case we're trying to portray the *other* side
as the extremists, not ourselves. We're talking about tactics
here, son. Not to mention the fact that you have disobeyed
me."

"Dad, look, it's simple. CMA will simply distance ourselves
from the action. *We* didn't do it, just a few of our followers
who got carried away by the idea of that evil doctor killing innocent babies. What I suggest you do is give out a statement
expressing regret, etcetera, etcetera. How CMA would never
dream of breaking the law. But meanwhile it's really that bitch
doctor's fault, and anyone who kills babies is at risk for stirring up the natural anger of moral Americans everywhere. This
way we get the best of everything. Deniability on one hand.
And some fear and respect, not to mention media coverage, on
the other."

Every parent comes to this moment eventually. They look at
their child and see a stranger, an adult they do not know. Fred
Doron continued to stare at Dwight, his youngest son, uncertain if he should be proud or horrified at what he had raised.

"You're assuring me, you're absolutely goddamn *assuring*
me that Betsy, Arnold, and Alice aren't going to blab?"

Dwight smiled. "Not if they want to go to heaven," he said.
"And incidentally, not if they want to collect five thousand
dollars apiece at the end of the year."

"You've offered fifteen thousand dollars of our money!"
Fred roared.

"CMA can afford it, Dad."

"Boy, you're way out on a limb here. *Way* out!"

For a moment Dwight thought his father was going to hit
him, as he had done so often in the past. Dwight steeled himself to get whopped good. But instead Fred Doron turned to his
oldest son, Luke, who had been sitting rigidly in the front seat
of the Caddy without uttering a word. Fred worried about
Luke. The boy was his stepson, actually, but that was a complicated story and part of the discomfort between them. More
and more recently, Luke's behavior frightened him.

"So what do you think, Luke?" Fred asked softly. "Are you having one of your headaches?"

"No, Father, I'm not having one of my headaches." Luke Doron turned his gaunt face toward his father and smiled sadly. "I'm feeling very sorry for the lady doctor."

"Are you?"

"Of course I am. Can't you see how unhappy she is living her life of pleasure? In her shallow vanity she is like a plant that has cut off its own root. She has denied there is a God, she believes she can do whatever feels good. But there is a God, there are laws, Father. Terrible laws. And I fear she is about to discover His retribution."

Luke Doron spoke quietly, but the very calm of his words worried Fred more than all his younger son's bluster. He didn't like it when Luke became too serious. It seemed to him that his best bet at the moment was to lighten things up a little. So he grinned, thinking about the scene in the restaurant up north.

"That must have been some sight, boy—a damn bloody cow's afterbirth on that doctor's table! Did she scream?"

"The whole restaurant screamed, Dad," Dwight said from the backseat. "It was one of those faggoty places where you probably can't even get a damn piece of meat!"

"Hey, I don't want to hear you use language like that!" Fred said sternly.

But his tone wasn't stern enough. "What language?" Dwight taunted, knowing the signs were right for joking. "Damn? Or faggoty?"

Fred smirked like crazy and put on a fake English accent, like the kind very uppity butlers used in old Hollywood movies. "Don't say faggoty . . . say ho-mo-sex-ual."

The two Doron men, Fred and Dwight, laughed loudly at the picture in their mind of a lot of elitist liberals sitting around in a fancy restaurant and what the arrival of a bloody mess on the table might do to their appetites. But redheaded Luke, the son with the face of a tortured saint, turned and whispered something toward the closed window, fogging the glass.

"What did you say?" Fred asked him.

Luke turned back to him. He seemed exhausted, worn thin, his skin so pale it was almost translucent.

"I said, Father, even this will pass."

* * *

As in every war it is the innocent who suffer most. That night five-year-old Angela Hampton had a screaming nightmare and woke at two in the morning, terrified that the thin woman she had stuck her tongue at earlier in the day at the clinic was now hiding beneath her bed, waiting to strangle her if she fell asleep again. Alison took the sobbing child to her own bed and held her tightly.

"I don't want to go to 'Kerky again!" Angela cried.

"Oh, sweetheart. It's okay . . . you don't have to go to Albuquerque ever again. . . . I won't go to work tomorrow, I promise. I'll telephone Suzie to cancel all my appointments. We'll do something special together, just you and me. . . ."

"I'm frightened, Mommy!"

"Shhh . . . shhh . . ."

At last the little girl fell asleep again, leaving her mother to stare at the ceiling and wonder what to do. Should she get out of family planning and specialize in some medical practice that was less controversial? But that would be giving in to the bullies. It was intolerable to her sense of justice that these fanatics should beat her through intimidation.

At close to four in the morning, Alison decided, the hell with them—let them win, if they liked! They could have New Mexico, America too. She would go to Africa and live on the veld with the elephants and zebras, taking care of people dying of AIDS. Alison fell asleep thinking of a movie that had affected her passionately when she saw it as a young girl, *The Nun's Story,* in which Audrey Hepburn played a nun who fell in love with a handsome, cynical doctor, Peter Finch, in the Congo.

The elephants stood by the river, the zebras galloped through tall grass . . . and Peter Finch whispered that he loved her. Alison slept soundly into the early morning hours until she heard distant voices murmuring in her dream:

Baby killer! Baby killer! . . . You can't hide from God!

Over and over again in sleepy rhythm:

Baby killer! Baby killer . . . You can't hide from God!

Then Angela was shaking her awake, and yellow morning light was streaming into the bedroom.

"Mommy, there's some funny people outside."

Alison sat up in bed, her stomach instantly in a knot. Outside the window she could see more than a dozen people standing on the road just beyond her front yard. The protesters had followed her home to San Geronimo, intensifying their siege. They were chanting, *"Baby killer! Baby killer . . . You can't hide from God!"*

8

Howard Moon Deer was getting into hospital life. No need to think or plan. Just lie there and let the world go by. His roommate, the Spanish man who had fallen off a horse, had been discharged, and for the moment Howie had the room to himself. He was in the lap of luxury.

About noon on Friday Howie ate his tray of hospital lunch and read through *The San Geronimo Post,* which came out once a week. The *Post* was everybody's favorite reading in town, always entertaining. For a town of less than ten thousand, the people of San Geronimo had an amazing ability to get themselves into hot water. The main story this week concerned the murder/suicide of Donny and Crystal Henderson. Apparently the police were taking the two deaths at face value, and there was quite a bit of talk about the pressures and problems of a marriage that had gone very bad. Howie had spoken with Jack on the phone earlier that morning, and Jack held a very different opinion. As far as Jack was concerned, it was a double murder, and he was pissed that his best witness had been killed before he could question her.

Howie studied the photograph of Crystal Henderson in the paper. She was the Nose Ring Girl without a doubt, and now he knew where he had seen her: on the ski patrol at San Geronimo Peak. But what was she doing that day in Colorado Springs? Howie was still wondering about this mystery when Alison Hampton and Angela appeared unexpectedly in his hospital room. The little girl came up shyly to his bed and regarded him gravely with her huge blue-green eyes.

"Hey, Angela! How's it going, kid?"

"I don't have to go to 'Kerky today," she told him.

"No, 'Kerky, huh? Well, that's great."

"Al-bu-quer-que," Alison corrected patiently. "I never talk baby talk to her, Howie."

Howie let his gaze travel from daughter to mother. From the toes upward, she was wearing ratty tennis shoes, tight faded jeans that were torn at one knee, a white T-shirt that had some writing on it about an AIDS foundation, and a light wool jacket that was a patch of muted colors and must have come from Tibet or Bolivia or Guatemala, take your pick. With the huge dark glasses perched on her pert little nose, she looked like a slumming movie goddess. For the first time since his accident, Howie felt the call of the real world.

"You look scrumptious enough to eat," he assured her.

"Isn't the hospital food agreeing with you?"

"I love it. And you *know* you're brain-dead when you start looking forward to the meals here."

She took off her dark glasses and smiled at him. But it was a sad smile, and she did not look happy. She pulled up a chair and sat close to his bed.

"How would you like to come live with me?" she asked.

"Uh, er . . . live together?" he gulped.

"Does it scare you?"

"Well, maybe just a little. But they don't call us braves for nothing."

"Howie, stop being a clown. I'm scared to death. Those damn antiabortion people appeared outside my house this morning, here in San Geronimo. It's gotten so I'm afraid to leave Angela alone, and I don't want to take her to work. I feel like I'm going crazy!"

To his surprise, Alison burst into tears and buried her face against the upper part of his good leg. Meanwhile, little Angela started crying too, overwrought and frightened by her mother's tears. Howie managed to pull the child to him, and she buried her head against his shoulder. He was glad he could be useful, at least, a human handkerchief. But he couldn't help wondering how he had gotten himself into this sea of weeping women.

"Listen, of course I'll do anything I can. . . . If you need me, I'm there . . . though I don't know how much good I'm going to be with my leg in a cast. . . ."

Howie made various comforting sounds, and one by one they stopped crying—first Alison, and then the little girl.

"You know, there's something about you, Moon Deer," Alison said speculatively, drying her tears. "I don't know what it is—but you're reassuring somehow."

"Like an old sofa," he agreed.

"I'll just feel better having you in the house—both of us will. I have a Spanish woman, Viola, who comes in and does everything, so you can just get well and hang out."

"But if there's trouble, Allie, what am I supposed to do—go after the bad guys with my crutches?"

"There won't *be* trouble, not if you're there. I know these people, Howie—they're cowards. They won't try anything with a man in the house."

Allie had it all worked out. She had even spoken in a professional capacity to his doctor and been given a copy of all his charts. The hospital had originally planned to keep Howie another two days, but she was able to convince them to release him into her care.

"I can look after you much better at home anyway," she assured him. "We'll get to work on your rehabilitation. You know, it's important that none of your limbs or organs remain inactive for too long a time. Or they'll wither."

"Are you saying we can play doctor, Dr. Hampton?"

"We can play doctor all you want, Patient Moon Deer."

"Mmm . . . you're making me very *im*patient for it to begin."

She smiled. "Well then, let me go and make you an *out*patient immediately!"

Howie checked out of the hospital and moved into Alison's downstairs guest bedroom late on Friday afternoon. He liked the guest room, even though it seemed a catchall for spare furniture and all the odd things that Alison had not quite been able to make herself throw out, but didn't know what to do with.

There was a chaste, single bed with a virginal white cotton bedspread. An old beanbag chair whose innards were slightly leaking. A pair of cross-country skis forgotten in a corner. Ice skates hanging by their laces from a hook on the wall. Trophies from junior ski competitions long past. A desk with a personal computer. The computer was an antique as these things went, four years old, an IBM clone with an early version of Windows on it—Alison had a much newer setup in her office upstairs. But the downstairs computer was on-line, and she gave Howie her access code just in case he got bored and wanted to surf the Internet or send e-mail to his friends.

Make yourself at home, she said. Anything you want, you only have to ask.

All in all he could see that there were advantages to having a girlfriend who was a doctor. Alison gave him his medicine, his shots, brought him dinner and breakfast on a tray. She made him feel that if he were to break his other leg walking to the bathroom on his crutches, she would fix him up again in no time. She even crept downstairs to his bedroom in the wee hours for a bit of creative hanky-panky—and it *did* take creativity to commingle with an unwieldy cast on his leg. Life would have been idyllic except for the cast, and except for the dozen antiabortion protesters who had taken up a vigil outside on the road. The large front curtains of the solar living room had been closed to erase their visual presence, but Howie found he could not forget them completely. Occasionally, when the house was very quiet, he could hear the distant blur of voices: *"Baby killer! . . . baby killer! . . . You can't hide from God!"*

On Saturday afternoon Alison needed to go into town to run some of the many errands she had been putting off since before her father's death—buy two new tires for her car, pick up her camera from the repair shop, shop for groceries, even drive out to her accountant's house to drop off some papers. Viola Suazo, the all-purpose Spanish cleaning woman, had come by to help look after Angela and Howie, so there would be two adults in the house in case "anything happened," as Alison delicately put it. Even so, she had an attack of nerves before leaving the house.

"You're going to be okay?" she asked, sitting on the edge of his bed.

"Believe me, any of those Christians try to sneak in here, I'll feed 'em to the lions," he assured her.

"Howie, I want to show you something. Come into the living room with me for a minute."

Howie had done some practicing in the morning with his new crutches, and he was getting about with more confidence all the time. He followed her at a lilting three-pronged gait down the hall into the high-ceilinged living room, darkened

now because of the closed curtains. She led the way to a tall
bookcase along the western wall. Howie saw there were a lot
of classics—*Anna Karenina, Great Expectations,* and company, most of them in well-thumbed paperback editions. Alison reached up to the middle of the top shelf and pulled out a
hardcover edition of Norman Mailer's *The Naked and the
Dead.*

"Mailer's not really my bag," he told her. "But if you have
any Kurt Vonnegut . . ."

"Howie, this is not a literary conversation. Do you know
how to use a .38?"

"Are we talking about .38, as in pistol?"

"I don't want to take it out, but it's on the shelf directly behind the book. A .38 revolver with five bullets in the cylinder.
The hammer is on the empty chamber. . . . I've never had to
use it, but I like knowing it's there. If there's any trouble while
I'm gone . . ."

"Don't worry, Allie. I'm not much of a gun freak, but I can
always wave the thing around and look like a damn scary Indian if I have to. . . . How in the world did you decide to put it
behind *The Naked and the Dead*?"

She smiled. "I thought the title would help me remember
where it was. It's up high, of course, so Angela can't reach it."

"I like the naked part, anyway."

She kissed him lightly on the lips. "Get your strength back,
Howie," she whispered. And then she was gone.

9

Howie and Angela spent an artistic afternoon together. She was the artist, that is, and he the canvas—the white blankness of his plaster cast inspired the little girl's imagination. Howie sat sprawled out on the living room sofa with his bad leg propped up on a stool while Angela worked on him with a box of colored felt pens.

"Remember, I'm going to have to live with this cast for the next few months," he cautioned.

"Don't move," she told him.

"Can I look yet?"

"No."

Like all true artists, she was a touch imperious. Howie really got a kick out of her. Her face was serene, yet extremely concentrated as she worked; Howie doubted if Michelangelo had set to work on the Sistine Chapel with a greater seriousness of purpose. He glanced through an old *New Yorker* while she drew, but his mind wandered. It worried him a little, playing house with his snow maiden. He couldn't help but wonder where this was leading, and how it would end—if she was only using him, and if at the end of it, he was going to be one unhappy Indian.

Yesterday, just before he left the hospital, Howie had phoned Jack to say he was moving in with Alison Hampton for a while, and that's where he'd be if Jack was looking for him. Howie told Jack the news in his best aggressive/defensive posture, prepared for a battle. But Jack had surprised him.

"You should do what feels right to you, Howie," Jack said mildly. "But as long as you're there . . . frankly there are some aspects of this case that puzzle me, and it could be very helpful to have you on the inside of things."

"You want me to spy on her?" Howie asked, outraged.

"Exactly. You can be a sort of male Mata Hari on crutches. You're still on salary, of course."

In the end Howie agreed to it, more or less. He would pass on to Jack anything that might bear on the case, at least, with the provision that personal stuff was none of Jack's damn business.

"Fine, fine! That's all I want," Jack said reasonably.

So there he was: spy, lover, and invalid. The little girl was the only part of this whole scenario that seemed entirely right to him. He enjoyed hanging out with her.

"Now can I look?" he asked.

"No-o-o!" she told him moodily.

"Look, my leg's going to go to sleep if I don't move it pretty soon."

"Okay," she said suddenly. "You can look now."

"Well, well . . ."

His plaster cast had been transformed into a bright, multi-colored panorama. There was a little girl with blond hair and a red hat and red dress walking along a path with a basket on her arm, about to enter a forest of decidedly phallic trees—a girl-child's Freudian trees, if ever there were any. Howie saw a house in the forest, narrow and dark, and a blue river running nearby. A funny brown furry animal with long ears stood on a rock by the river.

"So who is this guy? A rabbit?"

"That's not a *rabbit*!" she told him. "That's a *wolf*!"

"Isn't he a bit round in the stomach for a wolf?"

"He just ate Grandmother."

"Ah!" said Howie with sudden understanding. "Was Grandmother tasty?"

Angela shook her head with great solemnity. "No. She tasted bad."

"And what does Little Red Riding Hood have in her basket?"

Angela had to think for a moment. "Ice cream," she decided.

"What flavor?"

"Brazilian Rain Forest Crunch."

Howie laughed. When he was a kid, he would have been hard-pressed to fantasize anything more elaborate than a cherry popsicle. He had to stretch and turn his cast from one side to the other in order to see all of Angela's creation.

"Who's this guy with the long black hair and the ax over his shoulder?"

She was astonished he didn't know. "That's the Handsome Woodcutter."

"He looks sort of like an Indian."

"He *is* an Indian . . . that's *you,* Howie."

"Me? *I'm* the Handsome Woodcutter?"

She nodded.

"You mean, *I* get to rescue Grandmother and Little Red Riding Hood?"

"Yes," she assured him. "That's your job."

Later they watched a Walt Disney movie together on the VCR in the den. It put both of them to sleep—Angela on the oversize pillow on the floor, and Howie on the couch. Howie woke up when his leg started bothering him. He covered Angela with a crocheted blanket and then moved the curtain aside to peer out the window. The dozen protesters were walking in a lethargic elliptical pattern along the road, holding their signs with a noticeable lack of energy. These Christians for a Moral America intrigued him. Who were they really? What sort of lives did they lead when they weren't camped out in front of some doctor's house?

Howie had an idea how he might find out more about them. He let the curtain fall closed, and then he hopped with his crutches along the hall to his bedroom, leaving the door open so he would hear Angela when she awoke. He pulled off the plastic dustcover from Alison's old computer, and spent a few minutes trying to figure out how to turn it on. He poked and prodded until the machine fired up with an electronic whoosh, and the screen began scrolling and chattering with information about bytes and other esoteric matters. Howie had used computers often enough in his academic life, but he had never had the patience or interest to learn much about them. Mostly he did an Information Age version of hunt and peck, simply trying different things and seeing what worked. At the C-prompt Howie typed "win" for Windows, and then waited while various messages and flashy graphics appeared and disappeared.

His first choice came when he had the Program Manager in front of him. He tried clicking onto the icon, "Accessories"—got nowhere that he wanted to go, went back, examined his choices more closely, and this time brought the mouse onto "Netscape Personal Edition." When he double clicked, a new group of icons appeared, various e-mail choices and something that said, "My Account Dialer." This seemed like a promising direction, and in a few moments he had typed Alison's password into the computer and was connected to the World Wide Web.

This was where Howie was liable to get lost and frustrated. Computer nerds who cry the glories of the Internet, usually don't mention the hours of wasted time waiting for connections to be made, watching the annoying little hourglass on the screen, arriving all too often at an inglorious electronic nowhere. Howie typed out "http://www.yahoo.com," punched ENTER, and soon found himself in Yahoo, one of the few Internet servers he knew. Yahoo was a good starting place for computer illiterates like himself. He put the cursor in the search box, and after brief consideration, he typed three words: "Christians Moral America." Then he tapped ENTER and waited for a match.

To his surprise, there were sixteen sites on the Internet that contained these three words, more than what he would have imagined. Number eleven was what he was after: Christians for a Moral America. He moved the cursor finger beneath the name, clicked once again, and a few moments later he was on their home page.

The problem with the Information Age, Howie had always thought, was simple: A world in which there is more and more information, but less and less meaning, is a world in which a person can quickly go mad. No wonder there were so many self-help gurus and cults. Mankind couldn't inhabit the vastness of this limitless world without a search engine, some Grand Yahoo in the sky to make sense of it all. This was the void that http://www.cma.com—Christians for a Moral America—tried to fill.

Their home page had slick graphics, and Howie could see that they had gone to some expense and trouble to present themselves in a positive light. Whoever had written the copy was very big on capital letters: "Welcome to Christian America!" Howie read. "Our Goal is nothing less than to Obey, Proclaim, and Demonstrate the Word of Jesus Christ! And to bring this Great Nation under God into Full Accordance with the Law of Christian Principals that our Forefathers Envisioned."

Howie found himself staring at a color photograph of Dr. Fred J. Doron and his wife, Cathy, who were apparently the guiding spiritual force behind the group. Dr. Doron was a rugged, deeply tanned middle-aged man who had a square face that was made even squarer by his crew cut hairstyle. His wife, Cathy, was a plump blond woman, also deeply tanned, though slightly older in appearance than her husband. The doctor and Mrs. Doron were standing on their patio with a swimming pool in the near distance. They stood side by side smiling into cyberspace with an almost insane amount of sincerity.

Beneath the photograph there was a caption: "A Word of Welcome From Our President, Dr. Fred J. Doron, and his Wife, Cathy." In this word of welcome—a paragraph, in fact—Dr. Doron took a decidedly folksy tone. He was a simple man himself, but he just wanted to say that it seemed pretty obvious to him that Jesus had Great Plans for America. We all had to do our part and live by the Bible so that this could become the Great Christian Nation that God had intended. Somehow, and it was no secret, the country had got offtrack recently. Pornography on television. Lesbians in the White House. Foreigners allowed to run things. What kind of America was it when children were taught that homosexuality was okay? Where our kids weren't even allowed to pray in public schools? It was the goal of Christians for a Moral America to set these things right, and Dr. Doron hoped that every right-minded American Person would be a part of this Exciting Crusade.

"I know you are asking yourself, What Can I Do To Help?" the doctor continued. "I would like to make a Special Appeal to each and every one of you to open your wallet, your checkbook, your purse—break open your Piggy Bank, if you need to, but please give generously to this Important Work! We are on the verge of a Great Victory, but unfortunately, the Elitist Liberals are gathering their forces to fight us to their dying gasp. I know that many of you Good People are far from wealthy, but remember this: Every dollar you send to Christians For A Moral America, means another bullet in the war against Satan!"

All in all it was mildly amusing stuff, though this last bit

about another bullet in the war had an ominous tone. Howie
kept scrolling through the web site. There were individual ar-
ticles describing various projects the CMA had undertaken.
The group was fighting to make homosexuality a criminal of-
fense in Colorado, and to highlight the urgency of this task,
there was a story, meant to be terrifying, of a Denver restaurant owner who had been required by law to hire a gay cook
who had the AIDS virus. CMA was active on many fronts.
They were waging an expensive legal battle on behalf of a
seventh-grader named Polly Warden to teach Creationism at
public schools in the Liberal Elitist stronghold of Boulder.
They were also active in the issue of "Parental Rights"—the
right, that is, to raise a child as a Christian rather than an
Atheist Humanist. (As shocking as it might seem, the Liberals were trying to make it a crime for a parent even to hit his
own child!) Of course, all these battles, legal and moral, were
expensive to wage, and each article called for renewed gen-
erosity from Christians everywhere.

   At last Howie came to the protest action against the infamous child killer, Dr. Alison Hampton, in New Mexico. He
clicked onto the lead sentence and found himself looking at a
photograph of the Women's Cooperative Family Planning
Clinic of Albuquerque—the name itself was an object of
ridicule—with protesters outside on the sidewalk waving their
banners and signs. The article estimated that the clinic murdered over four hundred innocent babies each year, and also
encouraged rampant immorality by supplying free condoms
and birth control information to teenagers. The language was
very heated. Dr. Doron himself had a few urgent words to add
to the debate:

   "We must always remember what Holy Scripture tells us:
'Defend the cause of the weak and fatherless . . . Rescue the
weak and needy'—Psalm 82:3. 'Rescue those being led away
to death!'—Proverbs 24:11. And as Jesus Himself said most
eloquently in the Gospel According to John, 'I have come that
they may have life, and have it to the fullest.' Nothing can be
clearer, my friends, and no work today is more important for a
True Christian than stopping this Satanic butchering of innocent babes. To date we have spent nearly $24,000 in inciden-
tal expenses to support our six-month vigil against this
so-called 'Women's Cooperative.' Please support our impor-

tant work in New Mexico! If you are unable to come march with us but you want to show how deeply you are concerned about the murdering of God's children, please put your urgently needed donation in the mail today. . . ."

Jesus certainly seemed to need a good deal of American greenback currency so that His Will might be done on earth! The web site was starting to depress Howie, and he scrolled quickly to the end. He couldn't resist clicking one final heading: DON'T FORGET BIBLE CAMP THIS SUMMER! As Alison's computer received the transmitted information byte by byte, a photograph gradually began to appear, apparently showing some summer fun from last year's Bible Camp. Howie smiled at how hokey all this was. The snake-oil salesmanship, the constant, ill-concealed greed for cash donations. But his laughter died abruptly when the photograph on his screen was finished: It showed a tall young man with a pale complexion and red hair standing with a group of children on a summery meadow near a lake. Howie's stomach went tight with remembered pain. The last time he saw this face, Howie had been lying in his own vomit in a Colorado Springs parking lot.

It was a strange face, almost medieval. An El Greco face, Howie had thought in Colorado Springs. But now, looking more closely, he considered Brueghel as a better choice of artists. This was one of Brueghel's mad redheaded peasants from some crowded revelry in hell.

What did he say to me? Does it hurt? What a bizarre question! Of *course* it hurt! He had just been kicked in the face! Howie felt such a wave of nausea at seeing this redheaded man pop up on the screen so unexpectedly that he hardly even wondered at the intricate web of connections: what the Millennium Investment Corporation, the San Geronimo Peak ski resort, and the fundamentalist Christians who were marching outside Alison's house might all have in common.

Howie was so shaken that it took his eyes a moment to absorb the entire photograph. *Good God!* he cried out loud. The redheaded man in the photo stood with a bow and arrow in his hand. He was showing the children gathered around him how to shoot. The caption read: "Luke Doron demonstrates archery at last summer's Bible Camp. Luke, who holds a silver medal in the annual Rocky Mountain Archery Competition, is one of the many fine people who volunteer each summer to help instill Old-Fashioned American Values in our children. Says Luke to his young friends:—'A Christian always takes True Aim!' "

Howie found that his hand was not completely steady as he dialed Jack's number. But no one answered at Jack's house. The phone just rang and rang.

10

Jack Wilder was in the jaws of a feeding frenzy beyond conscious control. This often happened when he was depressed. By ten o'clock on Saturday morning, he had gone through an entire tray of scones, and was pulling a second tray from the oven. Katya watched with interest, ears pointed, tongue lolling from her mouth, as he set the scones on a side table to cool.

"So what do you think, Katya? Maybe we'd better try a few of these suckers? Make sure they aren't poisoned."

He used a knife to cut two of the scones in half, and then spread unsalted butter and strawberry jam on each of the four halves. With the death of Crystal Henderson, Jack's investigation had come to a crashing halt. He had pinned everything on finding her, certain she would prove to be the key to unraveling the mysteries of Kit Hampton's final morning and why he and Howie had been summoned to Doobie Rock. Jack was not entirely unaccustomed to investigative setbacks; he had suffered plenty in his more than twenty-five years on the San Francisco police force. But this setback was particularly annoying, since his means of functioning as a detective had become so limited. He felt utterly stuck. With Howie out of commission, it was difficult even to imagine how he could develop a new angle of attack.

Being stuck was only one part of Jack's depression. There was also the way Captain Gomez of the state police had treated him at the crime scene in Donny and Crystal's blood-spattered living room. Unfortunately, Jack in his blindness had stepped into some of the blood, disturbing the evidence, making quite unforgivable footprints on the carpet. Captain Gomez no longer even pretended to be polite or respectful. He had taken a statement from Jack—and Emma as well—in a crisp, unfriendly manner, and since that afternoon had not bothered to return Jack's phone calls. This was frustrating for Jack, because he wanted to know the results of the various forensic tests.

"He treated me like I was some sort of interfering old fool," Jack said to Katya. It was not a good sign, he knew, to be having a conversation with a German shepherd. "Well, maybe I *am* in the way. Face it, if I was Gomez, I'd hate it if there was some blind ex-cop bumbling around, thinking he's some hotshot detective when he can't even see to avoid stepping through the evidence . . . my God, Katya! How did I ever turn into such a ridiculous figure? Well, hell with it! Whad'ya say we whip up a batch of brownies, my friend?"

Katya thumped her tail with encouragement. As far as she was concerned, Jack Wilder was still a very great man, a wise master, and a fabulous cook.

The telephone was Jack's last remaining investigative tool. At the moment it was his sole connection to the outside world, and he had left messages on a number of answering machines in several states over the past several days. A few minutes before eleven, Special Agent Kevin Neimeyer from the Denver office of the FBI returned one of those calls. Fifteen years earlier, Jack and Kevin Neimeyer had spent three days together on a particularly boring stakeout, holed up in a San Francisco hotel room, and they had done some male bonding, filling the time with endless hours of conversation—discussing everything from wine, women, children to Zen Buddhism.

"Hey, Jack!" he cried into the receiver. "How are you doing, buddy?"

Kevin couldn't have sounded more friendly. But with Jack's heightened sensitivity—paranoia, was it?—he heard a subtle note of guilt in Kevin's voice. It was the discomfort of the perfectly healthy for the infirm and handicapped.

"Oh, I'm fine, Kevin," he lied. "Not quite like the old days when I could see, but there *is* life after blindness."

"I'm glad to hear it. I've been so damn busy! I've been meaning to call for more than a year now, see how you and Emma are getting on down there in New Mexico."

"We love San Geronimo, Kevin. The weather's great, we have a fabulous garden, Emma has a job she likes with the local library. I've even opened up a private investigations of-

fice with a bright Indian kid who functions pretty decently as
my eyes."

"And it sounds like you've got yourself quite a case
here . . . look, Jack, I'm in the middle of a monster day, so I'm
going to skip the small talk. I ran those names through the
computer, the ones you wanted me to check—Donny and
Crystal Henderson. Her maiden name is Hauptman, by the
way. Crystal Hauptman. There's nothing on Donny; he's clean
as a choirboy as far as we're concerned. But Crystal has a
sheet. Nothing big, and most of it comes from when she was a
minor. I had to call in a favor to get a peek at her juvenile
file . . . are you ready?"

"Yes."

"Okay. Crystal Gale Hauptman—apparently she was named
after the country singer, which may account for some of her
troubles in life. Her father is Sergeant James Hauptman, who
teaches small-weapons training at the Air Force Academy. Her
mother, Tina Hauptman, is a housewife."

"Crystal grew up in Colorado Springs?"

"She and her family moved to the Springs when she was
eleven. Before that she was all over the world, an air force
brat—Germany, Guam, Hawaii, even a stint in Saudi Arabia.
Probably it's not so easy to grow up in these military families,
moving every few years. When the Hauptmans settled in Colorado Springs, Dad and Mom became very active in the local
Christian scene. The Springs is quite a gathering place for
right-wing Evangelicals, as you probably know. Crystal's
problems started in high school. She was the family rebel, apparently. In 1989 she was picked up for selling two ounces of
marijuana in the school parking lot. She was fifteen at the time,
and the court gave her a suspended sentence. Six months later
the same judge sent Crystal away to a youth camp in the mountains for a three-month stint. It seems her father beat the shit
out of her one night, and the judge thought it best to get her out
of the house for a while."

"He sent *her* to reform school because her father beat her
up?"

"Well, it was a conservative judge, Jack, and he happened to
be a member of Sergeant Hauptman's church. Apparently Dad
had found a box of condoms in Crystal's closet, and so the
judge thought it was understandable, maybe even commend-

able, that he had applied some serious moral wrath. Probably he believed a few months in a youth camp would turn Crystal back into a blushing virgin. Naturally, it did just the opposite. She came out wilder than she went in. Got busted the following year selling Extasy to an undercover cop. Spent another six months at the youth camp. And that's the end of her juvenile record. Apparently she behaved herself during her last year of high school, and even became something of a skiing star. There was talk that she might try out for the Olympic team, but she never quite got around to it."

"What about her adult record?"

"There's only one mark against her there. She was arrested for prostitution in Lake Tahoe in 1994. Apparently she was working as an instructor at Heavenly Valley and trying to turn a few extra bucks in the evenings by cruising the casinos. Heavenly was where she met her husband, Donny—he was a ski instructor there as well. And that's all I got. Your girl seems to be a mixed bag—not exactly a nun, but she seemed to straighten out in recent years. If she was still seeking the lush life, I don't see her working a ski patrol gig. That's a lot of exercise, Jack, the pay's not great, and it wouldn't leave the lady much time for trouble."

"Yet trouble found her in the end."

"Well, I guess it did at that. Listen, Jack, I have a guy in my office, an agent who's a real ski nut, and he knows tons of people in that world. I could set him loose a bit and see what he comes up with. Maybe he can find out something more about Crystal . . . maybe not. But I'll give it a whirl if you'd like."

"I'd appreciate it, Kevin. Thanks. I owe you."

"No, I still owe *you,* Jack. For about a million and one things . . . shit, my other phone's ringing. I'll talk to you soon. . . ."

After he put down the receiver, Jack sat quietly for some time. He was still at the kitchen table when Katya thrust her long nose into his lap, hoping to inspire Jack to further culinary endeavors.

"Nice guy, Kevin," he said moodily to Katya, scratching her velvety ears. "But he feels sorry for us, Katya . . . like this whole investigation is some sort of basket-weaving therapy for the blind! . . . . Well, we'll just have to show that son of a bitch, won't we?"

*   *   *

It was noon when Jack's phone rang again. He and Katya were just finishing up a few open-faced tuna sandwiches on homemade whole wheat green chile bread, piled high with avocado, sprouts, and melted Jarlsberg cheese. Jack and Katya were not exactly having a low-fat day.

"Jack, it's Josie Hampton . . . I'm sorry I've taken three days getting back to you. But I've been crazy busy, and this murder/suicide has really got me down. I bet it's Donny and Crystal that you wanted to talk about, right?"

"You bet. Mostly I'm interested in Crystal. Are you aware that she was seeing your father?"

Josie snorted. "*Screwing* my father was the way I heard it from the state cops. Apparently it's why Donny freaked out. Somehow he found out, and it drove him over the edge."

"Did you ever see your dad and Crystal together?"

"Never. I didn't have a clue it was going on. Not that it surprises me. It's like I told you, the women just kept getting younger and younger."

"How well did you know Crystal?"

"Not well at all. She and Donny have been employees the past three seasons. They did a good job, and we were all very pleasant to one another, and that's about it."

"You never had a personal conversation with her?"

Josie paused for a beat. "Not really. We rode the chairlift together once or twice. Mostly we just talked about skiing."

"You hesitated for a second. Is there anything on your mind?"

"No, I'm sorry. I was just trying to remember, that's all."

"Tell me, Josie—who were Crystal's friends up on the mountain? Someone she might have confided in? I'm looking for anybody at all who can fill in the blanks about her."

"Well, there's Craig Watts, of course. He's the head of the ski patrol. Craig would probably know as much about Crystal as anyone."

"Where can I find him?"

"He's at home. Actually, I just talked with Craig five minutes ago about some equipment I need to order for next season . . . Jack, I tell you what. Why don't I swing by your house, and we'll go see him together? I have to pick up a list from him, anyway. Then, if you'd like, we can stop by my office up on the Peak, and I'll pull Crystal's employment file for you. Maybe there'll be some information in it you can use."

"That would be very helpful, Josie. Thank you."

"No problem. Believe me, I want to put this incident behind us before the bad publicity starts to hurt our season next year."

Josie pulled by Jack's house half an hour later in her Jeep Grand Wagoneer. Jack buckled himself into the passenger seat, Katya jumped into the cargo area in the rear, and they set off into the mountains. She was a fast driver—too fast, as far as Jack was concerned. He tried to tell himself he shouldn't be nervous. But, my God—she was a child, a mere thirty-one years old! What did she know about tragedy and sorrow, let alone how to drive a car?

"Josie, could you slow down just a little, please."

"Are you nervous?" Was there perhaps a small note of glee in her voice?

"Only a little," he assured her. "Anyway we're not in such a hurry."

She said she would slow down, but from the rush of wind outside the window, it seemed to Jack as if they were going faster still. He was thrown against the door by centrifugal force as they sped around a long mountain curve. Jack was almost glad he couldn't see. He had meant to use this time to ask her a number of questions, but now he thought it best to allow her to concentrate entirely on the hazards of the road.

Craig Watts, the head of the ski patrol, lived in a high mountain valley a few miles from the chairlifts. The air grew colder, and there was a scent of imminent snow in the sky when Josie finally brought the Jeep to a stop. At this altitude spring was still only a fragile promise. Jack could feel the looming presence of tall trees. They parked, and Josie came around to open his door.

"Craig's cabin is up the side of a steep hill," she told him. "We have to climb quite a few steps. Are you going to be all right?"

"If you just go ahead of me, I'll put a hand on your shoulder and follow behind."

Katya ran free, ecstatically sniffing and peeing wherever she was able, while Jack followed Josie up a long flight of outside stairs.

"Craig built this cabin himself. There's no running water or electricity, but it's very picturesque."

"He lives alone?"

"Yeah. Craig's one of those woodsy bachelors who's a little too eccentric for any woman to put up with for long."

At the top of the stairs, Josie used a brass knocker on the front door to announce their arrival. Craig was expecting them, and the door opened with a creak of tight-fitting wood.

"Well, well, it's the infamous blind skier!" said a growly male voice. Jack had met Craig Watts on April Fools' Day, in the aftermath of Senator Hampton's death. From his voice Jack pictured a big, gruff mountain man with a beard. "Come on in," he said. "I got a pot of coffee on the stove."

The cabin smelled of smoke and the rough woodsy aroma of a bachelor who lived alone. Josie guided Jack into a musty armchair that was greasy to the touch. Craig poured them all cups of strong black coffee.

"I'm trying to reconstruct Senator Hampton's final morning," Jack began. "I'm hoping you can help me, Craig."

"I'll be glad to try. The cops sure haven't done shit, and I hate to see something like this drag on and on. It's not good for morale at the Peak, and when morale is down at a ski area, accidents happen."

"Do you have any idea who killed the Senator?"

"Television!" he growled.

"I beg your pardon?"

"Television! Man, it's all that friggin' violence on the boob tube! It makes people crazy. To tell the truth, I'm constantly amazed that *more* people don't murder each other."

People who live by themselves in remote mountain cabins tend to hold strong opinions. Jack nodded and did not contradict him.

"What can you tell me about Crystal Henderson?" he asked.

"Crystal was a good worker. That's about all I can say. I have no idea about her personal life. I guess she was married to some ski instructor—assholes, everyone of 'em! As far as I'm concerned, the Peak would be a whole lot better off without a goddamn ski school."

"Craig, my sweet—people come here to ski, and they want to learn how," Josie told him patiently.

"Better they should learn on their own—*I* did!" he bellowed.

"Did you know that Crystal was having an affair with Senator Hampton?" Jack asked.

"I make it a point *not* to know stuff like that. But of course, after that nose ring business, it was hard not to suspect something was up."

"I don't follow you."

"Her nose ring. It was the only run-in I ever had with Crystal. It was around Christmastime when she showed up one day with a damn gold ring through her nostril. Now, I don't have any aesthetic or social problems with this, you understand, but we have a rule. No earrings, nose rings, no dangling jewelry when you work ski patrol. The reason is safety, because we ski in and out of some pretty close places, through trees and rocks, and it would be easy for a piece of jewelry to get caught on something. It would be a real drag for a patrol person to be rescuing somebody, and then need to get rescued himself."

"So you told Crystal to get rid of it?"

"I surely did. And I told her the same thing a week later when the damn thing was still in her nostril. That's when she pulled her little Kit-says-it's-all-right routine. And if I didn't like it, I was just being an uptight male chauvinist pig. Artistic people need to express themselves, she said. Hell, I told her she was suspended from the job until the damn thing came out!"

"I see," Jack replied judiciously. "So she went to Kit."

". . . And Kit came running to me. Saying this was getting close to the twenty-first century, and we all had to be sensitive about matters of hairstyle and personal adornment. Besides, we didn't want a lawsuit on our hands. I told him, screw that, Kit, forget *sensitive*!—this is a safety issue, man. I don't want to see that girl take a tumble and come out of the snow with her nose ripped off. We had quite a discussion about it. Old Kit stood his ground, and I stood mine. But you know, when push came to shove, he was the boss. There wasn't much I could do except resign, and frankly, I wasn't in the mood for unemployment last winter. So I said hell, all right, we'll chuck the whole thing if *that's* the way you feel about it! From now on, the ski patrol can come to work in hula skirts if they want. . . ."

Jack felt the conversation was getting out of hand. He tried to pull it back into focus. "Let's talk about the morning of April first," he suggested. "Did you see Kit that morning?"

"Sure. I saw him take the seven-forty-five chair to the top. It runs just for ski patrol and lift employees at that hour. He was alone about four or five chairs ahead of mine."

"Isn't that unusual? To ride a four-person chair by yourself?"

"Not really. At that hour of the morning, everyone's just waking up. I prefer myself to take the first ride alone—just me and the mountain, no friggin' bozo skiers anywhere in sight."

"Sounds very peaceful. Did you see Kit again that morning?"

"Not up close. Just a glimpse of him skiing."

"Skiing where?"

"He was coming down El Lobo Ridge through the new powder. I was on a chair riding up the back side, and I just happened to look up. The public's not supposed to ski there, so I got him in my binoculars—it was Kit all right."

"He was coming down from the avalanche hut on the ridge?"

"Possibly, I don't know."

"What time was this?"

"About nine-thirty, I'd say. He liked to ski that chute—it's steep, man, but there's a hell of a view."

"Surely there wasn't any view on April Fools' Day. It was snowing hard that morning."

Craig made a dismissive sound. "That wasn't what *I* call snowing hard! Just a little spring fluff. Anyway, the clouds were moving pretty fast. A day like that, the visibility changes from second to second. I saw him when the clouds had lifted a little."

"Who was the ski patrol person assigned to the number three avalanche hut on April first?"

"Crystal. Probably I wouldn't remember, but she was up there alone, and generally that's a no-no."

"How did she happen to be alone??"

"Her partner missed work that day—Dennis Abrams. Normally, you understand, everyone on ski patrol works in pairs for safety reasons. Crystal shouldn't have been up in that hut by herself but we were shorthanded because of the storm, and she convinced me that she would be okay."

"And her partner," Jack asked in a neutral voice, "did you ever find out why he missed work that morning?"

"Well, it was the damnedest thing—his car was vandalized the night before outside his house down in town. The tires were slashed. It took him all morning to get it fixed."

"I bet it did!" Jack agreed, allowing himself the smallest smile.

11

Jack sat in Josie's office while she read aloud to him from the two separate employment files that the ski resort kept on Crystal and Donny Henderson. The building was quiet, and her voice seemed unnaturally loud in the empty space. There's something sad about a ski resort after the season is over, Jack was thinking. Like a party the morning after, or a carnival that has closed.

There was nothing of interest in Crystal's file that Jack did not already know. She had lied in a few places on her job application, leaving out her various stays in a Colorado youth detention center and her arrest for prostitution in Lake Tahoe. But such omissions were to be expected; few people admitted the darker episodes of their past when applying for a job. Jack listened to the bald statistics of her life: Born January 9, 1974 in Munich, Germany. Height, 5'6". Weight, 122 lbs. He heard about her schooling, her interests ("computer graphics, astrology, learning more about first aid and mountain rescue techniques"). But at the end she was still a blank, this pretty skier with a nose ring, Crystal Hauptman Henderson. The slashing of her partner's tires from the ski patrol suggested careful planning for the murder of Senator Kit Hampton, but Jack had suspected careful planning all along. He sensed someone behind her, some guiding intelligence. But who . . . *who*? . . . goddamn it, he wished he had gotten to her when she was still alive!

Her husband, Donny, was from Menlo Park, an upper-middle class suburb of San Francisco. He had lived a less adventurous life than Crystal: elementary school and high school in Menlo Park, then an inconclusive year and a half at San Francisco State. Jack visualized a slouchy young man with few interests and goals, who spent his winters at ski resorts and his summers in various low-paying jobs, often working as a waiter in restaurants. It was hard for Jack to imagine what had brought Donny and Crystal together, except they were both more than a little lost and they liked to ski.

Josie had finished reading the two files and was waiting for Jack to comment. With difficulty, Jack pulled himself out of his reflective slumber.

"Millennium Investment Corporation," he said. "Can you tell me who they are?"

"They're Colorado people, a real estate development outfit of some kind. But I've never had any contact with them myself. They own approximately two thousand shares of the Peak. Dad had dealings with them, of course, but I'm only just learning about that side of the business."

"How much is two thousand shares worth?"

"A bit over two million dollars."

"Have you come across any correspondence between your father and Millennium? Any memos? Contracts?"

"Nothing. Dividends are sent out on a semiannual basis to all of the investors, but that's done by our accountant in Santa Fe."

"Did your father travel to Colorado Springs recently?"

"Not that I know of. I never heard him mention Colorado Springs at all except in a derogatory way. He hated the right-wing politics there, naturally."

"So you really can't tell me anything about Millennium?"

"Well, only that Dad didn't like them very much. He once told me he wouldn't have let them into the business at all if it had been up to him. Unfortunately, they invested back when the Peak was still in a blind trust."

"A blind trust!" Jack repeated with a smile. "Actually, I'm not certain how trusting we blind people really are."

"It was when Dad was in Washington," she continued. "So he didn't know anything about it until he lost his reelection and returned home."

"What wasn't there to like about them?"

"He said they were pushy. They expected to have too much say in the day-to-day running of things. I remember there was something unpleasant about six or seven years ago. Someone from Millennium came down here and tried to convince Dad to expand the back side of the mountain with a new chairlift and a year-round resort village, with condos right on the slopes. That sort of thing is very big in Colorado. Dad squelched the idea in a hurry. He tried to explain these things just don't fly in New Mexico. The water regulations alone are hellish down here, and we'd never get approval for something like that anyway."

"Who did your father talk to from Millennium?"

"I don't know. I got this all secondhand from Dad when he grouched about it a few times over dinner. I'm sorry to be so vague, Jack, but at the time I was concentrating all my energies in an entirely different direction—lift maintenance, restaurant supplies, making sure the payroll got out on time, all the thousand little details that go into an operation like this."

"Is there anything else you remember about Millennium? Anything more recent?"

"Not a thing . . . I'm sorry."

"Well, I still can't understand it!" Jack told her. "Fortunately, I have an FBI friend up in Denver who's looking into Crystal's background a bit more closely. We'll just have to hope he can uncover what she was doing up in Colorado Springs last week with the Millennium people."

"The FBI has become involved in the case?"

"Not officially. This is only a friend doing me a favor."

Josie caught her breath; for some reason this news seemed to bother her. "Look, I'd appreciate it if you let me know if they come up with anything dirty on Crystal. I don't want a scandal here. It's our reputation, Jack. Skiing's a dangerous sport, and it's essential that the public has a high level of trust in the ski patrol."

"That's reasonable," Jack agreed. Nevertheless, there was something in her voice which he could not entirely fathom. Why was she suddenly anxious? Was there something about Crystal that caused her fear? For the moment he drew a blank and decided to let it pass. "Let's talk about your half sister, Alison. You've given me a pretty good idea of your family history, but I'm interested in the last month or two. How would you characterize the relationship between your father and Alison this past winter, after she moved to San Geronimo? Was it warm? Strained? Any difficulties between

them? . . . I'm trying to get a better fix on Alison. She's illusive in my mind."

"Being illusive is a big part of my sister's fatal appeal for
men," Josie said dryly. "Anyway, as far as she and Dad go, I'd
say they were on good terms recently, though there was a bit
of a blowup right before Christmas."

"What sort of blowup?"

"She asked him for a loan of a hundred thousand dollars,
and he turned her down."

"Really? Do you know why she needed the loan?"

"For her clinic, naturally. A worthy cause, I'm sure, but it's
also a huge money loser. Alison has been operating that clinic
in the red for years, and this winter she came very close to
closing down. So she tried to hit up Dad in order to stay afloat.
Actually, I was surprised when he said no."

"I'm surprised too. I understand he donated quite freely to
various nonprofit groups."

"Yes, he did. And I believe he gave Alison the money
originally to get the clinic started. But Alison has no business sense at all, you know, and for Dad, it was starting to
seem like throwing cash down a well. Half of her patients
never bother to pay, and her records are chaotic, if she both-
ers to keep them at all. Dad was generous, but it worried him
to see Alison being so careless about money. He said it was
her upbringing, that she didn't know the value of a buck,
etcetera. And he wasn't going to bail her out anymore, because it was time she grew up and became more responsible
about practical matters. The whole thing was full of parental
overtones that had nothing to do with the original matter of
the loan. Alison was furious and accused him of being a
'pseudo-liberal' —that's the phrase she used, and he didn't
like it one bit."

"So if Alison didn't get the loan, how did she manage to stay
open?"

"Well, this is a secret. Alison has let her medical insurance
lapse. That's always been her major expense, you know, the
real killer of running a small clinic like hers. Without the
monthly premiums she's been able to limp along for the time
being. She's hoping to get her insurance up and running again
as soon as possible—and with her inheritance, that shouldn't

be too long now, of course. Meanwhile she's just keeping her fingers crossed that someone doesn't sue her."

"Sounds like a dangerous gamble."

"It's insane. I tried to tell her it was crazy to go without insurance, but apparently her premiums are outrageously high due to the fact that she does abortions. This is all so typical of Alison! She thinks she's on some sort of holy mission to help poor women take charge of their bodies—which is very admirable, of course—but she has a tendency to let everything else in her life go to hell." Josie snorted with disdain. "Somehow these high-minded people always leave the rest of us to pay the bills!"

"Yes, I see what you mean," Jack murmured in agreement. But he was thinking more of Josie's manner. She was agitated, talking too quickly, too loudly. Something was bothering her. Even her smell wasn't right; there was a scent in the room, the musky odor of fear. After twenty-five years of interviewing suspects, Jack had a second sense in these matters—a sense that had become even sharper with his loss of sight.

What the hell is bothering her? The success of an interrogation depended entirely on taking advantage of such small openings as this, and Jack didn't want to make a mistake. Was she holding back something about Alison? He paused to let his mind roam the possibilities. Then he had it. This wasn't about Alison at all. Josie had become agitated at exactly the moment when he had mentioned the FBI was looking into Crystal. *Josie was hiding something about Crystal!* Jack struggled to keep his poker face, but his heart beat faster, sensing he was onto something.

"Tell me, Josie—when's the last time you spoke with Crystal?"

"I thought we were talking about Alison."

"We were. But let's go back to Crystal now."

"Well, I told you, we rode the chairlift together once or twice. I guess the last time I spoke with her must have been February. But maybe it was earlier than that."

Jack decided it was time to gamble: "No, I think you spoke with her a lot more recently than February," he insisted gently. "Tell me the truth."

"I *am* telling you the truth. Why should I lie?"

Jack had no idea why she should lie; he knew nothing at all.

But at this point he could only press forward and pretend he was omniscient. "Listen to me carefully, Josie. I helped you out of a jam once, right? You know you can trust me. But you've got to tell me everything."

"I'm telling you. I remember now—the last real conversation I had with Crystal was at the end of January, on the Martin Luther King weekend. We took the chair together up the back side of the mountain, and she told me about some Texan the patrol had to sled down that morning with a broken back. Martin Luther King Day is always our biggest weekend, and the ski patrol keeps pretty busy."

Jack shook his head sadly and pressed his bluff: "You can't hide the truth from me. I *know* about you and Crystal. Why can't you trust me, Josie?"

"Jack, you're starting to piss me off a little," she said angrily. But he heard a note of doubt in her voice, a crack in her defenses.

"I've got to warn you about my FBI friend, Kevin Neimeyer," he told her, leaning forward in his chair with intimacy and warmth. "He's really good, incredibly thorough. This isn't like dealing with the local cops or a blind detective like me. Kevin's going to put half a dozen agents combing through Crystal's life, finding out everything about her. All her relationships. Everyone she's telephoned. All her incoming and outgoing calls—particularly the most recent. There are records of these things, Josie. So whatever you're holding back, this is the time to tell me. Do you understand? If you made a single telephone call to Crystal that you haven't told me about, or she to you, it's going to look very bad."

Jack felt her increased agitation, and he knew that she was going to break. He recognized the signs. The denials, the evasions might go on another hour, but it was like landing a fish you had on the line. She could still get away if he wasn't careful, but he was confident of his skill and very patient. Josie lasted nearly another twenty minutes, but in the end it was a much bigger fish than he had imagined.

"This is such a nightmare for me! But I can't tell you, Jack. I just can't."

"Yes, you *can* tell me, Josie," he insisted. "If you're in trouble, I can help you."

"But it's not really trouble. It's just so . . . well, it's embarrassing!"

"In my time I've heard everything. Believe me, there's no way you can shock an old cop like me."

"This is more something where I think I shocked myself. It's, well . . . I was seeing a guy for a while last fall. Nothing too serious. His name's Donald Kasenberger, a nice Jewish lawyer in town. But then he dumped me in mid-September, and it left me feeling just slightly bitter about men in general. So I had an affair . . . this is extremely difficult for me to admit, Jack. . . ."

"You had an affair with a woman?"

"Yes," she said softly, almost a whisper.

A few bells went off in Jack's mind. Lights flashed. The truth dawned.

"You had an affair with Crystal Henderson?"

"Yes," she said again. And burst into tears.

After Crystal's death Josie Hampton had been living in fear, a horrible, gnawing fear that the truth would come out. It was all so humiliating. And perhaps it might even implicate her in crimes she knew nothing about. She pleaded with Jack to help her. Yes, there were telephone calls—at one time, quite a few telephone calls. But she was innocent, she swore to God, of every crime except foolishness when it came to sex and love.

Jack listened carefully to her confession as it poured forth. As romances go, it was not a huge affair. It lasted less than a month, in October of last year. In today's world, many men and women would feel no shame—would, in fact, be proud to admit to a homosexual relationship. But Josie Hampton was not comfortable with what she had allowed to happen. Nor did she particularly think of herself as gay, or bisexual, or any of the words that people seemed to use these days with such astonishing ease. She was just . . . drifting . . . experimenting. She wasn't even sure what, exactly. And then at the end of October, on Halloween after a gay costume party, she became disgusted with herself and broke it off.

Did this mean she actually "knew" Crystal any better than she had admitted to Jack earlier in the day? No, Josie said. Crystal had been a mystery from start to finish, almost more of a mystery after they had been to bed together than before. The whole thing had been entirely sexual, nonverbal. They had spent a few weekends at a discreet gay lodge in the Colorado Rockies, where they rarely ventured out of bed. At the end Josie felt almost suicidal, like she was drowning in something.

"I just couldn't keep it going. Deep down, I'm too conservative, Jack. So I told her it was over, and that was the end of it."

"Did she accept gracefully your breaking it off?"

"Oh, absolutely. We never referred to it when we met at work. It was like it never happened. Only it did."

"Then it must have been disturbing to you when you discovered she was seeing your father afterward?"

"*Disturbing?* Jack, ever since Captain Gomez told me on Wednesday evening that Crystal and Dad had been lovers, I've been feeling half-insane. It's hard to describe exactly how claustrophobic this is for me. Incestuous, really. I feel so dirty and confused."

"Now, Josie, I don't see anything at all in this business that should make you feel dirty," Jack told her. "But let's talk more about Crystal. Would you say that she was the one who seduced you?"

"Oh, yes. Absolutely. When it came to sex, she was a predator."

"Then she probably seduced your father as well."

"Do you think . . . maybe I'm being paranoid, but do you think she had us marked in some way? Dad and me?"

"I think it's entirely possible. She must have set out deliberately to seduce you both. Did she ever ask you about business?"

"Well, yes. Now that you mention it, we talked about the ski industry quite often. I thought it was just a way to avoid any really personal conversation. But I wonder if she was pumping me?"

"What did you tell her?"

"Basically everything she wanted to know. She was curious about the Peak's income, taxes, insurance, how many skiers we average each year, the kinds of environmental regulations we deal with, how a private corporation is set up . . . none of this is secret information, of course, and skiers can get awfully obsessive once you start talking shop. But come to think of it, we talked about business a whole lot."

"Did she ever mention Millennium?"

"You know, she *did* once. She asked me about them, who they were—just like you did. But I couldn't tell her anything more than what I told you. I said I'd look into it, but that was just before we broke off, so I never got around to it."

"Apparently she just changed Hamptons—I'd imagine she began to ask your father the same kinds of questions she had been asking you, probably with more success."

"This is *so* strange!" There was a shiver in Josie's voice. "I wonder what she wanted from me and Dad? What the hell was this all about, anyway?"

Jack had to admit he was wondering exactly the same thing himself.

Josie drove Jack and Katya home later in the afternoon. They had not been in the house five minutes when the phone rang. It was Kevin Neimeyer calling to say that he'd managed to pick up a few interesting tidbits he wanted to pass on. The first item was that Crystal Henderson had received a traffic ticket in Aspen last October for an illegal U-turn; not exactly the crime of the century, but when Kevin's agent dug a little deeper, trying to learn what exactly Crystal had been doing in Aspen, he discovered that she had spent several weekends at a small but expensive lodge that catered to the gay world. A little more digging, and the agent learned that Crystal had been in the company of Senator Hampton's daughter, Josie. Jack thanked Kevin for the information, and mentioned (just a tad smugly) that yes, he had come across this same information himself.

Jack was so pleased with himself that he missed what Kevin was telling him next.

"I'm sorry, would you say that again?"

"This is something we picked up from your New Mexico state cops," Kevin repeated. "I wasn't entirely certain if they were keeping you up-to-date with their investigation. . . ."

"They're *not*," Jack admitted unhappily.

"Well, that's their mistake. Anyway, this may mean something, or it may only be a coincidence. But Crystal's autopsy showed she had an abortion approximately two months ago—

a rather late-term abortion, as a matter of fact. Second trimester. And guess who the doctor was?"

Jack took the plunge, not at all liking the increasingly close family weave.

"Dr. Alison Hampton?"

"You got it," Kevin agreed. "Dr. Alison Hampton."

12

On Sunday morning Howie played gicket with Angela in the sagebrush behind the house, out of sight of the protesters who were still keeping their vigil in front. Gicket was a game that Howie had invented, a cross between golf and cricket, played with one of his crutches and a nerf basketball. Howie was feeling pretty chipper all in all, batting the spongy orange ball to Angela and making silly Tarzan noises as he swung around the sagebrush on his crutches. Angela was delighted with his clowning; she glowed with laugher and a little girl's flirtatious excitement at finding herself in the spotlight of male attention.

Howie bet Angela that he could beat her to the piñon tree at the back edge of the property. They were racing across the sagebrush—Howie galloping on his crutches with Angela in the lead—when Jack and Emma pulled into the driveway.

"Looks to me like Howie is rehabilitating just fine!" Emma remarked, describing the scene to Jack.

"Youth," Jack told her enviously. "It heals quickly."

Emma walked Jack along the path to the rear of the house where Howie and the child were playing.

"I'm just dropping him off," Emma called to Howie. "But don't worry. I'll be back in an hour."

Howie sent Angela inside the house, saying they would play some more gicket later. Then he and Jack sat down on an old-fashioned patio swing that Alison had set up on the desert behind her house.

"You're recovering fine, I take it?" Jack asked.

"Sure. I'm getting pretty good on my crutches. So good, I'm going to be a parent volunteer at Angela's preschool this Tuesday. One of the other kids is having a birthday party, and the mother called last night to see if Angela can come. Alison's

been keeping Angela out of school, you know, ever since the
pro-lifers showed up in San Geronimo."

"So you're going to stay with Angela at school?"

"Yeah. That's me, bodyguard to the tots. Alison says she'll
feel easier if I'm there keeping an eye on things."

"Is this going to be a steady gig, then?"

"No, just Tuesday for the birthday party. Alison's still not
sure what she wants to do with Angela in the long term. I think
she's hoping for some sort of miracle, that maybe these Christians for a Moral America will pack up and find someone else
to terrorize."

Jack began pushing the swing with his foot in a restless, dis-
satisfied way. Howie wasn't at all certain what he was thinking.

"If you want me back at work, maybe Wednesday is the day,
Jack. As I say, I'm getting pretty good with these crutches, and
the leg isn't hurting too much. I'm thinking I could even drive
a car in a pinch, as long as it was an automatic. Have you
thought about replacing the Toyota?"

"Maybe next week. We'll go down to Santa Fe together and
pick something out, probably another truck. Meanwhile I think
it's best for you to stay here and look after the little girl. I can
understand why the mother is worried. And since you're here,
there's something I'd like you to look into for me."

"A little more snooping, huh?"

"Listen, Howie—Alison knew Crystal Henderson. At least
she performed an abortion on Crystal this past winter. I want
to know more about it."

"Alison has performed a lot of abortions, Jack. It doesn't
mean she had any special connection with Crystal."

"Well, that's what I want to find out. It's starting to bother
me how closely everybody seems to be interconnected in this
case. Why should Crystal go all the way to Albuquerque to Alison Hampton for an abortion?"

"Why not? My guess is Dr. Hampton knows her stuff. And
these days women prefer going to a lady OB-GYN."

"Yes, but I understand there's a perfectly good woman doctor here in San Geronimo, so she could have saved herself a
long drive. And here's something else—Crystal was having an
affair with Josie Hampton."

"With *Josie*? . . . you've got to be kidding! Josie's gay?"

"It sounds more like a bit of lifestyle experimentation. Still, it's a curious coincidence, particularly since her father was having an affair with Crystal as well. In fact, there's a chance the child that Dr. Alison Hampton aborted would have been her half brother or sister, had it lived . . . so you see, it's hard to imagine that Crystal just came across the Women's Cooperative Family Planning Clinic in the phone book."

"This sounds a little tangled, Jack."

"Yes, it is. And we're going to untangle it."

Jack went on to tell Howie about Alison asking for a loan from her father to keep her clinic going. Howie's undercover mission was to snoop out anything he could learn of these matters. Howie was uncomfortable with the role of spy, but he said he'd do his best. Then he told Jack his news.

"I found some interesting stuff yesterday on the Internet. Guess who won a silver medal in archery?"

Howie told Jack about the Christian web site, and how he had come across the photograph of Luke Doron, son of Dr. Fred J. Doron, with a bow and arrow in his hand. And how this same Luke Doron happened to be at the shopping mall parking lot in Colorado Springs, sitting in a car having a conversation with Crystal Henderson. Which meant one more loop added to the knot: San Geronimo Peak, the Millennium Investment Corporation, and now the Christian group that was making life hell for Alison Hampton.

Jack listened, deep in thought, rocking the swing so violently with his foot that Howie had to hold on to the armrest to keep from falling off.

That night, after Angela went to sleep, Howie and Alison played Scrabble in the living room in front of a burning log in the fireplace.

"What about a prize?" Alison suggested. "The winner gets a blow job. Okay?"

It was more than okay; Howie had trouble concentrating on the game instead of the prize. Still, they were neck and neck until Alison scored a decisive lead with the word "zygote" placed in the upper left-hand corner of the board, covering the red triple-word square. Howie told her it was unfair using her medical background to come up with a biology term, but Alison's smile only deepened to a warm glow. The final score: Alison 197, Howie 171.

"Time to pay up, Howie," she told him with a smile.

The prize giving took place in the guest bedroom. Howie was always astonished at the beauty of her naked form, the delicate, sculptured smallness of her shoulders and legs and breasts. He lay on his back on the bed, and she straddled him, bringing herself down upon his mouth—it seemed the easiest way to arrange matters with the inconvenience of his plaster cast. Howie found her clitoris with his tongue; he knew he had just the right place when she exhaled sharply. There was something very soothing, he found, in the rhythmic licking and lapping of an oysterish labia. A slippery meditation, these wet lips rubbing against his face. Mankind crawled out of the sea millennia ago, and to the sea he must occasionally return. When she became more excited, she pressed down harder upon his mouth and rode him back and forth. This went on for a long time, and as far as Howie was concerned, it could go on forever. But after a while Alison told him to put two fingers up inside of her, and then he watched as she masturbated herself with her own fingers to a shuddering climax.

"Oh, my God!" She cried, she laughed, she moaned. And then she stretched out beside him on the bed. Howie meanwhile was hard as a rock and suffering a certain degree of physical distress. But a deal is a deal, and he did his best to think of something unsexy in order to calm down. He remembered he was supposed to be asking Alison all sorts of ugly questions, and this did the trick. The flag of his desire went down to half-mast.

"Was it all right?" he asked her.

"Howie, it was more than all right," she assured him. "When you die, I hope you'll donate your tongue to science."

Howie smiled. But the more he thought of the snooping Jack wanted him to do, the more unhappy he became. What was half-mast a few moments earlier, was now entirely limp.

"Honey, you're looking a little deflated—what's wrong?"

"It's Jack," he told her. "There are some things he wants me to find out about you. To be honest, I'm supposed to be spying and learning all your deep, dark secrets."

Alison propped herself up on one elbow and regarded him with interest.

"Really?"

"I'm afraid so. Only I'm no good as a spy. I don't even know how to begin."

"I wouldn't let that worry you. Frankly, Howie, you're so good in bed that it's easy to forgive a few deficiencies in other areas. So why don't you just ask me what you want to know."

"Just ask you, huh?"

"Well, why not? Here you've got me naked and vulnerable and so satisfied with sex that I can hardly think straight. So go ahead and take advantage of me—I don't mind."

"Well, okay. Jack wants to know if you knew Crystal Henderson?"

"Crystal Henderson." Alison repeated the name dubiously. "Isn't that the girl in that murder/suicide? I heard about it on the radio while I was driving to Albuquerque the other morning."

"Did you know her?"

"I don't think so. Should I have?"

"She was Josie's lover for a while last fall. Jack just found this out."

"*Josie*?" Alison cried. "Josie finally had her lesbian fling? I don't believe it!" Alison howled with laughter. "Actually, I *do* believe it!"

"Why do you say *finally* had her lesbian fling? Did you see this coming?"

"Absolutely. Think about it, Howie—Dad deserted her as a child, he treated her mother like shit, then she had a stepfather who was a drunk and pretty much abused her. She's always carried a lot of really deep anger, mostly about men. All her boyfriends were creeps—at least the ones she's told me about. It's like she was reenacting all the negative feelings she had about men. I think every single one of her boyfriends dumped her in the end. Frankly, I think it's a great thing she's finally come out of the closet. Maybe she'll be happy now."

"What about Crystal? Did you ever meet her when she was with Josie? Or any other time?"

Alison shook her head. "No, I don't think so."

Now it was Howie's turn to prop himself up on an elbow and study her. "She was a pretty girl. Dark blond hair. She worked on the ski patrol. A nose ring through one nostril?"

Alison continued to shake her head. "Sounds like a thousand

other girls you see in ski resorts. Tell me something else about her."

"She had an affair with your father too. How long an affair, no one really knows. But she and your father managed to screw on the very morning he was killed."

Alison laughed again. A sharp, unkind laugh. "Poor Josie!" she cried. But there was something gloating in her voice. "My God, she must have been devastated when she found out she was sharing her little romance with Dad!"

"So Crystal Henderson still doesn't ring a bell?"

"The girl sounds fascinating, Howie. That's quite a feat, after all, getting it on with both father and daughter! But no, I don't think I ever met her."

"You gave her an abortion, Allie. Probably sometime two months ago. She was in her second trimester."

Alison still look mystified. Then her mouth opened. "Ah, Crystal! . . . You know, I *do* remember now! But Henderson wasn't her last name . . . Hauptman! That was the name she gave me. Crystal Hauptman."

"Hauptman was her maiden name."

"Well, I guess that's why I didn't make the connection earlier. But I remember now. She came to me in mid-February. A pretty girl with dark blond hair. But you know, Howie, I see so many of these girls, they all sort of blur together after a while."

"You can see why Jack is curious about this. Here's this girl who before she gets murdered has an affair with your half sister, and then with your father, and then goes to you for an abortion. The baby . . . well, it could have been your father's child."

"Aha!" said Alison. "The plot thickens! How positively baroque! I can see why Jack's wondering why she came to me. Of course, I *do* have an excellent reputation as a doctor, you know. I get women referred to me from all over New Mexico, even some from Texas, Oklahoma, as well as Arizona from time to time. I'm good at what I do, Howie."

"I know you are. But you can see how odd this is. Even if you didn't know who she was, she certainly knew you."

"You think so? Maybe it was just a coincidence her coming to me?"

"Not with your name, Allie. You don't have an affair with someone named Josie Hampton, then Senator Kit Hampton, and then go to a Dr. Hampton for an abortion without suspecting a family connection."

"Well, maybe you're right, but I just don't have a clue about it. For me, Crystal Hauptman was only one more patient. Probably I wouldn't even remember her name, except for one thing. It's a little kinky, actually."

"What's that?"

Alison smiled mischievously and ran a fingertip lightly down Howie's chest. "Her nostril wasn't the only place she was pierced. She had a small gold ring through her clitoris. She told me it was a wedding ring."

"Ugh!" said Howie.

"Oh, it could be put in without any pain. Though she would certainly be sore for a few days afterward. Have you ever made love to anyone with a ring through her clitoris, Howie?"

"Not once," Howie assured her. "Though I knew a lot of people into body piercing at one time. It's quite the fashion among a certain set in New York. I even heard of body-piercing performances down in the East Village, a kind of theatrical event where you can watch people cut themselves in various places. Personally, it was never quite my thing."

"What do you think it means, Howie?"

"*Means?*" he repeated. "Well, I don't really know. At first I thought it was like our Indian Sun Dance—you probably know about that."

"No, I don't. Tell me. I always thought a Sun Dance was very . . . well, sunny."

"Not so sunny really. The way it works, a brave will pierce himself and thread leather thongs through his chest, then suspend himself by these thongs from a wooden beam. Some of the guys hang like that for hours, even days. It's a way to transcend pain and take a walk into the spirit world. A kind of out-of-body experience, I'm told."

"You've never tried it?"

"We Ivy League Indians generally just drink a little too much chardonnay when we're looking for that out-of-body high."

"Well, whatever turns you on," she said, her fingertip tracing downward to his soft tangle of pubic hair. "Would you like to screw a girl with a ring in her pussy?"

"Are you saying it's supposed to be sexy?"

"You know, you really are awfully innocent, Howie! Of *course* it's supposed to be sexy! That's what it's all about!"

Howie was meditating on the mysteries of gold rings and vaginas when he felt Alison's fingertip very softly stroking his cock. The flag began to rise.

"Now, I find *that* sexy," he admitted.

"Of course, you do. But this is only the meat and potatoes of eroticism. Don't you feel an occasional desire to explore new frontiers?"

She flashed him a most feline smile and then moved her head so that her tongue could take the place of her fingertip. She licked upward from the root toward the tip, as though he were a popsicle.

"Ah!" he groaned.

"That's right, a little pleasure," she told him. But then she did something insane. She bit down sharply on the tip of his penis with her neat, bright teeth. It was only a jab, a quick snakebite; she didn't actually break skin. The hurt was abrupt and exquisite, and made Howie jackknife to a sitting position.

" . . . And a little pain!" She laughed triumphantly at his distress.

"Allie, for chrissake!" he cried angrily. He didn't like it, but he was so horny and overfull, he was afraid he might explode in her face.

"Well, that's your lesson for today. Now, just lie back and relax, Howie. I've always believed that Scrabble is a game in which everyone should come out a winner. . . ."

13

Bright Rainbow Preschool was located in a converted adobe house on the edge of the historical part of town. It was a pretty building set in a large playground behind an old wooden fence. Howie had always heard that this was *the* preschool in San Geronimo, very progressive, a trendy parent's co-op of enlightened ideals where all the kids seemed to have names like Chelsea, Brittany, Dylan, and Mesa Moon. These favored children were encouraged to discover their inner worth, to eat hot vegetarian lunches, and even dabble on kiddie computers to get a jump start on the information age. Very nice, but it made Howie wonder about the poor kids in town—all the Hernandos and Billy Bobs and Ritas, who generally stayed home with someone's grandmother in front of the TV, eating junk food and getting whacked whenever they did something wrong.

"The divisions of a class society are planted early," he told Angela on Tuesday morning as they walked together into the school. She grinned at him and crinkled her nose. Angela looked awfully cute this morning in a Babar the Elephant sweatshirt and green corduroy pants. She didn't know what he was talking about, but just about everything that Howie did and said made her laugh.

Alison's maid, Viola, had driven them to the school in her huge old American car. It was a sunny, spring-perfect morning. Even the wind, often so savage in New Mexico, had died to a complacent murmur. There were geraniums by the front door and the sounds of high-pitched, overexcited children's voices within. It all conspired to put Howie in an idyllic mood.

Won't it be fun to be part of a kiddie birthday party? he thought in ignorant bliss. Unaware that as he passed through that pretty preschool doorway, he was entering the very jaws of hell.

* * *

Angela was in the Chamisa Room, and her teacher was a young woman with frizzy brown hair and huge worried eyes named Phaedra Holbrook. Phaedra and her assistant, Heidi Schlumberger, both appeared on the verge of collapse. They had fourteen children between the ages of four and six to look after, and they were hugely grateful for help. *Any* help at all, even an Indian guy on crutches.

"Look who we have here, everybody!" Phaedra announced to the children in an exaggerated happy-happy voice. "This is Howard Moon Deer! And guess what? He's a Native American!"

Phaedra, of course, knew exactly why Howie was here, and she had promised they would keep a particular eye on Angela. Probably she meant it too. But as the day wore on, Howie saw how difficult it was to keep on top of anything. Two of the children in the group were the objects of bitter custody battles, and there were special instructions to remember about them as well—which relatives could pick them up, and which were banned by court order from even appearing at the school. Two other children required special medicines; a third was allergic to nearly everything; a fourth must be watched with particular attention because he had recently bitten another child so badly that the victim's father, a lawyer, was threatening legal action. And as if this wasn't enough to keep in mind, there was always Shanti, the youngest, who at the age of four had somehow missed toilet training and at odd times of the day had a sweet way of announcing she had just gone ca-ca in her pants. With so many possible calamities at hand, a child who might become the target of Christian wrath was just one more disaster waiting to happen.

On Tuesday they were overwhelmed nearly from the start. Two of the boys, Christopher and Colin, had just seen a new Batman movie, and they were eager to reenact for the other children the fabulous ways that the grown-ups had killed one another. Brittany's parents were getting a divorce, and the first thing Brittany did when her mother dropped her off was throw a yellow building block at Chelsea, who burst into tears that didn't stop for fifteen minutes. Her parents were getting a divorce too. The situation was made even more hectic by the birthday party that was planned for little Buffy Fletcher later in the day. Buffy was turning five, and her mother, Shannon, had wanted to make it a memorable occasion, with games, prizes, and an enormous cake. Since they were having such fine spring weather, Phaedra had decided days ago to hold the party itself at Ernie Martinez Municipal Park, which was five blocks away and had swings and slides and an open field. Buffy's mother had agreed to deliver the cake and various birthday treats to the park at noon exactly, and then remain to lend additional adult supervision.

Such, at least, was the plan.

At eleven o'clock, after Circle Time, fourteen small human beings were lined up in pairs holding hands on the sidewalk in front of the school. Phaedra led the procession toward the park while Heidi took up the rear, constantly on the lookout for stragglers. Howie, hobbling at an easy gait on his crutches, minded the middle, and for a while things went fairly smoothly, as excursions go with fourteen children of preschool age.

They arrived at Ernie Martinez Municipal Park at approximately eleven-forty-five, entering from the parking lot. Ernie Martinez, Howie discovered through a bit of research, was the only native son of San Geronimo to lose his life fighting Nazis in the Second World War, and as a result the town fathers had named an acre of brown patchy grass after him, a few dusty cottonwood trees, a dilapidated set of swings, a jungle gym, and a tennis court with a sagging net and weeds growing up through the cracks.

The kids ran directly to the swings, slides, and jungle gym to await the arrival of Buffy's mother with the cake and a lasagna she had agreed to bake. But this was the first serious glitch in the day: Shannon Fletcher was nearly half an hour late, and by the time she arrived, the kids were already over-hungry and overwrought. Mrs. Fletcher was full of exasperation and apologies. She said it had been a hell of a day, and she was terribly sorry but she had a major crisis at home—her hot water heater was broken. The plumber could only come this afternoon to fix it, or she would have to wait until the end of the week. Clearly, she could not live that long without hot showers, laundry, and her automatic dishwasher. So she would have to drop off the cake, the lasagna, the party favors, and run. She could not stay to help supervise the party after all.

Phaedra blew up. She would never have brought fourteen

children to the park for a sugar-fest birthday party with only
two fully mobile adults to supervise, and one volunteer on
crutches. But Shannon Fletcher was adamant. She could not,
would not stay—and that was the end of it.

"Well, I guess we'll just have to cope, won't we?" Phaedra
said to Howie and Heidi through clenched teeth. Her happy-
happy voice was showing serious strain.

The preschoolers began running every which way around the
park, enough to make a sane adult dizzy with despair. Later,
there were a lot of things that Howie could not account for in
that day, the most striking of which was the child he was there
to watch: Angela Hampton. In a preschool setting, Howie discovered, it is the destructive children, those who are about to
"act out" and bonk each other on the head, who occupy ninety-
nine percent of a teacher's attention. Sweet little Angela was so
good-natured and well behaved that she became more or less
invisible. Even Howie hardly saw her.

Lunch was a free-for-all fiasco. Pieces of cake ended up on
the ground accompanied by hot tears. Christopher and Colin
had to be restrained from throwing lasagna at each other. At a
climactic moment four-year-old Shanti pooped in her pants,
and Heidi had to take her off into the bushes to get her cleaned
up. Unfortunately, they had forgotten to bring an extra set of
pants and panties for her, and the little girl most definitely
could not be allowed to run around naked in a public park—
not in today's climate of sexual paranoia. This meant that
Heidi needed to return to the school to fetch some extra clothing. "If the school van is free, drive it back to the park," Phaedra told her frantically before Heidi took off on foot. "At least
it'll make it easier to get the kids home."

So there were two adults now, Phaedra and Howie, to look
after fourteen children. By the time lunch was over, they were
both nearly numb with stress and exhaustion. One of the boys
said let's play hide-and-seek, and Phaedra decided this might
be a good idea, a chance to let them all run off some steam.

Hide-and-seek was the final undoing of the afternoon.
Howie was "it," since he was on crutches. This gave the kids
an advantage in whooping in around him and safely touching
"home"—a languid cottonwood tree that was in the first stages
of its spring bloom. For each round Howie closed his eyes and
counted to twenty in a loud, melodramatic voice. The children

scattered with screams of excitement throughout the park. They hid in gullies, behind trees, sometimes in the shrubbery clear over by the parking lot. Phaedra allowed the game to go on for over a half hour, and still Heidi had not returned with the school van. Every now and then, the two adults counted heads: one . . . two . . . three . . . four . . . all the way to fourteen. Fourteen little bodies running around like maniacs in their colored T-shirts, like an abstract painting in motion.

Phaedra finally decided they'd have to walk back to the school, and she called all the children together from their various hiding places with a kind of pagan chant: "All-y, all-y in, free! free! free!" When they were gathered around, she did a head count: "One . . . two . . . three . . . four . . . five . . . six . . . seven . . . eight . . . nine . . . ten . . . eleven . . . twelve . . . thirteen . . ."

But this was the wrong number, and she and Howie both counted again. "One . . . two . . . three . . . *stand still everybody!* . . . four . . . five . . ." But again they arrived at the unlucky number thirteen. Howie felt the first cold fingers of panic. Phaedra shouted, actually shouted at the children, and told them to line up together and not move. The children had never been shouted at before, and they were so surprised that they did precisely as they were told. Then the adults counted again, one to thirteen. There could be no mistake this time: Number fourteen was missing.

"Who's not here?" Phaedra cried.

It took only a moment now to identify the missing child: the quiet one, the nearly invisible Angela Hampton.

Howie told the children, don't move, don't move an inch if you know what's good for you. Then he galloped around the park like a madman on his crutches calling for Angela. He looked everywhere, and so did Phaedra. They searched behind bushes and trees, gullies and picnic tables. They shouted until their voices were hoarse. "Angela! . . . Angela! . . . the game's over! . . . Angela, I'm not joking . . . *come in, wherever you are!*"

But she did not come in wherever she was. It was inconceivable. Could a child simply evaporate? Howie was nauseous with fear and outrage. There must be some mistake, he kept saying to himself. He had to be dreaming this. The thir-

teen remaining children stood in a small forlorn group, some
of them crying, feeling the panic in the air.

"I don't think I checked that clump of brush by the tennis
court!" Howie cried, taking off in his three-legged hobble
across the park to the spot he had in mind. But Angela was not
there. While Howie was poking at the brush with his crutch,
Heidi finally returned with the school van. She said the van had
had a flat tire that needed to be changed, and the jack hadn't
been in its proper place; it was all very frustrating.

"The hell with the van!" Phaedra screamed. "Find a goddamn telephone and get the police!"

It was a New Mexico state trooper, nearly an hour later, who
discovered the fate of little Angela Hampton. There was a note
folded in a thin strip, sticking out of the end of a soda can, like
the fuse of a bomb. The can had been sitting unnoticed near the
jungle gym, half filled with pebbles to give it weight. The message inside was in capital letters, a computer printout:

REPENT BABY KILLER AND YOUR DAUGHTER WILL BE SPARED

The can, Howie noted, was a diet Dr Pepper.

PART THREE

THE GHOST DANCER

1

Midnight, Tuesday, April 13th:

Josie Hampton sat by herself in the haze of Rio's Lounge getting drunk on tequila and grapefruit juice. The room smelled of beer and cigarettes and the urinals from the men's room nearby. There was music coming from the jukebox, an old Janis Joplin tune, and the sound of pool balls colliding on green velvet. Rio's Lounge on the south edge of town was the best San Geronimo could offer in terms of sin and late-night sleaze, catering to a mix of druggies and gays and people of all persuasions who lived on the edge, everybody cruising for brief bouts of satisfaction.

Josie couldn't remember the last time she had been so drunk. And, man, it felt great!

"What's up?" she said to a guy with long, stringy hair who was passing her table. She knew him from someplace, probably the Peak.

"Hey, I heard about your sister's kid," he said with sympathy. "It was on the TV news. A real bummer, man!"

"A bummer?" she repeated incredulously. "A *bummer*?"

"Some pedophile, huh?" the guy said, shaking his head.

Suddenly she was furious. "What the hell do *you* know about it, asshole?" she snarled.

He forked her the finger and walked away.

Josie held up her empty glass to the waitress. " 'Nother tequila grape," she said. The jukebox went from Janis Joplin to Grace Slick singing "White Rabbit." There were some retro-sixties freaks in here tonight, putting down their quarters for the old songs. Josie slipped out of her seat and glided toward the few square feet of open space in front of the jukebox that served as a dance floor. She clapped her hands and shimmied her body in rhythm to the beat. She was getting loose when she noticed a dark-haired woman come onto the floor to dance nearby. At first they were separate orbs, two different people dancing to "White Rabbit." But then the woman came closer and shimmied when Josie shimmied, and shook when she shook. They made eye contact, and in a moment they were dancing together.

"Well, why not?" Josie thought. "Get me drunk enough, I'd screw a grizzly bear tonight!"

When the song was over, the dark-haired woman whispered in her ear, "Let's get out of here. Go someplace."

"In a little while," Josie told her. "Right now I want to dance."

"You like to shake those buns, darling?"

"That's right. I love it . . . I *love* to dance!"

Midnight at Garden of the Gods Park in Colorado Springs was another matter. As Dr. Fred J. Doron walked with an over-size flashlight along the path to the special place, he was thinking angrily that it was cold as a witch's tit and dark as a well-digger's asshole! This was no night for a Christian to be out of bed.

"You're in serious doo-doo, boy!" he declared aloud after he stumbled on the uneven ground. The special place where he was headed was a hilltop in the park from where there was a great view of the mountains, at least during the day. He and Luke used to come here when Luke was a little boy. Just the two of them, for Fred had been the sort of father who spent a lot of time with his boys—Luke most of all, because Luke had been his favorite. This is what hurt Fred beyond measure. Lord, they had tossed footballs and gone on overnight hikes! Why, one season they even drove clear up to Denver to see every single home game the Broncos played that year, watching from seats that were pretty damn close to the fifty-yard line. And now the kid was trying to destroy him.

"You're trying to *destroy* me, Luke!" Fred bellowed as he climbed the path. "I know you're up there, boy! I just *know* it!"

Fred was breathing hard by the time he reached the top of the hill. Sure enough, Luke was standing in the clearing, in the exact spot, the special place where Jesus had appeared to the boy when he was nine years old. Luke always came here when he needed to think. Always. Fred had been with Luke on that

long-ago afternoon; he didn't see Jesus himself, of course, because he was an adult and had committed a few sins in his
time, and though his heart was in the right place, he was no
longer what you might call entirely pure. But even Fred had
felt something that afternoon, he honestly had, when his stepson had fallen to his knees and his unblemished child's face
had filled with utter radiance. Lord, it was spooky! It was like
there were angel wings beating in the air. Afterward, neither
Fred nor Luke ever told a soul about what had happened. Not
Dwight, nor Fred's wife, Cathy. Nobody.

"Turn off the flashlight, Father," Luke told him.

"I hope you're praying, boy! I *seriously* hope you're praying," Fred told him sullenly. But he flicked off the flashlight,
and now they were both only shadows in the velvety darkness.

"It wasn't my doing," Luke said. His voice was even and
calm.

"Hell, it wasn't! Where have you hidden that child? . . .
damn, I'm out of breath!"

Fred found himself gulping in air. Being so angry and shouting and climbing the hill all at the same time had completely
tuckered him out.

"Careful, Father. Anger is a sin," Luke told him.

As Fred's eyes became accustomed to the dark, he could see
Luke better the longer he stood there. The boy had become a
stranger to him—this tall, pale young man with the face of a
saint.

"Why are you trying to destroy me, son? My God, I had
cops in my office all afternoon. The damn FBI even! They're
going through all our records, everything! . . . do you understand what I'm telling you? These people, because of what
you've done, they're going to put us under a microscope. And
they're not going to stop until they know every damn thing
about us! . . . I mean, are you crazy? Didn't this cross your
mind even slightly before you grabbed that lady doctor's
brat?"

"This isn't my doing, Father. This is the Lord's work."

"Don't lie to me!" Fred thundered. He had gotten so he
hated it when Luke spoke of Jesus. But he forced himself to
keep his voice down, since he didn't want to broadcast family
problems to the entire world.

"Worse even than the cops," he hissed, "I had a dozen phone

calls this morning from some of our biggest contributors asking what the hell we're up to, calling attention to ourselves
right at this time when there are all kinds of deals in the
works . . . all sorts of things you don't even really know
about. . . ."

"Oh, I *know* . . . I know all about your big contributors too.
And the money, money, money you get from them. That's
what you're all about, isn't it, Father?—money. You're all getting rich, you and your friends. And the tragedy is, the kingdom of heaven is slipping away, so far away. . . ."

"I don't need any damn sermon from *you*, Luke!"

"No? Then perhaps I should save my sermon for your small
contributors, all those sad, beguiled souls who keep sending
you their hard-earned cash to do Jesus's work here on earth. I
wonder how they would feel if they discovered their money is
being invested in shopping malls and ski resorts. . . ."

Fred Doron was hardly able to breathe. It was unbelievable,
hearing Luke speak to him like this.

"You've done this deliberately, haven't you?" he cried in
astonishment. "You *are* trying to destroy me!"

Luke Doron narrowed his cold blue eyes to his father's, and
a cruel smile appeared on his lips. "Dad, let me tell you something," he explained quietly. "*You* are the only person destroying yourself. You don't need me to do that, you don't even
need Jesus. You're greedy, you're ignorant, and you're absolutely empty inside. "

Without thinking, Fred Doron slapped his stepson hard
across his face with his open hand. Luke staggered and fell to
his knees, with blood around his nose and mouth. He seemed
dazed for a minute and unfocused. Then he rose to his feet, and
when it looked as if his father was going to hit him again, he
calmly offered his other cheek.

This was more than Fred Doron could bear. Terrified, he
turned on his flashlight and jogged heavily down the hill to the
safety of his Cadillac DeVille.

Midnight at Dr. Alison Hampton's house, Howie sat exhausted, almost catatonic, at the wooden table in Alison's
kitchen. There was a uniformed state policeman on one side of
him, and Jack Wilder on the other.

None of the three men heard Alison as she came barefoot

down the stairs from her bedroom—not even Jack, though his hearing was very sharp. Alison was dressed only in her white nightgown, and she moved with the stealth of a jungle cat. She stepped quietly to the bookshelf in the living room and stood on tiptoe to reach for Norman Mailer's *The Naked and the Dead* on the top shelf. She pulled out the novel and then the .38 revolver that was hidden behind the book.

Jack was the first to hear something wrong.

"What's happening in the living room, Howie?"

Howie looked in time to see Alison running toward the front door with the gun in her hand. She looked so much like a hallucination, it took a moment for him to move. By the time he found his crutches and went bounding after her, Alison was already outside in the driveway running quickly toward the road.

She had decided to kill a few Christians for a Moral America. As many as she could get. It was the only thing she could think of that might give her a little relief. She began firing the revolver as soon as her bare feet touched the main road. The first shot was a disappointment, as the hammer came down with a dull click on an empty chamber. But the next round fired with a deafening roar. The kickback of the pistol made the barrel fly upward in her hands. She lowered the barrel more carefully, pointed the gun toward the place in the road where the protesters had been marching so relentlessly during the past few days, and began firing round after round, all five bullets in the gun. It was an orgy of smoke and noise. But when the smoke cleared, she saw that the road was empty.

The Christian vigil had pulled up camp and gone home hours earlier, at the first news of the kidnapping. Alison screamed in frustration as Howie came up alongside her and took the gun from her hands. She fell to her knees, she pulled her hair, she howled with rage. But her rage was futile. Like shooting bullets at a ghost . . . some unseen spirit of midnight air.

2

The great media invasion of San Geronimo began on the day after the kidnapping. By morning an army of sleek vans with satellite dishes affixed to their roofs appeared in town and could be seen cruising the streets, stopping occasionally to interview anyone who had anything to say about the crime, no matter how trivial or repetitious. It was a huge story, the kidnapping of an abortionist's child, stirring up anger on both sides of the contentious divide.

On the afternoon following the kidnapping, Howie sat with Jack around the same heavy wooden table in Alison's kitchen, where they had sat the night before; it seemed to him that time and motion had ceased. Howie had missed a night of sleep and exhaustion gave everything a dreamlike clarity. Sunlight was streaming in the large solar window, filtering through Alison's private jungle of green growing plants. He knew he would remember these things forever: the banana tree in a huge pot by the window; the orange tree near the refrigerator. And on the kitchen table itself, among their cups of coffee, a half-dozen avocado pits sprouting in jars filled with dirty water, like a science experiment gone amok.

Howie blamed himself desperately. How could he have let Angela out of his sight in the park? The enormity of his failure burned in his chest and gave an unhealthy glow to his cheeks. Alison was upstairs sleeping, thank God. After her raging hysteria last night, shooting at shadows in front of her house, a doctor had been summoned to give her an injection that knocked her out, and he had returned with another needle in the morning. Outside in the front yard, the driveway was crowded with police vehicles. Farther away, on the road itself, stood a dozen media vans and cameras trained on the house waiting for something, anything to happen. It was hard for

Howie to conceive of such perfect specimens of humanity, these squarely handsome six o'clock newsmen and women with their superb speaking voices and plastic bodies. Howie hated them on principle and wished they would go away.

It had become a waiting game now for Howie and Jack, just as it was for the reporters outside. Waiting for the kidnapper to make the next move. Waiting for a forensic report from the police lab. Waiting for some big shot to show up from the Denver office of the FBI. Howie felt that at any moment he might start shooting at shadows himself; it would be better than sitting here endlessly, staring at the dismal avocado pits on the table. He closed his eyes and must have fallen asleep in his chair, because suddenly there was a commotion and several strangers had appeared in the kitchen.

"Jackerooni! You old son of a bitch! Good to see you, man!"

"Kevinski, my friend!

Jackerooni? . . . Kevinski? Was this some sort of strange tribal greeting between law enforcement personnel? Through bleary eyes, Howie saw Jack shaking hands with a mild-looking middle-aged man who was dressed in a tweed sports coat and brown slacks. Howie wondered if they were giving each other a secret handshake.

"Kevin, this snoring kid is my assistant, Howard Moon Deer . . . Howie, say hello to Special Agent Kevin Neimeyer."

Special Agent Neimeyer looked to Howie more like a small-town pharmacist than his idea of an FBI investigator. He had a bullet-shaped head that was bald and shiny on top, with a narrow ring of dark curly hair around the ears. He wore thick glasses. Howie was struck by his sheer ordinariness, yet he must be important because there were two young FBI agents in suits hovering around him in a very respectful attitude, waiting to do his bidding. All three men pulled up chairs to the table and sat down.

"Howie, you'd better put on another pot of coffee," Jack suggested. "We're in for a long haul."

Three hours went by while Kevin Neimeyer's two aides took notes, and Jack and Howie recounted every detail of the events that had led them from Doobie Rock to this table in Dr. Alison Hampton's kitchen: from the murder of Senator Hampton to the apparent murder-suicide of Crystal and Donny Henderson, Alison's troubles with the right-wing Christian group, the kidnapping, the mysterious Millennium Investment Corporation, and the shadowy figure who had tried to kill Howie as he was driving home from Colorado Springs. Kevin had heard some of this before in pieces over the telephone with Jack, but he wanted to put the story as much as possible into a clearer sequence.

Kevin Neimeyer was a careful listener, cocking his head thoughtfully to one side, chewing on the end of a ballpoint pen and interrupting occasionally to ask a question or give an instruction to one of his two aides. Once Jack and Howie had told their story, Kevin recounted what the Bureau had done so far. There was still a forensic crew examining the crime scene at Ernie Martinez Municipal Park, but it would be several days, perhaps weeks, before all the information was sifted through and sorted out. Meanwhile the area around the park had been canvassed, and neighbors asked if they had seen or heard anything unusual yesterday afternoon. So far no witness had come forward with anything helpful.

All these facts seemed very tedious to Howie. Personally, he was in a mood for something big and conclusive. Grand deeds, a daring rescue. But Jack and his law-enforcement buddies were more into a painstaking study of minute details. Particular attention was being given to how the kidnapper had arrived at the park, where he (or she) had hidden while watching the children play, and how the "perp" (as Jack and Kevin tended to call this genderless individual) had delivered the note in the Dr Pepper can. The park apparently had two entrances—the main entrance was by the parking lot along Martinez Street, but there was also a small back gate from Carson Road, a narrow street that bordered the eastern edge of the park. A rusted chain-link cyclone fence enclosed the park, but it was old and sagging, and there were many places where a person could easily climb in and out, and be hidden in the dense brush. There was also an overgrown path that passed along the outside perimeter of the fence and exited into Carson Road, where a car or van might have been waiting. It was possible that this was how the kidnapper had managed his or her invisible approach and escape.

It was a struggle for Jack in his blindness to visualize the dimensions of the park, the precise distances from the parking lot to where the children had been playing, and to the various entrances and possible hiding places. It took a good deal of time for Kevin and Howie to describe to Jack every possible detail of Ernie Martinez Municipal Park, so that Jack finally had a clear picture in his mind. Another hour went by in this manner, and Howie was astonished to see that Jack and the FBI agents showed no sign of wear. As for himself, he was starting to feel the way he had in college after studying three nights in a row for final exams. All the facts were starting to swim in his head.

"Okay," said Jack at last, holding the immensity of detail in his mind, like a juggler performing a difficult act. "Now, the Dr Pepper can—that was found thirty-five feet west of the back fence, and twelve feet north of the jungle gym?"

"That's right."

"Well, I don't see how it got there," Jack decided. "On the face of it, it's downright impossible!"

"It was weighted down with pebbles," Howie reminded him. "It could have been tossed from the fence."

"Without attracting anyone's attention? I don't believe it. You were hardly more than thirty feet away yourself, Howie—don't you think you would have heard the can hit the ground?"

"Under normal circumstances, sure. But not necessarily with all the noise those kids were making."

"Even so, I still can't imagine that the perp would have risked giving himself away like that." Jack frowned behind his dark glasses, the furrows of his forehead converging into a V above the black plastic frame.

"Well, I'm glad to report we have an honest-to-God clue," said Kevin Neimeyer with a smile.

"A clue, huh? Well, don't keep it from me, please."

"We're talking fingerprints, Jack. On the Dr Pepper can. That's the good news. The bad news is that we have a whole bunch of 'em, too many—maybe the grocery clerk who sold the thing, maybe a bunch of friends who passed it around taking swigs after a game of tennis. God only knows. But here's the intriguing part. One of the prints comes from the right thumb of a young child. It's only a partial, but we should be able to get a match."

Jack's frown grew deeper. "Damn! One of the preschoolers

must have picked up the can at some point during the game of
hide-and-seek . . . probably *moved* the thing!"

"That's about the size of it. So now we need to find out
which kid it was, and where exactly the little darling found the
can originally. We have two child psychologists flying in from
California—we've been holding off interviewing the kids until
they arrive. If their parents don't object, we'll fingerprint the
preschoolers and see if we can get a match from the can. All
this is going to take a few days at best, maybe longer. As you
know, Jack, it's tough as hell working with very young children, not to mention their parents, and unless we're careful,
any evidence we get from a four- or five-year-old will be
thrown out of court anyway."

"You know, Kevin, I can't believe this was just a crime of
opportunity—someone had to plan this snatch carefully, and to
do that they would need advance knowledge of where Angela
was going to be yesterday afternoon."

"I agree. And we're making up a list of everyone who knew
about Buffy Fletcher's birthday party. But take a guess, Jack,
just how many people we have so far?"

"Well, with fourteen children and their families . . . and of
course the teachers at the school . . . I'd say you have maybe
forty names so far."

"Fifty-two, and it's still growing. You have to take into consideration the people who baked the cake—who are fundamentalist Christians, by the way. Even the plumbers who came
to fix Shannon Fletcher's hot water heater, they knew about
the birthday party too . . . it goes on and on. I have a team of
ten agents down here, but I still think we're looking at two or
three weeks just to lay the most basic groundwork in this case.
Unfortunately, that little girl may not *have* two or three
weeks."

"Can you requisition more help?"

"I have another ten agents on their way. This kidnapping has
national priority. Even the President has made a statement
about it. The damn thing's very political, of course. But I still
think we're out of time . . . what we need is a little bit of luck.
And maybe an inspired hunch. That's where I'm hoping you
come in, Jack. You've always been good at hunches. So give
me one now."

"You want a hunch?" Jack asked bleakly. He sighed and

then remained silent for quite a long time. "If I were you, I'd be looking for a Ghost Dancer," he said finally.

Kevin smiled thinly. "Are you talking about an Indian, or some religious nut, or what?"

"I'm talking about a metaphor. Not necessarily an Indian, nor even one of the Christian protesters—though it might be someone from either of these groups . . . I can't give you anything very precise, because this is still too shadowy in my mind. But I'm picturing someone who is dispossessed, angry. There's a chance this is a hate crime against the entire Hampton family. Killing the Senator, terrorizing the daughter, and now snatching the granddaughter. Someone who wants to bring this family to its knees, Kevin. Punish them for being the elite . . . anyway, you asked for a hunch and that's as close as I can come."

"No, I like it, I like it!" Kevin said agreeably. "So let's give our shadow a name and call him the Ghost Dancer—why not? He certainly managed to spirit away that little girl in a ghostly fashion . . . so this Ghost Dancer, tell me, Jack—is he crazy? Is the person we're looking for a madman?"

"Crazy?" Jack repeated. "No, I don't think so. I would say rather that he's . . . inspired."

"Inspired by what?"

"The voice of God. A burning bush. I don't know. But he's following a master plan."

Kevin's smile grew broader. "Well, then, that's just fine and dandy. Because as it happens, I have a candidate I'd like to nominate for the role. A guy who sees burning bushes everywhere he looks."

Special Agent Neimeyer opened his attaché case and pulled out a file. He opened the manila cover to a photograph that he gave to Howie. Howie had seen the picture before: a tall young man with light red hair and cold blue eyes who was standing surrounded by children, with a bow and arrow in his hand.

"Jack, I have a guy here I'd like to describe. Allow me to introduce you to Luke Doron."

3

It was turning into an unpredictable day. Less than an hour after the gargantuan bull session with Kevin Neimeyer, Howie found himself staring out the rear window of a huge American station wagon as they made their way northward through the high empty desert into Colorado.

Howie had the backseat to himself, and he sat sideways with his leg propped up. Jack was asleep in the front passenger seat with his head against the window. This was VIP treatment, Howie supposed, to have use of an FBI car and driver. The driver was a sullen young agent with wraparound dark glasses named Corky Roth. Corky spent the entire drive chewing gum and looking as if he wished he were doing something more useful than driving two physically challenged individuals to Colorado Springs. Certainly the FBI had to be in dire straits to seek the help of a blind detective and an Indian graduate student who had his right leg in a childishly painted plaster cast . . . a cast that Howie could not bear to look at, with its colorful drawing of Little Red Riding Hood and a very pregnant-looking Big Bad Wolf.

Howie tried to stretch out in the backseat and get some sleep, but his leg hurt and his mind was racing. He had been reluctant to leave Alison alone, worrying that she would need him when the tranquilizers wore off. But then Viola, the old Spanish woman, offered to sleep at the house for a few days, and Jack seemed to think this was a good idea. There was something very comforting about Viola; the old woman had an earthy, peasant strength that might be just what Alison needed right now.

Howie felt so useless he wanted to scream. He had failed in his role as bodyguard to the tots. Alison didn't need him, and he wasn't certain how he could be of any help to Jack. Not

knowing what else to do with himself, he reached for the FBI
file that was in his green day pack and read carefully through
it one more time. Hoping for a clue, a miracle . . . anything at
all that might save Angela Hampton.

The patriarch of the family, Dr. Fred J. Doron, was a dentist, it seemed, not a theological doctor as Howie had always
assumed. The man was six feet three inches in height, according to the FBI file, and 240 pounds in girth. There was a color
photograph stapled to the file that Howie found fascinating. It
showed Fred and his two boys, Dwight and Luke, standing together on some perfect summer day in the green foliage of a
park with barbecue smoke rising behind them. In the background there was the blue hint of a lake. Fred was wearing a
frilly apron that looked pretty silly with his huge shoulders and
square beefy face. The top half of the apron had some writing
on it: "JESUS LOVES . . ." But what Jesus loves was cut off by
the frame, leaving this great theological question unsolved.
Does Jesus love his hamburger medium rare? Or would He
love another diet Dr Pepper, please?
    The photograph was evocative, so clear in detail that Howie
could see Fred's nose was crooked from an old break, perhaps
the result of some long-ago game of hardball catch with his
boys. Dwight, the youngest boy, was wearing a tank-top shirt
and a baseball cap backward on his head. He was about to
chomp down on a hot dog; the photograph caught his hunger,
that greedy moment before the first bite, the bun and wiener
poised with relish and mustard, raised expectantly to his
mouth. Luke meanwhile stood on the far side of his father,
taller, slighter in build, more pale in complexion. He was
dressed in a dark blue polo shirt, and there was an enigmatic
smile playing on his lips.
    Despite their godly inclination, there was nothing sancti-
monious about the Doron men. The photograph captured an
outdoor-loving Colorado clan, the sort of all-American family
that would have a speedboat in the yard for tearing up summer lakes, and a fleet of snowmobiles in the garage to roar
through the silent snowy woods in winter. Everywhere they
went, they would leave behind a whiff of gasoline. As for
Jesus, Howie imagined they thought of Him as someone
pretty much like themselves—a big outdoorsy Rocky Moun-

tain Jesus, a kind of Paul Bunyan swaggering through the woods with chain saw in hand.

Howie turned his attention to the text. According to the file, Dr. Fred J. Doron had been born near Alamosa, Colorado on October 24, 1941. His parents operated a small farm that went bust in the mid-fifties, leaving Fred to make his own way in the world. After high school he got a job as a vacuum cleaner salesman in Pueblo, Colorado and supported himself through two years of junior college. Then a stint in the marines, a tour in Vietnam, and an undergraduate degree (bachelor of science) from Adams State College after his release from the armed services.

Fred had then drifted for a number of years before discovering his true calling. He managed a restaurant, sold automobiles, and drove a cement truck, finally deciding to enroll in a small dental college in Colorado Springs. He was thirty-five years old when he opened his first dental office, a late bloomer, but at this point the unique talents of the man came bursting forth. Within five years he had three offices in different sections of Colorado Springs; five years after that, there were eighteen Dr. Doron Dental Emporiums throughout Colorado, mostly in shopping malls. He advertised on radio and television with a clever jingle and a cartoon logo of a dancing tooth with a big smile and a cowboy hat. "The Home of Happy Teeth" was his well-advertised motto. His goal was to be the McDonald's of the tooth trade. You never needed an appointment at a Dr. Doron outlet; you could walk right in off the street. There soon came a time when Dr. Doron personally did very little actual dentistry; it was more expedient to run his growing empire from an office high in a new office building in downtown Colorado Springs.

On the personal side Fred married Cathy Lindstrom in 1971, a pretty blond woman of Norwegian descent who had a seven-year-old child, Luke, from an earlier marriage. Luke's real father was in prison at the time on mail-fraud charges and tax evasion. Left on her own with a young child to support and her ex-husband in prison, Cathy had found Jesus; it was her influence that eventually brought religion to the rest of the family, giving Fred Doron his first inkling that there was a spiritual dimension to life beyond the tending of teeth. For a number of years Dr. Doron appeared quite willing to be a Sunday-only sort of Christian, but all this changed in the early eighties when the evangelical movement started to blossom in Colorado Springs. For Dr. Fred J. Doron, a whole new career was about to begin.

He founded the group, Christians for a Moral America, in 1983, and eventually his two sons, Dwight and Luke, became his lieutenants. The stated purpose of CMA was to unite the dozens of fundamentalist sects in town, from Southern Baptist to the more trendy New Life Church, into a political advocacy group dedicated to creating change in America consistent with Christian belief. Money was necessary for the work—a good deal of money—and once again Dr. Doron proved his genius in this area. It was very clear to him, for example, that Jesus was opposed to environmental regulation, which enabled him to convince various logging and mineral interests in the state to contribute generously to the cause. It was the same with the gun lobby. There were blatant references in the Bible, if you understood them properly, to the need for Christians to arm themselves for the coming Armageddon, the fast-approaching millennium, the year 2000 in which good and evil would battle for supremacy and Jesus would walk again. The National Rifle Association was always pleased to support a cause like this, so in harmony with its own agenda. But most of the money the CMA collected came not from large interest groups but individual donors who were concerned about two terrible sins that were sweeping America: abortion and homosexuality. Whenever it came to either of these hot issues, the money flowed and flowed. And when the flow slowed for even an instant, it was enough to send out brochures with photographs of mangled babies and men with gold rings through their nipples kissing on the streets of San Francisco, for the floodgates to open once again.

How much money, exactly, the CMA had amassed, the FBI could not say. They had various holding companies and investment branches, the chief of which was the Millennium Investment Corporation, which owned shopping malls, an amusement park, an automobile dealership, and several office buildings. The existence of Millennium was a closely guarded secret from the rank-and-file CMA supporters, few of whom suspected the vast extent of the group's financial holdings. But in private, to special donors, Dr. Doron had been heard to say

that Christians could not afford to be dreamers in this terrible
time of sin and sodomy; money was power, and through an aggressive investment policy, the kingdom of Jesus could be
made manifest—if not to the world at large, at least to certain
parts of Colorado, Wyoming, Montana, and Texas.

The FBI file included two interesting paragraphs about the
boys, Dwight and Luke. Dwight, it seems, had been a star receiver on the University of Colorado football team and had
great hopes of being drafted by the NFL until an incident his
junior year put an end to these dreams. He had caught his
sweetheart at a frat party necking with another guy, and with a
few beers to fuel his anger, he threw her down a flight of stairs.
In normal times an incident like this would hardly affect a
young man's football career—the requirements of a winning
football team, of course, supersede all other law and morality
on an American campus. But there was a new woman dean
who was on a personal crusade, and she made a stink about the
episode. The football coach—a man who earned three times
the salary of the university president—naturally was furious to
lose his star player, but in this instance there was nothing he
could do. Dwight was benched for the rest of the season, and
although he played once again his senior year, his heart
seemed to be gone from the game and the NFL passed him by.
In the years that followed, Dwight carried with him the sullen
mark of a man whose true ambitions had been obstructed. He
was a victim, he believed, of international Marxist-lesbianism.

Luke Doron, who had adopted his stepfather's last name,
followed a more gentle path through life. He was a graduate of
Oral Roberts University, where he played no sport more ferocious than archery, shooting at leisurely straw targets with a
colored circle marking the bull's-eye. He seemed a truly pious
young man, volunteering his time to a variety of Christian or-
ganizations. Which was why everyone was surprised when he
married a buxom blond cheerleader from Houston, Texas
named Darlene Higbee, who sang a sultry alto in the Houston
Christian Youth Choir. They met during a Sing For Jesus Fes-
tival in Dayton, Ohio—Luke was a tenor in the Oral Roberts
University Choir.

Such was the extent of the file: a clever dentist and his boys,
their women, and a whole lot of money. The FBI had not been
able to find the CMA guilty of breaking a single law; the file

existed only because the Bureau had made it a policy in recent years to keep a watch on militant right-wing groups. Howie was pondering these matters when a small color snapshot fell out of the file—somehow it had gotten loose and been stuck between the pages. It showed Luke and Darlene Doron marching together outside an abortion clinic in Oklahoma City, probably a romantic occasion for a zealous Christian couple. Howie was surprised to recognize Darlene; she was the blond receptionist from the Millennium office at Manitou Mall, the one he had thought of so amusingly as a Republican sex goddess. But there was something about her, and Howie was so spaced-out he didn't remember at first what it was. Then he remembered. My God, she was the one . . .

The car phone began beeping. Corky answered and then handed it over to Jack.

"Yeah?" said Jack with a loud yawn. Then he closed his mouth and listened carefully. "Hmm . . . yeah, that's interesting . . . no, I'm getting sort of accustomed to coincidence in this case, Kevin. When will you know for sure? . . . okay, we'll talk later."

Jack handed the phone back to Corky and turned around to Howie.

"Try this one on for size, Howie. It's looking very possible that CMA was the right-wing group that funded the smear campaign against Senator Hampton in 1984, the one that got him unelected. That was Kevin—he's in Santa Fe right now, checking it out. This case is like a ball of yarn that keeps getting tighter and tighter . . . are you awake, Howie?"

"Wide awake."

"It's going to be tricky, getting any hard facts about these people. Groups like CMA have turned paranoia into a fine art. What we need is some sort of wedge. Some way to get inside these people, pry them open . . ."

"I got one."

"What do you mean, you got one?"

"I got a wedge, Jack. I know how to make them talk."

"You do?" Jack asked skeptically.

"I do," Howie assured him.

4

_____

What they did really wasn't very nice. This disturbed Howie when he thought about it later because he considered himself a civilized person, someone who took the high road. In desperate moments it was worrisome how easily the pretense of fine behavior crumbled, and for the sake of expediency one took any road at all.

At six o'clock on Thursday morning, after a brief night in a Colorado Springs motel, Agent Corky Roth drove Jack and Howie to a town house in an expensively manicured subdivision of homes near the Garden of the Gods Park. Dawn was still only a gray hint in the eastern sky, and the air was cold, blowing into town from the direction of the Front Range Mountains. Corky parked the station wagon across the street from the town house, and then the three of them settled back into companionable silence and waited, sipping coffee from 7-Eleven in paper cups, and munching on donuts that were hardly anything but sugar and air. Howie was surprised to see Jack, who was one of the world's great food snobs, consume such empty calories—hardly what Jack would condescend to call breakfast back home. Was it de rigueur, Howie wondered, perhaps an old law enforcement tradition to eat junk food on a stakeout?

The town house they were watching belonged to Luke and Darlene Doron. It had a redwood exterior and a patch of lawn and a few shrubs in front, exactly like every other house on the block. It appeared to Howie the perfectly generic home for your young professional, two-car, two-job, we've-only-just-begun suburban family. At seven o'clock a light went on in the upstairs bedroom. More lights followed downstairs in rapid succession. Howie yawned and waited. He imagined they must be taking showers inside and eating breakfast. Grape-Nuts,

Howie decided, and big glasses of reconstructed, glow-in-the-dark orange juice. Perhaps even some nice microwave waffles smothered with margarine and imitation maple syrup. Howie filled the long minutes by pondering such diabolic culinary possibilities. Luke's father, Fred, would doubtlessly prefer a dinosaur diet of eggs and bacon, high in fat but at least you could call it more or less natural; it was the new generation that was sliding down the path of plastic inevitability.

Jack interrupted these meditations, asking Howie to read him the most recently updated FBI report, a computer printout that had been delivered to their motel at five o'clock that morning. In flat governmental prose, the report gave a detailed synopsis of a series of separate interviews with Dr. Fred J. Doron and his two boys. All three Dorons vigorously denied any knowledge of either the kidnapping, Senator Hampton's murder, or slitting the throat of Rusty, Alison Hampton's dog. A good deal of effort had been taken to establish the exact whereabouts of each of the Doron men during the time these crimes had been committed. The father had a fair alibi for each of the three incidents; he was snowed-in in a Montana cabin with a well-known Colorado industrialist at the time of the April murder and the night the bloody words were written on Alison's window; as for the time of the kidnapping, he had been involved in a long business lunch with three other men at a steak house in Colorado Springs from twelve-thirty to nearly two-thirty on Tuesday afternoon. On the face of it, it appeared as if Dr. Doron could not be directly involved in any of the crimes.

The boys were another matter. Luke was covered for the time the dog's throat was slit, but he claimed to be driving by himself from Colorado Springs to Albuquerque on the morning of April 1; on the Tuesday afternoon of the kidnapping, he admitted being in San Geronimo giving a pep talk to the protesters outside of Alison Hampton's house. As for Dwight, he could account adequately for his whereabouts on April 1 and the evening the dog was killed, but he also was in San Geronimo on the afternoon Angela was kidnapped—running various errands in town, he said, at Wal-Mart and other stores. But so far, no witnesses from these stores had been found to support his alibi for the vital time.

Along with these notes on the Doron men, there were also

nearly fifteen pages concerning the ongoing investigation at Ernie Martinez Municipal Park. Most of the information seemed inconsequential to Howie—endless interviews with neighbors, some of whom might have seen something, or might not. One old lady reported a suspicious-looking panel truck parked near her house on Tuesday about noon; two agents checked it out, and discovered the truck belonged to High Desert Satellite TV, who were installing a satellite dish in a nearby house. More promising: two teenagers who had skipped school on Tuesday had observed a gray van parked on Carson Road about eleven-thirty a.m. Agents R. Browne and T. Lester had spent half a day tracking down this lead, only to discover that the van belonged to a certain elderly gentleman, Kenneth Montoya, who had parked briefly on Carson Road to read a girlie magazine away from the prying eyes of his wife. Poor Mr. Montoya was still being checked out, but it appeared that he and his aging libido had simply been in the wrong place at the wrong time.

And on and on it went. Naturally all the really gung-ho CMA protesters would be investigated as well, starting with the three individuals who had burst into the Blue Mesa Café with the animal afterbirth. Howie was astonished at the dull, dogged persistence of a criminal investigation. So many men and women knocking on doors, gathering odd, unrelated facts. It seemed impossible that he and Jack might come across anything the others had missed. Howie was still reading the report when Luke Doron stepped out of his front doorway dressed in a well-tailored light gray suit, looking every inch the model young businessman. Howie was tempted to jump out of the station wagon, pound the bastard senseless, and simply demand where Angela was.

"Easy!" Jack murmured, sensing his rage.

"I'm cool, Jack. A model of restraint . . ."

Luke carried a black leather attaché case in one hand, threw open the garage door with the other, and in a moment pulled out of the driveway in the dark blue late model American car that Howie had seen in the Manitou Mall parking lot. Howie hated to let him go, but Luke was not their prey this morning.

Ten minutes later—at exactly 8:23 a.m., according to their log—Darlene Doron came out the same front door and made her way to the second car in the garage, a compact Chevrolet convertible. Darlene was wearing a beige skirt with a tight green sweater, and her yellow hair was tied back in a ponytail, more simply arranged than when he had last seen it. Her breasts seemed to lead the way as she walked to her car, and Howie once again found himself doubtful that they were entirely the work of nature.

"Man, look at *that!*" Corky said appreciatively. This was plainly his sort of girl: a silicone goddess, a pinup dream.

"Stop her!" Jack ordered curtly.

"My pleasure."

Corky fired up the engine and swerved quickly across the street into the driveway, blocking her exit. He jumped out of the station wagon, holding up his badge. "FBI, ma'am!" he told her. "We'd like to have a few words with you."

She looked unhappily from Corky with his badge, to Jack with his dark glasses, to Howie with his broken leg and crutches.

"Who are you?" she demanded, turning her attention upon Jack. "I talked with people from the FBI yesterday, and *you* don't look like FBI to me . . . and you neither," she said turning to Howie. "You're that Indian who came into my office with that cock-and-bull story about building a ski resort in the Black Hills!"

"Darlene Doron," Jack announced in his most official voice, "look at me, and listen very carefully to what I'm going to tell you. You are in serious trouble."

"Oh, yeah? And why am I in trouble?"

"Because I know everything about you."

She laughed in his face.

Jack lowered his voice delicately. "Darlene, I know about your affair with Dwight, your sexual relationship with your brother-in-law."

Her mouth opened in astonishment. "My *what?*" she cried.

Jack repeated his accusation, but not so delicately. "You've been screwing Dwight. And that really isn't very nice."

Howie noticed that Darlene's orange tan had turned a kind of lemonade pink.

"You . . . you take that back!" she sputtered. "I'm a decent Christian woman, and I refuse to listen to these insinuations!"

"You *are* going to listen, and do you know why, Darlene?—

because if you *don't* play ball with me, I'm going to tell your
husband exactly what you do in your free time. Can you imagine the scandal this is going to make for your Christians for a
Moral America? You think people are still going to mail in
their checks once this gets out?"

"Luke won't believe a word of it! You're nuts, mister. And
you can't prove a thing."

"You don't think so? As it happens, the Bureau has some
very explicit photographs of you and Dwight together. At this
very moment the photos are in an envelope on an airplane that
is flying here from Washington . . . what time are those photographs due to arrive, Corky?"

"The ETA is within the next hour," Corky said crisply.

They were both lying, of course; there were no photographs,
and Howie didn't think this was going well. It certainly wasn't
like the confrontation he had imagined in the car yesterday
when he remembered the flirtatious body language between
Dwight and Darlene at Manitou Mall. After watching them together that day, it had been quite a surprise for Howie to discover that Darlene was married to Luke, not Dwight. But
maybe he had misread the signals. Who could say? Perhaps
there was nothing more at stake here than a mild attraction between a brother and sister-in-law. Howie did not have enough
experience in this sort of confrontation to realize how easily
someone could call your bluff; this great plan of his was looking like a total flop.

But then the conversation swerved in a new direction.

"Are you blind?" she asked Jack nervously. There was an
audible shudder in her voice, as though it was very spooky to
her that someone might be less than body perfect.

For an answer Jack removed his dark glasses, revealing his
dead eyes and scars.

"Dear Lord in heaven!" she cried, looking away quickly.
"What do you want from me?"

"I just want some truthful answers to a few questions."

"Will you put your glasses back on?"

"If you answer my questions."

She seemed to be furiously calculating the odds. She had no
idea, of course, how little they really knew. Howie was certain
she was about to laugh and drive away. But between his threats

and his blindness, Jack had succeeded in unnerving Darlene Doron. Quite unexpectedly, she caved in.

"You'll give me the photographs and go away?"

"That's right."

"You have to protect me. He'll kill me if he finds out."

"Luke will kill you?"

"Not Luke . . . *Luke* doesn't care! Luke is impotent, for crying out loud! Or celibate, or whatever the hell he calls it. My God, I'd still be a damn virgin if it had been left up to Luke Doron! . . . it's *Fred* who'll kill me!"

"I sympathize, Darlene," Jack slipped his dark glasses back onto his nose. "Shall we go inside your house and talk this over?"

"You know what this is? This is downright blackmail, mister!"

Jack nodded. "Yes," he admitted. "That's it exactly. Blackmail."

She wasn't very bright, Howie decided. A blond Texas cheerleader in the youth choir who had been impressed by the Doron money and thought she was moving up in the world when she married Luke. But what she got was a sexless marriage, a horny brother-in-law who had finally seduced her after a long siege, and a father-in-law she described as "a bad man."

"Bad in what way? Tell me about Fred Doron, please," Jack urged.

"Well, he's a fake, that's all. He doesn't care about Jesus, or the Bible, or the Commandments, not really —all he thinks about is money. Luke's the only real Christian in the whole family! But of course, Luke's kind of crazy, I guess, so maybe it doesn't count. . . ."

They were sitting in Darlene's living room, which was as perfect as a department store showroom: matching settees, a coffee table and lamps that looked as if they had been bought all together, part of a pre-packaged living room suite. The motif was Early American as visualized by Sears.

"You say Luke is a little crazy? What do you mean exactly?"

"Well, take the sex thing. I mean, I *tried* to have a normal married life with Luke, but whenever I . . . you know, did stuff to sort of get him in the mood, he'd only get angry. And I mean, *angry,* like I was the Devil or something. He said bodies were impure and that he was following the immaculate path of Jesus Christ. Sometimes I almost think Luke believes he *is* Jesus! And, I mean, *that's* a sin—isn't it?"

"I would think so," Jack agreed. "Certainly, he should have at least warned you that he planned to remain celibate before you got married."

"Yes, that would have been nice!" she said archly. "To tell you the truth, I think it was his father's idea that he get married in the first place. For appearances, you know. Luke probably didn't want to at all . . . you know, I'm not really such a bad person. But what's a girl supposed to do after a while?"

"Anyone in your situation would do the same." Jack had done a neat job of transforming himself into the sort of person a young woman might confide in. "So Luke is extremely religious. . . ."

"*Saint* Luke, I call him!"

Jack laughed obligingly. "It must be difficult for Saint Luke to put up with Fred and Dwight's cupidity."

"Cupidity?" she asked. "You mean, like in Cupid?"

"The word means avarice, Mrs. Doron. Greed," Jack told her. As his politeness increased, he had gone in an odd backward motion from her first to her married name. "I'm talking about Christians for a Moral America raising huge amounts of cash under false pretenses. As a true believer, this must have caused Luke some anguish."

"Oh, you bet it has! Why, Luke gets just about beside himself whenever he thinks of all those decent Christian people getting milked like that! And you know what the money is for, don't you? All those millions of dollars that Fred's been raising?"

"No, what is it for?"

"Well, this is the absolute worst of it—it's for a *ski* resort!" she confided to Jack. "Can you imagine that?"

"Why, that's terrible," he agreed. "But I don't quite understand. From what I know, your father-in-law's company, the Millennium Investment Corporation, put a bit over two million dollars into San Geronimo Peak in the early eighties. But surely that doesn't have anything to do with the money he's concerned with now?"

"Oh, that was *other* money, that was just some small

change. I guess you haven't heard the news, what they're building now?"

"Down at San Geronimo Peak? No, I don't think I have."

She lowered her voice: "A casino! Can you imagine that? For gambling and all."

"A casino!" Jack exhaled. His brain was racing like a roulette wheel, looking for a lucky number. "Ah, yes! A casino!" he repeated softly. He leaned closer to Darlene. "But, of course, gambling's not legal in New Mexico."

She leaned closer to him. "But it *is* legal," she assured him. "At least, on Indian land."

"Yes, that's true. Unfortunately, San Geronimo Peak isn't on Indian land."

"Well, that's the funny thing. Just a small part of it *is*—way up high on the mountain. At least that's what I've heard Fred tell Dwight. I've never actually been down there myself."

"I think I know the spot, Mrs. Doron. It's called Phoenix Rock. Sometimes the locals call it Doobie Rock."

"Yes, that's it."

"But surely it would be impossible to build a casino up there? Why that must be—what, Howie? Eleven thousand feet?"

"At least," Howie agreed. "And I've seen people there get higher still."

Jack raised a disapproving eyebrow at Howie for this remark. But Darlene didn't notice. She continued:

"The plan is to build an aerial tramway so people can go up and down the mountain to the casino all year-round. I understand there's really a lovely view from on top."

"Why, yes, there is, Mrs. Doron. You can see for miles."

"Besides the casino, they're going to build a restaurant, a hotel, a gift shop. Turn it into a kind of theme park, you know."

"Who exactly is going to turn it into a theme park? You're talking about CMA?"

"Fred's hoping to finance it, yes. And have much more direct control of the management down there. That's why he's been working so hard to keep the donations coming in just now, because it's going to take a huge amount of money. But he says it's going to be a real gold mine. And being on Indian land and everything, they won't even have to pay normal taxes."

"It sounds like quite an opportunity," Jack agreed. "Of course the status of Indian gaming is a hot issue in New Mexico. The laws could easily change."

Darlene shrugged. "Fred doesn't think so. CMA controls a lot of politicians down there who will vote the way he says. It's all those Spanish people in New Mexico," she confided. "You can buy 'em a dime a dozen—that's what Fred says anyway."

"I'm not sure he can entirely count on that, Mrs. Doron."

"Well, Fred says that even if Indian gambling is outlawed eventually, a few good years and they'll never have to worry about money again. After that, the aerial tramway will make a bundle even without the casino."

"Very interesting. But what did Senator Hampton think of all this? From what I know of the Senator, he was quite an environmentalist. I can't imagine him in favor of turning his mountain into a kind of Las Vegas in the sky."

"Oh, he was against it. Dead set against it . . . but of course, he's no longer around to object."

"Yes, and isn't that convenient?" Jack observed. "Have you heard your father-in-law say anything about the particulars of Senator Hampton's death?"

Darlene shook her head. "Only that the Lord's hand was clearly at work there. He thinks the heirs will be much easier to deal with."

"The heirs. You mean . . ."

"I believe there are two sisters who have inherited the resort. Meanwhile, Fred's been pushing Dwight and Luke to intensify the protest in Albuquerque. Without breaking any laws, of course."

"You're going too fast for me. What's the connection between the ski resort and the abortion clinic?"

"Oh, that's where all the money is coming from! Don't you understand? They have to march around there to stir up the faithful and get the donations coming in. To tell the truth, CMA really needed to make a kind of showy Christian gesture right now, because some of the members have begun to grumble about how commercial everything's become. The antiabortion protest was just what the doctor ordered, you might say. . . ."

"The doctor?"

"Oh, I don't mean *her*. I'm just speaking in a general way. What was needed to get everybody opening their checkbooks to give to the cause."

"A lot of your money just arrives in the mail?"

"A whole lot. This is big business we are talking about. Anyway, that's what Luke tells me. He really hasn't been very happy about it. Fred keeps saying, you have to be practical, this is what we need to finance some big changes in America. But Luke says, how can you talk about change when you're building a house of sin? Of course, the Bible says, 'Honor thy father.' So Luke feels he doesn't have much choice except to go along."

"That must be quite a dilemma for Luke," Jack agreed. "Mrs. Doron, you have been very helpful. I know I'm going to have more questions for you later, but as I'm sure you'll understand, right now our primary concern is for the safety of Angela Hampton. Can you tell me where she is?"

"The little girl? You think . . . oh, my God! CMA would never, *never* do something like kidnap an innocent child!"

"But you've just been telling me, Mrs. Doron, how corrupt they are. Why wouldn't they kidnap a child?"

"Because it's the opposite of what Fred wants! Don't you see? This is going to ruin him! No one's going to give a dime now to a bunch of crazy extremists . . . or maybe a few people will, but not the really wide support Fred needs to raise the sort of money he's counting on. The goal I've heard Dwight mention is twenty million dollars, and I know they're short. That little girl may not know it, but she's pretty much killed this deal for CMA!"

Jack was nodding energetically. "Yes, I see! . . . you know, I've been looking at this whole thing backward. Kidnapping Angela wasn't meant to *further* CMA at all—it was meant to ruin them, to stop this casino and tramway from ever happening. And there's just one person I can think of, Mrs. Doron, who might be angry enough to want to wreck everything."

"Luke?" she asked anxiously.

"Luke," he agreed.

5

Howie knew he had been in mid-America too long when he found himself salivating at the thought of an Egg McMuffin. Half an hour later Corky was pulling up in front of a McDonald's drive-through window for a bag full of breakfast goodies when his cell phone began making a strange *cheep-cheep* sound, like a sick plastic chicken. It was Special Agent Neimeyer. Corky answered and passed the phone to Jack.

"Jack, I'm in the air right now flying up from Santa Fe," Kevin said quickly. "I'll be in the Springs in half an hour. We got a break, and we're moving fast."

"What's up?"

"It's the state police lab in Albuquerque. They got a match for one of the prints on the Dr Pepper can. It's Luke Doron, all right—he obliged us by leaving a nice impression of his left index finger. The print's mixed in with a lot of smears of other people who touched that can at one time or another, but it's good enough for me. I've got a warrant, and we're going to pull him in as soon as I arrive."

"Wouldn't it be wiser to wait and see if he'll lead us to Angela?"

"We debated that one, Jack, and decided it was too risky. This particular decision came from above, that it was best to pick him up now, let him know the game is up and that if he can produce the little girl, it will be *very* much to his advantage."

"Uh-huh," Jack said thoughtfully.

"Why don't you sound thrilled?"

"No, I *am* thrilled. I think Luke's our boy. But you know how I hate loose ends. Like what about the child's partial that was left on the Dr Pepper can? Any luck chasing that one down?"

"We've managed to print ten of the preschoolers, but so far none of them are a match. With the other three kids, their parents are holding out, saying their precious darling might be traumatized by having their fingerprints taken. And what guarantee do they have the prints won't be used one day by Big Brother to trample little Brittany's civil rights? . . . you get the picture."

"Do me a favor, Kevin—check if that child's partial matches up with Angela Hampton. You have Angela's prints, I presume?"

"Just got them this morning from one of her toys. But they're not in the computer yet." Kevin was silent for a moment. "Are you onto something I don't know about?"

"No, no . . . it's just a wild idea, a real long shot."

"Okay, I'll put someone on it. Listen, I gotta go now, Jack. Let's rendezvous at the Ramada Inn on Academy Boulevard in forty-five minutes—we're going to make that our base for the time being. You can come along when we pull in Luke Doron, if you like."

"Thanks, Kevin, but I'd only be in the way. I'd rather use the time to check one of those loose ends that's nagging at me."

"Oh, yeah? And what loose end is that?"

"Her name is Crystal Henderson."

By late afternoon Howie sensed that this particular loose end was going to take longer than a single day to tie in a tidy knot. Crystal's parents, Sergeant James Hauptman and his wife, Tina, had recently left the Air Force Academy and retired to the Philippines, where the sergeant had once served for several years. This was a disappointment for Jack, since he wanted to talk with them. A few more frustrating hours were wasted trying to track down some of Crystal's old school friends. Jack had come up with several leads—a girl named Robin, who had supposedly been Crystal's best friend in the eleventh grade, and a guy named Tony who had been her boyfriend senior year. But Robin, it seemed, had moved to Phoenix six months before, and Tony had drifted away years ago, God only knew where.

All these minor discoveries took time. By six o'clock that evening, after hours of fruitless conversations, Jack had learned only one item of interest. It came from Crystal's juvenile probation officer, an elderly woman who was willing to talk now that Crystal was dead.

The item was this: When Crystal was fifteen and had her first run-in with the law over drugs, part of her probation was to attend a regular weekend day camp that was organized by one of the local churches to benefit at-risk children. There was a good deal of outdoor recreation designed to keep youthful bodies occupied in healthful ways. One of the activities Crystal was required to attend was archery practice given by a young graduate of Oral Roberts University named Luke Doron.

As it happened, Crystal showed a real talent for the bow and arrow. There was a contest at the end of the year, and she won a bronze medal. Luke was inspired to write a short note to the probation officer that was still in her file: "This is a girl who will hit a big bull's-eye in life, if we can only provide her with the proper motivation!"

At a few minutes past six, Howie took the cell phone to the far end of the Ramada Inn parking lot in hope of privacy. He leaned up against a Dodge van and dialed Alison's number in San Geronimo. To his surprise, Josie answered.

"Josie, it's Howard Moon Deer. I thought I'd give a call to see how Alison was doing."

"Howie! I'm so glad to hear from you. Alison was asking for you a few hours ago, wondering if you and Jack had come up with anything."

"You're staying at the house?"

"Yeah. I came over a few hours ago and sent Viola home. This seemed like a good time for Alison to know she has a sister. Anyway, it's sure better for me—it beats getting drunk at the bars, going crazy with worry about her and Angela."

"How is Alison doing?"

"Not so great. She spent most of the day just pacing back and forth in her bedroom like a caged tiger. I gave her another sedative a little while ago, and she's asleep now, or I'd put her on the phone herself. Do you have any news?"

"Some good news, actually. The FBI is about to arrest Luke Doron, one of the CMA boys. They've found his fingerprints on the soda can where the note was found."

"But what about Angela?"

"Well, there's nothing yet. But we're all very hopeful that once Luke is in custody, he'll tell us where she is. The consensus here is that Luke's a religious nut, but he has a history of mentoring children, and it doesn't seem in his character to harm a little girl . . . look, Josie, do you think you could wake up Alison for just a few minutes? I'd like to tell her this myself, if you don't mind. It might do her some good to know that things are looking brighter."

"You know, Howie, I'd really rather let her sleep. I know your news is encouraging, but it almost seems cruel to wake her when she is just settled down to a few hours of peace. But look, as soon as she stirs, I'll tell her you called and pass on what you've told me. Okay?"

"Well, okay," Howie agreed reluctantly. He added impulsively: "Give her my love, will you? Tell her I'm going to bring Angela back to her . . . tell her I'm not going to let her down."

Josie's laugh was gently mocking. "Of course, Howie. Call back as soon as you hear anything definite."

Howie was leaning on his crutches, turning off the cell phone, when he saw Jack and Corky walk quickly out of the Ramada Inn office toward the station wagon.

"Come on!" Corky shouted to Howie. "Get your ass over to the car! We got a situation on our hands."

"A situation?" Howie asked dumbly. His mind was a little dreamy, still on Alison.

Corky was excited. "Jesus!" he said, "this whole damn thing is about to blow sky-high!"

Josie put down the phone in the living room just as Alison appeared on the second-floor landing.

"Who was that?" Alison asked.

"A reporter. Can you believe the nerve of those people? I told him to get lost."

"There's no news, then? I was hoping Howie would call."

"I'm sure he'll phone as soon as he can, Allie," Josie said in a patient tone.

"I just can't bear this waiting!" Alison bit down hard on the knuckles of her right hand. "I think I'm going to go insane if I don't hear something soon!"

"Oh, Allie! Allie! It breaks my heart to see you like this. Why don't you let me give you a nice back rub? You're just so uptight right now—and it's not going to bring Angela back any sooner, you know, for you to get so stressed-out that you can't function."

"Actually, a back rub sounds wonderful," Alison agreed. "My neck too. I'm so tense I can hardly breathe."

"You just let your sister Josie take care of you . . . good, good care. . . ."

6

Sir Galahad's Castle was located at the edge of a strip mall near the Pro Rodeo Hall of Fame on the north end of town. It was a theme-park restaurant with fantasy turrets, a drawbridge at the front entrance, and a doorman dressed up in medieval armor. As a castle, it owed a good deal more in spirit to something you might find on a miniature golf course than one of those drafty stone buildings in Merry Olde Englande. But authenticity was beside the point. The main reason people went to Sir Galahad's was for its All-U-Can-Eat $5.99 dinner buffet.

It was twilight when Agent Corky Roth drove from the Ramada Inn with his siren screaming and a flashing red light stuck to the top of the station wagon. He pulled into the parking lot outside Sir Galahad's just at that bewitching moment when the multicolored city lights were coming on against a backdrop of red-orange sunset still flaring in the western sky. Howie was struck by the odd beauty of the scene: dozens of white Colorado Springs police cars blocking off the parking lot, their red and blue emergency lights broadcasting a revolving light show against the cartoonish facade of the castle. Overhead a helicopter was beating the air, making slow circles around the besieged building. As Howie watched, the helicopter's searchlight came on for a moment, shining down for some reason upon a huge green inflatable dragon near the drawbridge. The dragon was grinning happily, munching on a giant drumstick. A neon sign near his head constantly wrote, erased, and wrote again: "ALL-U-CAN-EAT . . . ALL-U-CAN-EAT . . . ALL-U-CAN-EAT. . . ."

It seemed to Howie a most peculiar setting for a climactic moment of any kind. Nevertheless, Luke Doron had barricaded himself inside this castle along with Dwight and Fred and several hundred moral Americans, men and boys. They had been feasting and listening to speeches about Christian family values when all hell broke loose. Kevin Neimeyer looked like a man on the verge of a heart attack. He was waiting for Jack and Howie in the parking lot, dressed in a blue blazer with the words FBI written on the back; his tie was askew, his complexion was ashen. When he saw Jack and Howie, he walked quickly to their station wagon.

"Welcome to the nightmare," he said in greeting. "Everything's gone wrong. I'd better fill you in. . . ."

Apparently more than twenty FBI agents had spent most of the morning and all afternoon trying to apprehend Luke Doron, but somehow they kept missing him at his usual haunts. It was difficult to know if he was on the run or simply having a lucky day. Then, after making himself invisible all day, he suddenly appeared at Sir Galahad's Castle. This was a gala night, apparently, the annual CMA Father-and-Sons Banquet, and not an event a Doron boy could easily miss.

The first word that Luke had been spotted came from the two agents who had been tailing Fred Doron all afternoon. They followed Fred to Sir Galahad's from his downtown office, arriving at the restaurant at close to 5:45; a few minutes after that, Luke drove up and went inside. The agents called for help and within ten minutes, every FBI person in Colorado Springs had converged upon the spot.

Kevin, who was one of the first to arrive, debated his options and decided they would simply wait in the parking lot for the banquet to finish and then take Luke into custody as he was leaving the building. After Waco and Ruby Ridge, the Bureau had a horror of situations of this kind; a besieged cult, children inside the building, it simply didn't get any worse. Kevin called in the Colorado Springs police, who sealed off the entire area. When this was accomplished, the law enforcement officers settled in to wait at a discreet distance.

But then the unexpected happened: a ten-year-old kid named Chris Donaldson became restless over dinner, and at 6:12 p.m. walked outside to the family car in the parking lot to fetch his Walkman cassette player. He was a quiet child—worse yet, an observant child—and he managed to get a good look at the small army of law enforcement personnel with riot guns and flak jackets surrounding the building.

A few minutes later a small contingent of men came out to investigate for themselves. They were angry and jacked-full of adrenaline; they demanded to know the meaning of this outrageous assault upon their rights as American citizens. Kevin did his best to defuse the situation, explaining that he wished only to talk with Luke Doron.

"Talk!" one of the men exclaimed. "When you need a whole army to *talk* with a good Christian boy, that's the moment decent people gotta band together and say no way! As Jesus is my Savior, I'm telling you we've had it . . . do you hear me, *had* it with all you people in Washington trying to tell us what to do!"

"Amen to that! . . . Praise be!" said the others. And they marched back inside the castle walls.

The situation went downhill fast. The people inside the restaurant actually seemed to want a confrontation. It was as if they had been preparing for this day for so many years, the inevitable moment when the FBI would appear on their doorstep in riot gear, that now they simply jumped the gun. As far as Kevin was concerned, none of this was necessary. But stopping it was another matter. He got on the bullhorn and did his best to talk sense and be reasonable. He called upon Luke Doron to come out peacefully before anybody got hurt. But a few minutes later, all the lights went off inside the restaurant, and someone fired a pistol shot from a window.

It was insane, but the Christians for a Moral America had decided to make a stand. A single FBI agent had managed to get in a back door into the kitchen, and he reported over a cell phone that the group inside had at least twenty handguns between them, and they were vowing to resist to the end. A mood of hysteria and defiance had taken over the crowd. Many people were praying. Dwight Doron was standing on a table by the All-U-Can-Eat dessert bar, giving angry speeches in which he called upon every free American to stand up and be counted in the war against that evil dictatorship, the federal government.

"How many children are inside?" Jack asked.

"A hundred, at least. Man, we just seem to get drawn into these situations whether we like it or not. Once again, the Bureau is totally up shit creek!"

"Just walk away, then," Jack suggested. "Tell all your agents and the cops to go home, and the CMA will be left with no one to be angry at. It'll make them look pretty silly. And you can pick up Luke Doron another time."

"You know, I'd *love* to walk away—that's the first sane advice I've heard in an hour! But it's too damn late now, Jack. We lost that option when whoever it was fired a shot from the window. Nobody got hurt, but if we leave now, it'll look like we're giving in to intimidation, etcetera. And in the future anyone can push us around. Meanwhile, I've had three calls from Washington in the past ten minutes, and I understand even the President has been apprised of the situation. My orders are to do nothing offensive until the hotshots arrive. We have psychiatrists coming, religious experts, crisis negotiators, the works . . . it's going to be a regular zoo."

"My experience, Kevin, is that the bigger the audience, the more difficult it becomes to back down and lose face."

"Yeah, yeah," Kevin said gloomily. "But what can I do?"

"When do you expect the hotshots to arrive?"

"Within an hour."

"So there's still a little time for common sense. Kevin, I've got an idea. You FBI boys, you know you're sort of a scary lot to an average citizen. But a blind old fart like me, and an Indian kid on crutches with a silly plaster cast—I've been getting the impression recently that we don't frighten anybody much at all."

Kevin stared at Jack in astonishment. "What are you suggesting?"

"When you can't send in the cavalry, sometimes it's the right moment for the lame and the blind."

Kevin scratched the back of his neck. "You know, I could lose my job over this."

"And that would be dreadful, wouldn't it?"

In all his life, Howie had never imagined that one day he would be required to wear a bulletproof vest to enter a restaurant. The vest reminded Howie rather unfortunately of the magic shirts the Ghost Dancers wore to deflect the white man's bullets; he only hoped they were more effective.

He was standing with Jack behind a line of police cars, getting himself fitted up for this new sartorial experience, when Kevin Neimeyer came over to them with a cell phone in hand. Kevin looked exasperated.

"Will you talk to these people, Jack? It's the police lab in Albuquerque—they ran that match you wanted on the diet Dr Pepper can. Frankly, I just don't have time for this right now."

Kevin gave the phone to Jack and then headed off quickly to yet another urgent conference. Jack held the phone to his ear, listened a few moments, grunted several times, then handed the device to the nearest agent. There was an odd expression on Jack's face.

"It's the child's partial on the soda can," he said. "The print belongs to Angela Hampton."

"That's crazy," Howie replied.

"Is it? . . . come on, we'd better get going. A whole lot of people are waiting on us."

Howie led the way, hobbling on his crutches across the asphalt parking lot toward the drawbridge to Sir Galahad's Castle. This was not his idea of fun things to do in Colorado Springs. Jack held onto his arm, and he was certain that together they made a pathetic sight. Jack had taken off his dark glasses to show his scars and let his disability become more obvious. The idea was to make his appearance less threatening, but Howie was afraid it might have the opposite effect. He expected a firestorm of bullets to cut them down at any moment; he was theoretically protected between his neck and belly button, but this still left a lot of body parts he cared about woefully exposed.

"You see what this means, don't you?" Jack asked as they were walking.

"You bet. It means I can be shot in the balls any second. Why the hell don't they make these vests a few inches longer, Jack?"

"I'm talking about Angela. The kidnapper simply *gave* her the can with the note in it and asked her to take it over close to the jungle gym."

"That's crazy. Why should she help someone abduct her?"

"Because she *knew* her kidnapper. She went willingly. Haven't you figured out yet who our Ghost Dancer is?"

"Well, sure. It's Luke Doron. Luke's doing a fine rendition of Jesus driving out the moneylenders from the temple. The thought of his daddy using Christian donations to build a casino was just too much for him. So he flipped out in right-

eous indignation, and now he's bringing down the house—
CMA, Daddy, everything. Busting up the whole damn show."

Jack stopped walking and tugged on Howie's arm. They
were halfway to the drawbridge, and frankly this did not seem
to Howie a very good place to stop.

"That's what we were supposed to think, of course. But
don't you see, if Angela knew her kidnapper, it changes the
whole scenario. . . ."

Just then a high-pitched voice shouted hysterically at them
from inside the building: "No closer! No closer! Or I'll shoot!
I'll shoot!"

Howie recognized the nebbishy figure of the small, nonde-
script man who had carried the bloody surprise to the Blue
Mesa Café. The little man stood in the open doorway with a
huge pistol in his hand. There were two lances with medieval
banners crossed above his head, lending a cartoonish absurdity
to the scene. But the pistol looked horribly real.

"No closer! No closer!" he repeated. Hysteria had given him
an echo; he said everything twice. "I'll shoot you, I'll shoot
you! I will, I will!" he declared.

"We're not armed. We've come with peaceful intentions,"
Jack said in a calm, resonant voice.

"God is watching! God is watching!"

"I'm counting on it," Jack told him. "Would you please inform Dr. Doron that we would like to speak with him? As you
can see, I am blind and my friend here has a broken leg. There
is absolutely nothing about us that should cause you any alarm.
I am certain we can work something out, and no one will get
hurt tonight."

"Wait there! Wait there!"

Jack and Howie waited, and they waited. Eventually the little man returned to bring them inside the castle.

"Okay, okay," he said. "Come in, come in."

It was dark inside the restaurant, only dimly lit with a few
candles and the heat lamps from the buffet line. The heat
lamps sent an eerie orange glow into the room, reflecting off
the food—turkey, roast beef, mashed potatoes, macaroni, fried
chicken, and breaded fish that looked as if it had swum a long,
long way from any ocean. The room was crowded with half-
seen figures in the shadows. Everywhere Howie looked, there

was a mood of repressed excitement, an oddly festive air, as though a long-awaited adventure was about to begin.

In one part of the room, an older man was leading a group in prayer. In another corner someone was saying excitedly, "You see, they're afraid of us really. They sense our power, they know their world is about to collapse, they know they can't prevail against the Lord's wrath . . . don't you see? It doesn't matter if we die here! They *know* we've won! . . ."

This was boys' night out, a Father-and-Sons Banquet gone berserk. There were only a few women in evidence, several terrified waitresses dressed as medieval serving wenches in loose-fitting blouses and long skirts, and they did not seem happy to be working this particular shift. Howie noticed Dwight Doron walking about self-importantly with a pistol in his hand organizing the defenses. There were clearly people in the room who were glad the final Armageddon battle between the forces of good and evil had come at last.

The nebbishy little man led Howie and Jack across the dining room to where Fred Doron was sitting at a table by himself with a candle and a half-eaten plate of food in front of him. Howie noticed he had left his peas on his plate uneaten. Probably it was okay to do that on boys' night out.

"I've brought them, I've brought them!" the little man cried excitedly.

Fred looked up at the small person with a repugnance he did not bother to conceal.

"You should take a deep breath, Arnold, and try to calm yourself. We have a long night ahead of us."

"But I'm so happy, Dr. Doron. I'm so happy! Those people outside think we're laughable just because we believe in the Bible and Jesus Christ. But we're going to show them, aren't we, Dr. Doron?"

"That's right, Arnold. We're going to show them."

Arnold turned his bony face toward Jack and Howie. He was positively gleeful. "You think you're so much better than we are, don't you? But we're going to have the last laugh! We're going to go to heaven, and *you're* going to go to hell!"

"Arnold, *please*!" Fred exclaimed. He seemed at the end of his patience. "Do me a favor and just . . . go . . . away." Arnold scurried away into the shadows. Fred Doron watched him leave with a disgusted look on his face. Finally he turned his attention to Jack and Howie. "Jesus Christ!" he swore profanely. "They send me a blind man and a cripple!"

"A few things for the record," said Jack. "First, my friend Howie here is not a cripple, he merely has a broken leg. Second, it's fine with me if you want to stay in Sir Galahad's Castle forever. You can go through the all-you-can-eat line until you burst on Jell-O salad, as far as I'm concerned. My only interest is finding Angela Hampton."

Fred smiled slightly. It was a very haggard, wary smile, but the corners of his mouth moved in an upward direction.

"Sit down," he offered. "I'd suggest you make yourselves up a plate of food, but frankly the food's pretty god-awful in this joint. We do our Father-and-Sons Banquet every year at Sir Galahad's because it's cheap and the kiddies like it. But I usually have indigestion for days."

Howie helped Jack into a chair, and then he sat down himself at Jack's side. Fred stared at them from across the table, a neutral, contemplative expression on his face, like a poker player trying to figure out a hand. He had removed his sports coat, rolled up his sleeves, and loosened his necktie.

"Let me lay down the ground rules," Fred said. "I'm not exactly sure how this situation is going to resolve, because as you may have noticed, my people are a little riled up. But whatever happens, I'm not giving you my boy, Luke. I want you to understand that from the start. He didn't kidnap the little girl, and I'm not going to hand you any goddamn scapegoat so a bunch of liberal TV reporters can have a field day making him look like some kind of extremist idiot. Do you get that?"

"I do, and I agree completely," Jack told him. "The last thing I want is a scapegoat. It's clear to me that Luke did not kidnap Angela."

Fred was about to say something, but this stopped him.

"What kind of game are you trying to play here?"

"No game at all. I only want to talk with Luke and ask him a few questions that I hope will help me locate the child. Once he answers, Howie and I will be on our way."

"And what about that small army of storm troopers outside?"

"I'll see what I can do to get rid of them. Basically, as far as I know, you people haven't committed any crime except a few weapons violations. It's a pity one of your group fired a pistol

out the window, but under the circumstances, I think I can get
the FBI to overlook that particular fact."

Fred glanced nervously across the room to where Dwight
was organizing a platoon of men to pile up tables and chairs
against the windows.

"I don't know. This has gone a little too far to turn around
easily," he said with a sigh. "Who's going to pay for the damage to the restaurant?"

Jack smiled thinly. "I think I can convince the government
to restore Sir Galahad's Castle to its pristine condition. Personally, I don't see any problems here that can not be resolved.
Unless, of course, you people really are determined to die."

"Hey, *I* don't want to die!" Fred Doron said fervently.
"Look, I tell you what. I'm willing to try to work something
out, but I want my lawyer present, and I want something in
writing that completely exonerates me and my family from this
mess. I run a completely legal, respectable organization, and I
want you to know that I deal with senators and congressmen
and other *very* important people. It's certainly not *my* fault that
a few lunatics have gotten involved with the CMA and are
prone to getting a little wild. Personally, I'm not responsible
for *any* of that. I'm a hardworking Christian businessman
who's trying to make a buck and maybe do a little good for the
world at the same time. . . ."

"Oh, Father! Listen to what you're saying!" It was Luke
Doron, stepping out of a shadow into the dim light of the candle on the table.

"Luke, I told you to let me take care of this, boy."

"Yes, I know what you told me. But I would rather get finished with this comedy. So I suggest I answer the blind man's
questions and perhaps help him see the light. Who knows?
After that, the rest is up to the Lord. As far as I'm concerned,
if this is Judgment Day, so be it."

"Luke, please! I know I haven't always been the father you
wanted to have. But I got a plan, son. We'll leave the rest of
these damn idiots to have a shoot-out with the FBI if they
want, but I'm going to get you and me and Dwight out of this
mess."

Luke Doron laughed joylessly. "Father, you really are piti-
ful. But let me tell you what I'm going to do. I'm going to take
these gentlemen somewhere we can talk without any fuss.

Then I'm going to answer all their questions and see if we can come to some understanding. Personally, I'm not afraid to die, but I don't see what we'd accomplish by dying in Sir Galahad's Castle."

"Amen to that!" muttered Jack.

"Well, what do you want to know?" Luke asked in a surprisingly gentle voice.

They were standing in a circle in a back pantry, an area with boxes full of crackers, candles, salt and pepper shakers, napkins, and other items the waitresses used in the dining room. There were two candles burning on a table next to an automatic drip-through coffee machine—to Howie it looked like an altar to the God of Caffeine. Luke was wearing a tan suit and a blood-red tie that went nicely with his hair. In the candlelight, his gaunt face was almost handsome. He stood calmly watching Jack.

"Tell me about Crystal Hauptman," Jack asked.

"Crystal? Well, poor Crystal . . . she was certainly part of the Lord's plan for me. She taught me everything a young man needs to know about sin."

"Would you mind explaining?"

Luke smiled wistfully. "I met Crystal when she was fifteen and I was twenty-four. I was volunteering time on my weekends to help with a local youth program. Oh, I was very stern in those days, very righteous! But I didn't know a thing about women. Not even a woman of fifteen."

"Am I to understand that you had an affair with Crystal?"

"Yes, that is exactly what you are to understand. She seduced me, I suppose. It wasn't very difficult, of course. She was a pretty girl . . . there was something about her that's hard to describe. A kind of playfulness, I guess. Me, I was as rigid as a brick building—but you know, rigid brick buildings are the first to collapse in an earthquake. It all started when I drove her home one Saturday afternoon in my car. I was a virgin, which she found amusing. After that, we met regularly for a while. The irony, of course, is that I was supposed to be the teacher, not her. But she taught me about sex and a whole lot of things for which I will be forever in her debt. It was quite an education, believe me. I smoked marijuana with her, we even took LSD one time . . . I can tell you're surprised."

"I am, frankly," Jack admitted.

"Well, marijuana, LSD, even the brief ecstasy of sexual union . . . all this intoxication is nothing but a misguided longing for God. We live in such a materialistic age. Young people especially grab at anything that promises even a temporary lift from the emptiness of their daily lives. It's the Devil, of course, just a brightly colored mirage. Only God brings lasting peace."

"How long did your affair with Crystal last?"

"Long enough. Let's just say we had our forty days and forty nights together. And then I saw I was on a false path and that what I was seeking could only be found in Jesus Christ. Part of my personal atonement is that I have never touched another woman since that time."

"Isn't that a little hard on your wife, Darlene?"

Luke shrugged. "Well, marriage was something my father wanted for me. My celibacy worried him—he's always hoped I would be more 'normal,' as he likes to call it. He said it would look better for the folks in Colorado Springs if I had a little woman at my side. It would help with the fund-raising, you see. So I did it for him, and I think Darlene has gotten something out of it too, in her own way. She was very poor as a child, so she appreciates having a nice house and money. And when she wants her fleeting carnal pleasures, there's always my brother, Dwight."

"You know about her and Dwight?"

"Do you take me for a fool?"

"No, I certainly don't take you for a fool," Jack assured him. "Please tell me more about Crystal."

"Well, I didn't see her for quite a few years. She went away. She lived for empty pleasures, and she became hardened. It was depressing to see how she had turned out. At fifteen there had been a spark to her, but by the time I saw her again, the spark was gone."

"When did you see her again?"

"It was about a year ago. She phoned and said she was in Colorado Springs and asked if we could have lunch together. She said she had something to discuss. Even on the phone, I sensed the evil that had overtaken her. We met at a Mexican restaurant, and at first she was very friendly. She told me she was working on the ski patrol at San Geronimo Peak and that she had a business proposition she wanted me to pass on to my father. I told her she should go to my father herself, since I was not interested in business propositions. But she wanted my help, she thought I could open the right doors and get things moving. Then she said that unless I helped her, she would tell everyone what had happened when she was fifteen. It was blackmail, pure and simple. Apparently I was supposed to be terrified that CMA would look like a bunch of hypocrites, and no one would donate any more money. I rather surprised her when I admitted that yes, we *were* hypocrites and if she would kindly do me the favor of exposing CMA, I would be much obliged."

"Let's go back a second," Jack said. "Obviously a girl on the ski patrol isn't in a position to make business propositions concerning the resort. Did she say who she was acting for?"

"Yes. She claimed she was representing Senator Hampton. The story she told was that the Senator was her lover, and he had sent her as an intermediary in order to keep everything strictly secret until all the details were arranged."

"Did you believe her?"

"I believed she was Senator Hampton's lover—I could well believe that! But no, I did not believe he had sent her to us with this supposed business proposition. Senator Hampton hated CMA, you know, and with some justification. After all, it was my father who was mainly responsible for his losing the 1984 election. We targeted Senator Hampton that year, along with about a dozen other liberal politicians in western states."

"I've been told that. But how did CMA become involved with the ski resort in the first place? And why?"

Luke shrugged. "This happened before 1984, during the time the ski resort was in a blind trust. I believe there was some Swiss outfit managing it in those days. Dad didn't care if it was a veritable house of sin, as long as it made money! I'm not certain Senator Hampton knew exactly who Millennium Investments really was, but he must have sensed something about us he didn't like. When he returned to running the mountain himself, he tried to buy us out several times. But my father always resisted. I gather the profits were terrific."

"Back to Crystal's reappearance in your life. If the Senator hadn't sent her, who did you suppose had?"

"I didn't ask, and frankly I didn't care. However, I did take the proposition to my father. Despite my taunt to Crystal to expose us if she could, I actually do feel a certain loyalty to my father. Poor Dad, his money fountain would have dried up in a hurry if Crystal started telling people how she had been seduced and abandoned by Dr. Doron's son when she was just fifteen!"

Jack smiled. "You know, this all has a very familiar ring, Luke. You must have recognized a certain thematic unity to this blackmail attempt?"

"Of course. It was almost exactly how CMA destroyed Senator Hampton in '84."

"And you still didn't know who was behind Crystal?"

"Not then, at least. My father was delighted with the proposition, of course. A casino, an aerial tramway, a hotel, restaurant, and gift shop—it was just the thing for him. He was skeptical at first that it would be possible to get the various environmental approvals, but the more he looked into it, the more enthusiastic he became. The proposed complex was to be on Indian land, and this made some things quite a bit simpler—it wasn't even necessary to obtain county permits, for example, at least not for the primary structure."

"Even though the land is actually on a ninety-nine-year lease to the ski resort?"

"Legally, Doobie Rock is still sovereign Indian land from which the tribe draws important revenue, and so on. As for the question of Indian gaming, Dad is the eternal optimist whenever a fast buck is involved. Frankly, he has some well-placed friends in New Mexico—he does not anticipate any changes to the laws."

"So what happened next?"

"These things move slowly. I imagine there were a lot of meetings with some of CMA's big contributors—personally, I did my best to stay out of it. Crystal came up to Colorado Springs every few months or so, and as far as I know, everything was on track. Then it all blew up a few weeks ago. Senator Hampton phoned my father and said he had just found out what was going on behind his back. He was furious."

"Did he say how he had learned about the deal?"

"No. Only that as long as he was alive, there would be no casino, no aerial tramway, nothing at all up there but trees and snow and rocks. Dad was naturally upset, since he had already spent a lot of time and money on the project—almost thirty thousand dollars in lawyers fees and architectural drawings. He got in touch with Crystal, and they did some serious shouting at each other. But she told him not to worry, that the deal was still on target."

"But how could that be?" Jack asked. "If Senator Hampton was dead set against it?"

Luke smiled coldly. "Well, that's the thing, of course. Perhaps Senator Hampton would not live forever."

Jack nodded. "And you knew, of course, by this time who Crystal was really representing?"

"Of course."

"Luke, I see that you are a subtle young man. So there's one thing I don't understand. You knew, didn't you, that you were going to be set up for the rap? You must have known—how else could they have gotten away with it?"

"You're asking why I allowed myself to be the fall guy?" Luke shrugged. "Well, why not? I'm as guilty as anyone. My guilt began years ago when I allowed that fifteen-year-old girl to fill me with lustful thoughts. Who knows? Crystal might have turned out quite differently if I had provided a better example. Anyway, it is the Christian ideal for someone to be willing to take the rap, as you call it."

Jack turned to Howie. "You got it now?"

Howie still couldn't quite believe it. "Josie?" he asked tentatively.

Jack nodded.

Howie felt suddenly as if an icicle had been driven into his heart. "Josie! My God, Jack, she's with Alison!"

7

The small twin-prop Cessna lurched and dove in the night sky as it crossed the Sangre de Cristo Mountains from Colorado into New Mexico. Howie was afraid the wings would fall off if it got any rougher. They were racing back to San Geronimo, but he had little faith that they would actually arrive. Outside the window, he saw from the light of a misty half-moon that they were bobbing in and out of a silvery landscape of snow-capped peaks and granite cliffs that seemed close enough to reach out and touch. Howie was certain they were all going to die in this absurd little flying machine.

Kevin was in an improved mood, relieved that the Christians for a Moral America had vacated Sir Galahad's Castle without further incident; indeed, he was the hero of the hour within FBI circles. As for Jack, he was still deeply concerned about Angela, but he had been through many situations like this before and had learned to keep a certain distance from his work. Howie was astonished Jack and Kevin could appear so calm. It was unbearable to him that Angela remained missing and Alison's fate was hanging in a perilous balance.

Kevin spent the first part of the flight sitting in the copilot's seat talking on the radio, organizing the operation that would begin as soon as they touched down in San Geronimo. After a while he walked back to Jack and Howie. Howie watched his face carefully as he approached, anxiously trying to judge if his news was good or bad. But what he had to say was unexpected.

"Jackerooni, good buddy—guess what?"

"Lay it on me, Kevinsky."

(Howie wanted to vomit!)

"I've been speaking to my man in Santa Fe," Kevin said. He turned briefly to explain to Howie: "Jack suggested we contact

the accountant down there who does the books for San Geronimo Peak . . . you know, you're scoring pretty good today,
Jack.''

"Thank you. Now, why don't you cut the bullshit and tell us
what's going on."

Kevin grinned; it was hard to recognize him as the anxious
wreck of an FBI agent who had been pacing the parking lot
outside Sir Galahad's only an hour earlier.

"The accountant is a lady named Virginia Obrecht who
works out of her house on Cañon Road. My agent got to her just
a little while ago as she was finishing dinner, but she didn't
mind the late hour. She even offered him a piece of chocolate
cake. Actually, there have been a few things bothering her, and
for the past few weeks she's been debating whether she ought
to go to the authorities. She kept finding a reason not to do so,
but it wasn't hard to get her talking. This was a lady who was
bursting at the seams.''

"She'd found some irregularities in the books?"

"It's even more interesting than that. Toward the end of
March, Senator Hampton drove down to Santa Fe with a whole
bunch of computer printouts for her to look at. *He* was the one
who found the irregularities. She had never seen him so furious. He told her that a few days before, he had discovered that
Josie was going behind his back, trying to set up a development deal to build a casino at Doobie Rock. And now he had
just learned she was robbing him blind—if you will pardon the
expression.''

"Did he give any details?"

"He did indeed. Apparently part of Josie's job was to over-
see the four cafeterias and restaurants on the mountain, and
this is where she was doing her embezzling. The Senator suspected she had stolen as much as forty thousand dollars over
the past few years, but the actual figure turned out to be much
higher, closer to a hundred grand. She had done it by falsify-
ing accounts and adding a few phantom employees to the payroll. The Senator was really beside himself. The way he saw it,
he had taken in this girl, tried to do his best for her, and now
she was betraying him. This hurt on a gut level. He told Virginia he was going to fire Josie, write her out of his will, completely disown her. Virginia got him to calm down enough to
at least wait for the season to end before he did anything. It

would give her a chance, she said, to go over the books more carefully. This was a family matter after all, and a bit sensitive. Meanwhile, she suggested he hire a private investigator to discover what else Josie might have been up to."

"Aha!" said Jack. "This all becomes more clear. But I wonder how the Senator caught on to Josie in the first place?"

Kevin was still grinning. "Get this—he received an anonymous letter about Josie's plans for Doobie Rock. Virginia didn't see the letter herself, but the Senator mentioned it. After he got the letter, he stayed late on the mountain one night in order to go into Josie's office and see what she had on her computer—he was hoping to find her correspondence with Millennium. He didn't find a thing about Millennium, but her latest restaurant spreadsheets were lying on the table, and he had a peek at those instead. It was the phantom employees on the payroll that tipped him off that she was stealing from him. Apparently, she had two waitresses named Andrea and Ursula listed for the Winterhaus Inn—and being an old skirt-chaser, Senator Hampton was certain he would have remembered young women with such provocative names had they really existed!"

"Well, well, an anonymous letter!" Jack mused. "You know, this could be Luke's doing, but personally I wouldn't be surprised if it were Donny. He must have been a very unhappy young man. If he suspected something was going on between Crystal and Josie, it could have been his attempts to bust things up and get a little revenge."

"We'll find the note itself eventually," Kevin said confidently. "At least we know what we're looking for now. I love it when you get to this point in a case when everything finally starts making sense . . ."

Howie became more and more indignant as he listened to Jack and Kevin. They were having a grand old time being so wonderfully clever.

"Why don't you just jerk each other off?" he asked sourly.

Jack turned his dark glasses upon Howie. "What's the matter?" he asked.

"What's the *matter*? My God, Jack, *everything's* the matter! Angela's probably crying her eyes out right now, waiting for someone to come rescue her, and we don't have a clue where that child is. So it seems to me a bit premature to break out the champagne and sit around congratulating each other!"

"Nobody's breaking out any champagne," Jack said carefully. "But Kevin and I have been doing this for a long time, Howie. You learn to keep your emotions under wraps."

"It's just an intellectual puzzle for you, then, isn't it?"

"No, it's more than that, my friend. But if you don't keep your cool, you're not going to be able to function. And if you can't function, you are not going to do anyone a whole lot of good."

Kevin smiled tolerantly. He patted Jack on the shoulder and moved away down the short aisle to his own seat, allowing Jack the opportunity to explain the facts of life to his young assistant.

"I don't care about any of this shit," Howie complained stubbornly. "I only want to know where Angela is, and that Alison is safe." Howie was so upset that for a moment he thought he was going to cry.

"You *know* where Angela is," Jack said sternly. "We all do. The conclusion is inescapable."

"The hell with your inescapable conclusions!" Howie cried bitterly. "I don't know anything!"

"Then maybe we should go over this a little," Jack suggested.

"Let's start with April Fools' Day," Jack said in a deliberately calm voice. "Senator Hampton had just learned that his daughter was embezzling money from him and making secret deals behind his back that she knew he would oppose. He wanted us to find out all the gory details. He didn't know I was blind or that there would be a snowstorm that day to obscure the view, so he set our meeting at the very place on the mountain Josie wanted to destroy with a casino and an aerial tramway. Probably he thought it would be an object lesson for us to see the spot for ourselves. Unfortunately, he had confided everything to his girlfriend of the moment—having no idea that Crystal was Josie's girlfriend as well, and reporting every word.

"So Josie knew that her father was planning to fire her, possibly even write her out of his will. She realized she had to do something fast or she could be left out in the cold without a job and without a penny. At all costs she needed to stop him from talking with us. So she decided to go for it, to kill her father before he could meet with us at Doobie Rock. At the moment we can only guess at how exactly this was done. Somehow Crystal managed to get the Senator to Doobie Rock half an hour early—since he never wore a wristwatch, perhaps this was not as difficult as it seems. The extra half hour was vital in order to get the deed done and escape before you and I showed up. Crystal and Josie probably worked this all out between them, but my guess is that it was Josie who actually shot the arrow. It must have been very satisfying for her to do that, a settling of old scores.

"So Josie had the motive, she certainly had the anger and the resolve. But now she needed to figure out how to get away with it. Unfortunately for her, in the normal course of things, she and Alison, as the principal heirs, would be the first suspects in any murder investigation. So she had to figure out a way to set up someone else to take the blame. And that's where Luke Doron and the Christians for a Moral America came in. For Josie, they were the perfect fall guys and everything she did was designed to lead us to them. It's the reason the Senator was shot with an arrow—she knew from Crystal about Luke's skill in archery. It's why she killed Alison's dog and wrote hate words on her window. It's the reason Angela was kidnapped. Josie was desperate, she had to make up her plan in a hurry, and she wasn't able to think everything through to the end. But still, it wasn't a bad scheme as these things go. Somehow Crystal must have gotten hold of that diet Dr Pepper can with Luke's fingerprints on it during one of her trips to Colorado Springs, and that was supposed to be the clincher, just in case we still had any doubts about Luke's guilt."

"You're saying the CMA was only window-dressing?" Howie asked. "But surely Josie didn't have anything to do with their antiabortion protest or throwing that cow's placenta on Alison's dinner table?"

"No, of course not. These Moral Americans gave her that for free. As fall guys, they couldn't have been better suited to the role. Josie tried to steer us toward them from the start. Remember our first conversation with her at the Winterhaus? She managed to let us know all about some fanatic right-wing group that had destroyed her dad's political career in the eighties. We were meant to follow that up and discover it was CMA, and they were back to their old mischief, crazier than ever, trying their best to destroy the whole damn family."

"It's still hard to believe she thought she could get away with it!" Howie said, shaking his head.

"Well, what choice did she have? The moment her father made the appointment to meet us at Doobie Rock, her clock was running out."

Jack took Howie on a brief tour of how the subsequent events had unfolded. He was the first to admit that there were many things he did not know, and that much of what he said was conjecture. But it seemed obvious to him that Josie's greatest liability was Crystal. Certainly it was nice to have a partner in crime, and it would have been impossible for Josie to have arranged everything herself. And Crystal, for her part, probably believed she would share in the bounty once she and Josie ran the ski resort. But when Howie recognized Crystal in Colorado Springs, and saw her talking with Luke Doron, her usefulness was finished as far as Josie was concerned. The problem, as she saw it, was that anyone investigating Crystal closely enough would eventually be led all the way back to Josie. So first she tried to kill Howie so he would not be able to report what he had discovered. Possibly it was Crystal who had followed Howie as he drove home that night to San Geronimo, and she was the one who acted out the part of the Ghost Dancer on the lonely road. Or it might have been Josie herself with the shotgun; she could have been in Colorado Springs herself that day without being seen by Howie. Either way, when he survived the accident, Josie knew that Crystal had to go. Jack was certain, though it might never be proved, that Donny and Crystal's death was a carefully arranged double murder.

That brought Jack to the relationship between Josie and Alison. Terrorizing her sister must have had an emotional appeal for Josie. It was a way to avenge an old emotional wound—Alison had always been the legitimate one, the princess from California, while Josie had grown up with nothing. But there was also a calculated reason for the campaign of terror; it made it appear as if CMA was responsible for a *series* of bad things that were happening to the Hampton family, and in this way it disguised the one real crime, the patricide that would have been painfully obvious had it stood on its own. Kidnapping Angela was yet another attempt to implicate the Christian group, leaving behind as evidence a Dr Pepper can with Luke's fingerprints on it. But Josie was most likely starting to enjoy herself too much. If she had thought it out more clearly, she would have realized that the kidnapping would bring too much heat down on her. It was one thing to fool the local police, quite another to put it over on the FBI. Josie lost her clear-sightedness as she became more and more engulfed in her own destructive nature.

Howie listened carefully, but he felt like he was missing something important that Jack was trying to tell him.

"Back to the casino, Jack . . . I still don't understand why she would set that deal in motion when she knew her father would veto it."

"There are two possibilities. The first is that she knew she was going to kill her father from the start, so he wouldn't be around to veto the project when it got closer to being realized. She would be in charge of the ski resort by then, a very wealthy and powerful woman."

"The other possibility?"

"That she never cared about the casino at all. That from the very beginning this whole thing was an elaborate sham—just a clever way to murder her father and make it look as if someone else was responsible."

"So you think this whole thing is . . ."

"The rage of the dispossessed," Jack told him. "So you see, in a way, Josie is a Ghost Dancer after all. She planned to live out the remainder of her life in all the splendor she believed had been denied her as a child. It was a sort of deliverance, I suppose. Unfortunately for her, she got careless."

Howie sighed. "Okay, maybe you're right, Jack—I'm not sure I even care at the moment. What I still want to know is where the hell is Angela?"

"You aren't listening, Howie. I've told you that Josie is an extremely angry woman who is doing everything in her power to hide her tracks. Now, Angela certainly recognized her Aunt Josie as her kidnapper. Therefore there's no possible way that Josie could allow that child to live."

Howie felt like his stomach was sinking out from under him.

"But Angela's just a little kid, Jack! She's Josie's niece, for chrissake!"

"Howie! This is someone who killed her father—the fact that Angela was related wouldn't worry her a bit. Besides, what better way to get back at Alison?"

"So you think this has already been . . . done?" Howie asked tentatively.

"I think it was done almost immediately. You just have to harden yourself to the fact, Howie. It isn't your fault. That little girl had her own life and her own fate, and you're going to have to accept it. You've done everything you could to save her, but Howie—you're not God."

Howie turned away from Jack toward the dark window of the airplane and tried to force back the tears that were blinding his eyes. He tried to think about it all rationally. He knew children sometimes had to die. Yet it was too painful; he hated the very world in which such things were possible.

Howie was thrown back in his seat as the little plane fell precipitously in the unstable air.

"Go ahead! Crash! Take me!" he prayed desperately to the gods of the sky. "I'm ready to die!"

But the plane didn't crash. Instead it came down into a long safe glide onto the single runway of the tiny San Geronimo airport.

8

There was some confusion at the airport. Howie waited on the runway by the plane while Kevin conferred with a group of his agents a dozen feet away. The FBI people stood near a cluster of cars and talked in low voices among themselves. Howie had no idea what was going on, and at the moment he didn't much care. Kevin spoke on his cell phone for a few minutes, consulted some more with his agents, and finally walked over to Jack and took him aside. Now Jack and Kevin repeated the ritual; they spoke in quiet voices and then Kevin used his cell phone once again.

To Howie it all seemed meaningless, just a lot of strutting about and self-importance. These people with their damn cell phones were beginning to piss him off. He walked to the edge of the runway and with some difficulty lowered himself with his crutches so he could sit on the desert. The sandy earth felt good, it felt real. He stretched out on his back and stared up at the moon and stars. It was a beautiful, serene New Mexico night, but the beauty and serenity only made him more aware of his own jagged grief. After a while Kevin led Jack over to where he lay.

"There's been a complication," Jack said.

"I guessed that," Howie replied upward, not moving from his spot. "We may not all be Sherlock Holmes, Jack, but even I can make an inescapable conclusion from time to time."

"Do you want to hear about this or don't you?"

"What I want, frankly, has nothing to do with it."

Jack hesitated. "It's Alison," he said at last.

"Is she dead too?" Howie asked bitterly.

"Not at the moment."

"What the hell does that mean?"

"It means the team of agents surrounding Alison's house

started thinking something was wrong when there were cars in
the driveway but no one turned on any lights when it got dark.
A little while ago they heard the phone ring and no one answered. So finally on Kevin's instructions, they broke in. They
found Alison alone in the house, unconscious on her bedroom
floor."

"Was she shot with an arrow? Or was it something more
mundane this time, like a knife or a gun?"

"Neither. It was a suicide attempt."

This brought Howie to a sitting position.

"Suicide?" he asked. "Like Donny and Crystal?"

"No, this looks like the real thing. The agents found an
empty bottle of sleeping pills on her bedside table. Right now
Alison's in an ambulance being rushed to the hospital. I have
to tell you, Howie—she's unconscious and it's too early to say
if she'll make it or not. As for Josie, her Jeep is still in Alison's
driveway, but somehow she's managed to give us the slip."

The early morning sun flooded through a window into the
hospital waiting room. Howie was asleep in one of the chairs,
his good leg sprawled out in front of him, his head lolling to
one side. A nurse was trying to shake him awake.

"You can go in, Mr. Moon Deer," she told him.

"What?" He opened his eyes groggily.

"Alison is going to be all right. She's asking for you."

"Howie sat up warily, expecting some sort of trick. He had
become a cynic during the last few days. But the nurse was a
pretty young woman with sympathetic brown eyes, and she
was even holding his crutches for him, offering a helping hand.
Meanwhile there was no sign of Jack or Kevin or the FBI. To
Howie, this almost seemed too good to be true.

"She's going to be all right?"

"She had her stomach pumped in time. She's going to be
fine."

Howie swung up onto his crutches and followed the nurse
down a hall. Alison had a room to herself two doors from
where Howie had convalesced only a few days before. She
was sitting up in bed when he walked in, dressed in a funny
white hospital gown with ties in the back. The nurse smiled
vaguely and left them alone.

Alison started crying the moment she saw him. "Oh,

Howie!" She put her arms around his stomach as he stood by
the bed and sobbed softly into his belly. This tickled a little,
but he didn't laugh. Howie stroked her hair and shoulders and
didn't know what to say. She looked terrible. Her face was
bloated, her eyes were red, and it seemed to him as if she had
aged ten years since he had seen her last. Even her hands suddenly showed signs of age; they seemed birdlike, hardly more
than fragile bones covered by taut, translucent skin. He had always been impressed by her physical beauty—too impressed,
really. So it was strange to find her no longer so perfect, not
his mythical Lady in White, not even a snow maiden. The
woman he held was entirely human and vulnerable . . . and he
had never loved her so much. Every particle of his body and
soul wanted to encircle her with his love and protect her.

"Oh, Howie! Get me out of here," she cried. "Take me
home . . . please!"

"Yes," he said, stroking her hair. "I'm going to take you
home. . . ."

It felt as if they were survivors from a shipwreck, alone together in her house. Howie told Viola there was really no reason for her to come in for a few days. Frankly, he was glad to
do the cooking and cleaning; it gave him a momentary purpose. He put Alison into the guest room bed on the ground
floor, since he still had trouble climbing stairs, and he set
about taking care of her. Alison slept a great deal, and Howie
often just sat in the living room and stared out the window at
the trees, or picked out a novel from her living room shelves.
It was odd how life went on.

On the second day Howie carried a lunch tray with a turkey
sandwich and a glass of mineral water into her bedroom—an
acrobatic feat with his crutches, but he managed not to spill a
thing. Alison sat up in bed with her tray, but instead of eating,
she told him the story of Josie's strange visit. At first Howie
was worried that it might be dangerous, a mistake to relive
such emotional memories so soon. But she clearly wanted to
talk.

Josie had shown up unexpectedly on the morning that
Howie and Jack were in Colorado Springs.

"At first I was grateful she'd come. It was a surprise, you
know, because we had never been close. But it felt good to

have some family support. I thought, wow . . . I really *do* have
a sister! Maybe something positive is going to come out of this
nightmare. But then I started feeling these weird undertones.
It's hard to describe, Howie, but by afternoon I sensed something very creepy going on."

"She was, what . . . angry? Threatening in some way?"

"No, just the opposite. She was too sweet, overly solicitous.
It didn't ring true somehow. In the afternoon she told Viola to
go home, and when we were alone together in the house I
started getting a little frightened. I was pretty much out of it,
of course, loaded up on sedatives, sleeping a lot. I remember
waking up when the phone rang downstairs sometime toward
evening. Josie said it was a reporter, but there was something
about her tone . . . I didn't quite believe her. I thought maybe
she was keeping something from me. Then she offered to give
me a back rub, and frankly that sounded like a *great* idea. I was
so stiff and tense, I felt like I was going crazy.

"So I was lying on my stomach on my bed, and Josie was
straddling me, rubbing my back. And then she started talking
in this dreamy voice like she was outside her body, or very
stoned, telling me really horrible things. How unhappy she had
been as a child on the reservation. How she had hated everything—most of all, her creep of a stepfather, Manny Trujillo. I
remember saying, 'But your mother loved you, didn't she?'

"She laughed really bitterly when I said that. She told me it
was all Dad's fault—Dad had trashed her mother, destroyed
her self-respect, and by the time he was through dumping on
her, the only thing Maria loved was cheap booze. Apparently
she and Manny used to get drunk together, and go on terrible
binges that always turned violent. Every binge ended with
Manny beating Maria up. Josie used to hide under her bed
when they were drinking because she was afraid Manny was
going to come into her room and kill her. I told Josie I was
sorry to hear all this, of course—I never knew her childhood
had been quite so bad. Then she said that whenever her mom
wasn't around, Manny would make her jerk him off. She really
went on about this, how Manny taught her to put her hand
around his dick and make him come. Only he was such a
drunk, you see, it used to take her forever to do it. She was
seven or eight years old, and she would have to just sit there

for hours with his limp dick in her hand and Manny getting angry because he said she wasn't doing it right.

"I was shocked, absolutely horrified at what she was telling me. I sat up, and I turned around on the bed. I tried to tell her how deeply I empathized, that child abuse just made me sick. I said it still wasn't too late to report Manny to the police. But then she started getting angry. Saying how could *I* understand anything when I grew up in such a rich house and everybody loved me and treated me just like a little princess. It was a very disturbing conversation, Howie."

"Did she confess to killing your father?"

"Not directly, but I began to suspect it. She went on and on about Dad—how it was all Dad's fault that she had suffered such a dysfunctional childhood. And then she calmed down a little and said she had to tell me the truth about the phone call I had heard earlier—the one that woke me up. She said it was you on the phone, Howie, not a reporter, and that you had passed on some very bad news."

"It *was* me, Allie. But I told her things were looking a bit hopeful."

"Did you? Well, Josie told me she didn't know how to break it to me, but I'd better get a grip on myself. The worst had happened. Your phone call was to say that Angela was dead. You had found her naked body in a forest outside of Colorado Springs, and she had been . . ."

Alison took a gulp of air, unable to continue.

"Maybe you shouldn't try to tell me this yet," Howie cautioned. "It was all a bunch of lies anyway."

"But *was* it? That's what I don't really know! And it's just destroying me, Howie. I don't know if I can bear it!"

"Allie, we've got to wait until we learn what really happened."

"Josie said Angela had been raped . . . repeatedly . . . she said she was raped so many times in the anus and vagina that her little body . . . her little body . . ."

Alison was crying in convulsive sobs. Howie hobbled over to the bed and held her.

"It's all lies," he said again. "She was only trying to torment you."

"My God, she went on and on and on about it, Howie! I remember I tried to stand up from the bed, but with all the tranqs

I'd been taking, and the stress and anxiety, I fainted dead away
on the floor. Probably I wasn't out for long, but when I came
to, Josie was gone. I saw she had left a plastic bottle of sleeping pills on my bedside table. I knew she had put them there
for me deliberately. I just stared at the bottle for the longest
time—for hours I think, because it had got dark in the room.
There just didn't seem anything left for me to live for. Angela
was dead, raped hideously. My father was murdered, my sister
was a monster, crazy with hatred . . . I couldn't take it anymore. So finally I got a glass of water, and I swallowed the
pills. . . ."

Howie didn't have any idea what to do except hold her and
let her cry.

Later that afternoon Emma Wilder phoned Howie with a
message from Jack. Josie had been picked up in the Albuquerque airport attempting to board a flight to Mexico City
with a hundred thousand dollars in cash in her carry-on bag-
gage. Jack and Kevin had immediately flown to Albuquerque
to question her. The interrogation was still in progress, but
Jack wanted Howie to know that Josie had confessed to killing
Angela. Jack and Kevin were still trying to discover what she
had done with the body; when there was any word, they would
let Alison know. Meanwhile they were doing their best to keep
the confession from the media until the details were better established; there was no sense turning this into a three-ring cir-
cus. But Kevin was planning to hold a news conference at ten
o'clock the next morning, so Howie should be prepared. The
moment Josie's confession was made public, hordes of jour-
nalists were sure to descend on Alison's house in search of
some true-life grief.

Howie had taken the call in the kitchen. He put down the
telephone with a carnivorous emptiness in his soul. His eyes
had become dry, scorched rocks. Alison was sleeping so he
was just as glad to spare her for the moment of this final piece
of news. He was still sitting in the kitchen an hour later when
she appeared in a white terry-cloth robe. Howie felt paralyzed.
He sat staring at her from his straight-back chair, his plaster
cast resting on a second chair nearby.

"You don't look very good, Howie," she said.

"I'm okay."

"Have you been eating? Why don't you let me make you up a can of soup?"

"Maybe later. I'm not really hungry, Allie."

"No," she said stubbornly. "I'm going to make you up some soup, and spoon-feed it into your mouth if I have to."

It seemed that they had traded places emotionally. As Howie watched her futz in the kitchen, he became more and more depressed. He knew he should tell her about Emma's phone call. Several times he actually opened his mouth to speak, to form the words. But he couldn't physically make himself say it. And the longer he put it off, the more difficult it was to begin.

Allie heated up a can of lentil soup, poured it into a bowl, and placed it on the table in front of him with a spoon.

"Eat, Howie. Frankly, you're about the last living thing I give a shit about, so I don't want you to waste away."

It was good to hear her being a little feisty. A hint of the old Alison. He wasn't hungry, but he took a few spoonfuls anyway to encourage the trend. She sat next to him at the table, and her eye was caught by Angela's drawing on his plaster cast. Howie tried to remove his leg from the chair so she wouldn't see it, but Alison told him to leave his cast where it was.

"You know, I never really looked at this closely, Howie. It's the Big Bad Wolf, isn't it?" Alison studied the absurd, fat creature with big ears that Angela had drawn. She was doing her best to remain calm and speak in a matter-of-fact voice. "I was telling Angela the story of 'Little Red Riding Hood' just last week . . . she was always fascinated by the ending. The part where the Wolf eats Grandmother and Riding Hood, and then the Handsome Woodcutter comes along and kills the Wolf and cuts open his stomach with an ax—at least, that's the version of the story I told her, how I learned it myself when I was a little girl. Angela really got a kick out of how Grandmother and Riding Hood just step out of the stomach, and everything's fine. She always used to say to me, 'Mommy, how can Riding Hood be alive if the Wolf ate her?' And I would say . . . well, this was an *awfully* Handsome Woodcutter, a kind of Prince-in-Disguise. And a Prince-in-Disguise, you see, has the power to save Riding Hood. . . ."

Alison looked up at Howie, her intense brown-gold eyes fixed on him.

"You know what Angela told me once? She said that you were like the Handsome Woodcutter, Howie. She had you pegged as the Prince-in-Disguise who's supposed to rescue us all."

"She told me that too," Howie admitted. "She said it was my job."

Howie couldn't let go of this image of the Handsome Woodcutter, that somehow he had really screwed up his part of the fairy tale. He knew it was absurd, perhaps even self-delusionary. And yet the thought was like a seed that grew inside of him. He agonized over it. What kind of Handsome goddamn Woodcutter let the Big Bad Wolf get away with eating Riding Hood? All that evening he thought about it, as he and Alison shuffled around in her big solar home.

What kind of goddamn Handsome Woodcutter was it who couldn't save a little girl?

He felt like screaming. As far as Howie could see, he was entirely useless, and a coward as well. Because now too much time had elapsed since his phone call from Emma, and he was certain he could never tell Alison what she had told him, he couldn't voice the words that would put a final end to hope.

They slept together in the bed downstairs, but it was sexless, only the embrace of shipwrecked souls. Howie didn't think he would sleep, but he did sleep for several hours. He woke around two in the morning and stared wide eyed at the ceiling, still thinking about the Woodcutter. He had just had the strangest idea: A Handsome Woodcutter was, if you thought about it, a kind of Ghost Dancer. Their job description was similar to some extent, to bring people back from the dead—the Woodcutter did this by opening up stomachs with his ax, the Ghost Dancer by dancing until the heavens opened and the gods released the spirits of slain warriors. Howie lay on the bed for another hour, going over and over the idea in his head. He knew he could never have made a very good Handsome Woodcutter, despite Angela's expectations. *I'm afraid I'm just not handsome enough, Angela,* he told her ruefully.

But what if he could be a Ghost Dancer? Was it possible?

By three o'clock Howie was certain he was going crazy. Nevertheless, he gently disentangled himself from Alison's embrace. He got out of bed, hopped on one foot over to his crutches, grabbed his clothes from the chair, and hobbled into the living room. He really had no idea how to begin, but the living room did not seem the right place to try. So he dressed and went outside to the rear of the house, to the open desert where he and Angela once played gicket with her Nerf ball. It had been a long time since Howie had done any Indian dancing. When he was a teenager, he used to go to some of the powwows, mostly for the purpose of meeting girls. But that was years ago, and he wasn't even sure he could remember the steps. All in all, this couldn't be more impossible. The night was black, there was no one to sing, no one to beat the drum, and his crutches didn't help matters either.

"Ridiculous!" he said aloud.

But nevertheless, Howard Moon Deer began to dance. He found a patch of desert, and he danced in a clockwise circle around and around. Indian dancing is a kind of two-step to a beat that is strangely soothing, like a heartbeat. Howie felt very awkward at first with his cast and his crutches getting in the way. But after a while he found that his clumsy dance had a kind of power in its monotony, and he even began to sing. Not real Indian singing, since he had forgotten all the words, but a kind of made-up song of many vowels that was more like a rhythmic moan. He danced for a long time, for hours, around and around. He lost track of time. He danced until the sky turned gray above the mountains in the east. He danced until the pink dawn made the clouds above San Geronimo Peak catch fire. Around and around the circle he went on the small patch of desert that he had made his own. At one point he was surprised to see that Alison was standing in her terry cloth robe near the back fence watching him with a look of astonishment on her face. But still he kept dancing. A Ghost Dancer simply didn't have time to stop and chat with the girls.

Howie danced until the morning had fully broken. And then he tripped. He must have been exhausted because he fell hard onto his back, knocking all the wind out of him. He was lucky he hadn't landed on a cactus. As he sat catching his breath, he found he was facing San Geronimo Peak to the east. It was a beautiful sight: The early morning sun was breaking through some dark clouds that were gathering around the Peak, allowing a single swath of brilliant sunlight to hit the base of the mountain, shining directly onto the Indian reservation. Howie stared at the focused beam of light as though he had never seen the sun before.

As he sat on the desert, Alison approached with a mug of coffee for him.

"Allie, I have the craziest idea," he told her. "It's absolutely insane."

"I'm glad," she told him. "But next time can I dance too?"

9

The only way Howie could fit his broken leg into Alison's MG was to stick it out the passenger window as she drove. It was a half hour drive to the reservation, and they drove in silence. Alison seemed to have complete faith that Howie knew what he was doing, and he didn't want to disillusion her. Frankly, he knew this was nuts. As a final element of absurdity, he had brought along the small hatchet from Alison's downstairs fireplace that she generally used to make kindling. As a weapon, it was a mockery of the Handsome Woodcutter's long-handled ax. Howie certainly wished he had something more menacing, but unfortunately the police had confiscated the revolver Alison had once kept on her bookshelf behind *The Naked and the Dead.*

What was he doing with a hatchet in his lap and his plaster cast sticking out of Alison's car window? There was at least some small rationalization to this absurdity: It had occurred to Howie that when Josie had kidnapped Angela from Ernie Martinez Municipal Park, she would have needed to take the little girl someplace quiet where they wouldn't be seen or disturbed. What better place to take Angela in order to kill her than the Indian land where Josie had grown up? Certainly there were plenty of other wild places nearby where Josie could have taken the child, hundreds of square miles of wilderness and uninhabited desert. But wouldn't Josie be drawn to her own childhood haunts? She would know endless hiding places on the reservation. Not only that, the state police and FBI would hesitate to enter the sanctuary of Indian land, so she might feel reasonably safe there.

This, at least, was the rationalization. Howie knew it was only a guess—not a bad hunch, as guesses go, but it could easily lead nowhere. On a more emotional level, he felt that he and Alison would go crazy if they sat around her house another day. It was better to be in motion, to be doing something, anything. And if they found Angela's body . . . well, that would be devastating but it would be a sort of closure. Howie believed it better for Alison in the long run to take an active role in this discovery, than simply hear about it passively from his lips.

Probably it was a good thing Alison didn't ask what they were doing. She just followed Howie's directions and detoured around the touristy part of the pueblo, then drove along the dirt road toward the mountain valley. As they climbed in altitude, patches of snow appeared and the road became muddy. The last time Howie had come here, he was at the wheel of a four-wheel drive truck; Alison's small sports car was quite a different vehicle, low to the ground and not suited to this kind of terrain. A few times Howie thought they wouldn't get any farther, but Alison managed to race the engine and plow through the mud and standing water as though the car were a speedboat. Clouds were moving quickly across the sun, alternating mountain light and shadow; the air was scented with the fragrant smoke of cedar wood from the houses they passed. The road got worse until finally the MG couldn't go any farther. The wheels spun helplessly as they sank into a snowdrift that crossed the road. But Maria Concha's lonely house was in sight, nestled against the mountains a quarter mile away.

There was no one at Maria's home. No smoke in the chimney, no car in the driveway. No human sound at all, just the wind through the trees. Howie rested on his crutches while Alison watched him, waiting patiently for his next Inspired Hunch. Unfortunately, Howie at the moment was fresh out of hunches.

He was thinking he might have to do a little more dancing, just to keep Alison in the right mood, when he noticed the horse corral and utility shed that stood at the far side of Maria's garage. There were two horses in the corral, a black mare and a smaller palomino, and they were regarding Howie with serious horsey interest, their ears pointed his way.

"Do you know how to bridle and saddle a horse?" Howie asked.

"I should. I had my own horse when I was a kid, Howie." He was glad to hear just a touch of her old class arrogance. She was studying him almost as intently as the two horses. "Tell me something, do you actually know what you're doing?" she finally dared to ask.

"Not completely," he admitted. "Does it matter?"

"I'm not sure. But let's do it anyway."

Howie used the blunt end of his hatchet to break the padlock on the utility shed, and Alison found two bridles and saddles inside. Alison was looking better today. He watched her as she saddled the horses. There was more color in her face, and the puffiness around her eyes had disappeared. Howie took the larger horse, the black mare, and Alison the palomino. The challenge for Howie now was to get into the saddle. This took a little maneuvering. Alison brought the mare close to the fence and held the bridle. Howie dropped his crutches, reached for the saddle horn, raised his good leg into the stirrup, and swung his cast over the far side of the horse.

"Do you want your crutches?" she asked when he was safely in the saddle.

"No, leave them," he told her. "They'd only get in the way."

They set off along the trail, following the streambed into the valley toward the mountains. There was a good deal less snow than when Howie had been here on cross-country skis. Much of the trail was firm. Sometimes they needed to make detours around the deeper drifts. Once when the snow was impassable, they rode for fifteen minutes up the stream itself. As for his cast and broken leg, Howie found it was fairly comfortable to just let it dangle free.

Would they discover Angela's fate in this remote valley? Howie was doubtful, but he was glad to be here anyway in the vast peacefulness of nature with Alison riding behind him. They rode for more than an hour into the narrowing canyon without exchanging a single word. And then Howie saw wood smoke from Raymond Concha's adobe hut. The trail passed around a huge boulder, and the hut itself came into view. It was an idyllic setting, a huge cottonwood tree overhead and the stream gurgling close by. The old Indian was standing outside his front door, he seemed to be expecting them. He held a rifle loosely in his arms.

Howie pulled out the hatchet from his belt as he rode closer. The old Indian saw it and smiled faintly.

"Hey, where did you get your tomahawk?" he said mockingly. "You must be a real Indian after all!"

Alison rode up from behind Howie. "Where's my daughter?" she demanded.

Raymond frowned, but did not answer.

Howie was suddenly very angry. He raised the hatchet above his head. "Hey, old man—I'm going to throw this thing right at your goddamn head if you don't answer the lady's question!"

"Even if I shoot you first?"

"Go ahead and try!"

Howie's bravado was only skin-deep, and for a moment he was certain Raymond was going to shoot him. But then the old man let the rifle sag in his arms, and he turned his attention to Alison.

"So you've come for your daughter? Why are you looking here?"

Howie answered for her. "Where else would she be? This is the only place that makes sense."

"Perhaps she's dead."

"Is she?"

The old man remained quiet for quite a long time.

"This is not a simple matter," he said at last. "Josie brought the child to Maria, my niece, and told her to do the killing. But Maria took pity on the child and couldn't do it. So she lied. She told Josie the girl was dead. Then she brought the girl here and told me that I was the one to do the killing."

"And why should you do a thing like that?"

"For my people, of course. Josie promised Maria that she would tear up the ninety-nine-year lease and return all the Indian land to the reservation. But first this killing must be done."

"That doesn't make sense. Why didn't Josie kill the little girl herself?"

Raymond shook his head. "This may surprise you, but she couldn't do it either. Actually, it's not so easy to kill in cold blood a small, trusting child and live afterward with your memories. You have to be someone very stern, like me."

"So what did you do, Raymond?"

Raymond shrugged. "Well, I haven't really killed anyone for a long time, you know. To tell the truth, I've forgotten how.

So I thought I'd let the mountain decide, let her live here for a while and see what the spirits had to say. But it's a funny thing. When I was a young man, the spirits of this land were a lot more decisive than they are today. Maybe they're getting old, like I am. . . ."

Out of the corner of his eye, Howie saw a movement behind the cabin, then a blond head and a Babar sweatshirt.

"Mommy! Look what *I've* got!"

It was Angela, appearing from the streambed with a live fish wiggling in her hand. Her clothes were filthy, and it looked as if she hadn't had a bath in days. Alison jumped from her horse and then forced herself to walk calmly to her daughter. She picked Angela up and gave her a fierce hug.

"Oh, my Angela . . . my sweetest angel!"

Howie watched from on top of his horse. He was an honest-to-God Handsome Woodcutter now, and he didn't want to spoil his image by floundering around helplessly on the ground without his crutches. Angela obviously had no idea anything was wrong, or that anyone had been looking for her. She had simply gone off with her Aunt Josie and was now having a wonderful vacation in the mountains with her new friend, Uncle Raymond.

"Look, Mommy, I caught a fish! Look what I have!"

It was only a very small trout, but it looked huge to Angela. It was very much alive in her hand, gasping in the air.

"Do you want him for dinner, sweetie?" her mother asked.

"No-o," Angela said thoughtfully, scrunching up her nose. "I want to let him go."

"We'd better do that quickly, I think."

Alison walked with her daughter down to the stream and watched as Angela set the small trout alongside a slippery rock.

"Go away!" the child cried. "Go free!"

The little fish hesitated only briefly, and then darted off quickly into the cold current.

EPILOGUE

The Indian Who Lost His Tribe

On an afternoon late in June, Howie drove Alison and Angela to the Albuquerque airport in the old MG, the top down, the wind blowing fiercely in their hair. Howie's plaster cast had been off for nearly a week now, and he was feeling almost alarmingly light and agile. As they drove, Angela fell asleep in her mother's lap.

Somewhere in the open stretch of freeway south of Santa Fe, Howie felt Alison's eyes on him through her dark glasses.

"I'm going to miss you, Howie."

"You'd better write, then," he told her. "I'm expecting at least one letter a week. And lots of postcards of lions and tigers and elephants."

"I don't think they have lions and tigers and elephants in Ghana," she told him. "But whatever they have there, you'll get a postcard of it. Howie, will you write back?"

"Of course."

"I'm sure going to miss S-E-X," she said delicately, spelling out the letters in case Angela was not really asleep.

"We'll have plenty of that when I come visit you in September," he assured her. "We can S-C-R-E-W our B-R-A-I-N-S out in a romantic little grass hut."

"Actually, I'm going to be living in a house. They have them there, you know."

"Do they? With roofs, you mean? But what about indoor plumbing? We modern Indians don't go anywhere unless there's a Jacuzzi."

She punched his arm playfully, and then fell silent. This moment of separation, now that it was upon them, was difficult and bittersweet. Alison had closed down her Albuquerque clinic and was flying off to Ghana to work in a rural hospital. The AIDS epidemic was bad in Africa, and unlike the people in Albuquerque, Africans were glad to welcome an OB-GYN who was on a mission to promote responsible sex.

Howie personally was very much in favor of responsible sex, and wished to practice it as frequently as possible. Unfortunately, he had not seen a great deal of Alison over the past few months. At first it was because there were reporters and TV cameras everywhere; later because Alison wanted a few weeks alone with her daughter—to get to know each other again, she'd said. Then in May, Howie himself became very busy. Wilder & Associate suddenly had more work than they could handle, due to the publicity they had received in the media. In his free time—and there wasn't much—Howie was also working with a new spurt of energy on his much delayed dissertation, "Philosophical Divisions at the Top of the Food Chain."

As for Alison, her upper-caste hauteur had gradually returned, and even on the nights they spent together, Howie sometimes feared they were drifting apart. She was a very rich woman now, of course; due to the law that forbade criminals from profiting from their crimes, Alison was in the process of inheriting the entirety of her father's estate, including the San Geronimo ski resort. Howie was happy for her, but it was difficult to be the lover of someone whose economic reality was so enormously different from your own. Small moments, such as settling a bill in a restaurant, became awkward as he insisted on paying, and she insisted that he must not. Actually, Howie was feeling quite wealthy himself now that Wilder & Associate was a rousing success, but of course, it couldn't compare with Alison's millions.

"You'll never guess what Jack told me yesterday," Howie mentioned as they drove. "Luke Doron is setting up a defense fund, helping to raise money for Josie's legal costs."

"Is he?"

"Luke turns out to be a real Christian after all."

Alison sighed and shook her head in amazement. In the past few weeks, Howie and Alison had done their best to avoid speaking of "the thing," as they had come to call it, hoping to distance themselves. Now they were both trying out their sea legs, so to speak, seeing if they could talk about it calmly.

"I'm supposed to come back for the trial in October, of

course, but I'm hoping to get away with sending in a signed deposition," Alison told him.

"It's looking now as if the trial will be delayed until February. These things can drag on for years."

"You know, I don't feel sorry for Josie. I've tried, but I can't. Not after what she did to Dad. To me. To our dog, Rusty. To Angela . . . I don't want her to get the death sentence, but I hope she goes to prison for a long, long time. . . ."

"She will. I gather her lawyers are negotiating a complicated plea bargain, where she'll plead guilty to avoid the death penalty. But she'll get life."

"Life!" Alison repeated sullenly. "That sure doesn't sound like a life to me! My God, Howie, this has all been such a horrible business. And you know what I still can't understand?"

"What's that?"

"Why did she run? I mean, here she had set up this nearly perfect crime to kill Dad and make it look like someone else was to blame . . . but then she just sort of gave up."

"Basically, she had no choice," Howie told her. "The game was up for her . . . this is something Jack and I discovered only a few days ago. It seems she found the password to your father's computer, so she was able to download his e-mail and read all the messages he had been sending back and forth to Virginia Obrecht, the accountant in Santa Fe, about how Josie had been embezzling from the resort. She broke into your Dad's e-mail on the morning before she came to your house—the local Internet server here in San Geronimo was cooperative, and we were able to trace the activity on your Dad's account. As far as Josie was concerned, this was the last straw. If Virginia knew, there was no way to contain the damage. So she opted to run."

"Jack was clever to figure that out."

"Jack's a clever guy," he assured her. But Howie, in fact, was being modest. When it came to e-mail, Jack didn't know an in-box from an out-box; he was the wrong generation. It was Howie who had followed the cyber-trail, figuring out this particular angle to the case. Success had made him more confident as an investigator, and he was learning to follow his hunches.

"Poor Josie!" Alison said after a while. "She wasn't very lucky, was she?"

"No. But once you give yourself up to the Ghost Dance, it'll destroy a person in the end."

Alison smiled. "You did a bit of Ghost Dancing there yourself, Howie. It didn't destroy you."

"Yes, but I was lucky—I tripped."

Howie pulled up next to the busy airport curb. They had agreed in advance that he wouldn't park and come inside the terminal; long good-byes were too painful. He unloaded her luggage from the backseat and the trunk, and set it on the sidewalk. Then he picked up Angela and gave her a big hug. Finally he turned to Alison.

"Well, Allie," he said.

"Howie, Howie . . . my man in the moon Moon Deer."

He kissed her just once, lightly on her elegant lips.

"I left a little good-bye present for you in the glove compartment," she told him.

"You shouldn't have."

"No, I *should* have . . . you were a surprise in my life, Howard Moon Deer. I wasn't expecting to fall in love."

It was nice that she had said the L-word at last; but they both knew it was good-bye. She turned abruptly and walked inside the building, with Angela following and a porter pushing a trolley with all her bags. It reminded Howie of the way she had skied away from him so gracefully at the top of the chairlift on April Fools' Day. Gliding away in perfect form . . . she was good at that. She was even dressed in white today, a rough woven muslim blouse and loose drawstring pants.

Howie got back in the car and popped open the glove compartment. Her good-bye present was a pink slip—the ownership of the MG made out in his name.

"Damn you, Allie!" he exploded. He always knew she would leave him like this, an awkward tip pressed discreetly in his hand. He got out of the car to rush after her and give back her damn pink slip. Didn't she know he didn't want anything from her but love? But he stopped at the automatic door when he saw her through the glass. She was giving orders to the porter and moving briskly toward the first-class check-in, her mind already occupied more with what lay ahead in her life than what she had just left behind. So he let her go. He hardly knew her anymore, she was no longer his: just a wealthy Lady in White, her back to him, with her blond child in tow.

Howie returned a second time to the car, his new MG.

One day I'll find my own tribe! he vowed as he turned over the ignition. He knew they were out there somewhere: a whole damn tribe of bookish, misfit Indians. But meanwhile he felt so suddenly lonely he could hardly see the road through his tears as he drove away.

Don't miss the
next compelling mystery,
The Warrior Circle,
starring Howard Moon Deer
and Jack Wilder
coming from Signet in 1999

PART ONE

Disappearing Woman

Howard Moon Deer was in postcoital heaven when his world fell apart. It came when he was least expecting it, when he was a snug and sated satyr, feeling almost perfect: the sound of rain outside the cabin, skin against warm skin, his arm nearly gone to sleep beneath the weight of her blond sex-tossed hair. This was about as blissed-out as an Indian could be—post-Columbus, at least, and severed from anything resembling roots. But then unexpectedly Aria Waldman disengaged and sat up in bed.

"That was fabulous," she said. "But I'm afraid it's the last time."

"Say again?"

"It's over. I'm leaving you, Howie. This is quits."

She had succeeded in snagging the attention of his hormone-soaked brain. He sat up stupidly, a slow-moving male animal, gorged on pleasure.

"Let's start this again. What are you talking about, Aria?"

"Howie, you're the nicest man I've met in ages. But this simply isn't working for me anymore."

"Then, let's not work on it," he suggested reasonably. "Why don't we play instead?"

He put his hand on her thigh to illustrate exactly what he had in mind. But she pushed his hand away and rose decisively from the covers.

"Howie. I'm serious about this."

"Then tell me why?"

"There's no 'why' about it. I've just got to go, that's all."

Howie studied her as she walked about the room in search of her clothing. Aria Waldman was certainly a pleasant sight au naturel: blond, long legged, and rosy complexioned. A tad plump, perhaps, but interestingly so—Renoir-esque was the word that generally came to mind, though tonight she might just as well have been a Jackson Pollock, for she was unfathomable, a study of abstract motion that was making an unexpected exit from his life. Howie had a horrible sense of having missed some vital piece of information. Probably it was flattering that she had waited to call it quits until after they had made love one final time, but this added to his current vulnerability. With a discreet motion he moved the sheet to cover the limp, dejected, noodley thing he liked to think of as his manhood.

"Aria, talk to me. What have I done to make you angry?"

She shook her head. "Not a thing. You've been perfectly sweet. The ultimate cuddly lover . . . too cuddly, maybe."

"Too cuddly," he repeated, chewing on the concept. "Well, I can change, you know. Work on myself. Would you like it better if I was mean and macho? I can be a real son of a bitch if you'd find that more interesting. Wanna hear me growl?"

"No, I do *not* want to hear you growl," she told him firmly.

But he growled anyway. He even beat his chest a few times, sitting up in bed, coughing when he beat too hard—a mock show of blunted male force. She laughed briefly, for she had always found him a very funny Indian. It was a good thing to make a woman laugh, seductive in its way. Make a woman laugh and she's halfway to your bed, was Howie's motto. But not tonight clearly.

"Seriously," he said when the laughter was spent. "Why?"

"Some things just have to end, that's all. It's not your fault, it's not mine. It's the way things are. . . . What's that *n*-word you like to use?"

"Entropy?"

"That's it. Everything falls apart in the end. Everything runs down. Even you and I, Howie. I can't explain it any better than that."

"Sure you can. You're not even trying."

She shook her head. "It's no use trying. It's over, that's all. Don't you get it?"

No, he did not get it. There had been times in his life when he thought he had love all figured out; but the older he got, the more he realized he barely had a clue. Moodily, Howie watched her dress, stepping into a pair of bikini panties that had a design of red chile peppers on them—cute but they were falling apart, the elastic separating from the cotton material. Aria was a slob when it came to underwear, a trait he had always found strangely endearing. Mentally he said good-bye to the dark blond thatch of pubic hair as it disappeared from view. It was an exquisite triangle, his personal Bermuda Triangle that had spun his compass in a big way, sunk his ship. He watched as the bra went snap, covering her breasts. They were lovely breasts, evocative of some primal paradise lost . . . and such a restful place to lay one's head! But no more . . . *bye-bye, breasts*, he thought sadly.

Why did women make it so difficult for men? Poor men, lust-driven creatures, lumbering along; Tarzen was still swinging through the forest, but Jane apparently had taken a powder. Howie was twenty-eight-years old and starting to become awfully discouraged by gender games. He liked Aria Waldman, he truly did, and he had been under the impression that she liked him. Aria was a smart, attractive, funny woman—smart and funny, for Howie, being key ingredients of sexual attraction. She was great in bed; she even had an interesting job— she was the star reporter for the local weekly newspaper, *The San Geronimo Post*, with a particular talent for sniffing out the countless corruptions and absurdities of small-town politics.

Howie and Aria had been going out for nearly nine months. They were each very busy, of course, and the demands of modern life had not made it possible to be Romeo and Juliet exactly. She was not the love of his life; Howie had always known that. But what they had was rather nice—he thought so, at least—a modest, friendly sort of affair centered mostly around gourmet dinners that were followed inevitably by equally gourmet sex. Sometimes they ate at her house; other times at his. It was hard to say who was the better cook—she was more spontaneous, while he was the methodical one, working in a scholarly fashion page by page, calorie by calorie, through *The Silver Palate Cookbook*. Once a week on Saturday night, she would sleep over at his cabin. Sundays they generally spent reading *The New York Times* in bed and hiking in the afternoons. Howie knew he was going to miss her. This might not be great love, but as far as he was concerned, dinner, laughter, intelligent conversation, and a good screw made for a pretty decent consolation while you waited for the real thing to come along.

She was speaking to him now, trying to explain herself despite her avowal that this matter was beyond explanation. Her first inclination for silence had been the right one, for it came out now in hackneyed phrases. How she needed to find herself and be strong alone—all the usual things that people say when they break up, but don't entirely mean, and rarely succeed in doing. Howie struggled to be sensitive and understanding, but he found this heavy going. Occasionally, his mind wandered to the natural sound of the rain outside his cabin. He could smell the wet sagebrush, visualize the huge expanse of desert and mountains, the harsh, beautiful landscape of northern New Mexico. It was a stormy July night full of thunder and lightning. A dramatic night to end a love affair, the rain slapping hard against the windows. Howie wondered vaguely about the basil he had planted last week in a big pot outside on the flagstone terrace, how it was handling the storm. Basil was currently Howie's favorite herb and it would be tragic to lose both it and his girlfriend on a single night.

"Look, Howie, this has nothing to do with you," she was saying. "It's *me*. My clock is running. I'm going to be thirty next week and I've been putting off too many things that I need to accomplish. Unfortunately, you've been a major distraction," she added with a rueful smile.

He studied her with an uncomfortable sense that he had never really seen Aria Waldman until this moment. Her eyes were cold tonight, without lustre; her mouth was set with grim determination. Suddenly he could see in her face the old woman she would one day become. It frightened him a little. He could see a hint of cruelty in her face, something hard and unattractive that had always been hidden before by the facade of romantic play . . . hidden, perhaps, by his own desire for her.

"There's another man, isn't there?"

"That's very condescending, you know. That a woman can't leave for her own reasons—that she always has to be in search of a man."

"But it's true though, isn't it?"

"No," she said. "It's not true. There's no one else." But she looked away as she spoke and Howie was not certain he believed her.

"I thought we had something nice together, Aria. I thought maybe this was something that would grow."

"Oh, Howie, you're hopeless!" she exclaimed. "You'll never understand, and I can't explain it any better—I just can't!"

"That's it, huh? Only some vague feeling you can't bother to explain?"

"Look, I'm trying not to hurt you. What do you want me to say? You don't turn me on anymore. I don't want to go to bed with you. I don't want to see you. I don't want to talk with you about books, or food, or anything else. Do you get it now?" She saw the hurt in his eyes and her tone softened slightly: "So just forget me, Howie. Forget this ever happened. Go live your life, be happy. Get your damn Ph.D., meet some nice girl and have a ton of children. . . . But it's not me, I swear to God. I'm not the one for you, you've simply got to believe me."

Aria was standing by the door, ready to leave. Howie watched her, feeling more confused, defeated, awkward, and hurt than he could remember being for a very long time. For a moment, he was tempted to perform a small show of savagery. Maybe leap naked in the air, give a war shout, grab her by the hair, and simply pull her back to bed. But the truth was, he was a very civilized Sioux; it just wasn't in him. And besides, he sensed this was already a lost cause, a corpse that could not be revived. It was best now to part without inflicting any more damage. He rose from the bed, turning discreetly to hide his maleness while he stepped into a terry-cloth robe. When he was decently covered, he walked to the door and offered his hand.

"Well, I guess it's good-bye then," he told her. "Frankly, this seems like a waste to me. But I wish you all the happiness in the world."

She took his hand, and her green eyes gleamed momentarily with some private irony.

"We had some great dinners together, didn't we?" She gave him an impulsive, platonic kiss on the cheek. "I'll miss your *paella*, Howie. You really are the King of Saffron Rice."

That was something, he supposed.

* * *

Howie watched from the doorway as she drove off into the rain in her powder-blue Jeep Cherokee. A jagged bolt of lightning filled the night sky, turning the landscape magnesium white for just an instant as she was leaving his driveway. In the flare of light, Howie saw her turn a final time and wave goodbye. It was an image he would try to reconstruct in his mind afterward. Was she crying, or was that only water from the sky streaming down her windshield? He could hear the muffled sound of her car stereo—she was playing Puccini's final opera, *Turandot,* which he had given her for Christmas. There was a tremendous crack of thunder as Howie closed the door and returned to his empty bed.

It was a state trooper who discovered her abandoned Jeep on a desolate stretch of highway shortly before dawn. The empty Cherokee was sitting on the shoulder of the road less than a mile from Howie's cabin with the headlights on, the engine running, the windshield wipers clacking back and forth, and Puccini's last opera going around and around on the cassette player. The driver's door had been left open, allowing in the rain. To compound the mystery, there was a small-caliber handgun left on the passenger's seat, fully loaded. Just as the officer stopped to investigate, the Jeep ran out of gas and the engine shuddered to a halt.

"Hey!" he called. "Anybody here?"

But there was no answer. Aria Waldman had vanished without a trace into the stormy New Mexico night.

SIGNET (0451)

MYSTERIOUS TROUBLE

☐**CHIP HARRISON SCORES AGAIN** *A Chip Harrison Mystery* by Lawrence Block. Bordentown, South Carolina, is ready with a warm welcome all right—by the local sheriff. But before long, Chip charms his way into the sheriff's good graces, a job as a bouncer at the local bordello, and the arms of Lucille, the preacher's daughter. Even Chip should see he is headed for trouble with a capital T.
(187970—$5.99)

☐**NO SCORE** *A Chip Harrison Mystery* by Lawrence Block. It is a mystery why a wily, witty, world-wise young man-about-town like Chip Harrison has to resort to elaborate arguments and intricate maneuvers to get as beautiful a girl as Francine to go to bed with him. But a big man with a big gun turns Chip's dream of desire into a nightmare of danger, threatening to make his ultimate moment of bliss the last of his life. (187962—$5.50)

☐**CLOSING STATEMENT** by Tierney McClellan. Sassy realtor Schuyler Ridgway is being sued by a sleazy lawyer whose deal went sour, and her boss is going ballistic. Luckily, she leaves the office to show two new clients a Louisville property but unluckily, there's a dying man on the living room rug. While calling the police, she notices that the victim is the lawyer who's suing her. His dying words will surely make her a prime suspect. (184645—$4.99)

☐**SKELETONS IN THE CLOSET** by Bill Pomidor. It takes Dr. Calista Marley's extensive knowledge of human bones and her husband Dr. Plato Marley's expertise as a family physician to piece together the connection between a headless skeleton found in an excavation pit outside a Cleveland medical school and the brutal murder of a med school professor. (184181—$5.50)

☐**NO USE DYING OVER SPILLED MILK** *A Pennsylvania- Dutch Mystery with Recipes* by Tamar Myers. Something is truly rotten when Magdalena Yoder's second cousin twice removed is found naked, floating in a tank of unpasteurized milk. Loading up the car with her free-spirited sister and her fickle cook, Magdalena heads to Farmersburg, Ohio, for the funeral...and gallons of trouble. (188543—$5.99)

Prices slightly higher in Canada

Payable in U.S. funds only. No cash/COD accepted. Postage & handling: U.S./CAN. $2.75 for one book, $1.00 for each additional, not to exceed $6.75; Int'l $5.00 for one book, $1.00 each additional. We accept Visa, Amex, MC ($10.00 min.), checks ($15.00 fee for returned checks) and money orders. Call 800-788-6262 or 201-933-9292, fax 201-896-8569; refer to ad #SMYS6

Penguin Putnam Inc.
P.O. Box 12289, Dept. B
Newark, NJ 07101-5289
Please allow 4-6 weeks for delivery.
Foreign and Canadian delivery 6-8 weeks.

Bill my: ☐Visa ☐MasterCard ☐Amex_____(expires)
Card#_____
Signature_____

Bill to:
Name_____
Address_____City_____
State/ZIP_____
Daytime Phone #_____

Ship to:
Name_____ Book Total $_____
Address_____ Applicable Sales Tax $_____
City_____ Postage & Handling $_____
State/ZIP_____ Total Amount Due $_____

This offer subject to change without notice.